When Ali Met Honour

RUTH AHMED

First published 2015 by Dahlia Publishing Ltd
6 Samphire Close Hamilton
Leicester LE5 1RW
ISBN 9780956696762

Printed and bound by Grosvenor Group

A CIP catalogue record for this book is
available from The British Library

Your love
has made me sure
I am ready to forsake
this worldly life
and surrender
to the magnificence
of your Being
Rumi

Bring me my bow of burning gold
Bring me my arrows of desire.
Bring me my spear, Oh clouds unfold,
Bring me my chariot of fire.

I shall not cease from mental fight,
Nor shall my sword sleep in my hand
'Til we have built Jerusalem
On England's green and pleasant land.

Blake

For Adam, Laila and Sami

Chapter One

HONOUR

There was a time when I was lucky enough to believe that 'There's this girl in Pakistan' would be the worst five words Al ever said to me. Years later, they would be totally eclipsed by 'They can't find a heartbeat'.

Today is the sort of day for reflection, a day where autumn starts to dampen down the summer and I can smell the first strands of cold in the air. It's my favourite time of year, there is something so special in the early leaves drifting from the trees – as if we are all to be allowed a chance to peel, to refresh, to start again. I walk through the wood, the dog at my side. I need to unfurl my past to make sense of my future.

A tiny copper beech tree trembles to hold its own against the wind, its candy-amber leaves hanging over a floor of tweed bracken. A brook, swollen to rolling froth by the recent rain, completes the picture. When we were looking for answers and for peace this was enough for me; walking in the woods tells me my place in the universe. It is, literally, my idea of heaven. It could never be that for Al.

Al had a pain in his soul that threatened to burn him alive, Islamic guilt at his conflicting cultures, his dichotomous identity. Where I wanted my eternity in carbon molecules, in being part of the trees, the sky, air itself – Al needed a concrete future,

5

something prescribed; the rubies and pearls of heaven written out for him in fine detail.

I didn't see that coming when we met. I didn't see the silent enemies or the unlikely allies. I didn't predict the booming role of Al's ancestors, thousands of years dead but livid in our present day. And if I was aware of any of it, I just thought it was part of his exoticness; part of what made him different, what made him perfect.

When I first met Al no amount of wise advice could have got me to recognise anything but our similarities; we were both young and educated, both boldly heading to a life after university where all the plans we had made would trickle into reality. We were the same age and born in the same country. We liked the same clothes, the same music, the same food. We were a match made in heaven; a heaven I didn't believe in but one that was very real to Al.

I met Al in a pub. He sat on a high stool, tapping one foot on the ground and dominating the half-moon stage of the bar – the same dingy and unremarkable university bar that I'd been to every weekend for the last three years. When he'd finished singing, Al moved out of the bright light and his face became visible.

He stepped down from the stage and walked towards the bar. I didn't take my eyes off him as he got closer; I didn't look demurely down at the sticky pub floor.

He looked straight at me and winked. On anyone else it would have looked ridiculous – 1996 had moved beyond the language of winking at girls. Coming from that face, shadowed below the dark fringe, centuries of civilisations unknown to me drawn in his defined eyebrows, it looked like the most natural thing in the world.

I made a straightforward and involuntary decision that took my breath away: *there is my future.*

He came and stood next to me at the bar, our arms separated only by a tiny puddle of lager – a spume of bubbles dying at its edges – and by a world of difference hidden beneath our skins, pale pink and smooth brown. We almost touched.

The noises of the pub were loud around us and the moment stretched out in awkward silence: one of us would have to speak. It wasn't like me to open a conversation. My clumsiness was evidence of my lack of practice.

I wanted to speak to him because he was cute, no more, no less. So simple, such an uncomplicated idea. Such a dream.

He was beside me waiting to be served. It was now or never. I had to summon my courage, hide my shyness and speak to him or stay silent and watch him walk away.

'I've never seen an Indian boy play guitar before,' I said, as if my mouth had taken complete leave of my mind and of any manners or standards I thought I had.

'I'm not Indian, I'm Pakistani.' He narrowed his eyes, he didn't like me.

'Don't sound very Pakistani to me.' I tried to rescue myself.

He just raised one defined eyebrow and looked straight at me with cow eyes.

'I've never seen a Pakistani boy play guitar before either.'

This time he smiled, straight white teeth, apples forming of his cheeks. His smile was deep and real. He was changing his mind about not liking me.

'I'm Honour,' I said. 'Honour Edwards.'

'Al, Al Hussain.'

I asked him if he wanted a drink. Even as I said it I cringed inwardly at the fact he was standing at a bar waiting to be served; of course he wanted a drink.

He asked for a coke.

'Are you driving?'

'I don't drink.'

'Oh.' It dawned on me that I was having a conversation with someone with a religious belief. 'For religious reasons?'

'No, antibiotics.'

'Oh God, sorry. I just assumed... I'm so embarrassed.'

He laughed, light and easy, very sure of himself. 'Yes, for religious reasons. I'm Muslim, I don't drink alcohol. I don't blaspheme either. As it goes.'

'God, I'm... Oh!' I coloured up, my cheeks burning, literally lost for words.

'And I'm dying of thirst.'

'I'm sorry,' I leant forward on my bar stool. My arm touched the sticky beer and I recoiled, bumping his arm as I did. We both jumped.

'I liked that song.' I couldn't think of anything else to say.

'My song?' He was holding his guitar case between his thighs, resting his elbows on the top of it. He blew upwards to move his fringe off his face, his dark lips in a perfect kissing shape. I knocked the thought from my mind before I started blushing again.

'Fields of Gold. Not many people have heard of Eva Cassidy.'

'It's not Eva Cassidy. It's Sting.'

'Really?' I didn't want him to think I doubted him but I couldn't back down. 'I don't think so. My cousin in America sent me the album.'

'She might have sung it but Sting wrote it.'

I looked at him. 'I've got the CD.'

'And I've spent hours poring over the music.' His eyebrows

gave a cool shrug. 'So trust me.'

I did trust him and the evening Al and I met became the night that we met. By the time we fell asleep at daybreak we were different people.

ALI

'There's this girl in Pakistan.'

Five words.

Five pillars.

Five rivers.

Five minutes.

Five words that I thought would be the hardest words I would have to say.

Five pillars of my faith. A faith I flirted with and then drowned in.

Five rivers, the *Panj Aab*, that flowed through my veins.

Five minutes is all it takes to change your world forever.

When I was a child I burnt the back of my right hand on a hot iron.

I can't recall the pain, but there's an eye-shaped scar as testament to it. As a teenager I used to think it was the all seeing eye of the anti-Christ and that I was the devil incarnate. Or at least a minion.

It was my right hand, innit?

What I do remember though is my father, or Dad as we called him, abandoning the polite *Abbu*, telling me not to cry and to be patient because the fires of hell were seventy times hotter than the fire of the iron.

Seventy times.

Something like that stays with you. Since that day the fires of hell and the damage they can do have been a reality.

Honour doesn't understand this.

How can fear make me love something?

When I met Honour, my love had nothing to do with fear.

Neither jabr *(impiety), nor* tafwid *(idolatry): but something between the two…*

The Sufis always had a treatise for love.

And it was something between jabr and tafwid I felt when I saw her. I didn't think I'd experience first love before I went home, but I recognised it immediately as it burned its way into me.

I fell in love with her red hair, green eyes and silvery skin much later. In the beginning, I recognised in her the same incompleteness that I hid inside myself.

Three years at uni had passed in dry study rooms, commandeered library desks, Islamic Society talks, and the company of others trying to get firsts. It was only just before graduation I realised that I had swallowed my only chance at living.

So I decided to pack my three years into my final three weeks. My release from the pressure had been taking my guitar to Green Park, sitting under the heavy canopy of trees, using the isolation, to sing into the wind, scared to even hear my own voice.

And then that night. I pitched up for an open mic session in the student bar, determined to have my own moment in a shaky spotlight, feeling reckless because it was foreign territory. I was fine, I was coping perfectly with my first experience of a crowded pub, slightly saddened that I hadn't done it before. But then, all the faces, distorted with drunkenness, and the level of shrieking chatter began to suffocate me: I felt a real panic.

It was in that instant that I saw her, standing at the bar. Each word I sang I imagined for her, I believed she was there waiting for me, and when I finished, it was only Honour that I wanted.

I watched her get us drinks, it should have been me, but I needed the time to collect myself. I steadied my guitar against the table, and steadied myself with it.

And forgot every rule I had ever known.

That first night was legendary. We didn't kiss, just sat talking. I remember her laughing, openly and honestly, at my dreadful jokes. So I kept on, trying to make her laugh and smile, trying to impress her by asking her philosophical questions.

The drunker she got, the more intense and lucid her answers. Around us the pub emptied, but we just talked and talked, holding on to our empty glasses as a rationale for staying.

'Do you always go out on your own?' she said.

'No,' I said. 'Only to bars. Secret drinker.'

She smiled, a shared memory from earlier, reached out, touched my hand.

'What's that scar?'

I couldn't speak, as she stroked the back of my right hand. No woman had done something so intimate for a long time and it made me nervous.

'Are you okay?' she asked.

I cleared my throat, aware of the strangled reply that was going to break through.

'I burnt my hand on an iron, when I was a child.'

I had to get my mind away from her touching my hand, her fingers still lingering.

'What are your plans for the summer?' I asked.

'I'm going travelling with my sister. Mainly in France, we've got some work lined up on a farm. It'll be a laugh. Then my sister's going to stay there for a bit – her degree was in French and she wants to get a job there – and I'll come back here for some work experience. We'll get a place in London together when she gets back at Christmas.

I envied the French and her sister.

'You?' she asked me.

'I have to go home. I'm starting my masters in September, can't afford London rents over the break. And my mum and dad will be expecting me, catching up on my news, checking I haven't gone off the rails, innit.'

It sounded so pedestrian, pathetic even.

'Where's home?' she asked.

Just thinking about Manchester, about my family shouting round the house in Punjabi, made me feel isolated from her. As if leaving her would cause me a physical pain.

The barman broke in. 'Seriously, pal, haven't you got homes to go to? There's only me and you two left now.'

I was immobile, I didn't know how to leave her.

'Sorry, mate,' I said, 'we didn't mean to keep you.'

Honour stood up, hooped gold earrings flashing through the curls of her hair as she moved her head. So this would be where it ends, I thought.

'You could come back to mine?' It was a question, not a statement. A question that left me fighting for words, that pitched my heart against my head.

'Everyone else has gone home,' she said. 'There are four spare beds.'

In the end it didn't matter, we only needed one.

We headed to Soho for breakfast as the sun rose on our first morning together. She ordered coffee and croissants, I ordered a vegetarian breakfast.

'We should have gone back to mine, I could have cooked you something better than that,' I said, glad at the same time that she

RUTH AHMED

wasn't seeing my tiny room, the trash my flatmates had left in the poky kitchen.

'You like cooking then?'

'Love it,' I said. 'My mum never let me cook at home, so it was something I did with a vengeance down here.'

'Ha.' She grinned. 'Same, my mum loves her kitchen, I can't get near.'

I stretched to hide my smile, my bones cracking in my shoulders.

'Well, let's get some sleep, you go back to yours for a bit, then why don't I cook us some lunch?' she said.

'Sounds perfect,' I said.

And it was.

Chapter Two

HONOUR

We never made it to separate beds on that first night. I thought I'd understood the message of his drifting into my room with me, sitting tentatively on the edge of my bed, chatting and wriggling his feet out of his shoes. I had waited for a lull in the conversation, a convenient moment where I had tipped my head towards his in laughter. And then, following convention and experience, I had moved forward to kiss him.

I hoped that the fact that my eyes were half-closed removed a little of the humiliation of his rebuttal. The tops of my cheeks burned crimson with clumsiness, embarrassment at putting myself, and him, into such an awkward situation. He was so gentle, it wasn't a put-down – he just moved his face away from mine and immediately cast his gaze down to the floor and, when he spoke, his words were fast, tripping over themselves.

'How long have you lived in this flat? Do you get on with your housemates? Are you keeping it on for next year?' He picked at invisible strands of cotton on my striped duvet cover.

I tried to talk the last few seconds out of history.

'We have a great laugh here, we really do. But everyone's going their own ways in the next few weeks. It'll be time for another group of students to go through it the same way we did.' I patted my pillow, intending to illustrate my fondness for the house and its contents – none of which belonged to us – but Al seemed to see it as an instruction to swing his legs round and lean back against the headboard. He was fully clothed, his legs out straight in front of him, and he nervously wriggled his toes inside his black socks.

I filled the awkwardness with more words. 'It was good for me to live here, with such beer monsters. They helped me get over leaving home – I missed my twin sister so much at the beginning of uni, I cried every night.'

'Wow, my sister and I just have a fight every time we're in a room together.'

I couldn't imagine him fighting with anyone, he was so quiet, his body language almost apologetic.

'Why didn't you go to uni together, you and your sister?' he asked. 'Wouldn't that have been easier?'

'It was my mum's idea, and she was right I think – looking back on it. She just wanted us to be individuals for once.' It had taken a lot of persuasion on my mother's part but, coupled with the fact that we couldn't decide on a college that suited us both, Connie and I had eased our way apart three years ago.

'I'll be right back,' I smiled and grabbed my pyjamas from under my pillow. 'Shall I make you a cup of tea?'

'That would be great, thank you.' He smiled and we both made an effort to forget the aborted kiss and the tension its ghost left in the room.

I shrugged myself into my pyjama trousers in the kitchen. With anyone else, I'd have just jumped under the covers in my pants and t-shirt, but I felt a little responsible for him, for not making him feel awkward again. It made me grin to myself. My pyjamas were decorated with images of Tintin. I thought Al might be relieved when he saw how harmless I looked; maybe he would be satisfied that no one wearing the Thompson Twins and Captain Haddock up and down their legs could have been that set on seduction.

I took the tea back into my room.

'Sorry, I didn't ask, do you take sugar?' So polite, so distant.

He shook his head.

I sipped at my drink too soon, burning my lips in the effort to distract myself. Al sat propped against the headboard, his t-shirt – a matte bottle green – had slipped slightly up from his jeans revealing a line of smooth brown skin and tufts of black hair across his belly. I longed to lay my hand on his warm skin but I didn't dare. There were new rules in this room and I had no idea what they were.

I looked down at my pyjamas again, focussed on the motif of the little white dog skittering around my knees and tried not to think about Al or how much I wanted him to kiss me.

Slowly we got more comfortable with the proximity, our questions and answers little beacons of hope across the summer air.

'Is English your first language?'

'Nope,' he sounded sleepy now, his voice smoother. 'My mum doesn't speak English so I just spoke Punjabi with her until I started school.'

'That's amazing. So will you spend all summer just talking in Punjarbi?'

'Pun-jabi,' he said, 'there's no r in it. Non-Asians always say *Punjharbi* but it's just Pun-*jabi*.'

'Cool,' I said, 'I feel a bit special now – like I'm in the know. So do you? Do you talk in Pun-*jhabi* at home?'

'No, there's more English speakers in our house than not. So the majority rule. As soon as my sister arrived and I started school, English kind of came into our house. And my dad speaks English properly. So we speak in English and our mum answers in Punjabi, that's how she likes it.'

He rolled on to his side, we were eye-to-eye. I didn't dare attempt another move on him. I was terrified that he'd just go home.

'What about the shops and stuff? Or going to the doctor's? Does she speak English then?'

He rolled his eyes. 'Don't get me started. My sister goes with her to the doctor's as a translator, unless she can get in to see the Pakistani doctor of course. And, God this makes me cringe, all our local shops are Pakistani. My dad or my sister go with her to Manchester city centre and do all her talking for her.' He rubbed his face with his hands. 'It sounds so awful when I talk about it, but at home, in Manchester, it's just normal. It's how people live. It's who my family are. And every other family around us.'

'God, you don't have to tell me about families.' Here was a subject I could support him on. 'My family are bonkers, nuts. They embarrass me every which-way.'

I dared edge my hand into the narrow no man's land between us on the bed. It cut through the shadow of the window frame thrown onto the bed by the streetlamp outside. I splayed my fingers out on the striped cover, my thumb on red, my little finger half on green, half on blue.

His turn. 'Is it just you and your sister? In your family?'

'Just us. They wanted more kids but it didn't happen.'

'I can't imagine how that must be. A family of four. It must be so peaceful.'

'My dad doesn't really do peaceful. He's a bit of a character. You'll have to come down to Kent and meet him.'

I stopped short, maybe that was too much, too soon. Was that the phrase it would take to make Al run, to make him vanish into the night leaving just the dent in the pillow where his head had been and a faint trace of his aftershave?

'That sounds cool. I like getting out of the city. Are they near the sea?'

I was so relieved. 'Just a few miles. It's crazy quiet there, a couple of pubs and a newsagent, that's it.'

'You're making me very jealous.' His arm fell forward, our fingers were millimetres apart. I swear I could feel the static between them. 'My summer will be spent, sweltering, in my parents' house, my brothers and sisters getting on my nerves, and nothing to save me but wandering around the streets and going to the gym or the...'

He stopped mid-sentence. I looked at him, my eyes questioning.

'I was going to say mosque, but it seems a bit silly. A bit *wrong* somehow.'

'Guilty wrong?' I asked.

He shook his head, rolled on to his back. I copied him and we stared at the spidery cracks in the damp-stained plaster.

'Not guilty wrong. Just another world wrong.' His fingers snaked across the sheet and wrapped themselves round mine. I squeezed his hand gratefully.

We peeled layers of fact and history away from one another, keeping them inside us as an intimacy. Each similarity was a magical note, each difference a thread of intrigue and interest.

'You haven't got a spare toothbrush, have you?' he asked as the dawn began to filter into our world. We were half-delirious with tiredness but I couldn't close my eyes in case I broke the spell and he disappeared.

'I haven't, but I've got these.' I reached into my bedside table drawer and pulled out a packet of Extra Strong Mints. 'You could just rub one over your teeth. Better than a poke in the eye with a sharp stick.'

'Maybe not,' he said, rolling the packet round in his hand, squinting at the tiny writing on the label. 'Ah, thought so. I can't eat these. But thanks for the offer.'

'Why? What's wrong with them?' I asked.

'Gelatine. It's made from hooves. And it won't be halal.'

'Hooves? I'm freshening my mouth with something made of hooves?'

He nodded, grinning. 'Where's your bin?'

I pointed to the corner of the room and he tossed the packet into the wicker basket, a perfect shot.

I was so in awe of Al. I couldn't take my eyes off him for the three weeks we had left at college, as if he was something I'd conjured up and he could vanish just as quickly. There was something about him that I hadn't seen before in anyone else. I had been more intimate with other boys, other men, and yet I felt I knew Al far more deeply, that there were layers and layers of him to unfold and uncover. He carried himself confidently, he knew his limitations. The strict sentiments of his life, the very tenets that stopped him from even kissing me, were the same things that made him so unique, so perfect.

I longed for more, for an invitation into something further, into the parts of him that were still secret to me. In only twenty-one days he became my best friend, but I had serious doubts whether he would ever become my lover.

I sent tentative emails to my twin sister, Connie, hoping against hope that she would have backed out of the trip we'd planned for years and I could somehow spend my summer with Al. I wished with every fibre of my being that something would go wrong in the organisation of the summer in France Connie and I had looked forward to so much and for so long. There hadn't – the plans had come together perfectly.

I left for France, the thought of being without Al a physical pain.

ALI

Almost every Bollywood film I'd watched involved love at first sight. The hero would see the heroine's sari pallu flutter in the wind, clock her coquettish look, and then a song would start expressing how they made each other feel, how they were terrified of the emotions that they stirred in each other, how the world was alive for the first time...

I didn't dare to make that connection between Honour and myself.

And my heart, traitorous thing that it was, flashed an image: Al Hussain, successful professional, working-class boy done good and all grown up at a work dinner, his beautiful, red-headed, vivacious, wife in his arms, dancing some slow ballroom number, envied by every man (and woman) in that room...

But my mind woke up and obliterated it with another image: a self-confident, infatuated seventeen year-old, declaring my love to a woman, called Mehreen, who I thought felt the same. Only to be rejected.

Every morning for three weeks, whether in my narrow bed or at her flat, Honour and I had woken up together, digging deeper, mining our pasts, more isolated from the rest of the world, more reliant on one another. I preferred staying at mine, even though it was far less comfortable. Somehow, I told myself, it wasn't intentional that we were sleeping side-by-side, that our skin occasionally touched, when the only option was a single bed. At her house, it was all my fault when I chose to share the double bed with her, the open doors of the other empty bedrooms a reminder of my decision.

We talked about everything, except how we really felt about each other. And if I ever got close to being brave enough to talk about it, I'd remember the pain on her face when I'd turned down her kiss that first night. Every part of me had wanted it to happen, every part except the shamed boy inside me, the one who had kissed Mehreen before she walked away. I couldn't take it happening again, I couldn't kiss Honour until I was sure she wouldn't walk away.

We were in a nightclub watching other people our age – people who barely knew each other – snog and dance, gyrate with strangers as if it was the easiest thing in the world. I wanted to pull Honour hard against me, I wanted to be able to shout above the music that it wasn't *her*, it wasn't that I didn't want her.

When I turned around with our drinks, she smiled at me, it was genuine and without guile, for me only. I unsteadily carried our drinks back, trying not to spill her alcohol on my hand.

I shuffled into the booth next to her to make more small talk, to try and keep her attention a little longer. 'Have you got any pictures of your twin?' I said. 'I'm curious.'

She dug in her purse for a photo-booth-style pic of two red-haired girls pulling faces. Only one had Honour's smile.

She was shocked, unable even to pretend I was wrong when I pointed her out.

'I'd know you anywhere,' I said making eye contact as I clinked my glass against hers.

We danced until we were breathless, I was surprised at how much I enjoyed it. It was an opportunity to touch her, to be with her, letting the pounding music take the place of the pounding fear for a few minutes. She was a good dancer, made it easy for me to follow her. Over her shoulder, I watched other men look her up and down and I curled my hands protectively round her delicate fingers.

'Time to go?' I asked her. 'Hungry?'

She turned and nodded, her eyes a little glassy from the alcohol.

We climbed the stairs up from the subterranean club and collapsed out onto Charing Cross Road, leaning against some railings, I offered her my bottled water.

'Al, have you seriously never had a girlfriend?' she said between gulps.

'No...' I felt the heat of embarrassment creep into my face, despite being outside.

'But someone must have asked you out,' she leaned close to my face and my heart raced. 'You are actually fucking gorgeous.'

'Honour Edwards,' I laughed. 'You're unbelievably drunk.'

'I'm not, Al, not that drunk.' She struggled to her feet, wobbling slightly.

'There was someone, briefly, at college. I thought I was... I had feelings for her, but it didn't work out.'

'Why not?'

'We were young, seventeen, she wanted different things. She didn't feel the same way.'

Honour was silent, her fingers lacing through mine, holding on.

'Her loss,' she said. 'What was her name?'

'Doesn't matter, she doesn't matter.'

'I'm curious. Was she English?'

'No, her name was Mehreen.'

'She broke your heart?'

I nodded, but Honour didn't see.

Instead I turned the conversation away from the danger of intimacy and failure.

'What about you?' I asked, 'how many boyfriends?' The question was like a knife in my side. God only knew what the answer would feel like.

Fate protected me from finding out. The hot oily air of a kebab shop wafted across the street – the combination of the heat, the smell and the alcohol leaving Honour hunched over a black and gold litter bin. I held her beautiful hair away from her face and rubbed her back while she threw up and afterwards, I half-carried her back to the bus stop. On the nightbus she cuddled into me on the musty-smelling seat, her tiny hiccoughing sobs of humiliation making me love her more every second.

I helped her clean her teeth and tucked her into her bed, stroking her face and waiting till she was asleep. I leant over her, her perfect face pale and streaked with mascara. Gently I stole a kiss from her passive mouth.

The three weeks ended and I headed home to Manchester.

I thought maybe 'us' had ended before we'd had time to crack the surface, like something that doesn't grow, never was. She said she'd keep in touch. It gave me hope.

Write to me.

Those were her last words. I felt empty as my train pulled into Piccadilly, as though I had forgotten how to breathe without her there to show me.

I tried to shake off my infatuation for Honour as the domestic reality back in Manchester hit me. Dad had a summer of DIY planned. Re-paint and re-furbish, make the house look new. First job was to do the lounge.

The paint was thick, magnolia, spattering my old jeans and shirt, bobbling on my arm hair. The roller was causing a pain in my shoulder and a local Asian radio station played in low volume behind us. The furniture had been put in another room, the carpet covered in the sheets that we used when there was a gathering, religious or cultural.

'I'm thinking of preparing Zain and Aaliyah for the grammar school exams,' said Dad.

He was on his knees doing the skirting boards, wearing a white shalwar kameez, now with the bland yellow blotched all over it. My dad was in his late forties, his hair grey streaked but still black, a short beard covering his face. I didn't think he had aged, but when I looked more closely, his eyes had circles around them that hadn't been there when I had left home.

'That's a good idea. My tutor helped me, so maybe you can use him,' I said.

Dad spoke in accented but good English. 'For Zain, yes. I will find a lady tutor for Aaliyah.'

We carried on painting, the only sounds the radio and the roller.

'You were right, I should have done the skirting boards and ceiling first,' Dad said. 'The gloss is going to mark the walls.'

'It's okay, we can do the walls again,' I said.

'I haven't painted in a long time. What happened to flowery wallpaper? That was easy to paste on.'

'I'll finish the ceiling,' I said.

I exchanged rollers, picking up the white emulsion covered one, and steadied myself on some dodgy wooden step ladder.

'I was speaking to your cousin Abdul. He said you can do Accountancy,' my father said. He had his back to me still, painting the skirting boards. I guessed it was uncomfortable discussion time.

'Why would I want to?' I said.

'He says there are very few economic jobs here. But if you do Accountancy, do the exams, you can practice back in

Manchester.'

The radio started its news in Urdu. Dad listened, tutting over Pakistani politics.

'That nation was created with the blood and sweat of your grandfather, and this is what they've done to it,' he said.

My mother came in to see if we wanted tea. She was dressed in a maroon shalwar kameez, her head uncovered, a dupatta, in case of guests, draped around her neck. She looked too young to have a son as old as me.

'Be careful on that ladder,' she said, speaking Punjabi.

'I'm fine, Mum,' I said, answering her in English. 'And, yes, tea would be great.'

'Do you want English tea or normal tea?' she said.

'Normal is fine,' I said.

Normal meant boiled with teabags and milk on the stove. English meant the tea would have cold milk added after the teabags were boiled. I wondered how Honour might have coped with that. Would it taste foreign to her?

Get a grip, Ali, she's not here, innit, she's in France, it's all over.

It just wasn't so easy to shake her now she had been so close to me.

'So what do you think?' Dad said. 'About the Accountancy? Especially if I'm sending your brother and sister to a grammar school.'

'Dad, I'll help out with their fees, don't worry about that. But I haven't changed my mind. I'm doing my MA and then, inshallah, I'll join an Islamic bank.'

My mother brought us tea and we sat cross-legged in the middle of the floor to drink it. She had brought a plate of jalebis too.

'There is always the Law,' he said, putting a jalebi dipped in hot tea into his mouth.

'Maybe for Jamal?'

Jamal was my middle brother, a teenager with gangster identity issues.

'Jamal will be lucky to get even one A Level. Even the tutor said maybe education is not for him. I think I'll send him to a polytechnic, and then we can see what he does.'

'They're all universities now, Dad. He must have an interest in something.'

'Huh,' was Dad's response.

'Let's not give up on him just yet,' I said. 'People change.'

Honour seemed so distant, and I felt more trapped than ever in the gilded ghettos of suburban Manchester.

I sat at my mother's kitchen table for family dinner; we all ate together every evening. I couldn't quell thoughts of Honour though, wondering how she would fit in, imagining scenes of conflict and comedy. Honour cooking her first curry and my mother taste-testing it, adding salt or even worse, extra chilli, just to spite her. I hated hot food. Or my mother daring my dad to say he liked what Honour had made.

'You feel well, Ali? You have a very faraway look on your face, beta,' my dad said. 'Like you have left your heart behind.'

He fixed me with eyes as liquid black as mine and for a moment I felt exposed, like he could see right through me. That irrational childhood thought that he could read my mind maybe.

'What nonsense, his heart is here with his mother and his family. Tell him, Ali,' my mother said.

'Begum, this generation of boys and girls, you know how they are.' My dad never said my mother's name; she was always Begum, the generic term for 'wife'.

'Nothing's changed, we know best, don't put ideas into his head when there are none. Ali is a good boy, he knows what will please us.'

At least Dad had tried to find out if there was 'someone'. Mum just believed in the power of her chappatis that I wouldn't stray.

Too late Mum, your Ali went and got corrupted.

At least I had hope that Dad would support me… except that was redundant. I had to keep reminding myself, Honour was in France, it probably didn't matter. I'd end up confined to a life half-lived. Get over it.

Eric Cantona and Imran Khan posters looked down on me, as I sat in my single bed, pen poised, ready to write something to Honour.

I wanted to write to her every day. Secretly I did, and then threw away bits and pieces. They always seemed to be so raw, on the sleeve, poetic nonsense, declarations of love. Honour had never said she was in love with me, or acknowledged what I felt.

We parted as friends. No, worse than that, as pen pals.

Every letter of hers I would open with trepidation, wondering if some guy called Jean-Claude or Anton had whisked her off with his French-ness, his natural lover's ability and his accent. Bastard. I grew up in a world where brown women had a moral code and white women didn't.

Luckily that letter never came.

Instead along came Billo. The girl from Pakistan.

'Look, my son, she is so beautiful, she has fair skin and green eyes and brown hair.'

'She's English?' I asked cheekily, holding the cheap photo print with trepidation.

Which unfortunate victim had they found for me to marry in what backwater, *unbeknownst that my heart was not for trading*? Honour would quote Shakespeare to make a point: for me, it was always Rumi.

'*La hawla wala kuwwat...* May God protect us from such misfortune... you think I have lost my senses that I would marry you to a white girl?' My mum used the word gori as an insult and yet when she talked about Billo she said, 'Look how gori she is.'

Oh, Mum, the irony.

'Well, you seem pretty obsessed with green eyes and skin colour,' I mumbled.

'She is so gorgeous.' Mum went on ignoring me. 'Think how beautiful your children, my grandchildren, will be? They will have cats' eyes, just like Billo.'

Honour has fair skin and green eyes too, and just think how beautiful your grandchildren will be if they're mixed race, I thought.

I didn't say that to my mum, obviously.

'She is the youngest daughter,' Mum went on with the sales pitch, 'the same caste and a Sunni. She is fresh out of school, only sixteen and is studying...'

'She's sixteen? Mum, are you crazy?'

'What? I was fourteen when I married your father, and it's right the girl should be a few years younger than the boy...' She patted her shalwar kameez on her lap with a gesture of righteousness.

'Sixteen? Mum, she's a child, she's way too young.'

'Well, we can wait then for two years and she will be eighteen, it will all be well. Her family are okay with that option.'

'What do you mean? You've already got to that stage? Mum?' Instinctively I moved further down the sofa, away from her.

'Well, I knew you would fall in love with her, look her hair is red-brown, and your sisters said that you like that Sally from the TV.'

'Sally?'

'The one in your poster.'

'You mean Scully? So, what? Does the entire family know about this?' I was fuming.

'Marriages are between families. We know what's best.'

'Are you all going to get into bed at night with us then?'

'Don't be so shameless,' she said.

'It's between a man and a woman,' I said.

'That lasts maybe a year, then you become part of the family, that's what matters.'

'What about Dad? What does he have to say about this?'

'He will do whatever I tell him,' she said thrusting the picture into my hands again. 'Look at her.'

I couldn't let this go on, there was a young girl in Pakistan somewhere thinking she was about to get onto a plane and start a new life in Manchester. That was not going to happen.

I refused to go along with it, and the battle lines were drawn.

Mum wrapped her dupatta tightly round her face and looked mournful – teary-eyed on cue whenever I came into the room. Dad kept chuckling to himself at her behaviour. All my siblings kept telling me how old I was and how I needed to get married and that Billo was beautiful. It was like a pressure cooker of familial duty and expectation, added to which were haranguing images of the love of my life being chatted up by strange French men.

I thought my refusal would be enough to end the Billo saga, but what did my opinion on it matter? I was just the groom. There were much bigger machinations behind the scenes; politics and family dramas on a global scale.

Turned out Billo had an older brother, Bilal. And Bilal was going to marry my younger sister, Farzana. It was choose one get one free. People said they could tell Farzana was my sister, even though she didn't look like a boy and I definitely didn't look like a girl. It was in our features, in the tone of our skin, different to the colour and look our other siblings had. I joked she was made from my leftover DNA, she said the crap came out first.

Naturally she hated me, but still I didn't want to see her shipped off.

'No way, Dad, Farzana's only twenty, she is not marrying someone from back home.' I valiantly came to my sister's defence, appealing to my father's liberal nature. He had never struck me as being one of *those sorts* of men. The sort that got their kids married back home. I always thought he would let us have a choice, that he interpreted his religion properly.

'*She* can speak for herself,' Farzana said.

I ignored her.

'Girls are different to boys,' said my dad, 'they grow up faster and it's also difficult to find someone decent here. It's my duty to get my daughters married, and with you also married into her in-laws they will treat her well.'

'I don't need my big brother to ensure my in-laws treat me well,' Farzana said.

'Dad, this is nearly the twenty-first century, this is England. I can't believe you're saying this. And I thought I had a choice? You're taking it as a given that I'll marry Billo?'

'Ali, you are a man now, you have four younger siblings to think of. You need to accept your responsibilities. Until you are married your brothers can't be. Your cousin, Abdul, told me to wait until after your masters, then speak to you about marriage. But your mother can't keep anything quiet.'

Abdul, sanctimonious and leader of the cousins, always getting a say in my life. He was the oldest son of the oldest son, born to even more pressure and duty than me.

'What about Farzana? What about her degree?' I reasoned.

'Do you even know what I'm studying?' she said narrowing her eyes at me.

'She can carry on after marriage. I'm not sending her over there, I'm bringing her husband here,' Dad said.

'This is insane. And she's okay with this, is she?'

I looked at Farzana but couldn't read her expression. Maybe she was embarrassed to fight with our father?

'She's staying here, at home, for university and her head hasn't been turned by London. And Billo's grandparents came over with yours in the Partition. This will just cement that bond. It was your grandfather's dying wish our families be bonded.'

'I only stayed because the money went on this house, your tutor, your studies and Dad couldn't afford to send me away to uni. I would have paid back my own student loans, you know.' Farzana pointed her long fingernail at me, accusingly. 'And my head would have been my own whether I was here or in London, Dad,' she said, one face for me, another – more pious – for my father.

'Well, I'm not going to marry Billo,' I said.

I was adamant and thought myself the hero. The biggest shock came from Farzana after my father had left us alone.

'Why are you messing up my marriage, you freak?'

'You want to marry some bloke you've never met? Are you crazy? I'm doing this for you.'

'Oh please, Ali Hussain only does things for Ali Hussain. Or Al is it? You're so up yourself, totally selfish.'

I just stared at her. She was wearing an ankle-length denim skirt and maroon polo neck, her thick black hair falling over her shoulders. Nothing about her said Pakistan except her skin and fiery black eyes. I didn't understand women, that was clear.

'Fine, you go ahead and marry a freshie, but I won't.'

'They won't marry me without you. Just do it; you've got to fucking marry someone!'

'Do me a favour, Faz, and learn how to form an opinion.'

'Pretentious fuckhead,' she said.

Next up was my brother, Jamal.

Like some bad stereotype he had taken to chillin' with the boys in pool halls, learned to drive and become a man. All in the three years I hadn't lived at home.

'Look, bro, you need to just chill n get wiv da program, innit. You is the eldest, so you do the right ting, you marry the virgin gyal from back home, innit. Means me and Zain can marry gyals from here, innit. We can mess about. You got born first, you got spoilt and you is the one who our parents love the most. Now it's payback time. You marry da gyal from Pakiland and she looks after dem in der old age, innit.'

'You're an idiot,' I said.

Who made this deal? This trade off where the first-born son has to conform just so everyone else could take the piss? Well, I wasn't putting up with that.

So I sat sullen at dinnertimes, and it didn't matter. My mother sat on her prayer mat all night, whispered conversations with the local women on what remedies worked to stop the black magic that was clouding my head.

Dad had the final word: 'Unless you are married by the time you finish your masters, I will propose your rishta to Billo. Men have needs, and I won't have you fulfilling those outside of marriage. The longer I leave it, the more temptation there will be.'

'Dad, that's really unfair, I'm not an animal…'

And so I ran. Took to a treadmill and spent as much time as I could in the gym just to get away from it all.

Inside, the thought was forming. I had a year to convince Honour to marry me: when my masters was over, so were my chances of freedom. My desperation gave me courage.

To my relief, Honour wrote to me, and I found myself on a train to Kent.

This had to be significant. I imagined how Honour would be when I saw her again. Hoping she would say something that would reflect the affection I had for her.

I had to cling to those ever harder to remember moments Honour and I had shared in the last three weeks of uni. I had to read meaning into them, hope I wasn't delusional. That she had begun to love me a little at least.

A summer apart had meant those reminisces were torture. I couldn't believe how easily I had planned a whole life around Honour, and had made it the life I wanted. Despairing of resenting a wife and kids that wasn't her, weren't hers. Until she had invited me down.

TO MEET HER PARENTS.

That had to mean something, right? Yeah, okay, me and Honour hadn't seen each other in months but this was proof she was taking this seriously, she in fact was taking it to the next level?

I didn't know the rules, so was guessing.

This was BIG and SIGNIFICANT though. It had to be.

Chapter Three

HONOUR

I spent the summer travelling through France with my sister, working on vineyards with our backs screaming and our minds numb, my skin plastered in the thickest sun cream I could find. Al and I wrote most days, long old-fashioned letters on real paper; we sprayed them with whatever was to hand. Mine to him smelled of sun lotion and wine, his ones back of curry and cheap aftershave.

Al had moved back, temporarily, with his parents whilst he waited to start his master's degree in September. If I sent him postcards, I had to put them in an envelope. If I'd sent them with my name on, or if my return label on the back of the envelopes showed the letters were from a woman, they would have gone straight in the bin, unopened, when his mother found them on the doormat in the morning.

By the time I got home I hadn't seen him for thirteen weeks and when his letter came back saying that, yes, he'd love to come and spend some time at ours, I was trembling with excitement. At the same time, I tried to stifle a disquieting fear that it was all imaginary, that it might be a longing whipped up by our written words.

I thought I was cool, sophisticated, telling my parents I was bringing someone called Ali Hussain to their house. I felt very grown up not elaborating on his ethnicity or eulogising on the colour of his skin. My politically correct mother played her part; not asking me for details of Al's background or querying my statement of 'He's from Manchester'. My father's lip buttoned with a lack of experience. I felt a frisson of interest in knowing Al was the only Asian person who had ever been in their home; not through any intent, we simply didn't live in a multi-ethnic area. Our family friends were white, all of them; interesting, diverse people, well-travelled and well-educated but, to a man, Anglo-Saxon.

My parents' house was messy but in a middle class, almost fashion-statement, way. I wasn't sure what Al would make of it as I'd nothing to compare it to; the chances of my meeting his mother were slim to non-existent at that time. If I'd only known what happiness lay in that particular cold war, I'd have kept it that way.

I met Al at the station, the wheat fields that lined the lane waved with waist-high golden stalks. Three fat, fluffy, clouds hung leisurely in a sky so blue it could have come from a picture book. It was the first time I had seen him since uni had finished back in June and three months' absence had turned into a longing on my part. I knew that this was the weekend I would talk to him about our future; that I had decided staying 'just friends' would be more painful than never seeing him again. If I'd been older and bolder, I'd have simply asked him what the Qur'an said about a quick bunk up in a wheat field.

I was too excited to wait in the car and I'd arrived stupidly early at the station. I wandered through the peaceful lanes a little and pulled flowers from the hedgerow to make him a welcome bouquet. Early September favours Kent, bringing out the best of its sights and smells, the sun no longer fierce, just generous and reliable.

I heard the clicking from the train tracks that said he would be there any second and rushed back to the platform.

When Al stepped down from the carriage I realised I had been holding my breath waiting for the doors to open. He saw me straight away and paused, head cocked to one side; I saw the familiar raise of his eyebrows.

He looked older. He'd said that he'd been running a lot and going to the gym in an effort to avoid his mother's wailing and gnashing of teeth. Beefing-up suited him, turned him from boy to man. I felt the now-familiar stab that came with the thought of losing him.

The pale pink commuters scurried round him and along the platform. He looked magnificent.

'Are those for me?' He took the flowers and made a comedy gesture of smelling them. 'You look fantastic. Is that a... a... tan?' He rubbed my arm with his thumb and I heard my heart beating. 'You've lost your blue tinge.' He hugged me. 'Seriously, you look gorgeous.'

I drank in his smell, I'd missed him so much more than I'd realised. Despite dreaming of him every night, besides my secret habit of writing Honour Hussain in curled scripts on every scrap piece of paper, I surprised myself by how much I needed him. He held me tight, the side of my face against his chest.

'Been working out?' I smiled. 'It suits you, especially with the flowers.'

A ladybird crawled from the posy onto his hand. He pursed his lips to blow it gently away.

'You have to sing to it first,' I said. '"Ladybird, ladybird, fly away home, your house is on fire and your children are gone." Then it can go.'

'What's that from?'

'I dunno, I've always done it. My mum does. Then it goes "All except one, and her name is Anne, and she's hidden under the frying pan."'

He laughed and reached out for my hand. 'I've missed you so

much.'

I thought that was going to be the moment, I thought he was going to kiss me there and then. I could hear my own fast breathing and really hoped he couldn't.

But he just smiled. Wide, deep, meaningful, his perfect lips framing his boy-band teeth, but no kiss.

'This is weird,' he said in the car.

'What is?'

'You driving for a start. Like a grown up. I can't believe I still haven't learnt to drive.'

'You're a city boy; you don't need to.'

'And when I'm at home, someone would only steal my car. That's why I won't stay there. I'll bring my kids up somewhere like this. Not Manchester or London.' He stared out of the open window, squinting his eyes against the breeze and the sunlight. He ran his fingers through his fringe to straighten it.

'I thought you were urban till you die. You'd be so bored out here in the sticks.' I'd picked up a vague idea from something he'd said in one of his letters that he might be a bit of a secret smoker. I hadn't run with the clues and asked for answers; weed is my bête noir and it would be just my luck to end up with a stoner. A fundamentalist Muslim stoner: I added it to my list of Qur'an queries. 'My parents' house is at least five miles from the nearest club.'

'I mean for schools and stuff. Things kids need. Fresh air, sunshine, not being called a paki in the playground. I bet your childhood was well different to mine.'

When we pulled up in my parents' drive, I apologised for the size of the house. Al had a kind of told-you-so look about him; smug that his class prejudices and assumptions had been confirmed.

'Nice house,' he said, a note of laughter in his voice. 'How old is it?'

'My sister went out with an archaeologist for a bit, he said the cellar's Roman. Then it's got bits from every century since, I suppose. The shit is all my parents' though. It's a little dodgier inside than it looks from here.'

The house was charming, even to me and I'd lived there all my life. A dark amber roof of Kent Peg tiles swooped almost down to head height, the stuccoed walls were painted a white that had seen so many better days. The gate was rotten and hung, impotently, on one hinge. My parents had caused more decay in this house with their benign neglect and lack of hoovering than all the advancing armies of Cromwell, Hitler and nature put together.

The porch of my parents' house always reminded me of my childhood; the glass panel that my sister and I smashed with a football years ago had never been replaced. That was the way things worked in their house. My parents had always spent their money on food and art and travel. Altogether, it painted a quaint picture of rural life but it was not to everyone's taste. My student digs were so tidy that everyone remarked on it; my silent little rebellion.

I opened the door and Teddy bounded out, tail wagging, pink tongue hanging out his happiness. The next few seconds blurred into a mêlée of sight and sounds. Al screamed and stumbled backwards. Teddy barked with delight. Al flung his backpack hard at the dog and I just wondered what the hell was going on.

I grabbed Teddy by the collar, his tail wagging fit to come off. Al was sprawled on the drive, his head against the gate which had slipped a few more centimetres from its moorings. He was pale and shaking.

'I'm, I'm a bit... I don't like dogs.' It came out in a rush, like a spell that would magic Teddy into a cat or a hamster or at least something smaller. 'And he's huge. Is he a Rottweiler?'

'He's a black Labrador.' I tightened my grip on the smelly emblem of middle class England. Teddy wagged his tail some more for want of any more constructive role.

'I'm sorry, I just... Oh, I feel a bit sick.' Al put his head on his knees, curling his arms round his legs and hiding his face.

My dad came out of the front door at that exact moment. I looked angry, the dog confused and the man-of-my-dreams rocked backwards and forwards, close to tears and taking loud, ratcheted breaths.

Like so many moments of my life with Al, it wasn't quite as I'd pictured it.

'Bloody Hell,' said my dad; a phrase he believes covers most situations. 'What on Earth is going on here?'

Al tried to scramble to his feet, holding onto the gate, ready to vault it if I let go of Teddy.

'Put the dog in the house, darling,' said my dad and walked towards Al. 'David Edwards, how do you do?'

Al recovered enough to shake his hand. He rubbed his sweaty palms on his trousers first. 'Ali Hussain, pleased to meet you.'

I was interested that Al made himself Ali to meet my dad. He was Al to all of his or my college friends.

'Not a fan of the canine then?' My dad was grinning.

'Terrified,' Al said, 'absolutely terrified.'

'Teddy's the dog to start with then. Absolutely bomb-proof.' Nothing could shake my father's commitment to his way of life, least of all someone else's opinion. 'Dog! On your bed!' he roared as he led Al into the house.

Teddy obediently skulked onto the festering pile of blankets and broken basket-weaving piled against the Aga. Ali sat at the kitchen table, as far from the dog as he could. They watched each other intently.

'He won't hurt you,' I said, as the dog closed one eye in boredom.

'I know. It's not that. It's a culture thing. It's in the hadith that you can't bring a dog indoors. Can't have them in the house.'

'Quite right too,' said my dad, 'filthy things. That one stinks.'

'Muslims?' I wanted to pay my dad back for taking charge.

'Labradors. And you're not funny.' Embarrassing my father always makes him cross.

Al moved fractionally out of his terror to wink at me from under his fringe. My heart went straight back into the uncomfortable claustrophobia it had been surrounded by for months.

I looked at the piles of bills on the kitchen table and sniffed the grimy kitchen with a fresh nose. I began to wonder if I'd made the right decision in bringing Al here. Then I remembered the inelegant way he flailed in terror in the driveway and it occurred to me that, perhaps, my parents and the man I was horribly in love with were all as completely mad as each other.

My mother fluttered a little as I introduced them. I could tell she thought he was every bit as film star handsome as I did and her longing for frothing flowers at a country church wedding was thinly disguised. I could picture her vision of my titian curls tumbling onto a white dress, little brown-skinned girls in lemon-coloured frocks behind me: I'd known her too long. I wished my sister was there to take the pressure off but she was still floating round Provence leaving a trail of moped fumes and broken-hearted Frenchmen.

As my mother moved the old-fashioned kettle onto the Aga top to boil, she talked to me in her best stage whisper. 'I've made up the double bed in your room and the spare room too, just in case. I wasn't sure which you'd want.'

A tiny part of me felt sorry for her, having a daughter who wouldn't share, wouldn't let her in to the intricacies of her relationship. I might have, if there'd been anything to share but, apart from missing me and sending me messages, Al had given no indication that this weekend would change anything between us. His long poetic letters showed his soft side but never in conjunction with a reference to me.

'We'll share my room, thanks Mum.' That, at least, would give her hope. It would give me the chance to lie beside him, just touching our sides together where we had to and fully clothed, listening to the world go round like we had in those closing days of college.

There'd been a couple of guys in France over the summer; chance meetings with men who had laughed or charmed me into bed, men that I knew were players. I'd avoided anything that could have meant anything because of Al; Al and his lack of innuendo, Al who avoided any topic that wandered near relationships or sex. I hadn't chosen them over him, I just wanted to remind myself that there might be more somewhere, that someone might physically desire me, be overcome with passion.

It was inevitable that shock-headed identical twins were going to attract some male attention in the three months we were there, sweating over the vineyard pruning jobs in our shorts and bikini tops. I'd enjoyed the flirting, enjoyed the sex even, but I knew it was empty, that it was just play.

I did suspect Al of being as deeply in love with me as I was with him. I did feel the charged particles between us and I hugely appreciated his efforts to write charming funny letters and keep me thinking of him. What really worried me was the depth of his commitment to his way of life, to his religion and to his culture that seemed so far removed from mine. My real suspicion was that Al wouldn't have sex with anyone before marriage, something I didn't want confirmed by a conversation.

Mum tinged a teaspoon against a china cup. 'Do you?'

'Sorry, Mum, do you what?'

'Do either of you want a cup of tea?'

'Do you know, I think we might go for a walk.' I shrugged at Al and he nodded back with a distinct look of relief.

I went to pick up the dog lead off its hook on the beam but thought better of it. I grabbed the car keys instead.

'Shall we go down to the beach?'

'That would be brilliant, like a holiday. It was still raining when I left Manchester,' he explained to my mum.

There were many bays and inlets to choose from, on a clear day you could see France from some. I chose carefully and where I knew there were no dogs allowed until the end of September.

'This is amazing,' Al said as we wound our way down the narrow cliff road of St Margaret's Bay, the grey sea stretching out below us and piercing points of sunlight dancing on the top of each wave.

'It's even more spectacular in winter.'

'How did you manage to live in London? You must have missed this every day.'

'I did and I didn't, it's a long way from any culture or nightlife.' I patted his leg as I parked the car, centimetres from handbrake to thigh, making it look like less of a gesture than it really was. 'I'm sorry about the dog; I didn't know.'

'No, I'm sorry. You must think I'm a total idiot. It's always been a problem. Normally I just stay away from them. It didn't even occur to me that you'd have one. It's not the fear that's the worst thing, you know.'

'It's not?'

'No, it's the stink. You have no idea, trust me, how much that dog smells. You can't have or you'd shave him.'

As I gazed through the windscreen at the endless possibilities of the sea I had a sudden revelation of how different we really were beneath the giggles, the awkward touches and chaste gestures. If I captured this man, my children would grow up without a dog. I had been born into a family with a dog and we replaced each one as it died. It was part of our way of life; every day of my childhood had involved a walk, however grudgingly, however windy, cold or wet. I would have to raise my children differently if they half belonged to Al.

No, not if they half belonged to 'Al', it would be 'Ali' who made those differences.

I felt suddenly far more robust than him, as if my outdoor childhood had made me sturdy. I jumped out of the car and stood up; I needed to remember how much taller he was than me, how much stronger. He was in danger of fading.

We picked through the rock pools as children would, waved seaweed at each other, got our shoes wet and eventually took them off and rolled up our trousers. We had to hold hands to pick our way across the slippery rock; a soundtrack of 'oohs' and 'ahs' punctuating the sharpness underfoot. I took a picture of Al holding a tiny crab so close to his face that he was nearly cross-eyed peering at it. It is such a picture of happiness, such an image of promise; I still have it.

It was a relief to be alone, even though the weight of unspoken words hung between us like a storm. We lay on the pebbles, wriggling our way into dents the size and shape of our bodies. We trickled the stones through our fingers and listened to the seagulls sing to us with their ugly voices.

'This one has a hole in,' said Al, squinting through the sparkling middle of a white quartz.

'It's good luck. Bring it back to the house. My dad will be

pleased; he threads them onto a rope in the bathroom.'

'What if I want to keep it? I might want to wear it round my neck so I remember you for the rest of my life.'

My eyes filled up quickly with hot tears. I got up, brushing imaginary sand from my legs back onto the pebble beach. 'We'd better go.'

'Something I said?'

I shook my head and pretended to have trouble opening the car door to look anywhere but at him. He'd implied that he'd need a pebble to remember these days. I had convinced myself they were simply the prelude to our becoming inseparable.

I knew from his quietness that he had no idea what was wrong. I didn't enlighten him; the weight of my error in thinking he would fall for the charm of my childhood was drowning me.

'Your parents are very liberal.'

'I guess so.'

'I mean, offering us a shared room. When my parents talk about being liberal it means they wouldn't stone my sisters for picking the wrong boyfriend.'

I couldn't trust myself to answer him.

'I'm not the first boy to stay over, am I?'

'No.' The conversation was making me angry. These were the wrong circumstances. I wanted to explain about the days before I knew him but I wanted to do it in the dark, where I couldn't see his eyes or read his face. 'Is it actually any of your business?'

'Of course not, I'm sorry, I... I just meant, I thought. Never mind. It doesn't matter.'

We finished the journey in silence.

When we got back, the smells in the kitchen confirmed my worst fears. My mother is an incredibly accomplished cook but so much so that she has an overwhelming store of recipes to pick from and becomes panicked. She consequently suffers from a kind of culinary Tourette's; my French penfriend had to suffer a week of coq-au-vin and gallettes before she negotiated her way to a yorkshire pudding: every time my uncle arrives from Switzerland, she makes him a fondue.

My mother had made Al a curry.

'No, not just a curry,' she said when I petulantly took her to task on it. 'Samosas and dahl and chappatis.' She grinned like she'd discovered the cure for cancer.

'Smells amazing,' grinned Al, 'I look forward to it.'

'Do you want to bring your bag upstairs?' I asked him, gesturing with my narrowed eyes and angrily-set mouth.

'Whassup?' He laughed and jumped onto the bed, 'it's funny.'

'It isn't funny, it's embarrassing. Doesn't it make you feel awkward that they're trying too hard?'

'No, it makes me feel happy. As does being with you, as it goes. Except when you're being grumpy.' He pulled the pillow out from under his head and swung it at me. 'Stop being so mardy.'

The gong rang loudly from downstairs.

'No!' he gasped. 'You have a dinner gong? Just how posh are you?'

'Shut up. It's a big house and my mum hates yelling, that's all.'

He laughed all the way down to dinner.

The samosas steamed from our plates, faultlessly folded powdery filo which showed my mum's skill, if not her imagination. Food has always been a distinct currency in my parents' house, signifying approval or repudiation; she clearly loved Al.

'I've made a fresh raita and there's home-made mango chutney there that I did for last Christmas,' she said.

I don't think she ever got over her disappointment in his asking for ketchup.

ALI

I grew up believing dogs were dirty, unclean, that if they entered a house the angels ran out the other door, and if you touched one you had to wash with bleach and your clothes would become dirty if a dog licked them and you couldn't pray in them.

That was some seriously tough rhetoric and anti-dog lines to get past, so I never did. Well, almost never.

We were instructed to say a prayer every time we saw a dog across the street (because we crossed the street every time we saw one).

It was only as an adult I learnt it wasn't dogs per se, just the saliva. And when you see where dogs put their tongues, well, that's understandable really. By then though my aversion had turned into phobia and dogs were nasty, dirty creatures and, more than that, absolutely terrifying.

So my idyllic trip into the English middle classes had fallen flat pretty quickly. I barely had time to check out Honour's childhood home, examine the brickwork and decipher if there was a sea view out back, when a massive Rottweiler attacked me.

I thought her dad would be the biggest threat to this trip, the one I had to avoid and dance around. Instead it was the thing in the corner breathing funnily, mucous hanging out of its mouth, and eyes waiting for the rest of the family to go away so it could rip my throat out.

My skin was goose-bumped, the hairs standing on edge. I felt real terror, my left side palpitating. Was I having a heart attack over a dog?

You're a grown man. Stop it.

But this wasn't going well. I wasn't listening to a word that was said by Honour's parents, not even able to look them in the eyes. Ever since we had come back from our walk, and since the ludicrous gong, nothing else registered.

My inattention was hardly the best advert for the role of boyfriend. They probably thought I was shifty. My throat was seizing up too, they were offering me tea and Honour's mum had cooked a veritable Indian restaurant menu of food.

'I don't mean to be rude, and I know it's the dog's house… but do you mind if…'

Her dad just laughed in my face. But the dog was reluctantly led out, giving me huge eyes of betrayal and sadness as it did so.

'I understand phobias of course, I am terrified of spiders,' said her mum.

'Terrified? She regularly disturbs my sleep making me kill the tiniest of spiders in the middle of the night. I tell you, son, when you get married, wear ear plugs. If you want a good night's sleep, that is.' Honour's dad laughed at his own comment. I didn't think it was funny but I laughed anyway.

His laugh was a bit loud, oppressive even. Without the dog in the room everyone else came into focus.

Honour was playing obedient daughter (I would have to tease her about that later) putting things on the table for her mum or going off to check on the dog (giving me alone time with her parents?). Her mum was just putting food in front of me, and watching my face as I tasted everything.

When she plated up the starters for us of minced meat samosas ('We went into London especially to get you halal meat.') the beaming smile turned to absolute horror as I loaded them up with thick red tomato ketchup before I ate them.

My ethnic credentials were slipping fast. I can't stand raita at the best of times and always insist on ketchup. I say insist but at home it's always on the table.

Not sure how talk of curry and halal meat turned into talk of Partition but I found myself listening to David ('Call me David, what's this Mr Edwards nonsense?' another guffaw) talk merrily about it.

Mrs Edwards, who thought it was extremely polite of me to call her that, flitted around trying to bang things on the table or in the kitchen. I think she was trying to get him to shut up but without being too direct.

'I think we'll have our main in about ten minutes then, Paula,' he said.

Paula didn't respond, but didn't disagree either. Was he giving her orders?

'So, technically, you're from an Indian background then?'

'No, technically I'm British? English even?'

'I mean your family… your parents. They are Indian?'

'No, they're Pakistani, although both of them are British Citizens now,' I said wishing there was food to distract him.

'Did Pakistan exist when they were born?'

He laughed, the I'm-so-clever guffaw again. Where was Honour? She came in and smiled at me. Did she think this was a good thing, me and her dad having a tête-à-tête?

'Yes. Both of them were born in Pakistan as it is today,' I said.

'And your grandparents? Were they born in India?'

'I suppose… technically, if you're thinking like that…'

Did he just say Indja? Bloody hell. Why didn't he just call it the Raj? Or British India?

'No 'like that' about it, it's the facts. Partition was a lot of nonsense. You all have the same languages and culture, you all look the same and yet, based on religion, you all butchered each other. Thank God we stepped in and kept it from becoming a second Holocaust, that's all I can say.'

I couldn't actually believe he'd said it. A hundred thousand people were butchered on both sides, and millions displaced, by Partition. And the reason for most of the bloodshed was because an Englishman took his sweet time to draw the line that would divide Pakistan from India, then split Pakistan into East and West.

Wow, scratch the surface and, what do you know, I was a Pakistani through and through.

'Things are never that simple, Mr Edwards,' I said, just to show him he had crossed a line.

'I disagree. I think you'll find things are always that simple.'

If he wasn't Honour's dad I swear I would have swung for him.

'Well, history is a murky business. A lot of people died to create a separate homeland for those Muslims who wanted it. I think it denigrates their memory to say it was a lot of nonsense.' I was nice for Honour's sake.

'I didn't mean it quite like that; I just meant it's like the Irish and Us.'

'I think it might be more like the French and You?'

You and Us already?

'They speak a completely different language to us, have a different culture. They're Catholics for crying out loud.' He laughed again.

'Most people in India don't speak the same languages as those spoken in Pakistan and, well, the majority of them are Hindus.' I didn't bother trying to educate him in my Rajput culture. My particular Pakistani heritage is practically the same whether you're Hindu or Muslim. Rajput rituals are taken from Hindu tradition regardless of religion.

'I think, Paula, it's time for the mains.' Luckily, the rest of the evening I wasn't left alone with Mr Edwards.

'I'm glad you're getting on with my dad,' Honour said before we went upstairs.

Differences got me thinking about Honour's sulk earlier.

As dinner progressed, Honour's half-formed beach confessions began to consume me.

The jealousy that had pricked at me over her previous boyfriends was slipping into her French escapades – turning into pseudo-madness. Images of model-type men drifting in and out of this house filled my head. Rugby players with floppy blonde hair scratching the Rottweiler behind the ears, exchanging slobbery kisses with it (that grossed me out), swapping drinking stories with David and flirting with Paula. Then lying in Honour's sheets and...

'I have to go to the bathroom,' I said.

I practically ran up the stairs and turned the water to cold and splashed my face to kill that vision dead.

I wondered why her parents were so relaxed. Was that a sign of just how many there had been? What was I? Number five? Or, effing hell, was I number fifty?

I felt sick, like my insides were crawling out. It was a strange mixture. I was angry, jealous as hell, but mainly hurt that I couldn't be her first.

I wondered if her parents had a point system. Robert got a five, Caspian got an eight, Tarquin got ten because he was 'just like us'. We'll give Al a four? Not bad for a paki?

I couldn't focus. It was like the dog was in the room again. I had changed in the en-suite shower room before, unable to show my body to Honour, even in my boxers and t-shirt, scared that she would find me lacking after seeing so many perfect specimens of manhood already.

I should've trained harder in the gym, and that big meal would just make my stomach bloated. I hit the cold, watery tile floor and did fifty press ups and then fifty crunches.

It didn't make me feel any better.

I couldn't breathe, as the envy ate at me.

It was while sitting on the loo that my thoughts started to crystalise. Such a basic function, and yet it again screamed of the difference between us.

I didn't use toilet paper, so the shea-butter covered rolls were no good really. I had bought some bottled water at Manchester Piccadilly and sipped it carefully all the way to Kent, leaving enough so the empty bottle wouldn't get thrown out.

It was now my 'toilet bottle'.

Honour had thought it was hilarious and disgusting at the same time when she had first found out. I had friends at uni I had known for three years who didn't know about the 'toilet bottle'. But Honour and I lived so close for those three weeks, it was only a few days before she asked me why I had a measuring jug by my loo. I burned red and couldn't look at her when I explained.

'You just wash yourself? No loo roll at all?'

'Hey, at least we get clean. What's with trying to wipe it all away with flimsy bits of paper and tissue?'

'Do you think I'm dirty then?' she asked, 'Not me, but us, white people, non-Asians?'

'No...'

'Yes you do. I bet you think I'm unclean. Can I try it?'

'If you must.' I laughed.

I thought she was pretty cool to give my lota a go. Mine was pretty basic, just a measuring jug. The one at home was a plastic, Grecian-style watering can.

'Ooh, hoo,' she said, 'don't like it. You will never convince me that that's the more hygienic option.'

Now I was in Kent, away from my comfort zone and my familiar world, our differences were starting to feel like an issue.

Then I caught sight of an empty plastic watering can sitting in the corner next to the loo, red plastic and covered with swirly designs, clearly intended for an old lady's house plants.

A lota from Honour.

The tiniest gesture but overwhelming.

'Did you find everything okay?' she asked pointedly when I came back down to the kitchen.

'Thank you,' was all I could say.

Chapter Four

HONOUR

I didn't eat much during dinner. My mother kept glaring at me over Al's coke glass and making 'You're being offensive' faces every time I took a sip of my wine. I've never seen my mother drink so little. It would have mortified her to know that Al had had to carry me home from a nightclub, dragging me through the streets and laughing at my wobbling legs, holding my hair back from my face while I was sick in a dustbin.

My dad always says you should never marry anyone unless you like them when they're drunk; I suppose that's even more important when you are completely teetotal. Al just seemed to find it funny and then indulge his ego with how much I needed him in the morning, begging him to fetch McDonald's breakfast and bring me tea.

Al and my dad had a long conversation over dinner about Human Rights and 'Partition'. They seemed to make some headway towards friendship and I was glad, I know my dad can be quite overwhelming sometimes; a few of my school friends had been terrified of him. It felt like Al had always been there, sitting round our huge kitchen table, fighting for space to talk with the rest of us.

'Mum?' I stood up and started stacking plates, Al followed my lead. 'Do you mind if we nip out; I want to show Al the pier.'

'Isn't it closed?' she asked.

I shook my head. 'They open it for the night-fishermen.'

'Oh, bloody hell,' said my dad. 'You'll see all manner of human life down there. You not over the limit?'

'For God's sake, I've had half a glass of wine. Have we just become the Holy Order of Temperance?' I turned to Al. 'They've been stuffing wine down mine and Connie's throats since we were babies. They're just showing off because you're here.'

'That's a terrible thing to say,' said my mum who was already halfway to the wine rack in preparation for our leaving, 'We did no such thing. And if Constance were here she'd back me up.'

'Except she isn't here; she's in France getting pissed as a parrot every night.' My dad made himself laugh and we left to the sound of his loud guffaws.

I pushed my sunglasses up from my face so that they held my hair out of my eyes. For the few miles I'd driven from my parents' house to the beach, the evening sun had nestled just on the horizon, reflecting on the warm tarmac and dappling through the gentle leaves along the sides of the road. On the beach I didn't need the shade; the sun had slipped a few more inches, kissing the horizon, blowing ripples of silver to beckon us forward.

'I bet you've never been on a pier,' I said as I pulled on the handbrake. 'Do they have them up north?'

'Yeah, they do. Blackpool. Wigan.'

'But they're not very Islamic places?' I was getting the hang of it all.

'I suppose not.' The eyebrow raise, my heart flipped a beat.

'I've never been in a mosque, if that evens things up any.'

'Hmmm, they're not that dissimilar to Blackpool, minus the hen parties. The inside of your average Indian restaurant? Bit like that, flock wallpaper and too many fairy lights.'

'Really?'

'Almost. I'll take you when you come up to meet... When you come to Manchester.'

'Am I coming to Manchester?' I was fishing now.

He was silent.

I filled the space, the silence was crushing. 'Turner painted this view. From the pier back to Deal seafront. You have to apply for planning permission now to do anything to the houses on the front, they're iconic. See how different all the roofs are? They were all built at different times but joined up to each other, so they're higgledy-piggledy.'

Another loud pause.

I linked my arm through his and we walked down the pier. The sun was burning the impossibly straight edge of the sea in the distance and lines of faint cloud, like the patterns in sand, fanned out from it.

The steps that led down to the lower deck were damp from a high tide and the concrete reflected the sunset. I walked boldly across the metal grids set every now and again in the platform floor, the grey sea a metre below. Al walked round them, staying on the planked decking.

'That makes me feel sick, seeing you stand on those.'

'We used to give ourselves a thrill by doing it when we were little, Connie and me. They honestly won't go through, it's cool though, isn't it? Watching all that swirly water just under your feet.'

'No, not cool, terrifying. Get off, will you?'

I stayed on the grating, he pulled my hand, I resisted. He pulled harder, with two hands – we were both giggling, I moved towards him and, suddenly, there we were; a cinematic kiss situation. His strong arms round me, my chin tilted upwards, our lips no more than two inches apart. I could feel his breath on my mouth. The last of the sun caught the sides of his face in a halo, golden edges shaping his beautiful outline.

As our lips met, I closed my eyes. I couldn't trust my legs to hold me up, such was the relief, and I leant harder into him. He didn't hurry to take his mouth from mine but, when he eventually did, he held my shoulders and looked straight into my face.

'There's this girl in Pakistan,' he whispered, his voice catching, leaving on the wind. In the empty seconds directly afterwards, I believed that they were the worst five words he would ever have to say to me.

I kissed him again, but this time with the barest taste of a salt tear. Whether I cried for me or for the girl in Pakistan I wasn't sure.

We stayed there for a long time, looking back towards the town at the twinkling lights of the seafront. We didn't say much. And what we did talk about was related to the scenery, to the last few seagulls still awake, the fat old men casting futile lines into the sea, catching nothing the whole time we were there. We could smell their cigarettes over the dirty brine, and occasionally we caught the metallic blood scent of their bait on the breeze. We punctuated our watching with kisses. Holding him – my fingers curling up the fabric of his shirt, his hand tight across the back of my head – shook away the ghost of the girl, made her vanish for a moment. I didn't want to hear more about her, to share my moment by giving her the substance of a name.

It was dark, still just warm, the most romantic of settings for the handsome young couple kissing occasionally against the iron-railings of the pier. Passers by smiled and sighed; unaware of the poison ready to spread through all our hope, the tiny hook of difficulty stuck with barbs to our skin.

We tried to talk, tried to let the gentle salty wind unravel our thoughts on the way back to the car. We sat, a tiny distance apart, on the beach for a while; hoping our unhappiness would evaporate on the air gusting back across the Channel and take our misery somewhere else. To another country even. Desire pulled us back together like magnets and stuck us tight to one another.

My parents were already asleep when we got back. The house was dark and quiet.

We had shared a bed several times before; this time was different. This time we did without the barrier of clothes; skin on skin, heart on heart, gentle, intense, involved.

Afterwards I wished I'd done it Al's way; I wished he'd been the first, the only. For the second time since I met him, the world was different.

'What are you thinking?' I asked him in the dark, my auburn hair across his chest.

He propped himself up on one elbow, moved my hair from my face with his soft fingers.

'Do you mind if I don't tell you just now?'

Sometime later, the sound of the shower woke me. I could see the crack of light around the bottom of the bathroom door; it highlighted the emptiness beside me. This was what I had been afraid of, that Al would feel too much guilt. I worried that I had stolen something from him, something I would never return. My fear was that he might never forgive me.

When he came back into the room, I watched him pray through half-closed eyes. His worship was so intimate and yet I felt that there was a chasm between us.

ALI

Things were different when we were outside, the darkness threatening, dangerous, the air cold.

Honour almost skipped beside me, keen to show me her world. The sea, the pier, the smells she assumed was so alien to an urbanite. She was showing them off, sales pitch-like, this is me, this is where I come from, isn't it marvellous?

When she tried to make out I'd never seen a pier before I told her about Blackpool having one. She tried so hard to understand my background that I let her think I had never been to the beach, never been in the water or near it really, that I didn't really sunbathe. It was a complete lie but I had to see the excitement in her eyes.

Daytrips on a coach full of cousins erased from my memory, just for her.

As she skipped along again, putting my vertigo to the test by standing over flimsy metal grills, I wished I could erase her past as easily. All the men who had touched her, kissed her, been intimate with her, I wished they would disappear. I wanted to be back whenever it was she had discovered sex, and just have it be me.

I realised then I was already set on sleeping with her, that I had just assumed in my head that I was going to have sex with her. I was seduced by the woman whose hair looked gold under the pier lights then, as we got closer to the edge, almost black as it battered the sea breeze.

I had to stop myself suggesting we make it monumental, Bollywood, on the beach.

It was only years later I realised sex was about the moment, about who you were with. The best sex was never the first time, rarely even the first few times.

As I gripped her hands hard the thought entered into my head. I could be the one to kiss her from now, make love to her, cover her with my fresh desire. And that would mean no one else could. Ever again.

I tried to think of the million reasons why sex before marriage was wrong.

But fear became a victim to my human excuses: that I wanted to marry Honour. But to marry her I would have to sleep with her. I wasn't just going to get what I wanted and go, this was for life.

I stood there, holding onto her, and in my head I was having this debate, arguing my conscience into silence again.

Sod it, I was a twenty-two year-old virgin and all I knew was that if I didn't go through with this I would probably die: just the touch of her skin was driving me insane. When we kissed I knew there was nothing else to be done.

But my conscience had one last attempt and I told her about Billo, and the complication of her brother Bilal being engaged to my sister Farzana. I had to know, before I took a step that would leave me unable to marry Billo, I had to be sure that Honour was willing to give us a go.

'There's this girl in Pakistan,' I said.

I could see she was visibly shaken and upset by it.

'So what does this mean, Al? Why did you come here if you knew that?'

'I had to.'

'Are you engaged then? Congratulations.' There was no warmth in her face.

'No, of course not. There's just a lot of pressure on me that's all. Farzana's future, the expectations from me as first-born. My parents want my wife to look after them when they're old.'

'Right and only a girl from Pakistan will do that? English girls stick their parents in old people's homes? Fuck off, Al.'

'Stop presuming things, will you?' I said. 'Honour, listen to me, I'm trying to be honest. I'm trying to protect you, us.'

'Don't Al.' The scent of her hair swished past me as she shook her head in defiance. She looked beautiful with anger dancing across her face. 'My grandad lived with us most of our lives,' she said. 'We all looked after him, even when his Alzheimer's had advanced so far that he needed twenty-four hour care. We pulled together as a family until he died. So don't presume that you guys have the monopoly on the right thing to do.'

'I didn't. You're twisting things now.'

'Just fuck off and marry your little…'

'I'm not going to. I'm just telling you there's this situation, it's happening and it's real. Would you rather I lied to you? Whatever we decide tonight, it's not going to be easy. That's all. It would be dishonest of me to let you wander in blind.'

'Oh gee, thanks,' she said.

'Honour… if this isn't for you what it is for me, then it's not worth you getting involved. If you think we have something we might be able to fight for, then fine. This isn't just about one night. What we decide tonight, it will change the rest of my life. With you I feel as though I can have a life; without you, just an existence. It's your choice.'

'Such a romantic.'

'Stop it, why are you being so unkind? I'm doing my best,' I said.

'I just don't want to hear it,' she said and I realised that she was crying. I moved back closer to her, held her tight in my arms, kissed the side of her face with a confidence I didn't feel.

'I'm not trying to be difficult. But after uni I didn't know where we were, what we were doing. You ran off to France and I went home to my parents' and then what?'

'I was on holiday,' she said.

'No, you weren't on holiday. It was three months, three months of our lives. Don't you get it? When we parted, I had already planned a future for us.'

'We're here together, aren't we?'

'But in your head this is getting together again. In my head we were never separated. Those weeks in uni, they weren't the whole thing, some short affair for me. They were just the first days of how I wanted my life to be, of how I felt, of my love for you.'

She looked at me like I was an idiot or speaking some foreign language.

'Love?' she said.

'In France... well, when I wrote to you, those letters? What did they mean to you?'

'I didn't think a lot was going on. I just thought you were flirting, maybe saying we weren't off the table. You never actually said *anything*,' she said.

'Off the table? I was dying for you. Every day I thought about you and my whole world revolved around you. I was like some freaky messed up little teenager. Why did you call me here then? Was there someone in France? Is that it? Did you fall in love with someone?'

'No, not at all. I mean, I didn't fall in love. I did meet a couple of people but they weren't special, they weren't you.'

My heart was in my mouth. I realised that I had no desire to know any more about her past. What was behind her made me feel sick, petrified. Only the future mattered now.

'I tried to kiss you, remember?' she said without looking at me. 'You were the one who turned me down.' Her sadness was breaking my heart. 'And all the time in France, you were there, in my head. I never forgot you all summer, that's why we're here now.'

'I said I love you about a million times. Maybe not the actual words, but in every other way,' I said.

'But… you never said what you're saying now, that you wanted to pursue this. I thought I was just a friend, a flirtation, someone you weren't interested in like that. I hoped I was wrong…'

'How could you not know, Hon? You were my everything. You still are. Oh, eff it,' I said and stormed off to stare into the darkness.

We stayed apart for a few minutes, thoughts like the rough water crashing between us and in my head. I wanted to know what she was thinking, what was going to happen next. I didn't understand how this worked.

Okay, so I hadn't said to her that she was like my girlfriend or whatever, but she should have known – I did. Now she had clouded the in between phase, and my love story with her would never be boy meets girl and happily ever after. We would always have boy meets girl, girls meets other boys, girl comes back to boy and then…

Then what?

It was my fault. I should have told her before. Swallowed that horrible fear and stepped up, been a man. My brother would have. Instead I let Mehreen hold me back.

So what now? Was it all over? Had I shouted her into hating me? Had she gone? I was a tangled mess, unable to navigate the situation. I thought for a moment it wasn't real, everything was too intense, I was playing at something.

When she put her cold hand in mine and rested her head on my shoulder… I have never been so grateful. It was her way of telling me that she was in it for the long haul, that she was willing to fight our corner.

That this for her was what it was for me.

All the way back to the house, the journey up the dark stairs, entering her bedroom… the voice of conscience whispered.

I stepped over a line and like some virginal bride I was the one being led by her. She was the one removing our clothes, I could barely move. She showed me where to put my hands, my mouth – her own busy on my trembling body. I worried what she would make of me, how would I fit compared to the others who had taught her the things she was doing to me? Again that feeling of being cheated resurfaced. I wanted to scream at her: I waited, Honour, why couldn't you do the same?

But as she tenderly showed me the way, she told me she loved me, she told me just what I wanted to hear: that she had never felt this way about anyone before.

After that it was just me and her and the bed.

I woke up in the middle of the night and showered, trying to do it quietly.

When I finished I took a clean towel, laid it out like a mat and prayed on it. The noise of the shower and my moving round her bedroom woke Honour. She didn't say anything, just sat on her bed, the blankets wrapped around her, pulled up to her chin, staring at me.

'Sorry I just forgot to do my night prayers. I have to do them now,' I said, hoping my voice was steady.

I could feel her watching me as my forehead touched her carpet, as I did a sajda, a prostration. In every one of the twenty-four sajdas I begged Allah for Honour, and to forgive me for everything in between now and marriage.

When I finished my prayers and turned around, the look of desolation on Honour's face broke my heart. I could sense her misunderstanding, feeling as though I was disgusted with myself. Did she feel abused and cheapened by my reaction? Her lips trembled as I looked at her. Her eyes shining, full of tears.

'Are you done?' she asked.

After all that, the only thing I could do was make love to her again, show her that what I thought she might be thinking wasn't true.

This was my baggage, my guilt, my soul, my eternity. It wasn't fair to burden her with that.

We weren't two people randomly having sex, this wasn't my wild phase before I married Billo.

No, I had done it because I loved this woman, and because I wanted to spend the rest of my life with her. Things were never easy for anyone, and sure things would be twice as difficult for us.

But there was nowhere else I would rather be than in her arms. The poetry of Sufis swam around me. My beloved was not divine, just a woman made from flesh and bones and – in my eyes – perfect for her flaws, for her humanity.

But the fire within her, and her soul, were eclipsing my own. They say some couples are joined in heaven, and on Earth they look for their partner soul to be with.

I knew that I had found mine in her. And who can fight heaven?

Chapter Five

HONOUR

I never asked Al what he prayed about that night, after we made love for the first time. I knew I was too raw to cope if he had said that he had asked for forgiveness. We were both too rookie at the whole love thing. I like to think it was a prayer of thanks, a way of ensuring we could stay together for the rest of our lives.

We moved in together a few weeks later. It wasn't intentional; Al had started his MA back in London and neither of us could face being apart.

My dad offered to drive us up to Al's flat, grumbling the entire time about my possessions crammed into the boot, split bin bags leaking socks and necklaces, old suitcases stuffed too full to close and tied with grubby string.

'What have you got, Al?' he asked, yet again and as rhetorically as the first time. 'One rucksack and the same clothes you arrived in? All a chap needs.'

I looked over my shoulder at Al, he was smirking but at least he didn't join in.

'And I bet nine tenths of it is crap,' my father continued. 'You'll get there and throw it all out. Insist on new. Bloody women.'

'Dad, who are you actually talking to?' I asked. 'No one cares. They're my things and it's none of your bloody business. I'd have got the train if I'd known I'd have to put up with this. Jesus.'

I turned the radio up louder so that he could only moan to himself for the rest of the journey although I'm sure he treated the poor shop assistant at the service station to an earful of my failings as a packer.

Between them, Al and my dad lugged my bags up the steps to the new flat. I ran around behind them picking up lost pants and stray make up as the bags finally gave way and shed their contents on the way in.

Al seemed to find his grown up self as my dad left, shaking his hand and thanking him for all his efforts.

'Yeah, thanks, Dad.' I kissed him on the cheek. 'Next time I'll maybe sort through the bags a bit. Leave some stuff at yours.'

'No, no, darling, not at ours, just chuck it. That's the solution.' He waved as he got back in the car. 'Enjoy!'

'Shouldn't you have carried me over the threshold?' I asked Al. 'Technically, it's our first home.'

'Carried you over the threshold? I think I should be sending you to bed with no supper.' He smiled as he said it but there was a hint of sternness in his narrowed lips.

'Because?'

'Because of the way you just spoke to your father. And all the way here. Blimey, I hope he doesn't think I'd ever be that disrespectful.' He was heaping my bags on to the bed, looking backwards and forwards from the huge pile to the small chest of drawers and the less-than-generous cupboard.

'He likes it.' I started to open the first bag. 'And it's his fault.'

'Honestly, Hon, I'm not kidding – I've never heard anyone talk to their parent that way. Not ever. If that happened at home, phew, you've no idea.'

'Really?'

He nodded. Those beautiful brows raised up to his hairline, his face at its most expressive, almost comic. 'You were out of order.'

'I suppose,' I said without conviction.

'He drove us all the way here. It's Saturday, he could be out enjoying himself, not stuck on a motorway.'

'Oh, for God's sake, okay, I'll ring him later and say thank you.

Better?'

'Better.'

By the time I rang my father that evening, I'd thrown away at least half of the stuff I'd brought.

Within weeks of moving into Al's college digs, and to my delight, I bagged an internship at a West End graphics studio. Although it only just about covered my travel expenses, it was more than I could have ever hoped for in terms of work experience. A reference from there almost guaranteed me a place at the Royal College of Art for my own masters.

Al and I realised our CVs would be amazing if we could just hang on financially and academically. They were halcyon days; little time and even less money. Small gestures of making each other coffee during a late night study stint or leaving notes in each others' sandwich boxes or coat pockets, home-made cakes in an otherwise empty kitchen.

I would go straight to my West End waitressing job as soon as I'd tidied my work station in the studio each day. People who'd been polite clients in the day failed to recognise me once I was a ubiquitous waitress bringing more drinks. I used to wonder if the same men would have tried to grope my backside or pull me onto their knees if they'd known I was really a graphic designer, or that my boyfriend was smart enough to be at LSE doing a Masters in Economics that would have made their thick heads burst.

It was a relief when Christmas punctuated our routine. We needed a break, even with youth on our side we were exhausted. I didn't really give Al the option of going to his parents', it didn't occur to me that they'd make a big deal of Christmas and, anyway, Eid would be at the end of January and he'd go home for that. Without me.

We caught one of the last trains down on Christmas Eve, people jostling parcels and bags, a burr of excitement running through the carriage. The usual rules of engagement were off, passengers helped each other in and out of the train, held doors open and offered seats to the heavily laden.

I looked across the aisle to Al; it was too busy to get seats together. I'd tried to keep family gifts to a minimum but I'd splashed out on Connie. I hadn't seen her for the whole autumn – our longest ever – and every time I'd seen something that I knew she'd love, a notebook in Greenwich market, a tiny brooch on a bric-a-brac stall, it would make me feel closer to her and I'd add it to my Christmas collection.

A woman with a buggy forced her way into the carriage and Al stood up to give her his seat. The huge rucksack of gifts balanced against his leg and I carried our clothes in a much smaller holdall.

When I was a child, I'd asked for a clockwork mouse every Christmas; nothing more, nothing less, despite Connie's annual requests for ponies and luxury Wendy houses. It was still family tradition that I got a clockwork mouse at the bottom of my stocking every year. I imagined my mother wrapping the predictable stocking fillers, my father counting off his rows of spirits to make sure he had the ingredients of any cocktail any guest might ask for. This would be the first year he'd also have to make *mocktails*.

Al and I got to the house before Connie. Later I drove my parents' car down to the docks to pick her up. Al refused point blank to come with me and I had to cover my gratitude in a pretend disappointment.

She and I both squealed as she walked through the sliding

double doors of the arrivals hall. People turned to look at the racket, remembered it was Christmas, took a double take at the identical twins, and went on their way smiling.

'Oh my God, I've missed you so much. Just so much.' I hugged her tightly.

'You too. I'm so glad I'm here. And I've got so much to tell you. Stuff I didn't want to put in an email.' She stepped back to get her case and we looked at each other, laughing. 'Is he in the car? Al? I can't wait to meet him.'

The months in France showed. Connie looked fantastic; her coat was long and fitted – a far cry from my practical puffer jacket. She wore woollen gloves, hoops of subtle colour on her fingers, and her tight jeans were tucked into tan cowboy boots. Her hair was shorter than mine and straightened; it made her look more like our mother when, normally, she just looked like me.

'He offered to stay at home, bless him. He knew I needed you to myself for ten minutes. I can't believe you're back.' I took her arm excitedly and we headed out to the car. 'That suitcase is a bit grownup. I swear I left you with two Auchan carrier bags and Dad's ex-Army duffle.'

'It belongs to a friend.' She smirked over the word friend. 'I borrowed it. But you first, tell me about London, about Al. How is it really, living together?'

'It's fab, Con, it really is. Just having him there every day when I wake up, cooking together – when we're not at work – it's brilliant.'

'You look so happy,' she said. 'I'm so glad you got it right.'

'I did go out with some idiots, didn't I?' We both exploded with laughter, I opened the car boot and threw her bag in. We spent the next minutes rubbing frost from the inside of the windows – the car's hot air blower had died years before. 'He's much more sensible than I am, that really helps.'

'And?'

The car engine spluttered into life on the third try. 'He's just lovely. And unbelievably fit.' We laughed together, extra giggles rolling round our relief at being together after such a long separation. 'And you? Tell me more. Are you going to move to London now you're back?'

'Ah.' My sister opened her green eyes wide. 'Slight change of plan. Called Laurent. And I have to go back to France to give his suitcase back.'

'No way. When was this?'

'Just the last couple of weeks.'

My elbow moved out towards her as I steered the car left at a roundabout. She put her gloved hand on my arm. 'I'm really sorry but I can't come back. Not yet anyway.'

'What if I whine and stamp my feet and shout?' I was torn between celebrating her happiness and mourning the good times I'd anticipated; just Al, Connie and me hanging out in London.

'Could you leave Al to come to France?'

I breathed out hard, the warmed air from my lungs visible in front of me and leaving a cloud on the windscreen. 'Just the thought makes me shudder. I hate leaving him even to go to work.'

'Well then, you'll just have to put up with it. For now at least.'

We pulled into my parents' driveway, my mum waved excitedly through the kitchen window, soft-focussed by the steam of her Christmas cooking.

'Come on, you need to meet Al, and there's a vat of red wine with our names on it.' I grabbed Con's fancy suitcase.

'Have you managed to stop Mum from warming the wine and filling it full of leaves and orange and crap?'

I shook my head. 'Unfortunately not, but we'll soldier bravely through it over the next few days.'

I watched my mum tiptoe across the cold pebbles. From the back, she didn't look so different to Connie and me, one knotted vein at the back of her knee a giveaway.

'How old's your mum?' Al was obviously thinking the same thing.

'Fifty-three? Fifty-four? She had her fiftieth when I was in sixth form. Fifty-five or so.' I knew that when I shrugged off my boots, those same smooth stones would feel like hot coals beneath my feet.

'Same age as my mum. Pretty much.' He was taking the longest time possible to undo his shoelaces. 'You'd never know it though. They're so different.'

We looked at my mum, close to the foaming water's edge, my father holding one of her hands to pull her on. Behind them the sea rolled in a turmoil of battleship grey and weak edges of spume faltered onto the beach before being sucked back into the water. My father led the charge, his legs spindly in his swim shorts, his skin shining from the fine spray of the waves on the icy December wind.

'Come on,' Connie shouted, her fleece round her shoulders and her bare legs mottled with blue and purple.

'I can't believe I'm doing this,' said Al for the hundredth time. He folded his jeans over his shoes in a neat pile. I could see the goose bumps on his thighs, the black hairs on his legs rising up in an effort to trap some warmth on his skin.

'Just let your breath out in a rush as the water hits you. Then your body will instinctively breathe in again no matter what.'

'For fun, yes? We're doing this for fun?' I didn't know if he was shaking his head ruefully or because of the sheer cold.

I think Connie and I were probably seven or eight when we did our first Boxing Day sea swim, but we'd been to the beach every year of our lives to watch our parents and their friends do it.

It was the same bay I'd brought Al to on his first day in Kent, before we'd even kissed. The seagulls wheeling on the summer breeze then had seemed to fly voluntarily; the ones now were whipped up on the sharp wind, their angry shrieks in keeping with the colour of the sky.

Running into a freezing sea is an extraordinary experience. At first you notice only the pain, every pore filling with water, every microscopic area of your skin on fire. Then, as you start to reach out with your arms, kick your legs and gain control, the breath rushes back into your lungs and your head clears startlingly fast. You know you'll live. Almost everyone, at this exact point, yells out, whoops of joyous survival linking up across the surface of the water like steam. The elation sets in, the wakening of your body, bones, skin and hair, everything completely shocked into renewal.

I got the feeling back in my legs, still gasping in the cold. I tested the depth of the water with my toe, the sloping pebbles may have been just below me but I didn't have enough sensitivity in my feet to identify them if they were. I spat sea water, looking out towards France and the wild rollers of waves a little further out.

Al swam past me, his muscled arm proud of the water like a shark's fin.

'How long?' he bellowed over the wind. 'When? Out?' I couldn't hear the other words, the waves were too loud. His black fringe was slicked to his forehead.

'Now.' I pointed to the shore and we dragged ourselves out, bodies shining a burnt red – his deep and even, mine vivid and patchy.

Everyone was shouting, even Al, calling out in yells and short sounds like Martial Arts fighters, trying to rub ourselves with towels without taking off our fresh skin.

'That was amazing.' Al was laughing, a blue tinge on his lips, his teeth chattering.

'Just pull a fleece on and race to the pub.' I was already fighting my arms into my jacket, the material catching on my damp hands. 'Come on, grab your stuff and run.'

My mum and dad, hand-in-hand and half-dressed, were already sprinting across the car park, lifting their knees in an exaggerated dance as the small stones stuck into their cold bare feet.

We all got to the bar at the same time. A chattering line of everyone I loved; my mum and dad, Connie and Al. There were brandy glasses lined up along the bar as far as the eye could see. My father pressed them into our hands. 'L'chaim!' he shouted and around the pub other Boxing Day swimmers shouted it back, swigging the drinks.

My dad looked at Al, the brandy glass still in his hand, the liquid not even rippling and his blue lips dry.

'Jesus Christ, man,' my dad said, the sympathy in his voice overwhelming. 'Not even for medicinal purposes?'

ALI

Living together revealed aspects of Honour that I'd never have seen at a distance; her kindness, the way she thought so hard about other people. She'd even made me proud of carrying empty jars and bottles down to the recycling bin in the car park, gathering together bits of cardboard and feeding it, piece by piece, into the hopper in an effort to make a better world. My family would never pick this habit up, I was certain, the idea of my mother carrying 'rubbish' round the streets was a million miles from possible.

As Ramadan came round, I loved the tender way Honour fussed round me. I wondered if she'd feel the same after a month of me hungry and bad-tempered, low blood sugar stopping me concentrating and all of my energies spent on getting closer to God.

I could hear her clattering about in the kitchen.

'What's that? Smells great.'

'They're high-energy bars. Nuts and seeds and dried berries. Ramadan bars. They're to stop you getting hungry during the day, slow-release foods, you know?'

'Thanks. You're amazing, do you know that?' I said.

It was late, about nine-thirty at night; I had come back from the mosque.

'Can we go to the pictures tomorrow?' she said, her back still to me, as she cut the baked mixture into squares.

'I'd love to but if I miss a night I'll miss the bit of Qur'an they're reciting that day,' I said, coming up and resting my head on her shoulder, watching her slice cakes with a blunt knife. The landlord obviously didn't trust students with sharp ones. 'I do

75

appreciate your support. It's lovely having someone thinking about me like this. I promise when it's Lent I'll give up whatever you do.' I kissed her cheek.

'Why on Earth would I give up anything for Lent?'

'I know you're lapsed, but even lapsed Christians end up giving up something, don't they? You just did Christmas. Maybe you should give up chocolate,' I said.

'Everyone does Christmas. Even your family have Christmas dinner. I'm not a Christian, Al, I'm not giving up anything.'

'You must have been christened, or baptised or something. So technically you are. Like, when you were born.' Both my palms were resting on her hips. My stomach growled.

'I wasn't christened. I don't believe in God, neither do my parents. Why would Con and me be christened?'

They hadn't gone to church actually, at Christmas. I hadn't even thought about it then. What an idiot.

'You mean, for real, you're not a Christian? As in *at all*?' I said.

'Never have been and...' she said, laughing, 'never will be.' She moved away and started wrapping the high-energy bars in cling film.

I felt as though the ice had just cracked and I had fallen in.

Ramadan intensified my faith. I would wake up at 4am, pray, have my pre-dawn meal, fast all day, read Qur'an and visit the LSE prayer rooms for each namaaz. I would have a quick dinner to open my fast, then shoot off to the mosque for evening prayer, which lasted two hours in this month. Everything I thought, said or did reminded me of my faith, the faith of my father and his father before him, and of my duty to God and my family. It became extremely difficult to balance in the light of my real life.

It had been nearly five months since I had been back home and I had started to miss my family, even Jamal and Farzana. My plan had been to reveal my 'other life' to them after Ramadan, after I could convince them – and myself – that I was still a good Muslim, that I'd followed my fast in the tradition of the Prophet (peace be upon him). With their faith in me bolstered I'd tell them that I intended to marry a Christian woman, my mum would make a fuss, my dad would talk her down and point out that there's only one God, it's all the same.

And we'd all live happily ever after.

Except that my girlfriend wasn't a Christian.

I'd grown up believing that I should learn about the fires of hell from my father and look for heaven at the feet of my mother. I remember waiting for my mother to bow down in sujood, and trying to catch a glimpse of heaven on the soles of her feet, only to be disappointed by her dry and cracked skin. It was the first time I had learnt about allegory and parable, that literal interpretation would inevitably lead to misunderstanding. Meeting Honour made me interpret it all in another way, it felt like she was all I needed.

I had to make an honest woman of her. We had to make this proper, legitimate. Get married – there was nothing else to do – the only way to move on. I knew I couldn't face year after year of trying not to sleep with her during Ramadan to convince myself of my piety. Years of feeling that I was no good to either her or God.

And I'd assumed she was, at some level, a Christian, someone I could marry in my faith. I didn't know what we would do now, how my father would react.

I had just followed my heart. I had tuned out everything that might get in the way of me being with Honour. Maybe I'd purposefully not asked the right questions.

So did it matter what everyone else thought? There were two

people in our bed, and that's where it should begin and end.

'Al, are you okay?'

She rubbed her eyes, stretched... man, she was my world...

'Al? You're shaking? What's up?'

'Nothing, just a bit cold,' I said.

I moved closer to her, spooning her body, but I didn't make love to her.

'Do you mind if we don't have sex in Ramadan? I know it's a bit hypocritical, but are you okay if – just for these few weeks – we don't?'

I didn't say how the brothels in Lahore closed during Ramadan. That didn't sit right with us. We weren't doing that.

She didn't say anything, just kissed my hand, above the scar, and I held her tighter.

My heart was calm, and I felt a sense of peace again.

This was right, and the only thing I knew about my future, was that Honour would be in it. I would make the world accept us and live around us.

I felt invincible when I held her.

As for God, well, it was a merciful God I believed in... and He had created Honour the same way He had created me, whether she believed or not.

For whatever reason, she had been sent to me, given to me. Completed me.

We lasted about five days before we made love again.

Chapter Six

HONOUR

We squeezed into Al's college room while we could bear it then, as the spring ebbed, found a grotty but affordable basement flat in Woolwich. It was almost Blackheath with the wind in the right direction and good walking shoes on, and on damp days tiny frogs hopped through the air vents in the walls. We absolutely loved it.

Later, when the first year of living together had brought an edge of reality to our little home, the summer heat in the flat and the small window were suffocating. We would climb, weary, dusty and over-worked, onto the slow southbound train and head to Kent for the weekend, stuffier at first even than the tiny room as the bodies of commuters and students crushed together in the swelter. The rattling carriages took us out of London, grey buildings slipped into green fields, sometimes startling with vivid colour after our tired views of pavements. Swapping the miles of littered streets for acres of oil-seed rape that stretched into a blue sky lifted my heart on a Friday afternoon however much Al grumbled about being old before our time.

I couldn't see it then but we were pulling ourselves through a space carved between youth and adulthood. On some occasions we'd arrive at my parents' with a bin bag, splitting with washing – other times, I'd pick out an Australian Chardonnay to try and show my dad what we were drinking in London these days or Al would cook up a batch of spinach-speckled chicken pakora and wrap them as a gift for my grateful mother.

'We could have gone to the pictures or something this weekend,' Al's face scrunched against the scratched glass of the train window. His straight hair spidered out onto the rough velour of the seat.

'Bollywood? Or something not ridiculous?' I squashed up beside him. He'd met me at the station straight from work and his shirt smelled of coffee and faded aftershave.

'You'll understand Bollywood one day, you'll get it eventually. Maybe when you're more mature.'

'Maybe when I'm a middle-aged gay man?' I inhaled his scent, so different from last year, more delicate, more subtle. I stretched out my feet under the seat in front and leant against the wrinkled linen of his shirt sleeve.

He stroked my hair. 'I would like to stay in London some weekends though, you know. Much as I love the company of your family...'

'Liar,' I said, my eyes closed, my face relaxed.

'Okay, much as I'm learning to tolerate the company of your family, I'd like to chill at the flat more. Have picnics in the park. Go swimming in Hampstead Lido.'

'Sit on a tube for an hour so we can have a refreshing outdoor swim?'

'You know what I mean.' I could hear the tiredness in his voice.

'I do,' I kissed the dark shadow of his jaw. 'But this weekend is special. It's the closest we can get to being there on our anniversary. You'd forgotten, hadn't you? It's a year since we first spent the night together.' I dropped my voice, self-conscious and suddenly aware of the other commuters. 'Properly.'

'Sometimes I wonder if you get me at all. Of course I hadn't forgotten. It's the only reason I'm not kicking and screaming about the theft of my precious weekend.' He returned the kiss, gently and quietly onto the top of my head. 'And I won't ever forget.'

We'd been experimenting in our kitchen with some over-ripe mangoes that had been going cheap at the market. Once we'd emptied all the mouldy jars on the top shelf of the fridge we sterilised them and filled them with fragrant mango chutney, flecks of home-chopped chilli suspended in the sticky orange of the sauce; we were inordinately proud of our creation and that weekend Al carried a jar of it for my mother, the lid decorated in a gingham-checked paper, the label hand-written and with her name on.

'Oh, darling,' she gushed, 'you are marvellous.'

Al and the dog eyed each other warily as we sat down in the kitchen.

'What would you like for supper?' My mother clutched a tea towel that matched her apron.

'We're going out, Mum, special occasion.'

'Sorry, darling, you did tell me. Did you book anywhere?'

'No, don't be daft. It's not central London.'

'I know it's not, sweetheart, but there's golf on. The town's busy.'

Al stared at the dog. 'Let's just go anyway. Now. And wander around until we find somewhere.' He headed towards the door.

We felt like Mary and Joseph being turned away from restaurant after restaurant. We were even denied fish and chips on the seafront since the chip shop had gone up-market and decided to coat everything in 'beer batter'.

Eventually, we squeezed into a booth side-by-side in the only restaurant that would have us.

'Yum, yum,' Al said, his black eyes twinkling. 'Provincial seaside curry house. My favourite.'

'You never know,' I whispered, smiling at the over-enthusiastic waiter who handed us the greasy menus. 'It might surprise you.'

Al peeled a piece of dried onion from the back of the laminated card. 'Or it might not.' He leaned closer to me, blowing his fringe off his face. 'I don't really mind. I'm with the most beautiful woman in the room.'

I glanced round the darkened space, the ceilings low and tarred umber, noisy fans whirring downwards in an attempt to reconstruct a Bangladeshi nightspot.

'And I've woken up next to her every day for a year.' Al raised his coke glass to my wine. 'The food's the last thing on my mind.'

We ordered 'curry house staples', the Asian equivalent of scampi and chips, things that couldn't really go wrong; samosas and grilled tikka meats. Pre-prepared halal dishes that could be thrown into a deep fat fryer by even the least skilful chef. I wanted to chance a prawn puri but Al's solemn face warned me off.

Al wandered through the restaurant to find a loo. I watched him walk away, my chin propped up on my elbows, calm and happy to be here with him a full year on.

As he passed a table on his way , a man suddenly stopped him, his hand palm flat in front of Al's chest. I sat up straight.

'Four more poppadoms, please mate,' the man asked Al and I suddenly saw him as they saw him, black work trousers, white crumpled shirt, his jacket casually undone for a Friday night and a brown face in a sea of white and swarthy pinks.

'I don't work here.' Al's voice was low, he almost hissed at the man.

The man looked at his plate in a flurry of apology, embarrassed to the tips of his scarlet ears.

I didn't know what to say, I pretended I hadn't heard it but Al and I both knew I had.

In the dark of my old room, we lay side-by-side, not knowing quite how to start the conversation about the man's mistake. Al was already certain that he couldn't fit in to my parents' world; I couldn't bear for this to compound his insecurity, his suspicions.

I didn't know whether my concern helped him or just made it all worse; he was uncomfortable, tense. I kissed his shoulders, wishing that I knew what to do. I closed my eyes tightly and hoped that love was enough.

ALI

'Four more poppadoms please, mate.' A stereotype is a stereotype.

Me, in an Indian restaurant in Deal. Must be a waiter.

Him, skinhead and tattoos. Must be a racist.

It was a deep-rooted thing. We grew up with skinhead gangs marauding through our streets, threatening us to 'go back to where we came from'.

Nice.

Mistakes happen, all a bit embarrassing, this was Deal, he was just a man at dinner with his wife and a friend.

So I looked him in the eyes, nodded and smiled, coming close to him so others wouldn't hear his mistake, ready to laugh it all off.

'Sorry mate, I don't work here.'

Something inside me rose up, I was angry, felt labelled. I was here with Honour, a romantic night out, and no one had noticed. This man had not noticed. I was invisible to him, until I was to be of service.

I stared into his eyes, expecting disgust, the casual arrogance I see so many times amongst groups of drunken men in Indian restaurants. They seem to inhabit areas best left to burra sahibs back in their cool clubs, while the natives milled around them. I geared up for confrontation.

Instead, the man had turned the colour of the faded red napkins, absolute embarrassment reeking from his every pore.

'I'm so sorry,' he said, half-rising.

The woman with him looked away, just as uncomfortable. Me staying on would increase their awkwardness, and it threatened to turn into an incident. They would go home and turn it over in their heads, and it would be their memory of the night. So I put a hand on the man's shoulder, and smiled, while holding out a hand that he shook tentatively.

I walked away as the couple exchanged embarrassed looks. I knew that, no matter how wonderful the rest of the night was for me and Honour, this is the thing I would take away with me.

At the sink in the restaurant bathroom I splashed cold water on my face, and stared at my reflection. My white shirt, my brown skin, my dark eyes. They were there forever, I couldn't change those things. Honour would forever walk with me and I would be different to her.

Truth is, it made me feel sad. I was born in Manchester, I wanted to call myself English, but I had to use the term British, because there were people in this land who only saw being white as being English. To some people I would never be more than the colour of my skin, I would always be a 'paki', I would never belong.

'Where are you from?'

Immediately you know what the answer should be. Pakistan, India, Nigeria, St Lucia. You have a battle in your head, lasting milliseconds, well-rehearsed, well-worn. You know what they want you to say, and you know what you want to say. Then the long view – how difficult shall I make this? Shall I capitulate, say the name of a mother nation, or hold on and say, 'Manchester.' Only to find the answer inadequate, and the inevitable follow up questions: 'No, where are you from originally?' and 'Where are your parents from?'

You are born somewhere, grow up breathing the air, drinking the water, eating the grain. It is in the earth of England that I will be buried. And still they say I don't belong here.

Then there are the majority, the ones who say actually you do belong, you are British. Well, British Pakistani. Or British Muslim. Or even English Muslim. Always I have to accept another label, like some mongrel.

Except for Honour. The only person who ever referred to me as English, without any colour classification.

So I don't think about it. I don't care what anyone else thinks. I know I belong here. That my family belong here. That my children will belong here.

And the word paki washes off me, I don't react to it anymore. It says more about the person saying it than me.

It was a tough brown skin that our children would have to develop. I just hoped the realisation didn't make her run screaming the other way.

I shook my head, I was making too much of this. I went back to the table, the lingering thought pinching inside me, how I would always be on the outside, trying to justify my right to be here.

'Everything okay?' Honour asked, lacing her fingers into mine as I sat down.

She had seen me speak to the man. Was she afraid too, had she made her own assumptions? She didn't seem upset, not in the fearful sense. There was something else, hard, ready to fight?

'It was nothing, he thought I was a waiter that's all,' I said.

I hope the smile that I didn't feel in my eyes would convince her.

'Ignorant…'

'Come on, let's leave it. He was embarrassed, even more than I was I reckon.'

She nodded, but I sensed her thinking for the rest of the meal.

'It's going to happen. We're used to London, Manchester. Just wait until we end up in some Scandinavian village, where I really am the only pak…'

'Don't Al, don't even joke about something so serious,' she said.

'Come on, lighten up, let's have fun. It's nothing, okay?'

I tried to convince her, picking food off her plate, starting a mock argument. The food was surprisingly good for somewhere outside Manchester; even I had to grudgingly admit that. The lightness returned in drips, until it felt as though it was flowing again.

I had muted my own anger to stop the other diners having their night ruined, but when we were alone at home, it was all that I could think about. It was all I remembered from that night.

Chapter Seven

HONOUR

For three years, Al and I ducked below the parapet, safe from prying eyes. As the world ticked round into the new millennium, I still hadn't met his parents. He took day trips up to them, sometimes even stayed over, but we stayed mainly off the subject and were both happy to do that.

'We will have to move from here, you know,' Al whispered at me in the dark. 'We're twenty-five years old; we both have master's degrees as of today. Oh, did I remember to congratulate you?' He kissed me again, my mouth still sweet with the champagne I'd drunk earlier. 'I have a mega-top job, as of last month. Oh, did you remember to congratulate me?' He kissed me again and it was some time before we finished the conversation.

'And here we are, living in a subterranean grotto with a number of mature tadpoles.'

'They wouldn't like it anywhere else,' I told him. 'What about schools? What about their friends?'

'If we had a garden, we could build a pond. Find them some slimy rocks. You must have some left over that your old boyfriends climbed out from under.'

I put the pillow over his face. 'I have some that I keep by for when you get too annoying. To finish you off with.'

'Seriously though, we should start looking. I earn enough on my own to pay a pretty massive mortgage and I'll get preferential terms. You'll get snapped up in a second and you can pay for all our holidays and treats.'

I sighed, 'The Good-Muslim-Boy way?'

'I don't know why you mind. I would have thought it would suit a post-modern feminist.' I could hear his smile in the dark. 'It would be massively emasculating for me if you were paying the bills. Seriously. It would feel so weird.'

'I don't mind, I'm messing with you. While we can afford it. If things got tight you'd have to get over yourself.'

His answer was, 'Hmmm'. Enough for me.

My sister had met Laurent months after I met Al and yet they were already picking dresses and flowers, ready to marry on a French hillside festooned with secular happiness and guilt-free garlands. We would all share delightedly in their traditional French croquembouche; choux pastry buns piled high with crème anglaise and spun sugar. My father would make his speech first in English and then in atrocious French. We would laugh, we would dance, and the two cultures – even separated by water and language – would meet to declare the happy couple wed.

My mother harboured secret fantasies, hatched since our birth, of a double wedding for her twin girls. Luckily Con and I agreed that it would be in appalling bad taste.

My same mother who, despite her dedication to political correctness and ability to tell her identical daughters apart at a glance, was convinced that Al and Laurent looked like brothers. She based this on a furtive notion that all brown people look quite similar and that Laurent's father was dark-skinned. In reality, there was an obvious world of difference between Con's half-African fiancé and my own smouldering Rajput.

Laurent's father didn't take his commitment to Islam quite as seriously as some people and ran off back to Morocco leaving Laurent's white French mother holding the baby. I assured Connie that, from my point of view, the absence of the Muslim relatives was a distinct advantage.

There is one photo where they do look alike. Connie and I turned up to my dad's birthday party wearing similar outfits, something we do all the time, lots of twins do. Al and Laurent both happened to wear linen shirts, as men do when they're dressed up smart on a hot summer's day, in that year's particular favourite shade of baby blue. The effect is accentuated by the fact that we're lined up like wise monkeys, all faking grins.

If you saw the same picture in Al's parents' house though, it would more probably be an example of their BOGOF children deals, a daughter given away with a son, or two siblings marrying cousins.

'If I got married in a field like your sister and Laurent, my mother would drop to her knees and wail *"Mera Allah kithey*?" over and over. Where's my God? Where's my God?'

'Like Jesus being crucified?'

'You've heard of Jesus?' He rolled his eyes in pretend wonder.

'I did R.E. at school you know; I'm not a total savage.'

'Actually, he said *"Eli, Eli, lama sabachthani*?" – My God, why hast thou forsaken me?'

'Which you, of course, are going to tell me is Arabic.'

'Aramaic, actually. But you're improving. I may yet get you in a mosque.'

'Of course you will, just not in a wedding dress.'

Al's choice was bitter; live with me and fight the things his family wanted, had brought him up with. Or do what his mother wanted and lose me forever. If I converted, or reverted as Al would say – he believes everyone was born believing in Allah – he could tell them about me and then, with terrifying rapidity, we could marry in the mosque and everything would be fine. Except, of course, for the thorny issue of his previous betrothal and Farzana's marriage to Bilal. But I'm not a Muslim woman, I can't live like that; I don't want to. I don't even believe in that sort of a god, the beardy fellow, the omnipotent being with the ability to crush nations, flood hospitals, burn children, just to teach The Faithful a lesson. Fuck that.

I felt for Billo more than anyone. She was as innocent in this as Al. This was about the centuries and millennia that gave Al his majestic features, his strong jaw and flawless skin, not about Billo or Al. It was about the heritage that my children would wear with pride, his dominant genes dictating their colouring and stature. It was about money and passports and education, but it wasn't about Al or Billo.

There were solutions, ones that real people had tried, even members of Al's family. We knew they weren't for us.

'My cousin found a way round it. It's not, er, pretty.'

We were enjoying a lazy Saturday in our little flat, sprawled on our sofas and waiting for our coffees to cool down.

'Really? Did he pack her off on a banana boat and have her come back meek and R-E-V-E-R-T-E-D?' That was unkind, picking at Al's beliefs was below the belt but sometimes irresistible.

'You wanna know? Or not?' The eyebrows; sharp though, not amused.

'Sorry.'

Al took a deep breath. 'He married the girl from back home. His mum got her day, my other cousins got their freedom, and the family looked good, *saddi izzat bachgayi*, saved face. They moved in with my aunt, so his wife had company, help with the kids an' all dat.' His Manchester accent was coming out with his nerves. Even talking about his family and their intentions made his palms sweat. He picked up his coffee cup, flattened his hands around its heat.

'And his girlfriend married a nice white guy and never spoke to your cousin again?' I was on thin ice; insulting family was a red rag to Al.

He didn't bite.

'He's still with his girlfriend. She's lovely. They have two kids. She lives in Hale.'

'And his wife?'

'They have five kids. Gorgeous, all of them.' His speech was fractured; it was obviously hard for him to talk about. 'He can afford it. He pays for everything for his girlfriend, for their kids.'

'You're kidding me?'

He shook his head. 'It's terrible, isn't it? It happens all the time though. Honestly, I even know he'd recommend it to me if I told him about you.'

'Wow.' My jaw dropped. 'And they'd have you do that?'

'It's possible,' he admitted. He covered my hand with his, my thin fingers peeked between his. 'We'll have to wait and see. It's a world of heartbreak if you're on the wrong side of it.'

'Secrets and lies?'

'Sometimes people just give in. Abdul, my oldest cousin...'

I nodded encouragement, pressing my fingertips against the coffee table so that my knuckles rose up between his. 'Go on,' I said.

'His first love, a girl called Shahana, was already signed up to marry a freshie. She and Abdul met at uni, they were crazy about each other. Really, I mean properly in love. I met her a few times, really nice girl. Her parents just wouldn't contemplate changing the arrangements they'd made for her. I mean, there were other catches, she was Raeen bradary, and we're Rajput.'

I raised my hands in a shrugging gesture. 'And?'

'Well, they're different castes. Rajputs think they're better than everyone, that we're special."

'You're special, all right.' I grinned and threw a cushion at him.

He caught my wrists and leaned over me, kissing my face.

'And I'm not going to do what Abdul had to. I'm not going to walk away and marry someone else, someone I have to learn to love because we have children together, because people expect us to live a certain way. I love you. And you're my only option.' His dark eyes were solemn, he sighed loudly. 'And somehow I'm going to have to convince my family that you're their only option too.'

I was never sure whether these glimpses into Al's background emphasised his determination or my naivety. I had to remind myself constantly that the people he was talking about were just like us that they'd been to the same schools and universities, that they did the same jobs and spoke the same language.

When I thought about how easily his culture would absorb and accept any of those duplicitous face-saving decisions if Al had chosen to make one, it felt like someone walking over my grave.

ALI

Graduation itself had been another blip in terms of honesty, and I watched the grey area inside me spread into what was once black and white. Right and wrong.

And as I heard myself tell my father that I wasn't going to attend my graduation ceremony, I felt more uncomfortable than ever.

'Are you sure, beta, you won't get the opportunity again?' he said.

'It's okay, we did the whole picture thing when I graduated the first time,' I said. 'I can't be bothered with the gown again. And it seems a bit of a backward step now I'm actually working, it seems like it was a while ago.'

Honour sat on the sofa, wearing my hired gown and cap and I tried not to make eye contact with her as I lied through my teeth to my father.

She looked away, poured herself more Moët, topped up my Shloer. I'd been able to hear her from the stage of the Peacock Theatre at the graduation ceremony. Despite sitting all on her own, surrounded by strangers, she'd whooped her support to the rafters when I stepped on stage and shouted 'Mubarak!' at the top of her voice as I collected the scroll from the Chancellor.

'I'm proud of you. Well done,' my dad said and my guilt flicked to Honour's graduation in a month's time and to a mental picture of David, Paula and me sitting in a row like a family. 'So, now you're finished, am I okay to speak to Billo's parents?'

My face must have paled. Honour looked at me with knitted eyebrows, her head to one side.

'No, Dad.' I said. 'I don't want to, not yet. And definitely not to

Billo.'

I watched the redness creep up Honour's face. She moved her foot on the coffee table and knocked the glass, I couldn't tell if it was deliberate. She went off to the kitchen to get a cloth.

'Then who? It's time, Ali.'

I sighed into the phone.

'Dad, I've just started a new job. Banking careers take a lot of time, I can't have that pressure on me.'

Honour came back, started mopping up the spilt drink. She had removed the gown and cap.

'You have put me in a very awkward position,' Dad said.

'No, Dad, you guys are creating the awkward situation, not me.'

'I can't tell you how disappointed I am, Ali,' he said.

'I can guess. Okay, Abbu, I have to go. I'll call later and speak to Mum.'

I put the phone down and sighed loudly.

'Not good?' Honour said.

She brought me over a refilled glass, clinked hers against mine, and we toasted our future instead.

'Don't worry about it, Hon, we're all I need.'

I still had panic attacks in the night – about the future, my family – despite my outward calmness. I could never tell Honour; it wasn't her fault and I didn't want her to think that I was anything but crazy about her.

I still believed in One God, His Prophet (the voice in my head still said *peace be upon him* every time I thought or said his name) and His religion. I didn't drink, smoke, I didn't disrespect my parents, cheat, steal, kill, traffic whores or drugs. I prayed five times a day, fasted in Ramadan, gave to charity. Hell, I even worked for an Islamic bank, specialising in halal mortgages and investments. I did my bit.

My father called a couple of months into my new job.

'Zain passed his Manchester Grammar exams,' he said. 'Are you able to help with the fees?'

'Yes, Dad, I promised I would.'

'Okay. I am good for half of them, if you could maybe help out with the other half?'

'I'm okay for the full amount. You take it easy.'

That night I ran it by Honour.

'It's your money, why are you asking me?' she said.

She was sitting on the bed, painting her nails, cotton wool in between each toe. I sat at her dressing table, watching her, marvelling at her precision.

'It's our money. In Islam the wife gets to decide what happens to the money,' I said.

'Well, we're not in Islam. And I'm not your wife,' she said. Her tongue sticking out to the side as she reached a tricky bit.

'And whose fault is that?' I asked, taking the irritation felt at my father out on Honour.

She looked up at me and pointed her nail varnish brush at me like a dart. I could smell the chemical tinge from where I was sitting. A red blob fell onto our white cotton bedspread.

'Well, you have a plethora of women waiting to marry you for a passport. Feel free to pick one at any time.' She smiled, didn't mean it.

I felt foolish. Just the night before we had discussed the women in arranged marriages, girls like Billo. For the first time I was wondering about the rights of these girls they brought from Pakistan to marry my cousins – whether they liked it or not. They were someone's daughter, someone's sister too. A person in their own right. They too were God's creation, and yet I had never stopped to wonder whether the marriages they were making were the best thing for them. Whether they wanted to leave their homes and families to marry men sometimes thousands of miles away. I'd grown up thinking they'd just be grateful for the Green Card, for the British passport.

Messed up, innit.

'Sorry,' was all I could say.

I went home to sort out Zain's fees a couple of weeks later, and to try and make headway into my family's expectations.

I had ticked the boxes: Education, job, house. Next was marriage and kids. I couldn't see how Honour and me would get to that last stage, nor could I see how I could exist without her. The pressure of duty came back, it was always there, buried just under my life.

I was left alone with my father, tea steaming in mugs in our hands, the Manchester chill evident. This was lecture time, my mum had closed the door behind her.

'Ali, have you thought more about marriage, my son?'

Standard opener, quite calm, reasonable.

'Yes. I'm not ready yet, not for an arranged marriage.'

'I've had other offers. And Billo's parents…'

'Please Dad, let Billo go.'

He looked at me, slurped his tea, didn't blink. I felt like I had as a child; his look, the threat that lay behind it. Man, it still made me tremble.

I put my cup on the low table, got up and started warming my hands in front of the faux log fire.

'Have you met someone else? If she's not Rajput, it's okay to tell me.'

Not Rajput? Was that the only rule he thought I would break? This was the moment, a real chance, come clean about Honour. Tell him that the woman I love would be the worst option for him.

'Unless you don't want to get married... maybe there are other reasons? Unless you're like your cousin Tamwar?'

I froze, the small spark of courage in me faded. No, Honour wasn't the worst option as far as he was concerned, this was.

Tamwar and I had gone to school together from the first day of Primary, as close as brothers. Yet not close enough for him to ever openly tell me that he was gay. We both understood it though.

Unfortunately, other family members picked up on it too.

Tamwar's father, my dad's first cousin, heard the rumours of his son's secret life on Canal Street. He took the radical step of locking Tamwar in his house, barricaded into his childhood bedroom while his mother wept and wailed outside the door. Word got to my dad that Tamwar was being starved, that his family were refusing to feed him in an effort to get him to turn his back on his sexuality.

A group of men gathered at Tamwar's father's house, led by my dad. They had gone to explain to him that there must be another way; that his treatment of his son was barbaric, criminal even.

Upstairs, locked in his room, Tamwar only heard a mob shouting. His assumption was that the men were there to further his father's torture, that things would get worse. By the time the men persuaded his father to open the door and release him, Tamwar had taken his own life.

Under the carpet it went, with all the other aspects of Pakistani culture that we didn't talk about.

'No, Dad,' I said. 'I'm not like Tamwar. Not that there's anything wrong with that.'

My father flinched, obviously not agreeing.

'What would you have done if I had said I was?' I said.

I turned around to look at him. He stroked his beard, looked down at the mug resting on his shalwar-covered thigh.

'You're not, so I don't have to find out how I would fare in a battle between the love for my son, and the allegiance to my religion,' he said.

I didn't dare to raise the issue of Honour then.

Coming back from that trip home, I was more convinced than ever, that Honour and I would have to create our world, live by our own rules. My family weren't ready for her just yet.

I didn't know if they ever would be.

Chapter Eight

HONOUR

We'd held suppers before, invited friends round to sit on rickety chairs and play Trivial Pursuit on a table still laden with spaghetti bolognese but this was to be our first ever grown up dinner party. We were building a life around our limitations, our friends filling up the gap Al's family left.

Al and I had spent evening after evening sitting up in bed poring over cookbooks and Sunday supplements, finding ever more complicated recipes and imagining trying to cook them in our pokey kitchen, bashing into each other in every corner, frantically trying to keep the minuscule work surfaces clear for the next course.

The guests had been easier to choose than the food. Although Al denied it hotly, I knew I was pretty much a secret at his work – it didn't take a genius to pick up the omissions, the white lies. He did it to protect me although it served to compound our sense of isolation, of barely bridging two worlds. Of the very few who did know – the more progressive colleagues Al felt he could trust – most were married with small children and would find trekking across London on a precious babysitter night a chore. Al's friend Ruby was someone who often came up in conversation. She did the same bean-counting job as him but was single, a good Muslim girl waiting for the introduction to Mr Right by Someone Who Knew Best. I knew that she was very British though and had even been to the pub with Al and some of their non-Muslim co-workers.

I was conscious that it wouldn't be appropriate to put Ruby in any sort of situation that looked or felt like a setup; even in my narrow experience I'd come to know that that was the Pakistani way and something she'd be suspicious of. The field was even narrower for my friends; the people I'd done my masters' with had evaporated back to the corners of the globe that they'd come from and most of my co-workers in the little design agency couldn't be trusted to be drug-free after eight pm.

Just as I'd started to give up and consider inviting the scary family in the flat above ours, people who had to shout to be heard over their constant television, my boss suffered another heart-shattering relationship break-up and pleaded with the whole office to take pity on him and start asking him out.

Neil's romances were all doomed. He had the emotional attention span of a mayfly and, twenty-four hours after meeting the love of his life, would swan into the office, puffy-eyed and hollow-cheeked about the fact that another relationship had bitten the dust. He claimed that life for a gay man as handsome as him, in central London, was bound to be traumatic. I wasn't sure of the validity of that but at least he wouldn't try and get it on with Ruby. I gave him some lectures about behaving in an appropriate manner and crossed my fingers till Friday evening.

We were like children when we got home from work, Al and I. We were flushed with excitement and thrilled by legitimately playing house. We'd rushed back as fast as we could to give ourselves a clear three hours to cook; we even pinned up a schedule on the back of the kitchen door that listed which dish claimed the oven when. I went first with one of my mother's favourite canapés; crisp shells of choux pastry, almost red with cayenne pepper and filled with an oozing puree of peas and mint, the resulting graphic green seeped like putty through the cracks in the pastry.

Al had made the starter, spinach and feta in filo pastry, nutmeg dusted over them from the tiny silver grater he had bought just for the occasion. He put his finger to my lips and I licked the taste of Christmas from the end of it.

Bumping into each other was inevitable in the tiny kitchen and we giggled and apologised, squeezed past and dropped things. I burnt myself on a baking tray and Al paused from his instructions to hold my finger under the cold tap.

By the time the doorbell rang, our crises had been ironed out, our food polished and our sitting room cum dining room cum hallway was tidied and candlelit.

Ruby was stunningly small; she extended a bird-like hand and, at the same time as she shook mine, stretched onto her tiptoes to air-kiss my cheeks. Her eyes dominated her tiny face, lakes of deep brown set like jewels in her perfect skin.

'I've got mango juice, lassi, fizzy water,' I offered her, taking her coat. 'What would you like?'

She looked slightly embarrassed. 'Erm.'

'Tea? Coffee?'

She reached into the large handbag she held. 'A glass of this?' Ruby pulled out a bottle of red wine. 'Unless you've got something already open? This could do with decanting really and it needs to settle. Or a white, I like white too. Anything, to be honest...'

'I'm so sorry, I assumed... Oh, silly me.' In my embarrassment I appeared to have turned into my mother.

Al took the two steps from the tiny kitchen and saved the moment by pressing large cold glasses of Chablis into our hands. '*Et tu, Brute*?' he said to Ruby. 'I didn't know you drank.'

'Can you imagine if I did after work? Even when it's all us liberals out on the town? Professional suicide for a nice Muslim girl.'

'Well, I'm glad you feel you can be yourself with us,' I said. 'Cheers.'

When Neil arrived, twenty minutes fashionably late, Al and I threw ourselves with gusto into the role of gastronomes. Conversation lulled slightly as the dishes came out, the buns commanding coos of delight at their colours and Al's fresh light pastries flaking so softly that we all used our fingers to press up the last fragments from our plates.

'About ten more minutes for the chicken, I reckon,' said Al, a fine sheen of steam across the tops of his cheeks. He was in his element, we both were, and finally we felt like real adults with real jobs who lived together in a real relationship.

'Is the guitar yours?' Neil asked Al.

Al nodded, grinned slightly in a self-effacing way.

'Didn't think it would belong to that one.' Neil pointed at me. 'Far too creative a past-time for such a control freak.'

I kicked him under the table.

'Ow,' said Ruby.

'Sorry.' I laughed. 'That was meant for my boss.'

'She's a control freak at work, is she?' Al looked at me, that half-smile hanging on his mouth, his dark eyes dancing. 'She's so sloppy at home. I'll have to take some tips.'

'All good designers are obsessive.' I defended myself from behind an extremely large glass of Merlot. 'God is in the detail.'

'Oh, God "is" now, is he?' Al said. 'You have no idea how long I've been trying to get her to say that, guys.'

'He's a cruel and terrible God though,' said Neil. 'He allows fonts like Comic Sans to happen.'

Al laughed, his straight white teeth perfect, his chin faintly dimpling with the movement of his face. I loved him like this, carefree, happy. As the drinkers flew higher and higher on the wings of the alcohol, Al absorbed the mood, a vicarious kind of drunk; one that came without a hangover.

He brought out his chicken, the pan still sizzling, steam and rich smells filling the tiny flat. We'd seen some chef create this masterpiece on one of the many cookery programmes we were devoted to – horseradish, lemon and cream bubbling round the meat. Maybe Al was right, maybe we really were old before our time; we watched *Masterchef* with an almost indecent enthusiasm.

All four of us were quieter after we'd eaten, exhausted by the energy we'd expended mopping the last of the horseradish sauce from our plates, spent from wrestling the spatch-cocked chicken from its bones.

'Can we have a little post-prandial?' Neil raised his eyebrow suggestively at Al. 'On your guitar I mean? Do you fancy a tickle of the strings?'

I shook my head, swapping amused glances with Ruby. Neil's incorrigibility appealed enormously to Al's ego.

'Actually, I will play, but not the guitar. Honour bought me a sitar for my birthday. I'm not very good.'

'You are,' I said. 'You're brilliant.'

'I don't play it as much as I should; I have this mental picture of my parents walking in on me playing it and having some Bollywood moment where their favourite son returns to the fold, a good traditional boy with a lovely Pakistani girl.' He stopped speaking suddenly and blushed.

'It's repeated all over the world, mate,' Ruby said in timely rescue. 'It's not just you. Cheers.' She drained her wine glass in a defiant gesture and we all laughed.

Al sat on the floor cushions, the sitar sideways over his crossed legs, his head bent down over it checking the tuning.

'Hang on,' I said, 'complete the picture.' I hung a yellow tea towel like a dupatta round his neck.

Neil moved his chair to get a better view of Al. 'Honour, get your fat arse out of the way. You're completely ruining a middle-aged man's rugged-tea-plantation-owner fantasy.'

I knew what Al would play first – *Norwegian Wood*, a mesh of East and West, Ravi Shankar and George Harrison. I hummed quietly and we all joined in with his singing when he got to the chorus and we could trust ourselves to know the words.

'Oh, Al, make an old man very happy...' Neil said.

'Neil's thirty-three,' I said to Ruby.

'Leave this old witch and come and live with me.'

Al looked up through his fringe, the polished wood of the sitar reflecting a curved image of his face. 'Man, I'm so never going to leave her that I can promise you that if I do, you can be next.'

'That's so sweet.' Ruby put her hand on her heart in a gesture of romance. Her jewellery looked enormous on her tiny fingers.

'It is?' I wrinkled up my mouth. 'My boyfriend has just pledged that, after me, my elderly male boss can be The One.'

'Because I'm never going to leave you. Because you're the only girl for me.' Al grinned up at me.

'Unless I die, in which case you're in trouble.'

'Ah, I hadn't thought of that.'

'I had,' said Neil.

Distractedly, Al began to pick the first clear notes of 'Ek, do, teen'. Ruby clapped her hands in glee and gave a comedic wiggle of her head, Bollywood style.

I know the song now, can even sing it, but back then all I heard was the verdant Punjab, the striking primary colours of the five rivers, the intricate history of a complex land.

Ruby began to sing, '*Chaar paanj che saath aat nau das giyaran, barah tera, tera karoon, tera karoon gin gin ginke intezaar, aaja piya aayee bahaar...*'

I looked from her to Al and back, striking, singing the same language, sharing a culture that crept to the fore no matter where they were or what they were doing. I imagined slow-moving animals directed like traffic on the roads of Pakistan; children, doe-eyed and dusty calling out and playing in the shade of vivid trees that whispered with the wind. The words that Ruby sang wove the picture on; exotic, foreign, far away. It was pure Asia.

Part of me smarted at the link Ruby had with Al; anyone walking in to the room, at least if they were carrying my prejudices, would imagine them to be a couple. Neil's cropped blonde hair and bright blue eyes would mark us out as another.

I couldn't help but think of Al's pre-ordained betrothal to Billo and of how hard the match-makers had worked to find the girl beautiful enough to match this extraordinary man – this extraordinary man of mine.

ALI

At the core of my loving Honour beyond life itself, was one fundamental principle.

She let me be who I am.

With her there was never any pretence, I wasn't a blueprint for someone else's ambition. I didn't have to live as a cube with different sides that I showed to work, to my parents, to my friends. I was a whole person, and she accepted me.

Music was the perfect example of why we belonged.

Growing up, all instruments except drums at weddings were forbidden.

At university the fundas I hung out with in my first two years confirmed that.

Then I picked up the guitar again, and remembered how much I had enjoyed playing it as a teenager. And it became my weapon of seduction, what drew Honour to me, what I used to serenade her with.

Slowly I learnt that music and Islam, like most things, have a complex relationship. Pick your Islamic scholar and make your choice which interpretation and fatwa to follow.

As I played, Honour listened. As I became good, she revelled in it, choosing songs I should learn, making requests, confirming a vanity in me that maybe I could.

The lack of music was never about religion in my father's house. He just didn't want me to be distracted from my studies, the things that would get me a good job, bright future.

Worse than that, musicians were the underclass in Pakistan, called marassis and kanjars, their only regular gigs in brothels.

Not suitable for a Rajput boy.

When Honour got me a sitar for my birthday, I laughed at her, joked it was 'them Indians' who played sitars in their temples. My people played drums, did bhangra, sang qawwallis.

But she was the one who told me that some of the greatest sitar players in the world were Pakistani, and that there were workshops all over Pakistan where the instruments were still hand-made.

I was shamed. This woman had researched the cultural heritage of my parents to buy this gift.

Every time I touched the sitar, felt the wood under my hands, smooth and supple, I imagined it to be Honour – I caressed the strings and made love through my music.

It was like Prem Jogan from Mughal E Azam, where the Mughal Prince Saleem is caressing the courtesan Anarkali's face with a giant ostrich feather, as the raagas flowed in the background.

Uff, the passion.

It had been a distraction to have Ruby and Neil round for dinner, I did it mainly for Honour. Spending my work days understanding Islamic economics and dealing in data and numbers, all I ever wanted was to be home alone with her. She seemed determined to entertain so I had given in. It wasn't too bad, I even enjoyed myself, but there was a moment when Honour changed. Too subtle for the others maybe, but I could tell.

'Did I do something wrong?' I asked Honour when we were alone again.

I was washing up and she was drying.

'No. Why do you wash up like that? I've never asked. It really irritates me.'

'Like what?'

'You scrub everything and leave the tap running. It's such a waste.'

'Don't know. I don't diss you when you fill up the sink and soak everything.'

'That's the proper way of doing it,' she said.

'I'm sorry for flirting with Neil,' I said.

'I wasn't being serious. Anyway you flirt with everyone.'

'No, I don't. So then what is it?'

She looked at me through a glass she had just dried, unable to make direct eye contact as she spoke.

'It was just that song with Ruby... you two were so in sync, I thought you would be perfect for each other.'

'Me and Ruby? You *must* be drunk. She's crazy!'

'Don't say that, she's lovely.'

'Maybe as a friend, or as a dinner guest. But as an other half? No way. She'd probably take my credit card and go round the world, call me from Bangkok after two weeks to let me know where she was and where to wire more spending money.'

She laughed at the imagery, we both did.

'But that song... I bet it was some ancient love song, or some deep spiritual yearning for a homeland... some rite of passage...'

I laughed at her, and pulled her to me with my wet, soapy hands. I kissed her on the forehead, remembering Ruby aping Madhuri Dixit as she danced to *'Ek do teen.'*

'Honour, sweetie, that song is the Bollywood equivalent of the Birdie song,' I said.

She looked at me, biting her lips, then breaking into hysterics.

'If you can count from one to thirteen in Urdu, you can sing that song too,' I said.

Ruby kept my private life sacred, there was no commentary on the dinner party at the office the next day; only when we went off for lunch together, trading impressions over our Pret sandwiches.

We worked for the Islamic bank, an institution propped up by petro-dollars from the Gulf, aiming to break halal *Shariah*-compliant products into the Western market. There were a handful of branches providing commercial services, and a head office providing the machinations of investment in Aldgate, where I worked as an investment specialist.

It was an intimate set up, but also claustrophobic.

Hardly anyone knew about Honour. They all assumed I lived alone, the mortgage application for our flat was made under my name solely, just in case someone got bored and decided to go through the database.

My boss, Yacein, who led office prayers, had to authorise my mortgage, hence no Honour on the forms. I'd developed the usual Imam-crush on him, wanting his approval and advice in the absence of my father.

I did go out to bars with the non-Muslims though. The other brothers spent a lot of time trying to convert them.

The sisters ironically talked to the non-Muslim boys with more freedom than they ever spoke to us. We saw them chattering and laughing with them, and then being confrontational and argumentative with us. Maybe in their heads they would never marry a non-Muslim so they were safe territory.

Except Ruby Khan. She was the cleverest person in the office; PPE from Oxford followed by MSc Finance at LSE, the only girl in her year there. She had cut her teeth at two normal banks and then been lured by even more money to IB.

It was odd to think she had grown up in a terraced house in Derby, an only child, with tons of other Asians around her. It was the same background as me, working-class, oppressive. Her contemporaries were probably all married and breeding by now.

Luckily, we didn't have too many work functions. There weren't many situations where I felt the pressure of lying about Honour; just parties at Eid and when we hit targets or there was someone leaving. All very civilised with cake and soft drinks, but once a year we had a charity dinner in aid of Islamic Relief, where the entire bank (commercial and investment arms) would attend.

The others would turn up with their wives, husbands and children. My Moroccan boss, Yacein, with his Pakistani wife, Hadiqa. The single ones, like Ruby, would turn up with friends, or genuinely alone. I would be the great pretender, single except I wasn't really, all night wishing I had the courage to bring Honour.

Ruby was the only one who knew the truth, called me a spineless shit for lying about it.

I used to tell Honour that it was a male-only dinner, lying because I didn't want to hurt her or face up to the truth.

I was getting fed up though. I needed to marry her. It was getting ridiculous. I was working for IB because I was supposedly worried about interest and integrity, and yet here I was living a half-life. The most important part of who I was locked up in a flat, hidden away, making it impossible for me to be whole.

It had to stop. There was no honesty left in my life anymore and it was killing me.

So I pushed the marriage agenda again.

She pushed it away just as fast, so I decided to manoeuvre around her.

Fate brought my parents to London and with them, an opportunity to end the lies.

Chapter Nine

HONOUR

I couldn't decide at the time, just days after our dinner party, if it was serendipitous or disastrous to miss my first meeting with Al's parents but I actually had no choice. Connie's Matron of Honour emailed the final details of the hen weekend just minutes after Al had put the phone down, his face drawn, and said, 'My parents are coming to London.'

I imagined that my relationship with Al was well-known, if never talked about, within his immediate family; they must have noticed 'the Elephant in the Chintzy Sitting Room' and their missing son. We had, after all, got away with four and a half years of living over the brush. And I assumed they kept it, the filthy secret, from the aunts and uncles, the hundreds of first and second cousins. I assumed that as far as most of Manchester knew – and they all seemed to me to be related – Al was marrying Billo and the world would be well.

Their visit marked a turning point in our relationship, one where he was surprised that I was going to take the easy route, go along with the 'Good Boy Game' rather than digging my heels in and demanding he did it my way. We decided that I would remove the things that would actually upset Al's mother were she to 'chance' across them. I made sure that I scooped up all my make up from the dressing table and hid my necklaces and hair bands away in my knicker drawer. Tell-tale signs like 'Shampoo for Dazzling Auburns' and pink-handled razors were consigned to the cupboard under the bathroom basin. It would only take one moment of irresistible nosiness for his mother to be buried alive under an avalanche of tweezers, tights and tampons if she chose to snoop in the airing cupboard.

'Honestly, they're coming down because my sister's got a picture in an exhibition; proper reasons, like normal people have. But they'll do the whole thing like on one of those buses from old photos, 1920's style. What are they called?'

'Charabancs?' I said.

'Charabanc. They'll be that Asian family you see at the motorway service station, having a picnic on the grass. My mum will unpack plastic pot after plastic pot and they'll all sit round looking stupid eating chick peas.'

'I don't think that's stupid, motorway food's horrible. What will be in the picnic?'

Our two families, so disparate, share an obsession with food.

'Moong dahl, dahi palley and a big old chat, I'd imagine. And hard-boiled eggs and samosas,' said Al.

'Chapattis or naan?'

'Parathas.'

'Bollocks to a Spa weekend, I'm staying.'

'We used to go mental about it when we were kids, burned up with embarrassment. All those cars pulling in, other kids staring through their windows at the pakis. I hated it.'

'I wouldn't have stared. Connie and I would have run up like little fat ginger-haired pigs and scoffed the lot while my mother wrote down the recipes.'

I wasn't that sorry I missed the visit. I was scared of meeting Farzana most of all; I felt responsible for her getting caught up in the web of our complicated lives.

Instead of confrontation, I got to spend a weekend swimming and having manicures with my sister and her friends, indulging our own passion for food and a hefty one for alcohol along with it. My sister and I have never been great ones for friends; my mother says it's a twin thing. And, left to us, we wouldn't have invited anyone else on her hen weekend. It just would have been the two of us, talking nineteen to the dozen about things we couldn't remember afterwards and walking for miles and miles.

It had been the wedding photographer's idea to have someone else as chief bridesmaid; she'd done wedding photos for identical twins before and said that the more dissimilar their outfits and the further apart they stand in group shots, the better the pictures.

We could see the sense in this. Our mother had wallets of photographs that she couldn't identify until she looked on the back for the note that she'd written shortly after having taken it, before the memory of which baby or toddler was which faded. It would be nice to be different for the day.

Con had chosen a girl from college as chief bridesmaid. We both got on with Annie although I didn't see much of her.

'So, the guy you're living with is Pakistani? Let me get this right.' I'd already explained to Annie enough times but she was drunk, and on a roll. 'And he doesn't drink, and he doesn't smoke.'

'He smokes weed sometimes with a guy from work. He'd never admit that but he comes home stinking and chatting utter shite so I usually guess. He thinks I don't know.'

'So doesn't he mind you drinking? Or are you just delighted to be away from it and letting your hair down?'

I frowned.

'Honestly, Annie,' said Con, 'do you really see my sister living with someone who gives her a hard time over her general bad behaviour?'

We were sitting on the balcony of mine and Connie's room, below us fat men in golf carts zoomed across lawns laid like carpet and the 'thwack' of tennis balls punctuated the sound track of the Country Club. I was halfway ready for going out, wearing pants and a vest, a cigarette in one hand and a teacup full of champagne in the other.

'He likes me drinking. He thinks it's funny.'

'To be fair,' my sister said, 'you are a superb drunk. Never mean or moody.'

'And very funny,' said Annie.

'And you don't get maudlin and cry,' said our other friend, Claire.

'And,' I raised my teacup in salute, 'I become an absolute shag monster.'

'You're kidding?' Annie's eyes were saucers. 'He gets you drunk so you put out?'

'No!' I snorted champagne down my nose, choked a little on the cigarette, remembered why I hardly ever smoke, 'I meant more the – we get in late, he falls asleep because he's knackered and I start poking him and going "Al? Al?" in a drunk's attempt at a whisper until he puts out – version...'

'Doesn't he mind?' asked Annie.

'He's a twenty-six-year-old man,' I said. 'Of course he doesn't mind. Just because he's a Muslim, doesn't stop him thinking with the same apparatus as every other bloke, Annie.' I poured more champagne. 'He is actually a man.'

We laughed like drains.

My sister unwrapped her wet hair from the big white hotel towel. 'You up or down tonight?' she asked, a hair band on her wrist.

'You choose,' I said. When we go out, we try to look as different as we can to lessen the constant comments and grief we get. From women it's usually just questions, have we done any adverts, why doesn't one of us cut our hair? From men it's generally far more obscene. We did do an advert once actually, when we were six; it was for fish fingers. Our mother said we were so naughty and she was so ashamed that she could never bear to take us again.

'Make the most of it,' said Claire, 'I can't remember having sex since I got married.' She turned to my sister. 'Sorry to break it to you on your hen weekend, Connie.'

'He's not got a girl back in Pakistan that he has to marry then?' Annie wasn't giving up.

There was a moment's heavy silence. Con and I looked at each other.

'Are you silenced by that unbelievable racism?' Claire asked. Claire had gone to school with us, I preferred her to Annie; Con liked them both equally though and this was her night, the choice of guests was hers alone. My hen night, should I ever get round to having one, would probably just involve Neil and me getting drunker and drunker whilst Neil got lewder and lewder in his descriptions of how much he fancied the groom. Or maybe just Al; I'd probably choose to celebrate my imaginary nuptials just with him.

'You should be ashamed of yourself, Annie. If you wouldn't say it to Al, don't say it at all,' said Claire.

'I didn't mean it like that; I haven't met Al yet anyway.'

'I have,' said Claire. 'And I have to say that he is, possibly, the most gorgeous man I have ever actually seen in the flesh. Teeth from a dentist's billboard and smouldering eyes.'

'He is fucking gorgeous, I have to admit,' I said.

'More so than my future husband?' asked my sister.

'I'm not sure, it's fifty-fifty. But Laurent gets extra points because Al can't shrug.'

It was so strange. My sister was marrying a man from another country. He spoke a different language to her, he had been educated in a different system, his car had the steering wheel on the opposite side to hers. And yet, everyone was interested in my boyfriend. My English boyfriend. My parents' friends were the same.

'You will get married though, you and Al?' Annie didn't want to let up.

My sister moved the champagne bottle away from Annie, rolling her eyes.

'Why? We already live together. We've just got a mortgage and a lovely big flat. We can't have kids until I've got somewhere in my career or all my studies will have been for nothing. I'll be behind on software and finished.'

'Get married just for love?' said Annie.

'So Annie can get belligerently pissed on someone else's hen night?' said my sister.

'It's not that simple,' I said in the understatement of the decade.

'Has he got to marry a Muslim? I can't see you in hajib, Honour.' Annie would not let it go.

'It's "hijab", Annie,' said Claire. 'God almighty. Connie, shall I come and help with your hair? Honour, you need to get dressed unless you're clubbing in those huge pants and your scratty vest.' She was doing her best.

'He has got to marry a "believer", not necessarily a Muslim. And I don't believe in God. At all. Okay?'

'Please drop it now, Annie,' pleaded my sister. 'It's my fucking hen night. Can we go and just dance until we have blisters and no dignity?'

When we woke up, we were proud to say that our decency and decorum lay, shattered, on the dance floor of the Country Club. Every swoop of 'Rock Lobster' and every stamping foot of the Motown Classics had plunged us to new levels of discomposure.

We woke up with the worst hangovers of all time.

'Head?' I asked.

'Overwhelmingly painful,' said Con.

'This club will talk about us for years.'

'I do hope so. I would hate to die having achieved nothing whatsoever.'

'Your husband-to-be told me that French women don't behave like that.'

'French women thought that through. Your husband-to-be told me that you have paracetamol.'

'He's my boyfriend, not my husband-to-be. We're not engaged, remember? But I do have paracetamol.'

My sister looked serious for a moment; I assumed she was still drunk. 'Do you mind? Not marrying him, I mean.'

'I had to make a hasty decision, he wanted to get married when we were twenty-one, remember?'

'I think you should marry him.'

'I can't. I'm not converting.'

'I don't care about that; think of the food. The wedding breakfast would outstrip my French one.'

'An expert korma and some fresh chapattis are not a sound basis for a marriage. Anyway, when I get home my freezer will be stacked full of his mum's cooking.' I curled onto my side, burying my head in the sumptuous pillow and wishing my head would stop pounding with the imaginary beat of last night's music. 'Without me even having to marry him.'

'Do you wish you'd stayed to meet them?'

'Fucking hell, no.' I laughed. 'It was just a game. We both pretended that I was terribly sorry not to be there, as if I had to apologise to them for being away like normal people. But that's not really how it is. They don't know I live there, that we live together. And that I'm defiling their son every night of the week.' I sighed, imagining Al stroking away my hangover, fetching me orange juice and planting tiny kisses on my tired eyes.

'Con?'

'What?'

'Thanks again for last night.'

'Huh?'

'In the loos. For always sticking up for me. For always being there.'

'I'm your sister, it's my job. And I just pointed out what's true, nothing I didn't mean.'

I'd been sitting in the cubicle, digging in my bag for blister-plasters for the balls of my screaming feet when I heard Connie's and Annie's raised voices. I was about to call to them when I heard Connie's tone.

'For fuck's sake, Annie, quit it will you? What's got into you?'

Annie whined something I couldn't hear.

'He was playing a gig in a pub when she met him, to supplement his student loan at LSE on a course that, by the way, he got a Double fucking First for. But actually, do you know what? It wouldn't matter if he'd been the guy to serve her lime pickle for her poppadoms. He's clever, kind, beautiful and most of all...' She was livid. 'When you see them together you feel a kind of sadness because you know that one day, one of them will die. And then the other one, whatever age they are, will just shrivel away within hours – they adore each other.'

Later, I found myself back in the same bathroom with Con. We faced the mirror together, lipstick on our teeth, our hair a matching mess of sweat and tumbling curls despite our best efforts. Outside, the music pumped like a heart, the tone dulled to a thud, the rhythm relentless.

'Are you having a good time?'

She laughed into the mirror. 'So good. I'm loving it. That DJ is awesome.'

I span round on one foot, shooting my fist into the air, drunk enough to believe I cut a fairly dashing dance floor figure. 'It's kitchen music, isn't it? The old Motown and so on, it's what you put on in the kitchen when the neighbours are away and you want to get on down singing into a hairbrush.'

'I can see you and Al doing that.'

'Uhuh, never, Al only sings into the salt grinder. Centre stage.'

Connie pulled a scrunchie from her bag, wrestled it into her hair.

I put my hands on the cold porcelain of the sink in front of me. 'I heard what you said earlier.'

Connie cocked her head to one side, a bird-like gesture. 'When?'

'Here, with Annie. What you said about me and Al.'

'Ah, sorry if it was too personal, Hon. Annie's such a bitch when she's pissed.' Connie winced. 'She's dead nice the rest of the time. She really is. And when I first moved to France she used to email me every day, just to check I wasn't lonely or sad.'

'I don't care about Annie, really, I couldn't give a toss what she thinks. But it was lovely, what you said.'

I could feel a faint gloss of maudlin tears settling in my lower eyelids, sentimental drips of nostalgia and champagne.

Connie turned towards me, hugged me tight. 'He's the reason I can live in France. Be away from you. I never thought you'd find a better me. But you did, Al's it. He even more belongs to you than I do.'

'I love you, Con.' The tears were falling now. 'I'm going to miss you so much.'

'But you're not, Honour.' She kissed my cheek. 'You're not because you have him – Al – and a whole wonderful future together.'

ALI

I watched Honour hide all her women's products in anticipation of my mother and father visiting our home in her absence. We laughed and joked about it as we wiped all traces of her from the flat.

It was Mum, Dad and Farzana who were visiting. Farzana was gaining a reputation as an artist. She had an exhibition in London. How she had managed that from Manchester I didn't have a clue. But then I had never really taken the time to speak to her much, except to trade insults.

The three of them were coming down and I realised I had no choice but to tell them a few truths about their golden child.

Mum was in the kitchen washing up after cooking enough food to last a month. The freezer was jam-packed. I hoped Honour had remembered to throw away her bacon. As a favour to me she didn't put pig products in the fridge, but kept one pack of bacon frozen for emergencies when she was craving it so bad she would feel sick if she didn't have any.

Farzana was out hooking up with some artist friends.

Dad was watching the cricket, India vs. Pakistan, shouting Punjabi insults at the screen when someone dropped a catch or failed to hit the ball. Reminded me of when we were kids and I used to be the only one in the house who supported England.

Had I always been such an outsider?

'Dad,' I said.

Maybe it was the tone of my voice, but he muted the TV and looked at me. I felt like a four-year-old, telling him I had just broken next door's window with my cricket ball. I was petrified.

'I need to tell you something.'

There was silence. The words wouldn't come out. It was like I knew, once I said it there was no going back. The world would shift on its axis. Our personal Partition.

'Dad… I've met someone…'

We didn't realise the sound of water flowing in the kitchen sink had stopped. Mum was standing at the lounge door staring at us, the front of her kameez wet with soapy water, drying her hands on a dish cloth, her gold bangles making chinks of noise.

'Okay, who is she?'

'Her name is Honour…'

I heard my mother gasp, and fall into the sofa seat next to us. She knew Honour was no name for a Pakistani girl. She still tried though.

'Did you say Noor? Like my name?'

Clutching at cotton.

'No, Mum. Honour. She's white. English.'

My mother bit her lip, stared at my father, terrified.

'When you say you have "met her" what do you mean? As in last week? A month? Is she pregnant? Why are you telling us?'

'We met five years ago, in our final year of uni. When I came home after university, we were together. Sort of. And then, well, we stayed together. It's not some fling or affair or phase. It's…'

To my father's credit, he didn't freak out or go ballistic.

My mother was staring at him and then me, unable to comprehend, unwilling to believe what was being said.

'I see. So telling us you wanted to wait to further your career before getting married was a lie?' said my father.

Dad wiped his face with his right hand, like he did when he washed it during his ablutions before prayer. He played with his chin, his short beard bristling as his fingers worked it. He didn't look at me, or my mother, just the middle of the carpet.

He looked tired, but also in control. This was his job, to be father to his children.

As this was my job, to give Honour her rightful place in my family.

'I'm sorry… I know I should have told you the truth. But I didn't want to hurt you. Either of you.'

'Are you married to her?' His tone was resigned.

I felt even worse then. They had expected me to marry the unsuitable girl behind their backs, they still had that much faith in my piety.

'No.'

'Where does she live? What does she do?'

'She's a graphic designer, university-educated. Her parents live on the coast. But… she lives here, with me…'

'Oh, Ali…' he said.

'I'm so sorry, I didn't plan it. We fell in love and things just took their own course. I was so naïve and wrapped up, but Dad I love her, I really love her and I want to marry her. I can't live like this anymore. With you not knowing. I hate myself.'

'Where is she now?'

'She's gone to her sister's hen party'

'Where is she from?'

'From Kent originally.'

'Kent?' I saw his eyes make connections, the trips to Kent to visit 'friends'.

The look had been given though, Dad was disappointed, so I thought I might as well carry on and hit him in one blow. It was like jumping off a cliff. I told him everything.

He went to sleep early to think about it. My mother didn't say a word to me, but I heard her arguing with my father late into the night.

'Ha ha, I love it. You've fallen off your pedestal now good and proper.' Farzana had a field day when she returned.

Her hair was loose, her eyes lined heavily with kohl. She was wearing jeans with a long shirt and pashmina shawl. She looked bohemian, even slightly cool.

'It's not funny. I'm sorry, for you and Bilal. At least you won't have to marry him now,' I said.

'Are you an idiot, Ali? I love Bilal. I want to marry him. I've told you this before, get it into your thick head.'

'You haven't even met him.'

'I have met him. In London last year. And we talk all the time, he's great. He writes children's novels in Pakistan, he's like their Roald Dahl. In the making. And he used my illustrations in his last book. You never got it. You always thought he must be backward because he's from there.'

'Well, if the stereotype fits…'

'They live in a white-washed mansion, with tons of servants and are far more cosmopolitan than any of our family in this country, stuck in 1960. I will get more freedom to pursue my dreams and be my own woman married to Bilal than to any of the guys Mum and Dad might find for me here.'

I didn't know what to say: I had never bothered to ask her properly before. I always seemed to have a locked shield with her, as though we resented each other. I tried but failed to remember a moment in our lives when we were 'close' or 'loving'. I felt sad. Determined to change that.

'Well, I hope I haven't ruined your chances with him, because I wouldn't marry Billo.'

'Fuck's sake, you really are full of yourself, aren't you? You think someone as beautiful as her would sit at home waiting for you? She's got loads of other options. Billo's family gave up on you ages ago. Dad called them and told them you wanted to do your masters and they were good with that but, after the second year of you faffing around, they started to smell a rat. They're not quite as blind to you, Golden Boy, as Mum and Dad are.' A fleck of spittle from her fury landed on my cheek. I didn't brush it off.

'The only reason I'm not married yet,' she continued, 'is because me and Bilal were waiting for him to establish himself. You may think the world revolves around you but trust me, love, it doesn't.'

'Why didn't anyone tell me? Maybe I would have come clean about Honour before, if I didn't think the Billo situation was going on?' I could hear myself whining.

'We tried; you refused to get into a conversation about it. And I assumed you weren't too fussed what the girl you rejected would do with her life. I mean, you've been pretty selfish up until now.'

Was nothing about my life real? The Billo drama, the perceptions of my sister? Had I even imagined my parents and how they would react to Honour? At that moment Honour was the only real thing I was sure about.

In the morning my family left.

'We want to meet her,' Dad said.

'Oh, you bet we do,' Farzana said.

Mum was still silent.

Could it really be this easy? In the quiet of the flat before Honour came back, I debated with the empty spaces my family had left behind. I felt cheated. Why hadn't they given me an inclination at least that, hey, don't worry, we're so liberal now we'll accept Honour? I had driven myself half-crazy with the guilt. Was it all imaginary? A self-imposed prison? Had I exiled 'us' for no reason?

I wondered at time lost, the momentous weight of secrecy and lies. I felt betrayed by everyone.

But it was done. Now I had to tell Honour.

Chapter Ten

HONOUR

The flat smelled incredible when I got back from the hen do. This flat was four times the size of the one we'd rented, connected to the fact that our salaries were far more than four times what they had been in those early days. The first time Con and Laurent had seen it, sunlight flooding through the tall Edwardian windows, Laurent had whistled through his teeth in admiration. 'This place, it is beautiful.'

'It's bloody massive,' said Con.

'Of course it is, love, we're absurdly rich.' Although he was joking, Al sounded far more like my father than he'd ever want to admit.

We were, though, pretty well off. True to his word, Al paid the whole mortgage. I compromised in ways that I should have found controversial, squeaking the semantics of contracts and events to make them work for me. The bald truth was that the discounted interest rate Al was getting, alongside his ridiculous salary, gagged some of my previously vociferous politics with my own greed. It didn't make me particularly proud of myself.

Half of this flat was still a basement, but its wide and sunlit hallway pushed it sufficiently far up the food chain to be a 'garden flat' instead. The garden was just ours, shaded with wild shrubs and with a tall walnut tree keeping sentry over the lawn. On the second day that we lived there, I came home from work to find that Al had put a swing up for me, the dusty brown rope hung over the broadest branch. That night we pulled our mattress and covers outside and slept in the garden, waking occasionally to look for shooting stars.

Neil's graphic design agency was gathering bigger and bigger accounts all the time and I soon had a portfolio of clients of my own. We moved to an office in Frith Street and we all got salaries appropriate to our surroundings. We spent lunchtimes in Alastair Little's and stopped off in Ronnie Scott's after work. Sometimes coming home would be weird, I'd have spent the afternoon with Neil celebrating a deal with calves' liver and Chablis whilst Al and his colleagues marked a triumph with some extra prayers and a bit of pious gratitude. On days like that, it took us a while to unwind; he'd play guitar and re-inflate from his daytime meekness, back into the man I respected. I'd take a long bath and relax, sober up a little and climb down off my high horse.

My salary almost all went on holidays now that I had agreed not to contribute financially to the running of the house. We'd done New Orleans, New York, Cuba, all within the last eighteen months. With Con and Laurent we'd watched the Northern Lights in Norway, our mouths wide open and our place in the universe in perspective; with my parents we'd whale-watched in New England, even my father's ego dwarfed and humbled by the magnificent animals. On our own, we'd travelled from one side of Australia to the other, learning to dive and looking at sacred sites. We carefully avoided any Muslim countries and never even said 'Pakistan' out loud.

We were still decorating the flat, something we could have easily paid someone else to do had we wanted to. It was the kind of thing we liked doing ourselves, together. We spent hours poring over paint charts, laughing at some options, mulling over others. Then we'd take whole afternoons to browse the DIY shops for just the right brushes and rollers. We were still playing at grownups.

The curries Al's mum packed into the fridge drowned out the paint smell for the first time in ages when I walked back in, dropping my bag in the hall. The whole flat smelled heavenly; I knew Ali wouldn't like that.

I opened the fridge practically drooling; it would take forever to eat everything in there. There were cartons of creamy ras malai, plastic pots of curry and dahl, freezer bags filled with soft breads peppered with tiny black poppy seeds. On the top shelf, a new one on me, was a box of Indian sweets. Al counted some out onto a plate and we sat on the sofa together while he talked me through them. I tried, as I always do when we share food, to only touch them with my right hand. I failed, as I always do; in my house, we were brought up never to hold our forks with our right hands. 'Just for Americans and plebs,' my grandfather used to say. My being left-handed makes it even harder.

'Okay, so when anything good happens in a Pakistani house, like a wedding or a baby being born, we get ornate versions of these boxes and we deliver them, with the good news, to our friends and family.'

'Family being half the city?' I reached out with my left, then changed.

'Well, yeah, it gets expensive. So, for instance, when we have our first baby… ' He tried to bury the phrase in food details. 'My parents would get ladoos, ones like these round ones with the gold leaf, if it's a boy and jalebis if it's a girl.' He poked a little of the sweet into my mouth.

'Oh, yeah?' I kissed him with my sticky lips. 'Wouldn't they mind that they hadn't had the wedding sweets first?'

'You are kidding me?' His eyebrows almost disappeared into his hairline.

'What do you mean?'

'I've just had a conversation with my parents that I thought might kill the pair of them. Or at least destroy them, because I couldn't face one more day of hiding you away while we live together.' He didn't sound angry, just frustrated, a bit flat. 'And now you reveal that we're not even going to get married when we want to have kids?'

The tiny cake was over-sweet, a strong flavour of syrup filled my mouth.

'You know?' I spun round, lying across his lap with my feet up on the end of the sofa and talked up to his chin. 'God, marriage, it's all the same stuff to me. It's not my bag, none of it.'

He kissed his fingertips and put them gently on my petulant mouth.

'Laurent told me they have a saying in Paris that goes "*Il ne faut jamais dire 'Fontaine, je ne boirai pas de ton eau*".'

'And?'

'*Never say "Fountain, I will never drink your waters*".'

The following weekend we were summoned and took the train to Manchester.

I panicked about packing; I didn't have a clue what to wear. 'Should I take a scarf to put over my hair?' I was tearing through drawers, rattling coat hangers, desperate to find the right outfit to help make a good impression.

'Calm down, sweetie. It'll be alright. If you've got something nice, take it and wear it if we go to the mosque. But you don't need to wear it inside my parents' house. They're going to spot you're not a Muslim anyway.'

'By my horns and tail?'

'Something like that. No bare ankles though; don't wear cropped trousers. And long sleeves. And you'll have bare feet in the house.'

'What? You could have said. I'd have had my toes done.'

'You have green eyes and ginger hair. You went to church twice when you were at primary school and you seduced their eldest son, once their hope and glory. Do you think painting your toes is going to help?'

'It might make me feel better. I still can't believe your mum has changed her mind.'

'Oh, trust me, she hasn't. But my father wants to meet you. He's put his foot down and instructed his wife to welcome you into his house. At the end of the day, just like it is in this house, what *he* says goes.'

He ran out of the room as he said it.

ALI

Yacein Saykouk was my boss at the Islamic bank. Of Moroccan origin, the first things people noticed about him were his height, 6' 3", and then the charisma he had around him. He spoke in a heavy accent, which occasionally got him stereotyped as a foreigner who couldn't speak English, but he had the sharpest mind I had come across. At lunch it was behind Yacein that the brothers in the office prayed the daily prayers. With his perfect Arabic diction and his gentle manner, his obsession with football and the Middle East, he became a leader of men.

'You know, brother Ali,' he said one day while we walked back to the IB office after lunch. 'I'm married to a lady from your people.'

'My people?'

'Pakistani. She is British Pakistani.'

It was a Friday lunchtime and we had just been to pray Jumah, the only prayer we had to go to the mosque for. IB gave us a two hour lunch on Fridays just so we could.

'I know, I've met her, remember?' I said.

Hadiqa had come to our annual Islamic Relief benefit dinners. The ones Honour didn't know about.

'Yes, a most beautiful lady. Your women are just like ours, very stubborn and rule the roost at home.' He laughed openly, the sort of laugh someone with no deceit had.

'How did you guys meet?'

'Through mutual friends. But, brother Ali, I worry about you being so alone.'

I didn't say anything, as we plunged into frantic City workers. Suits and the unmistakable smell of money, clinging onto everything like a layer of grease.

'Or maybe not. Do you have a girlfriend?'

'No,' I said quickly.

Deny Honour again. Peter only denied Jesus three times. I must have denied Honour like three thousand times.

'Good, good. I have a proposition for you. My wife has a cousin, a very famous TV actress from Pakistan.'

'Okay...'

'My wife worries about her also, they are very close, like sisters. She is coming home to Manchester next week, and my wife wants me to find her a suitable husband.'

Manchester? Pakistani TV actress? It couldn't be.

'Is it Mehreen Khan?' I asked, excitement and disbelief in my voice.

'How did you guess? Did you read my mind?'

'No, not at all,' I said, laughing now. 'We were in college together. There aren't that many Pakistani TV actresses who are from Manchester.'

'So you know her? So I don't have to convince you then, my brother?'

'Convince me of what?'

'Look, brother Ali, you are a young man. I am not so old as to be naïve to the way of this world. You are good looking, earn well, are polite. Women must throw themselves at you, and it is easy for a brother to fall and give in to temptation. The devil does that, he is everywhere and the best of us can get tempted.'

I didn't say anything again. What was I meant to say? Too late, brother, I fell a long time ago?

'A man should not be alone. It was Adam and Hawa, brother, not Adam alone. Marriage, children, these are the real treasures of this life.'

I totally agreed with him. I had the wife. Well, sort of. And, well, kids would follow I was sure.

'You should meet Mehreen. You know her already. I get good points with Hadiqa and you get a beautiful wife. We all win. You made a good impression on Hadiqa when she met you.'

He laughed again. Honest, truthful, open.

'I will speak to my wife and we will arrange for the two of you to meet when you are next in Manchester. Now do not let me down or my wife will be cross with me.'

I was intrigued at the prospect of reconnecting with Mehreen or I would have made some excuse, not even bothered going through the motions. There was never anything underhand or solicitous about it. Honour would be my first word to Mehreen.

Part of me wanted to confront her, like a phobia, face her down after the hold she had had on me. Gloat even, show off that she might have broken my heart, but Honour had fixed it.

So I let Yacein arrange a dinner with my old friend.

Chapter Eleven

HONOUR

It was odd, I thought, as I got off the train under the vaulted arches of Manchester Piccadilly, that I had seen Grand Central station in New York and yet I hadn't been here; of course, spending almost five years avoiding my 'in-laws' was a factor.

Manchester surprised me. Coming from the South of England, I expect most cities to have lost their architectural heart in the Second World War. I had been to Birmingham and Coventry and imagined Manchester to be similar. I was charmed by its industrial brick and the vast hotels that Al assured me had once been cotton mills and warehouses that Marx and Engels had loitered in.

We'd arranged to meet Farzana in a Chinese restaurant, all chic tables and clean modern lines, one that featured often in Sunday supplement 'Best of' articles. I wondered if maybe the Hussains felt it was neutral territory, but Al said Farzana just liked the food.

The China Town was as pretty as Gerard Street in London but smaller and consequently less touristy. I held tight to Al's hand the whole way there, Manchester drizzle distracting me from talking too much.

'You okay?'

I nodded.

'I'm really grateful that you're doing this for me. Don't forget that. And don't forget that even if it doesn't go how we want, it's about us, not them. Okay?'

I assumed Farzana would be my worst enemy and the person I

would need to work hardest on to have an easy access to the rest of the family.

Her eyes were Al's eyes but elegantly edged with black kohl so that they looked even bigger, even deeper. Her clothes were as I imagined, elegant, co-ordinated shalwar kameez and sweeping dupatta but grey and worsted, made for an office, not the sequined patterns I'd pictured.

I hadn't envisioned her voice. This was a woman who was marrying a man her parents had chosen for her, without consultation, without her choice. A woman brought up and educated in the same city she'd been born in and still living with her parents into her mid-twenties.

Her voice was erudite, interesting; the voice of someone who straddled two cultures with a surety and style that I wished my boyfriend could find. She was smart, funny and, above all, completely capable of controlling her life and what happened to it.

She didn't have the irritating accent Al picked up when he was swerving from English to Punjabi and back again. Her enunciation was a cultured North East, almost indefinable apart from the flat vowels of words like 'castle' or 'ask'.

'I love what you've done with your flat; it's stunning,' was the first thing she said to me, after the perfunctory hellos.

'I'm just sorry I wasn't there to meet you.' And we both smiled in recognition of the circumstances and the platitude.

'Al, sorry, Ali, told me you were coming the same day my sister's bridesmaid finalised the arrangements for the hen do. I couldn't miss it.' My embarrassment made me rush. 'Look, I'm so sorry, about you and Bilal. It's all my fault.'

'Can we talk alone? Away from Mr Gallagher here?' she gestured towards her brother.

'Oh, please,' I said. 'If he says "innit" one more time, you can tell your mother that there isn't going to be any family crisis.' Al started adding 'innit' to every sentence as soon as we passed Watford Junction. It was driving me insane.

'I don't know why they do it, the boys. Especially now they're men. He went to the London School of Economics for goodness sake, then he comes back up here and talks like a "gangsta".' She shook her head. Farzana was, beyond a shadow of a doubt, a long way from the shrew her brother had conjured up.

'Jamal is waiting for you in the car outside,' she said to Al, dismissing him with a curt wave. 'Go be gangsta together.'

Al seemed relieved to be set free. Farzana had clearly planned this meeting with military precision.

'Have you had dim sum before?'

'No, but I'm desperate to try it; I've always meant to.' Already, I was beginning to feel like I would be lunching with a friend.

'Shall I just order for both of us, for now? We usually order in waves so you can have a go when you're feeling braver. It freaked me out at first; it's unlike anything else. Ordering off the Chinese menu isn't a good idea; it's not made for our palate. I have tried.' She pulled a face. 'Is there anything you don't eat?'

'Nothing,' I assured her.

The waiter asked me what I wanted to drink. 'Green tea, please.'

'And me,' said Farzana. 'First up, I'm sure, the same as all my 'English' friends, you can't believe I'm marrying a man my parents chose for me. Yes?'

'Yes,' I answered meekly, wondering if all my assumptions and prejudices were as obvious.

'Don't worry, I'm just getting it out of the way, then we can move on to interesting things.' When she smiled, she looked like Al, it made me more comfortable.

'Mothers, Pakistani mothers of my mother's generation, face a difficult dichotomy in this country. They've come here for the advantages, the education, the healthcare – although that's not the big decider it was in my parents' day.'

'Because of the NHS cuts?'

'Not at all,' Farzana touched her fingers to the front of her headscarf, checking her hair was neat and hidden. 'It's just that a little money buys a lot of healthcare in Pakistan. And we, they, have some amazing hospitals and doctors nowadays. It's part of why people in our culture send money home. It's all private, no waiting lists. Just as long as you're not poor; if you're poor, there's nothing.'

I let out a sigh, even after living with a Pakistani man for nearly five years, I felt like I knew nothing, I felt like a freshie.

'Asian women are keen to preserve some of the 'old ways', for their children. They look outside and all they see, in the media, on the TV, are ASBOs and hooligans – a lot of Pakistani immigrants read the Daily Mail.' She grinned at me, so much like Al. 'They shake their heads and say,' she put on a ridiculous accent and wiggled her head from side to side, 'oh deary deary me, what have we done? What would our families back home make of all this?'

I smiled, she was a good mimic.

'Ali has always been difficult as eldest sons go, always been what they call a coconut. Even why he chose the LSE, he felt it made him white. My mother was extra horrified because Mick Jagger went there apparently. She'd be more worried if she knew about all the fundas in those places.'

My cheeks began to get hot. I picked up my tea and blew on it, just to give my hands and my tell-tale face something to do.

'Oh God,' said Farzana, 'I don't mean to imply that you're some kind of fashion accessory.' She brought her hands to her mouth.

'You said "Oh God".'

I couldn't believe it.

'I'm not the same as my brother, I'm afraid. I'm a dutiful daughter and a dedicated believer but far more on my terms. In a twenty-first century way.'

'Sometimes I'd love Al to swear.' I smiled at her. 'In a blistering row, when I'm screaming at him. It would be such a... such a relief.'

'I seem to find myself swearing at him every time I talk to him.'

'Because of Bilal and Billo?'

'No!' She shook her head emphatically. 'Well, yes. Actually. But not in the way he thinks. Only because he thinks the whole world revolves around him. Oh, sorry...' That bright smile.

The first plate of food had arrived. Tentacles of squid, disguised in a batter but pointed and waved like fronds of seaweed, were piled into a mound on the plate. We tried to capture them with chopsticks but it was impossible to eat a whole one at once and I resorted to a fork.

'Fantastic,' I nodded my approval.

'The whole Billo thing, it started with my mum just trying to find a compromise to keep him happy. That's the story of her life really. Trying to keep everyone happy, but Ali? He's her pride and joy. The eldest son. Handsome and clever and so confused about his identity.'

'Isn't it the same for you?'

'My heart's a muddy brown colour, made of the middle ground.' She grinned. 'I've not lived in Pakistan yet, I'm English. A British Muslim but not a British Pakistani. Ali had to be the ground-breaker, test it all out for the rest of us. It's been hardest on him. It'll be our children's generation who really crack it. Who will build their own way of life.'

Platters of translucent dumplings and baskets of fried pastries were arriving at the table thick and fast. The flavours were amazing; I could pick up mace and ground nuts through the delicate heat of the chillies.

'I think it was some kind of nod towards his Western leanings that led my mum to Billo. She is very fair-skinned, green-eyed.'

'I thought she was Pakistani?' I interrupted. I had never asked Al any questions about Billo.

'She is, she's just unusual looking. Highly prized in our culture. Women who look like me are ten a penny.' She wrinkled her beautiful eyes. 'So my mum started talking to their family as a way of meeting what she thought of as his "special" needs.' She made little apostrophes in the air with her fingers and rolled her eyes.

She pointed at a plate of huge chillies. 'Eat some before I finish them, they're stuffed with prawns; unbelievable. And so hot.' She gasped a little and gestured at her watering eyes. 'So, the upshot of the whole Billo thing, was that the conversation between the parents somehow turned to my degree...'

'You did Art, didn't you?'

She tutted and sighed. 'See, this is why I swear at my brother. If I went round telling people he did "Counting" when he did Economics, he'd have gone mad. No, I did Illustration.'

She signalled the waiter. 'More tea?'

'Yes, please, and a glass of white wine actually.' I was coping well enough to risk it, the food and the company had taken the edge off the difficult situation.

'So, at some point, in all the match-making, some complete genius put Bilal and me together. He writes novels for children; he's pretty well-known in Pakistan. I met him when he came over here on a book tour, showed him some of my pictures. He loved my work, and me of course. The rest, as they say, is history.'

'Have you illustrated his book?' I was so impressed.

'The publishers took me on for a series of four; gold dust for an illustrator. Job, husband, nailed in one and I'm only twenty-four...'

I lifted my wine glass and clinked it against her tea cup. 'Bloody well done, congratulations.'

'So, yes, I'm marrying the man my parents chose but only because they chose brilliantly and it suits me. They used their experience and intelligence to make the right decision for me.'

'But not for Al?'

'Al had already gone off, was doing his own thing. And wandering between cultures. I don't mean to be rude but, you met him in a pub?'

I nodded, 'At a gig.'

'See? If he had been just a good home boy, like he was supposed to, he wouldn't have even been in the pub in the first place, the cycle wouldn't have started. In fact, if he hadn't been such a coconut with that bloody guitar... But, under the circumstances, I'm very pleased he did. I didn't always think it would end this well. I didn't really know until today, until I met you. And I'd have to be blind not to see the change in him when he's talking about you. He's like a man possessed.'

'I hope so and I hope it's enough. All this, it's so much pressure on him. On you, Bilal, Billo.'

'Well, let me help you out a bit. The media in Pakistan have picked up on the glamourous British illustrator and the gorgeous single author; we're under pressure from all sides to get married, and we're more than happy to yield to it too. The whole Billo thing isn't necessary to see it through any more. The problem is just the hysterical reaction of my mother and other people who haven't understood Pakistani culture since they last witnessed it at the end of the sixties. Things have moved on.'

'Oh.' I was finding this all quite complicated and was glad I'd ordered the wine. 'But what about stuff like the awful things we read about? Women's rights?'

'If you ask people over there about us Brits, they'll say "What about the BNP? What about the chip pan fires?"'

I shook my head. 'Chip pan fires?'

'It's a terrible practice that goes on all over Britain only we, anybody, don't talk about it. A girl meets someone from the wrong caste, the wrong religion and, one day, her sari just accidentally catches the chip pan and she burns to death. It's horrendous.' She looked down at her lap, shaking her head. 'It's an Indian thing mainly, the Pakistanis prefer the traditional honour killing.'

'That really happens? In Britain?'

'All the time. I volunteer in an Asian Women's refuge, in Oldham; it's near here. We help women who are victims of domestic violence, girls who are being sent abroad against their will, those kinds of things. All sorts really. It's a constant battle against funding cuts and bureaucracy as well as tradition. The work's invaluable; ours is a hard culture to stand up to. As you and my brother know.' She reached her hand across the table and put it over mine, squeezing my fingers in hers. 'The women need support from the whole community but, at least in the beginning, they need someone they can identify with too.' Her eyes were bright with passion. 'And it's work I'll carry on once I'm in Pakistan.'

'You're going to Pakistan?'

'As soon as we're married; for a few years, anyway.'

I couldn't believe how much I really didn't want her to go.

ALI

I had decided to put us up in a hotel, but I did pick the Midland in all its glory, simply to make it easier. It was one thing bringing a girl home, but another to expect my parents to put us up and let us share a room. It was also because Mum hadn't spoken to me since London. She would send messages via my dad asking after me, well, he said she did. Maybe she didn't. Maybe she was being a filmi mother and sitting at home cursing the womb that had given birth to me? Again.

I had seen her fall out with cousins and aunts over the years. Her modus operandi was to ignore them, while making my father stay in touch with them, so she could make a grandiose gesture of reconciliation later.

The fact is no one would have been *quite* good enough for me in my mum's eyes, even her own choice. And Honour definitely not.

Honour, in her modern self-confidence, had grown up never having to face actual raw, passionate, drop-down-dead-hostility. She didn't really understand what was going to happen.

She probably thought it would be comically awkward like when I met her family and friends. Un-PC comments, maybe my mum would make Yorkshire Puddings and a trifle, views of white people taken from *EastEnders* and *Corrie*. The sort of gentle introduction I had had in Kent, with her mother and her house.

No, what Honour would get was a wall of all-consuming animosity.

So I sent Farzana, to prepare Honour, give her insider knowledge. A sort of mini-Mum, a small indication to Honour of things to come. They would meet in China Town and talk about whatever it was that Honour would have to say, do, wear.

With her safely out of the way, I was left to hang with Jamal, but used him to drop me off to meet Mehreen.

Mehreen and I had been at Stockport Sixth Form College together. We had found each other and made a creative bubble to hide in. I used to dream that my 'music' would take me places, I was going to be the next Jimi Hendrix or Jim Morrison. Mehreen would sit patiently while I strummed clumsily at my guitar, listening to the bar chord horrors I had been practising overnight.

There came a point when I realised that I was practising just so she would listen, and I had spent about six months with a massive crush on her.

She had dreamed of being the next Bollywood superstar, odd since she wore thick glasses, and was studious, nerdy even. She would take part in all the college dramas. Unfortunately for her she always got bit parts and played mums, nursemaids and even males. I did script read-throughs with her, our relationship intensifying predictably when we went through Romeo and Juliet, rehearsing lines she would never get to say on stage.

I was in love with her by the end of it, thought she felt the same. Only to have my heart broken when I spoke to her of a shared future.

'For starters, Ali boy, I'm still not going to marry you,' she said.

We had decided to meet in Petit Blanc, away from Rusholme and any Asians who might recognise Mehreen from her time on Pakistani TV. The dramas were shown on satellite channels here and rented out at video shops.

'Good to see you too, Mehreen,' I laughed at her.

She did look good, I had to admit. The geekiness from her teenage years had turned into a sophisticated beauty. Her hair was smoothed back from her face, no visible make up I could see except kohl around her eyes and red lipstick. Devoid of NHS glasses, her eyes were amber, feline.

'Look, my cousin is a pain, she and the rest of my family are a bit worried. I'm in my mid-20's, kunwari, away working in Pakistan a lot. You know how it is, na.'

She clicked her fingers for the waiter, obviously used to ordering lesser mortals around in Lahore, and ordered drinks.

'So why did you agree to this?'

'I didn't until I knew it was you. Actually that's a lie, I usually do this with about three or four guys a year, just to keep them happy, give them the illusion that I'm trying. It's all bullshit though.'

'Charming. I see you grew up to be the star you always wanted to be.'

The waiter brought our drinks. Diet coke with ice and lemon for me. Something deep and red in a wine glass for her.

'Don't be facetious, this is who I am,' she said. 'I wanted to see you again, out of curiosity, see how my friend turned out. Plus, I already have a man. Unfortunately *he* has a biwi and bachey.'

I nearly choked on my drink. It hadn't been that long, Mehreen wasn't that removed from our combined starting point.

'Mehreen? Since when? A married man? With kids?'

'It's been a few years. Look, don't judge me, okay? He's a famous actor in Pakistan, in his early fifties. He's fabulous, you'd love him. I'll become his second wife when I'm ready.'

The waiter was back to take our order. I ordered lobster linguine. Mehreen asked for a starter salad. And more wine.

'Anyway it suits me. I don't want a husband to tie me down yet; I'm just getting to the peak of my career. The BBC want me in some Meera Syal drama and I'm in talks for a Pakistani movie. Plus married women don't do well as actresses.'

'Even now?'

'That's true for women everywhere, even in Hollywood. Marriage and age – the two killers of an actress' career,' she said

'So what then, is this bloke just for sex?'

'Don't be an imbecile, of course not. It's the company too, and I feel safer, knowing someone who's been in the industry a long time is looking out for me, na.'

I didn't know what to say.

What had happened to Mehreen? I had come hoping to face my first love with my current, and instead there were no traces of that girl left.

'What about you? Oh, I'm so sorry Ali, did you actually turn up thinking there was a chance? I don't give a flying whatever about the other guys' feelings, but really I didn't mean to play you along. I apologise, yaar.'

There it was. Her eyes genuinely concerned, even her voice sounded different. The real Mehreen, the one I had confided my dreams to, the one who had encouraged me. Meeting her was a pathetic attempt to regain Ali aged sixteen, and it had happened, for that moment at least.

'No, no, not at all. In fact I think I'm in a similar situation. Sort of.'

'Really?' She said, arching her neatly threaded brow inquisitively

The waiter brought our food over. Steaming pasta for me and leaves with a bit of cheese and lots of black pepper for her.

'Well, I'm here to please my boss, your cousin's husband. Yacein. No one knows about it in the office but I've actually been going out with a girl for a few years now.'

'Really? How sweet... Does she know about me?' She clicked her fingers again, ordered the waiter to bring more water and wine.

'She knows who you are. She doesn't know I'm here right now.'
I looked down at the table.

'So why aren't you married yet?' she asked.

'It's complicated. She's English.'

'So?'

So? *So*? She dismissed it. But it was complicated. Was Mehreen being obtuse or did she really not think it was a problem? I suppose compared to her own set up mine was pretty banal.

'What's the big deal,' she said. 'You're a boy, she's a girl, just marry her, get on with life. Do a for-the-sake-of-it ceremony and just move on. Honestly, Ali, it's no big deal.'

'Of course it is. My family are…'

'Just like mine. Sure they might sulk a bit, but they'll get over it. You're their son, flesh and blood, yaar, you'll be fine.'

'Come on, Mehreen, you make it sound so easy…'

'Do you love this woman?'

'Yes.'

'Do you want to marry her?'

'Yes.'

'Then there is no issue.'

'She doesn't believe in God.'

'So what? *You* believe in God, that's enough.'

'We can't even have a marriage though, not in Islam. Not unless we both believe in Him.'

'If you're so worried about Islam why are you with her?'

We ate in silence.

Mehreen was right of course. But then why were Honour and I here so late in the day? Why was I being such a coward? What had made us wait?

'Don't sulk, yaar. I didn't meet you so you could ignore me. I'm the drama queen, remember? Are you living with her?'

'Yes.'

'Congratulations then, you're practically married anyway.'

'Thanks. You say that as though it's all okay, all normal. But me and you, Mehreen, maybe we were never normal?'

She pushed away her half-eaten food, sipped on the drink that I could smell but didn't ask about, and pinned me with an intense stare. I felt vulnerable, naked, like she was looking through me. I put my knife and fork down, swallowed water. I don't know if it was rehearsed, an actress' trick, but she was making me uncomfortable.

'What's normal, yaar?' she said. 'You think everyone is perfect? Out there behind closed doors you don't know what goes on. People can go to the mosque twenty-four-seven, do everything properly, traditionally, and then they beat their wives or they're having affairs. You can't judge people, only God has that right. Thank God.'

'Technically, we're both having affairs,' I said.

'Don't be cheeky. Anyway I don't set myself up as a paragon of virtue, and I hope to God you don't either.'

'I don't think I do. But then what's my denial to Yacein and my work colleagues?'

'I deny my lover to my family. You make up your own rules. No soul is given a burden it can't bear, right?'

I was amused by her quoting from the Qur'an, the words incongruous with her scarlet lips.

'There are rules. We both know that. Come on, what we're both doing isn't exactly moral and Islamic is it?'

'Then don't do it,' she said.

'But I love her.'

'You're irritating me now. As far as I'm concerned, Ali, God will look at the entirety of my life and judge me on that. I pray, I fast, I've even been to Hajj three times and I give to charity.'

That was a shock. The glamour puss in a plain burqa, going

147

round the Kabah.

'Really?'

'Wow, what the hell happened to make you so sanctimonious? If you love this woman, be with her, na. If not then move on.'

'I want to marry her, but she doesn't believe in marriage either. She's meeting my parents tomorrow. She's with Farzana now, probably being grilled. I wanted her to get a taster of what tomorrow might be like.'

'You should have brought her to meet me,' Mehreen said clicking her fingers for the bill.

'I was set up on a potential marriage date with you, Mehreen. I only came because I wanted to meet you again. And pacify my boss. And get your advice about Honour...'

'Look, Yacein isn't a throwback, he'll be fine. You don't have to lie at work, especially to him. And especially if your girlfriend is meeting your parents. If Yacein's not cool I'll tell his wife to put pressure on in other areas.' She raised an eyebrow suggestively. 'But let me ask you, have you thought what denying this girl – what? nine? ten hours? – to people you work with every day does to her?'

My silence told her that actually I was a selfish knob and I hadn't given it too much thought.

'I'm not denying her...'

'Ali...'

'Well how do you feel? Doesn't your... *partner*... deny you?'

'No, he gets off on it, tells everyone. I mean look at me, right? I deny him. Anyway, this girl probably feels a little death every time you say she's not real.'

'That's why we're here,' I said.

I needed reminding, this was it, so the lies would stop. Mehreen picked up the bill on her Platinum card.

I waited with her while she hailed herself a taxi. I didn't feel bad when men looked at me with envy, accompanying this exotic creature.

'Trust me, I'll sort your boss out,' she said, 'and if he's okay your work colleagues won't bat an eyelid. Time to come out of the I'm-shagging-a-white-girl-closet, Ali. Because you're the only one left in it.'

'How far we've come from that sixth form common room,' I said.

'People don't really change, they just adapt to circumstance, but who they are inside? That rarely does. I still feel the same and have the same dreams and ambitions. Just I now have very expensive lipstick.'

I watched Mehreen get into a taxi and disappear into the Manchester traffic, her perfume lingering long after she was gone.

I called Jamal to pick me up from the restaurant. He wanted to do weed so parked up by Plattfields Park, I stared out at the black trees, while he lit up.

'Can you open the window at least?' I said.

'So who you know on Deansgate, bro? You messin' behind the missus' back, eh? Dirrrteee boy,' he said.

'I feel like feeding you a dictionary sometimes,' I said.

'Feed one a diction-ary,' Jamal said in a put on 'up-your-own-arse' accent. 'Oh, how proper one is now that one has a proper English girlfriend,' he said.

'Idiot, you know what? I'll get a taxi back,' I said.

'Chill, bro, I was just takin' da piss. She's cool, seems nice enough. Why you couldn't just shag her n marry back home, I don't know, man,' he said.

'You're not so old I won't smack you and then get you beats from Dad as well,' I said.

'Chill bro, come on. Jokes, innit.'

'Not funny.'

'Raas, you is well uptight. You want some weed to wind down?'

'Drugs are bad, and haram,' I said piously.

'Trust, if we're talking about haram…'

'What do you mean?'

'Well you n da missus, innit, tis not very halal.'

'Seriously? You're going to lecture me now?'

'What? I'm just sayin' bro. You shoulda done what we do…' Jamal blew out a huge puff of the purple-grey smoke. The air in the car was thick with it and I wound down my window.

'If you give me some bullshit speech about sleeping with goris and then marrying virgins again…'

'But it's tru,' he said.

'Yeah, maybe in 1970, not now. Grow up. They are women, human beings. They have families and morals and are people, not things. If I ever hear you speaking like that about white women again I swear, Jamal, you will be homeless in a matter of seconds. Do you understand me?'

'Yeah, whateva you ain't my dad,' he said.

'Just be glad, if Dad heard you speak like that he would cane you before throwing you out.'

'Whateva,' he said, but he went silent, obviously knowing it was true.

Dad had raised us to respect our neighbours, irrespective of colour. There was an old English woman who lived a few doors down from us back in the day, a widow, childless. We would be carted off to do her garden for free two or three times a year in the school holidays. Jamal's views were not learned under my father's roof, I was certain of that.

'It'll help take off da edge, innit,' he said, holding the spliff out towards me in his finger and thumb.

I had to admit the idea of having some of the pressure released appealed to me. I took the toke from him, and started inhaling.

'This should be the other way around, me corrupting you,' I said.

'Nah, man, you ain't ever been corrupt enuff.'

'When did you turn into a gangster?' I said.

'I ain't a gangster, bro.' He pushed the peak of his black cap up, the gold writing caught the reflection of the street lamp outside. 'It's just, you don't know what it was like for me, man. When we started at that school, all them posh white people an even de Asians, man. I don't mean white on the outside. They were like your sort of apney, innit, all proper n stuff. I never fit in man, I never had friends dere.'

'Neither did I,' I said.

'Yeah but, bro, you never fit anywhere, innit. You was always a bit of a' academic, like. N you got busy wid your books, getting your straight A's. I was thirteen, bro, I had to keep in touch wid da boys back in our hood, innit. They were my pals, my bros from other mos.' He made a ridiculous clicking noise with his fingers. I raised my eyebrows at him, he didn't respond.

I took a drag on the beedi, letting it fill my lungs. I was feeling light-headed. Maybe I should start doing this more often, I thought. Especially if stress was going to be so firmly ensconced in my life from now.

'For the first time I feel like I have someone I can talk to. Honour really gets me, and we were friends before anything else.'

'Well then, bro, hang onto her, innit,' he said.

'Dad worries about you, you know,' I said.

'He shouldn't, innit. I know what I'm doin', I don wanna go to uni n get married n do all dat gay stuff like get a house n shit. Dis is just me havin' a laugh, fittin in.'

I let the smoke fill my senses. Tonight was a night for

revelations for sure.

'You're working in a butcher's?' I said.

'Yeah, but I'll go back to college one day, I'm just savin' up.'

'I don't mind helping you out if money's the problem,' I said. I held the spliff at arm's length. 'As long as you don't spend it on this stuff.'

'Nah, bro, dis is my life, I need to stand on my own two feet, innit. Dad should be happy I ain't spongin' off him,' he said. 'I got a friend wid a fried-chicken shop, I'll be doin' that while I study.'

Not sponging off him? Just eating his food, using his electricity, staying under his roof. I didn't say that though. I coughed, my lungs warning me to stop now.

'You never said anything about being lonely. Not fitting in,' I said.

'You never asked, innit. N then you pissed off down souf,' he said.

'What about Farzana? She was up here?'

'Please, she's so up herself, thinks her shit don't stink.'

I had to laugh, that had been pretty reflective of my own experience with my sister. Trying to pretend she wasn't a repressed Asian woman by acting out with her brothers.

'Yeah, she had her moments even when I was at home. Still, she'll be married off soon enough.'

'Not soon enough, bro, not soon enough. She's always grassin' on me, windin' Dad up over me. Makes me feel like a proper black sheep, innit,' he said.

'Well, forget about her, Jamal. Focus on your plan. Get your degree or get your job. I've seen what the world does to people who don't try, and it would upset me to see you be one of them.'

'Get over yourself, bro, I don't need a lecture.'

I was wary of Jamal's driving when he dropped me off back at the hotel. The weed didn't seem to affect him the way it had me. I wondered just how much of it he was smoking.

'He took your posters down you know,' said Jamal, referring to Dad, before I got out of the car. 'Painted your room dat magnolia shit. I was sleepin' in it anyway like, but now it's sort of officially mine, innit.'

I couldn't trust myself to speak, the high of the weed gone completely.

Chapter Twelve

HONOUR

I was entirely wrapped in Al when I woke. He had pulled me to him, my small blue-veined breasts squashed against his broad chest, his leg laced through mine, pinning me into safety. His palm was curled round a thick shank of my hair. I could sense that he was awake.

'Are you frightened?' I whispered.

'Not here. Not like this.'

The hotel bed dwarfed us, pressed together we left white plains of Egyptian cotton either side. I thought of the nights in my single bed at college, fully dressed and desperate. I moved my head, feeling the gentle tension of his hand in my hair.

'I think it'll go better than you imagine.'

'I've met them, you haven't.' He sighed and then added, a tentative smile in his voice, 'Innit.'

'I know this might sound hypocritical from a girl who drank herself almost sick last night but were you and your brother smoking weed yesterday?'

'Er.'

'Er is not actually a word. Or an answer.' I rolled a few inches away from him so that he could see my face.

'A little.'

'You know how you think my parents' dog stinks?'

He pulled me back towards him as an answer.

'Well, take that and times it by fifty. And then imagine what fish shit would smell like and add that. That's what you smelt of last night. And you were talking shit as well.'

'I'm sorry, babe, I'm under a lot of pressure. I was just going back to my youth a little with Jamal. Letting off some steam.'

'I know. It makes you really annoying though. That's all.'

'I can think of ways to make it up to you.' He kissed my face, ran his hand through my hair.

'Excellent, get dressed then.'

'What?'

'Bacon, black pudding, sausages. Yum, yum, pig's bum. Hotel breakfast.'

'You make me feel sick.' He took his hands off me in a disgust that was only part pretend, giving me a chance to jump out of bed and head for the bathroom. 'And you sure know how to ruin a moment.'

Al picked at a peach over breakfast. My gluttony for pork products always made him lose his appetite but sometimes I needed to visit the important milestones of my own culture; mainly bacon. I was notorious at work for always ordering whatever on any menu was pork or wild boar presented in any form, just because I could.

'You won't be able to do that in front of our children, you know.' He watched me soak up the last of the meat juices with the fried bread.

'I know that. It's going to be brilliant; I'll never need to have an affair.'

He furrowed his gorgeous eyebrows in confusion.

'If I want the frisson of lying to you and doing something immoral behind your back; I'll just go and have a sausage sandwich.'

He laughed. 'I love you so much.' He poured some coffee and three tiny drips bled out into the white linen tablecloth. 'It's going to be a minefield though, raising kids. I'll be all proud because I've managed to get the baby into a jumper without breaking it and you'll come in screaming, shouting "Oh, my ahem, you can't put him in a green jumper on a Monday. Green on a Monday? That's so common".'

'Oh my god, you cheeky bastard. How dare you?' I kicked him under the table. 'From the man who'd want his daughter in a full burqa as soon as she thinks about getting a boyfriend.'

'Well, luckily, we'll be doing her thinking for her, won't we?' His eyes had lost the teased up crinkle at the sides.

'Meaning?'

'Well,' he knitted his fingers, the two index ones steepled and pointing at me across the table, 'I'd let my son marry who he wants, within reason. But not my daughter. She'd have to marry a Muslim.'

I didn't trust myself to speak. I made sure my lips were firmly sealed and no sound came out, I couldn't trust the sound to be rational.

'I couldn't bear watching her make all those mistakes. Not when I could help her out, direct her. I don't want her to...'

I got up from the table and walked away, dizzy, leaving the imaginary words 'sleep with as many men as her mother' pulsing in the air behind me, deafening both of us.

Back in the room, I poured myself a bath. I contemplated locking the hotel room door so that Al couldn't get back in; a couple of years ago, I would have done just that. But we were older, wiser, trying harder, even though real life continually bit us on the arse.

I knew his pattern, as well as he knew mine; a sulky silence that he wouldn't be able to penetrate until it had worked its natural course. The moments like these, the observations that had real substance, where he made a perfect point, were the most painful and by far the hardest to deal with.

I thought back to my own, tortured, teenaged years. As

reasonably attractive, long-haired identical twins, Connie and I were targeted by boys and inappropriate men; even one or two so-called-friends of my father's. I've read my diaries of that time and am so relieved never to have to live through it again. One week I was burying my face in my pony's neck and eulogising to my diary about his warm horsey smell; the next I was fucking the cricket team captain, wondering all the time whether the noises I was making were the right ones. Would I wish on any young girl the pain that captured me, floored me, when I discovered that Jonny Fillingham, first eleven, didn't actually love me? That what he'd really wanted was to bag one of the twins and it hadn't mattered which one? I fell for it, Con didn't.

The campaign of flattery, fuelled by drink, ended miserably in his parents' bed whilst they sunned themselves on the dark sand beaches of Malta. By the time they flew home, it was already over; Jonny moving on to the next girl and me crying myself to sleep at night.

What mother would deliver her daughter into the hands of such unhappiness if she thought she had a choice?

I understood the point of it all the first time I slept with Al. But it was a point of comparison; what did Einstein say 'There's no such thing as a mistake, only an opportunity for learning'? My daughters deserved the choice in their own experience, however painful. I'd use the benefit of hindsight to guide them but I certainly wasn't going to dictate to them. Connie's experience had been different to mine. Her first love had led to a halcyon summer of bike rides and picnics; would I want to deny my daughter those memories or that delighted experimentation of playing at being a grownup?

'Hey.' Al timidly pushed open the bathroom door. In his hand was a cardboard coffee cup from my favourite cafe chain. 'I went and got you coffee.'

'Thanks.'

'Have you been crying?'

I shook my head.

'Promise?'

'Promise.'

He looked relieved and sat down on the edge of the bath.

'No one said it would be easy, girl. But we will make it work.'

'I never doubt it.' I ducked my head under water so he couldn't see the lie.

I wanted to get a feel for the place my boyfriend had come from. He had spent five years meeting my family's friends, going to parties and sometimes funerals. I'd shown him the bridleways we'd ridden as children, my school buildings, the pub where I had my first drink, the neighbouring farmer's field thick with pea plants, where Connie and I used to hide, nestled down, in the days when we thought eating peas from the pod passed for stealing.

Now we were here, I suddenly realised how little I did know of his past. Our relationship was a wash of secrets, held together by the fragile pins of our belief in each other. There were things I kept even from Connie, a first for me. I had never told her that one day, in the street, Al had hissed at me, 'Just keep moving, don't look at me, just walk on. That guy was President of the Islamic Society at uni.' And I'd done it, wordlessly widened the gap between us so that I could have been anybody. So that I could only just catch the 'Salam alaikum' on the wind.

I never told my sister about the day we had to leave Waitrose when he saw his department head walk round the corner of an aisle. At least we lived in the anonymity of London; we didn't see these people on a daily basis. I looked at the central streets of Manchester, barely more than a town, and wondered how many more secrets we would have had to keep here.

We were meeting Farzana; she was primed to entertain me while Al spent time with the men of his family. At least I was no longer a secret from them.

Al took me round the sights, mainly focussing on the re-building after the IRA bombed the city centre in the year we met. Terrorism had touched both our families; Al and his parents had been shopping in the centre on the day of the blast and escaped terrified but otherwise unhurt. My parents' house had been far enough from the Royal Marine's barracks in Deal to keep our window panes, but the town, the families and the regiment lost eleven young strong bandsmen; musicians and soldiers. Television crews and cameras peered obscenely through the cracked glass of private houses, stalked widows and parents of murdered boys. Quiet people with no history of fear jumped when a car backfired or a door slammed.

The terrorist attacks straddled the North/South divide; no respecters of class, colour or religion, they touched us all.

Manchester had come back from the bombings, stronger and more gallant than before. In Deal, the Marines were withdrawn from the town, the barracks became a housing estate and the 'Green Beret' pub was renamed the 'Green Berry'.

The difference, of course, was that no one had been killed in the Manchester blast.

ALI

Death is the great leveller. Honour said that to me once.

Saturday morning I found myself at my father's elder brother's house, a sprawling detached property in Cheadle, where we were commemorating my grandfather's death anniversary.

It was odd wearing a plain shalwar kameez, the clothes so normal growing up, but I didn't wear them in my life away from home. I forgot how comfortable they were, although the naala to tie the shalwar was still fiddly even at my age.

The house smelled of agar batti and the ittar the men were wearing. The group coming to lead the prayers, to do the zikhr, were in great demand across Manchester and would carry out a number of circles before the day was done.

I hadn't realised the significance of the weekend when I had agreed to bring Honour up, and my father hadn't mentioned it either. Did he feel slighted that I didn't care about his father or remember these things? But it was his decision to meet us this weekend.

'Ali, man, where you been? Haven't seen you in years.'

It was my cousin Raqib, the one closest in age to me. He was the youngest in his family, me the eldest in mine.

My father had lost his oldest brother in the Partition and another two lived in Pakistan, so it was the youngest brother and the current eldest who were remembering their father today.

'Rocky, how you doing? How's life, man?' I said.

'Can't complain. The kids are growing up fast. Hey, Sohail, come and say salaam to your Uncle Ali,' he said. A boy of about four waddled over to shake my hand.

'Mashallah, what a cute child, man,' I said.

'Yep, looks just like his mother, thank God.'

'Don't want him getting your mashed up looks, innit,' I said.

'Hey, it's the kickboxing – it's not for wimps.'

'Big hero, are you?'

It was so easy to get back into a flow with Raqib aka Rocky. We saw each other when I came home twice a year for Eid. I realised I hadn't been to a single remembrance ceremony for my grandfather since I had left home.

Shit, did Dad feel that? How would I have felt if my kids didn't turn up or remember my father? I put a note in my diary to remind me of the date so I would make a point of it next year too.

Abdul, Raqib's oldest brother and the oldest cousin – de facto head of the family after our dads – joined us. He was more subdued than Raqib, but still had that streetwise confidence and banter than seemed endemic in Manchester.

'So what's new with you, Ali saab?'

'Nothing much. Still at the Islamic bank, still single.'

'Yeah, right, we all think you're shacked up with some gori down South. We aren't buying your single status,' said Abdul.

Raqib slapped me on the back and squeezed my shoulder at his brother's comments. My father looked on with a neutral expression.

'If I was would you still invite me to this?' I asked, only half joking, my eyes locked with Dad's, making sure he was paying attention.

'Don't be a bandar, monkey man. He was your grandfather too and you'll always be blood no matter what you do. Idiot, what a thing to say,' said Abdul.

'Even if I wasn't married to some girl? You'd still think I was okay to like sit in on these prayers?'

My father's eyes flinched ever so slightly.

'Hey, that's your business. We'd invite you. Then beat you afterwards and make you marry her,' said Abdul. 'Why are you saying this anyway? Is there something we should know?'

'No. Not at all.' Deny Honour again, why don't you? 'I'm just being weird. Tired after my journey.'

'Yeah, well, we should hook up before you go back.'

'That'd be good,' I said.

I didn't dare look at my father, but he came up to me, grasped my arm and whispered into my ear: 'Today is about my father, have some respect, don't make it about you.'

The group of men arrived to perform the zikhr so we all sat in a circle, the curtains closed to free the senses (normally this was done after sunset), and the leader of the group began chanting Allah's name. We all followed suit.

As the rhythm of our voices merged, ebbed, flowed, the very walls around us shook with the noise.

Seek your peace of mind, as I did find: I've found a haven of love requited. Whenever I stray, He draws near me. Whenever I draw near, He comes closer still.

Men may shut the doors on the faces of other men, but that's why I didn't worship any man, I worshipped God. This, the most sacred and intimate and secret worship. I was here, not excluded and no man had the right to ostracise me from it.

All that dwells upon the Earth is perishing, yet still abides the Face of thy Lord, majestic, splendid...

After the prayers for my grandfather were said, the men departed and the cousins all sat around trading banter, cricket scores, politics, Pakistani politics and just generally ripping each other up.

They kept asking me when I was getting married, and I sat there, knowing my brothers, Jamal and Zain, were sitting next to me, denying that anything was even in the offing. They, to their credit, kept straight faces, and Jamal kept cracking jokes to divert attention.

It felt good to be in this room, just us men, just the cousins and nephews, all tied by blood and family and history and all that. I wanted this for my kids too, they would miss out otherwise.

Why should my kids miss out? Who in this room would deny them that, just because their mother was different to all the other women in the family?

My father was in the other room with my tiaji, both men looking thoughtful as they came back to join us. Tiaji looked at me carefully, intently, conveying that he knew, maybe?

As we were leaving he grabbed me by both shoulders and said, 'Allah go with you, my son. And don't make it so long next time, this also is your home. And always will be.'

I had just been given approval by the head of our family. I felt humbled.

On the way home Dad got maudlin. Jamal and Zain were driving and staring out the window respectively.

'I'm glad you came, Ali. Your grandfather did so much for us,' Dad said.

I knew this. It was my grandfather's death that had led to his lands being sold, the money divided amongst his sons. It was that money that had paid for our new house, paid for my private tutor, my uni expenses. Some had been put away for Farzana's wedding.

By the time Aaliyah got married it was assumed I would return the investment.

'I always thought you would do that for me after I had gone. Have zikhrs and send blessings on to my dead soul.'

'I will, Dad. No matter who I'm with.'

'Don't worry pops if he don't I will fo'sho', innit,' said Jamal.

'You? What blessings will you send? Guns and bitches?'

I couldn't believe my father had just said the word 'bitches'. Jamal gave me a wounded look in the rear view mirror.

'I will, Dad,' said Zain quietly.

'Yes, I know, but it is Ali's duty as the eldest.'

'Dad, I will I promise.'

'And for you? Will your son do it for you?' he asked.

'I'll bring my sons up the same way you brought us up. Yes they will.'

There was silence in the car for the rest of the way home.

Raqib sent me a text saying: You bad boi I knew it, innit! Bring her round, innit, my wife will teach her how to cook. LOL. Good luck today.

Word had got round.

I texted him back saying: She cooks better curry than my mum. LOL.

Abdul texted next saying: This family is urs, she is welcome as u r, bro.

I texted him: Thanks, bro.

After Tiaji and Dad, it was Abdul's opinion that shaped the younger cousins and what we would do as a family.

Honour had been given the green light by the extended family.

But my father's decision would ultimately be the one they supported.

Chapter Thirteen

HONOUR

Farzana revealed within seconds that, although she was happy to babysit me whilst Al was at their uncle's, she had no intention whatsoever of spending the next couple of hours coaching me in Pakistani etiquette. She laid out her demands; coffee, shopping, more coffee. We went to a cafe next to the hotel for the first of her espressos.

'I like your scarf. Is that from Accessorize?' Farzana picked up the end of the scarf, rubbing the jersey fabric between her thumb and forefinger.

'It is. I love stripes.' I picked up my spoon and started stirring my coffee rather than look at her face.

'Yes,' Farzana looked suspicious. 'It's nice and wide too, isn't it? A bit, oh, a bit like… Hmmm. Oh! I've got it. It's a bit like a dupatta.' She poked her tongue out at me, scrunching up her dark eyes. 'I hope to God you're not going to put that on your head when you get round to ours.'

I was silent for a second too long.

'You were. Oh my God, you actually were. Does Ali know?' She was laughing and pointing. The people at the next table were staring at me over their cappuccinos.

'It's not funny, Farzana. I didn't want to offend anyone.'

'Oh, bless your little heart. I'm sorry, I'm being horrible. It was good of you to make the effort.' She wiped the corner of her eye where the kohl was running. 'Did you keep the receipt?'

'I like it anyway.' I jutted my chin in defiance.

'It's a bit big. For your frame. Perhaps we could go and get a smaller one. Something slightly narrower?'

'Look, I just don't want to get things wrong, make a bad first impression. And I don't know what manners are, you know, in your parents' eyes.'

Farzana patted my arm. 'Just the same as your parents' version of manners I should think. Good manners are just that, good manners. No matter where you come from.'

I sighed, the tension making my back teeth ache from clenching together. 'I just don't want to make some horrible, terrible, error that puts them off for life – reinforces everything they know about white girls.'

'I'd say normal rules apply really, don't list sexual conquests or talk about porn movies. You know; basic stuff.'

We'd finished our coffees and were collecting ourselves together to leave. Farzana held my arm. 'Look, my mum's old-fashioned. No one's saying she's going to jump for joy at her son's choice of wife.'

I blushed a little when she said 'wife'.

'But part of being old-fashioned is the belief that a visitor to the house is a gift from God. So she'll have to be reasonably nice, whatever she's really thinking.'

We walked out into the main street. People in various states of undress were making the most of the summer.

'She'll be scared, my mum.' Farzana pressed her way through the crowds, turning her head to make sure I was still with her and could still hear. 'We come from a culture where the daughter-in-law married to the eldest son takes on the care of her husband's parents for the rest of her life. They literally become her responsibility, her parents. And part of what my mum has to come to terms with in making her children British, is that that isn't going to happen.'

'Meaning me?' I asked, my eyes wide in comedy horror. 'I'm

only just coming to terms with Al, I'm not ready for your parents too. What about my job?'

'This is all part of it. We're twenty-first century working women. We wonder how we're going to manage jobs and children, let alone jobs, children *and* parents.' She put her arm through mine, steering me towards a side street.

'Are you coming back then? Not staying in Pakistan forever?'

'I'll come back when I have kids, God willing obviously. I'd want to be near my mum then. Bilal can work from anywhere, we both can really.'

'What did Bilal say about me? About the whole Billo thing? Is everyone furious?'

'Don't worry about it. They're sorted. His mum and dad have been getting annoyed at her for a long time. Billo's not a particularly easy person; very spoilt and they're getting too old to put up with it all. They've had countless offers of marriage for Billo, although Bilal says only from men who don't know her, and they're letting her sift through them all. She just wants to be rich and to travel; hence her 'thing' for the poor Californian plastic surgeon. She brings new meaning to the word "mercenary" I'm telling you. She's been stringing him along for ages but she insists on reading through the other proposals in case she gets a better offer. Even I wouldn't wish that on my brother.'

'Al feels terrible about it. About letting your parents down.'

She shook her head in exasperation. 'He doesn't listen. Not even to my parents. They aren't out of some backwater; they've been in this country for thirty years. They wouldn't force him into a marriage he didn't want. He keeps too many secrets from them because he thinks they'd never understand. He should try them once in a while. They love their children; they try to use their experience to help us make good decisions not to suffocate us.'

We'd left the main street now; the grey-slabbed pavements were far less crowded. The buildings around us were mainly pale stone, with the feel of a financial district. In the sun it was warm but pockets of empty cold hung around the shadows of the buildings. Walking the grey pavements of Al's past, feeling the whole experience of his culture, his city, had left me with so much to think about.

We realised that time had been slipping past whilst we wandered round the shops. I had a momentary panic; being late for my first ever dinner with Al's parents would be unforgivable no matter how hard Farzana tried to convince me of their gentleness.

We opted for the bus. Farzana had offered a short train ride with her father collecting us from the station. There was no way I could manage the claustrophobia of being in a car with Al's dad, sure that he'd be checking me out in the rear view mirror, looking for the integrity in my eyes or the honesty on my face.

I was struck with a terrible knowledge of my true worth when I realised that most of my terror abated when I thought of eating Al's mum's cooking. Even I was impressed by my shallowness.

The bus began to empty as we left the built-up urbanity of the red brick rows and moved into a more modern area. The main road was wide but narrow cul-de-sacs and neat drives edged off each carriageway. The high-rises of the centre's immediate periphery were out of view now.

The architecture of the area surprised me; its homogeny was disappointing. Al didn't talk much about his childhood or even his family and, over the years, I had illustrated them for myself. The shrewish, difficult Farzana; the irritating wide boy, Jamal and the two younger ones Zain and Aaliyah who I imagined as silent and blank-faced. They had all taken on an exoticism informed exclusively by television and the post-colonial literature popular in the 90's.

'Is Jamal going to be there too?' I asked Farzana as we rounded the corner into her parents' cul-de-sac. The road was wide and clean, each bungalow surrounded by a pointless wall, fence or looped white plastic chain: all only eighteen inches or so high. It could have been any town in the country.

'He's a law unto himself,' said Farzana. 'Probably less annoying if he isn't.'

'Al said he was just the same at his age.'

Farzana stopped dead in the street.

'He did not?' she asked me, wide-eyed. 'Ali said he was just like Jamal?'

'He grew out of it,' I ventured, sheepishly.

'He wishes.' She threw back her head and laughed, tidying the sides of her headscarf afterwards with her thumbs. 'That is so untrue. He managed one joy-ride to Blackpool, in a hired car.' She sneered the word 'hired'. 'And got a thrashing from my father. That was the sum total of his rebellion. Jamal, trust me, is a pain in the backside.'

We had reached the top of the short drive that led to the family home. A very new Mercedes was parked, slightly skewed, in front of the white garage door and around it small flower beds complemented the 1970's porch front. Farzana fumbled in her bag.

'I forgot to give you these.' She grinned at me.

I took the slim packet of wet-wipes from her.

'Lota for the 21st century,' she said, winking at me and reminding me of Ali and why we were doing all this.

Al met me at the door, his mother just behind him. She was small and thin, her handshake reluctant and brief. I tried to beam a smile without being patronising but it was clear from the curt nod of her head that she was not going to talk to me at all. I gushed words in response to her silence.

A mumble and a fleeting gesture with one hand were the sole constituent parts of Al's introductions. I walked along the line of people in the hallway making random small talk to accompany my firm handshakes, Farzana chatting away behind me.

The house in my mind had been brightly decorated, hung with the technicolour trappings of a seventies' Bollywood movie. I didn't expect the muted beige and magnolia on every wall, bright clean woodwork in a uniform white marking the edge of every door, the join of carpets and wall. Light-coloured Ikea frames hung dotted around, sheets of Qur'an quotations behind their glass. There were no silvered pictures of waterfalls and none of the stylized paintings of tropical birds that I'd envisaged.

Al seemed to have lost the power of speech. Anything he did say was mumbled, indecipherable. I wanted to shout at him to 'Speak up', try and get him to help me out in any way.

The Hussains were younger than I'd imagined. Their first names, if Al had used them at all in the introduction, didn't seem to be the appropriate way to address them. Of course, I already knew their names and how to pronounce them but, when I called his mother 'Mrs Hussain', no one stopped me so I carried on.

Mr Hussain was just an older, bearded, version of his sons; still handsome, white hair flecked through the dark, the faintest outline of a middle-aged paunch against his suit trousers. Mrs Hussain refused to look right at me. When I spoke to her, she just nodded her head forward; I wasn't sure whether she had acknowledged me or suffered a temporary bout of narcolepsy. She held her white-edged dupatta like a weapon, shielding her face with it and tidying it around her face as a way of finding something to do that wasn't looking at me. Farzana suggested we went through to the kitchen to help with the cooking. I was grateful to have something else to do rather than make strained and pointless conversation with Mrs Hussain (who wouldn't answer), Mr Hussain (who tried his hardest to engage me with his soft voice but couldn't dampen my embarrassment), and the two younger ones who stared at me from owl eyes.

In Punjabi, Mrs Hussain communicated to her daughter that everything was under control, her accompanying gestures proved we weren't needed. Farzana showed me the bowls and pots of waiting food anyway, her mother chipping in occasional Punjabi dialogue that could well have been cooking instructions or, just as easily, snippy comments about me. It felt incredibly uncomfortable.

A pan of oil bubbled away on the stove and Mrs Hussain dropped spoonfuls of pakora mixture in. She stretched out a newspaper on the work surface, scooped the pakora out and left them to drain into the print.

A gangly youth I knew had to be Jamal loped into the kitchen.

'All right?'

I put out my hand to shake his. He gripped it in some ridiculous handshake shape and shook it enthusiastically.

'Ha's it goin?'

He had a thick Manchester accent. His voice was nothing like his father's or any of his siblings.

'Honour, innit?'

I realise I'd not spoken, I was just staring at him with a perplexed look on my face.

'Whenever you see a stereotype on the TV screen, all bling and stupid voices,' Farzana said, 'it's because the producers have met my brother.' And then, facetiously, 'Innit?'

'Nice to meet you,' I said, sounding like the queen.

It was not going well.

We ate in silence, punctuated by my compliments to the chef. I could see Al's mother's eyes follow my left hand to my mouth every time I forgot. I tried and tried to use my right but, without a knife, I had no hope of bisecting the succulent lamb patties, the crisp and spiced potato cakes or the fiery hot samosas, using a fork in my right hand.

Towards the end of the meal, Mr Hussain started again with his polite questions, trying to show interest in me and who I might be.

'Your sister is getting married next week, my son says. Your parents must be thrilled.'

'They are. We fly down on Thursday. It's in the Loire Valley. Do you know France?'

'I don't.'

'Oh.'

'Ali tells me that your parents live on the coast?'

'Near Deal, in Kent,' I said enthusiastically, yellow rice from a piquant and perfect biryani doing its best to fly out of my mouth. 'In a village.'

'It must be lovely.' One of his trademark pauses. 'Your church, is it in the village?'

'There is a church there. They have fabulous bell-ringers. We say we'll go to Midnight Mass every Christmas. But we never do.' I smiled.

I found myself looking into a sea of cold faces, Al and Farzana looking the distinct green of the very poor sailor.

ALI

After the meal at my parents' house Farzana and Jamal went to drop Honour back at the hotel. I was surprised she agreed to leave without me, but maybe she sensed this wasn't the time, I needed to speak to my father.

Dad was happy, Honour had made the right impression, not his ideal daughter-in-law, but she was intelligent, beautiful, mannered. I could sense in him the same thawing, the same understanding, that had appealed to my own sensibilities.

So I decided to complete the picture, let my father into the secret, the dark corner I was still hiding Honour in.

'Dad, you have to know something,' I said, quiet but sure.

'Is she pregnant?'

Why was he so convinced Honour being pregnant was the only reason I'd marry her?

'No, she's not. Honour, her family, well... she's not a Christian.'

'Is she Jewish?'

'No. She doesn't believe in God. She wasn't born into a religion, she wasn't baptised or christened.'

'What are you telling me, Ali?'

'We can't have an Islamic marriage.'

Dad went off to pray. I sat staring at the wall until he came back.

'So what now?' I said.

'I don't know what to say, Ali. There are no choices really. You lied to me. You told me she was a Christian. Maybe you should have asked her to lie to me.'

I couldn't look at him, the direct stare, unblinking, the thing that had made us spill the truth and terrify us into behaving as kids. I felt like I had failed all my exams.

In a way I had.

'She wouldn't lie, even if I asked her to. And I never said she was Christian. I just didn't contradict you. I thought if you met her, maybe…'

'Well, that is something then, at least she is honest.' He ran his fingers through his short beard, pulling at the point on his chin, his contemplative stance.

Farzana and Jamal came back, bursting into the front room as though they were expecting bloodshed. Mum joined us too.

'Check da tension, innit,' Jamal said.

'Shut up, you idiot,' Farzana said.

'Check you, auntyji,' he said.

'Whatever. So what's been happening since we were gone? What's the verdict?'

Since when did Farzana become so feisty? Wasn't she meant to be respectful in front of me when my dad was around? I didn't want to know what my father was thinking.

'Mum? What did you think?' Farzana asked.

'Yes, she was nice. Very pretty.'

'Yeah, n she can learn to cook you chapattis n daal, innit, and if you're nice to her, Mum, she might not stick you in an old people's home,' Jamal said.

My sister answered him. 'Don't be such a dickhe… idiot. You're the only one who can't cook around here. As for homes – the madhouse is waiting for you, Jamal. Yes, Mum, she is pretty, isn't she? Her hair is such an amazing colour, so red and her eyes? Proper billi eyes, aren't they? And she is very sweet, really nice.'

I was still getting used to this new Farzana, the one Honour had introduced me to. It's funny how you can live with someone for a lifetime and not know them, until a stranger – in one night – can make you see them, like, really see them.

'I just say it like it is, innit,' Jamal said. 'She's cool tho.'

'You say it like you see it in your weeded messed up gangsta wannabe head. Which isn't the real world,' Farzana hissed at him.

'Sorry, auntyji,' he muttered.

Maybe I should say something to defend Honour?

'If I thought she was the sort of woman who wouldn't show my parents the same respect I do, I wouldn't be with her. When you see her with her own parents, sister, our friends… you know she is the sort of person who will also treat you both well,' I said.

'That's so true. I mean our own girls are a lottery as well, some will work out and some won't. So in truth it doesn't…' Farzana began.

'If I had a problem with her being English or white, Farzana, I would not have come to this country and I would not live here. Ali, you think you are the first boy to bring home an English girl?'

'No, Dad, but…'

'That is not the issue. The issue is how can I have you marry a woman who has no religion? What moral code will she raise your children with? I don't trust people who have no God. How can there be a nikah ceremony if she doesn't believe in God? There cannot be. And if there is no nikah then…'

'She can convert just for appearances' sake,' Farzana said, looking daggers at me, screaming silently that I should maybe find my spine and say something.

'Appearances' sake? Appearance for who, Farzana? You think I care what people say? Your mother may, but do not think I am a washer woman in some village.' My father was furious. 'My children are more important to me than anybody. Except my

God. And I could not face Him, knowing I had allowed a fraud to take place in His name.'

There was a silence broken only by the ticking of the clock above the mantelpiece, and Zain and Aaliyah rushing about upstairs, the stairs creaking as they took turns to listen in.

'Tru dat,' said Jamal.

'Maybe God will understand,' Mum said in Punjabi. 'He created us, He must know how much love a parent has for a child. Maybe He will understand what we do, and why. It is… Ali's soul and Ali's eternity. We have done our duty.'

'Begum, no, we have not. Not if we sit in on this drama.'

I knew I should be shouting, saying actually it didn't matter what they said, Honour was non-negotiable, but my father's volte face had left me immobile. I thought things had fallen into place when my mother had capitulated, but no, Mum came on board just as Dad took the lifeboat.

'In this house we know who our God is.'

'So do I. I haven't changed since I've been with her. Except for the better.'

'Who knows what you do when you are with her.'

There was a look of absolute disgust on my father's face.

'Dad, come on, if you don't budge on this you will lose Ali. Is that what you want? When I'm off and married, you'll be left with Tupac over there. Are you willing to trade in your eldest son?'

'You do not understand, Farzana. When you are as close to your grave as I am, then you will.'

'You talk about God, and then deny what He says?' I was spitting with anger. Was this the time to begin theological debate? 'We are all susceptible to die, anytime, without warning.'

Farzana ignored me.

'And what about his children? You lose Ali, and you lose your grandchildren. Can you trade them away so easily?' she said.

'What sort of children will he produce?'

'I'm not marrying a dog or a monkey, I'll produce children just like everyone else. So what, is this how it's going to be? You'll deny my children, with both our blood in them, any sort of right to their heritage? Can you really be so cold-hearted?'

'Ali…' It was my mother, telling me to shut up.

'Maybe I don't care what you say. Have you thought about that? Maybe I just did this because I didn't want to lie and hide anymore. I don't expect anything from you. I don't want a wedding, I don't want your blessing. I just came home to tell you, not to take anything. Honour is real and I love her and I will spend the rest of my life with her, and I don't care what you all think.'

The angry words echoed in the silence.

'You know, we don't have the monopoly on morality.' I think that was turning into my favourite phrase. 'She is a good woman, and she is here.'

'There are many good women in the world. Women who will suit this family better.'

'I don't want any of them. I can't help who I love. It's too late to pull out now. You have to accept that she is with me. So, what when Farzana gets married – then what? You won't invite Honour? Or when I come home at Eid she won't be allowed to accompany me?'

'Not unless she converts and marries you.'

'Then Farzana is right. I won't go anywhere without her. You are losing me if you don't accept her. I won't insult her anymore, she's been insulted enough.'

'Then there are over 3 billion women in this world, go and find another one.'

That was it. My father had spoken. Honour was no Christian, she wouldn't convert and there was no turning Dad. I didn't realise he had such a narrow view on morality. Religious people were some of the worst perpetrators of immorality in the world, but Dad couldn't see that. In his own way, my father was as infuriating as Honour's.

Mum hugged me and had tears in her eyes before I left. Farzana was livid with both me and Dad. Jamal said some gangsta sympathy words when he dropped me off at the hotel.

When Honour opened the hotel room door all I could say was, 'They absolutely loved you. Everything is good.'

The lies hadn't stopped, they had just stopped being to the world about Honour and were instead about the world for her.

Chapter Fourteen

HONOUR

My sister's new home, the village of Candée sur Beuvron, had been stolen from a story book. The impossibly narrow main street, white in the sun and flecked with tiny lizards sleeping in the dust; the quietly chattering river, so full of fish you could see the rings of their splashes although never quite catch one jumping with your full gaze, it all belonged in a novel about new lives, retirement in paradise.

The vivid red geraniums on every corner and every flat space, and the low stone bridge – history responsible for the dents and breaks in its contoured walls – came from a frightening tale of tyranny, of bullets and chipped brickwork, rhythms of marching feet and children with dark faces wide-eyed in doorways. When Paris had been given over to the Nazis in the Second World War to stem the hail of bombs and destruction that threatened the heritage of the city, promised to destroy its fabric and, with that, its whole point of being, the Parisians had begun a tortured exodus away from the incoming army. The coast would have trapped them, the south was already occupied and it was here, to the Loire Valley, west of Paris, that tens of thousands of Parisians had walked, their class and backgrounds levelled with the strafing, the punishment of armoury that came each night as they squatted by the roadside, ducked down in terror. The humble people of Candée sur Beuvron dug potatoes to try and feed them, filled jugs of water from the river for the refugees. That particular story played out up and down the banks of the river Loire.

The oak-beamed fronts of the roadside cottages belonged in a fairytale, their stooped roofs crouching low to the ground, encouraging children to touch the barley sugar slates, the tanned tiles. The tiny town cemetery, clutching the side of the hill, carried the touching stories of orphaned children, raised by ghosts inside the walls.

Everything about it contributed to the overall magic, the hidden hum of its alchemy, and I could see why Connie had fallen in love with it, with Laurent and with his country.

We arrived two days before the wedding to catch up and to indulge ourselves in the festivities for as long as we could before returning to the grind of London and work. Connie had booked us into the village bed and breakfast; a place so small and quaint that our eyes blinked and watered whenever we emerged back into daylight. The entrance hall was flagged with Caen stone, cool and worn underfoot, a relief of cold radiating from it as it had been laid to do, two centuries before. The tiny winding staircase was so perfect, so like the set of a film, that Al goosed my backside on the way up, his silent way of communicating his happiness with the whole set up.

The room was idyllic, carefully re-mastered in a twenty-first century way to look as if it hadn't been touched for hundreds of years. The walls were lazily crazed with cracked plaster and the floor beautifully finished with antique yellow wood. The windows opened inwards, and we squeezed together to look out onto the empty crossroads below.

'How gorgeous is this?' I asked Al.

'Like a dream.'

I felt closer to Al once I met his family; finally having a mental picture of the man as a boy built some bridges and cemented some links that, previously, had been tenuous and difficult to understand. My meeting them had spurred Al on to bring me out of the closet in a few situations, including work. His boss, Yacein, had been far easier about it than Al had expected; our mortgage was still in place and his career didn't seem to be suffering any. Al hadn't taken into account, of course, that discrimination legislation works two ways.

I hadn't seen my beloved sister since her hen weekend and that had been almost two months ago. We were meeting them at Laurent's grandparents' house at the other end of the village. Our shiny hire car stayed where we'd left it, drawn into the gravel at the side of the road, and we wandered through the soft September heat to find the house.

The main street of the village was barely wide enough to take a dustbin lorry and, had one tried to edge down it, the pedestrians would have had nowhere to go. The paths were marked out by shallow kerbs, mainly worn away under the weight of tyres they hadn't been built to take.

Al and I were both open-mouthed when we stood outside Laurent's grandparents' place. We didn't even know how to find the front door, whether to go in through one of the huge wooden gates set like drawbridges in the vast wall, or whether to push open the huge wrought-iron affairs we could see in the distance that led from the bottom of the terraced garden onto the river bank. The white stuccoed wall ran right the way along the road and disappeared round the corner. We counted three of the arched oak doors in just this side alone. We plucked up courage and pushed on one.

It swung open easily into a courtyard of neat gravel, expensive-looking cars and, in the centre of it all, a huge fountain. A bare-chested nymph stood awkwardly in the middle of the fountain, her chiseled stone legs twisted around marble robes. The tiniest hint of a rainbow played in the drops of water as they tipped over the scalloped edge of the fountain's bowl and onto the drive leaving a damp semi-circle on the sand. The front door of the house was easy enough to spot, flanked by pillars and sleeping stone swans.

The answer to the huge bell pull was a cacophonous barking of dogs, big ones. I watched Al's face blanch. He relaxed a little as a voice inside shouted in disembodied French at them.

I was so impressed when the French woman shouting turned out to be Connie. 'Oh my God, your French, it's like you're really, you know, one of them.'

'I am, as of tomorrow.'

We spent most of the rest of the day gasping in wonder at the delights of Laurent's grandparents' house, more like a museum than someone's home. The tiered garden had been laid out with long trestle tables, each seating at least a hundred people, in three rows.

'It's going to be glorious,' said Connie, clutching my arm. 'The day after tomorrow, these will be laid up with tablecloths, candles, flowers. It'll be amazing.'

She was right, as usual. The first wedding, on our second day in France, took place in the town hall, a long low municipal building of a few offices that seemed to be somehow annexed to Laurent's grandparents' house. It was short, efficient but thoughtful, even quite moving. In France, the documentation that accompanies the wedding comes in the form of a family book in which all of the events from that new family will be recorded. It seemed like a passport to the future; holding the 'livret de famille' seemed to cast a forward ghost across the faces of the happy couple, a vision that took in their children and their children's children, hundreds more weddings like this.

The secular nature of the French system means that you can't marry in a place of worship, or anywhere else, until you have married in front of the State. Connie was embarking on a three day wedding; her civil service and a family meal today. A church – just for the photos and Laurent's granny, Con said – followed, tomorrow, by a party so hard the guests were invited for breakfast the following morning. Al was fascinated. In exactly a week, we would be at Farzana's wedding back in Manchester; the rituals and roles of a Pakistani wedding, steeped in Hindu tradition and Indian etiquette, had seemed impossibly complex until we came to France.

'It's supposed to be all on the same day,' Connie hissed into my ear as we shuffled into the restaurant, 'but I thought our lot would be too pissed to manage.'

I looked around at my dog-eared family and knew immediately that she was right. My mother had developed a terrifying facial twitch which went hand-in-hand with her half-curtsey and repetition of the word 'enchantée'. She had fallen more than happily into the role of Duchesse, helped not in small part, by Laurent's Granny's Champagne stores.

'As a family, Con, we have no stamina.' I looked around the restaurant, the chatter of different languages filling it into every tiny nook. 'Is there a seating plan?' I dreaded sitting near one of Laurent's elderly relatives and struggling through the same sort of one-sided conversation I'd laboured on with Al's mum.

'You're with Claire,' Con said. Annie's drunken antics on the hen weekend had left relationships a little strained and, eventually, she redeemed herself by stepping down from her Maid of Honour role and passing it on to Claire. Our table turned out to be delightful, an English professor cousin of Laurent's and her, pretty much bilingual, husband and two junior relatives desperate to practise their foreign language skills. Claire and her husband spoke very little French although Al and I held the side up quite well.

Claire introduced us to her husband, explaining to him just how far back she and Connie and I went as she and I swapped stories of wounded knees and the painless childish versions of broken hearts.

'When I used to come round your house when we were kids, in the holidays or whatever, my parents used to take the piss out of me mercilessly. "Ere, Claire, you going up Buck 'Ouse again? Don't forget to doff your forelock to The Baron." They liked their mixed metaphors,' she grinned, 'The Baron was what they called your dad. In a nice way, obviously.'

I was staggered.

'I am also going to call your dad "The Baron" from now on.' Al grinned.

'If you dare,' I warned.

The wedding breakfast ran on and on through a warm haze of chatter, subtle scents wafting from the kitchen to the table. The gaps between courses grew longer, each pause filled with a speech or some home-grown entertainment. Connie had warned me of this, explained that even our family would be expected to contribute a song or a poem. Laurent's mother and grandparents had put together a play about things he'd done when he was little. Between the pungent cheese board and the perfect pale orange Tarte Tartin, we all shuffled out into the village square where seats had been arranged in an arc for the audience.

You didn't need to understand French to appreciate the skit. You did, however, need a love of slapstick and the Brits sat, in the main, with forced grins on their faces. The French stamped their feet and guffawed with laughter at each clumsy trick, each fake fall. I watched Connie laughing from across a growing cultural divide.

We filed back into the restaurant, swapping the scented

geraniums of the stone bridge in the square for the bitter coffee back inside. My dad had prepared a couple of jokes in French; they failed spectacularly in both languages and the assembled guests clearly wanted more.

One of the uncles, a shrugged little man, wizened with time and sunshine, announced a song and unsnapped the clips of a guitar case. I saw Al's eyebrows raise slightly in appreciation of the instrument he produced; a very old-looking twelve-string, its edges battered and its wood pocked and marked by the same ravages and experiences as its owner.

He sang in a reedy, warbling, voice for what seemed like hours. The French diners around us half-closed their eyes and swayed in their seats to the song; the English friends and family exchanged glances and began to feel a little uncomfortable at the amount of time the song went on for and just how bad it really was. None of the French seemed to notice the uncle strain to hit a note and then miss it.

After what seemed like hundreds of verses, he came to a stumbling halt. Family members jumped up to congratulate him, wringing his hands in an emotional exchange. I saw my father pointing at Al, talking rapidly to Laurent's grandfather who, in turn, beckoned the old uncle.

My father came over to our table, his cheeks flushed with brandy and a smear of chocolate on his face from the petit fours that had just arrived.

'I've volunteered you to hold up the family end, son,' he bellowed at Al. 'And Charles Aznavour there says you can use his guitar. You'll be saving us all from another thirty verses of that.' He clapped Al on the back, missing the panicked look he gave me.

'What shall I play?' He accepted the guitar from the old man, stroking its sides and making suitably appreciative noises about its wood, its age and its tone. The general clamour from our table, mainly in French, seemed to ask for The Beatles and, one eyebrow coolly raised in recognition of the general oddness of his situation, Al launched into a medley of tracks.

Later, when we couldn't sing, eat or laugh any longer, we excused ourselves from the wedding party and walked through the twilight along the river. Grasshoppers flicked in between the stalks of grass, calling to one another, and tiny flicking lizards lay in the warm gravel. We stopped under a picture book willow tree and lay on the grass, listening to the pops of water as fish reached up for insects before they fell, inelegantly, back into the river.

'I will never recover from the clapping as long as I live.'

Al clapped his hands together in a flurry of tangled rhythms. 'You should try playing through it. I couldn't hold on to a beat at all. I couldn't hear myself over them and I couldn't physically count because I was singing.'

It had started during 'All You Need is Love', first one, then a few, then a whole table of French people began to clap. At first, they beat out the rhythm and I tapped along on the tablecloth with one finger, a retiring English version of joining in. As more people started to join in, the clapping became a little more confused, as Al hit a chorus, all hell broke loose and the clapping became a cacophony, a chattering of hands with no more direction than a flock of crazed and confused birds swirling around the warm air of the restaurant.

Laurent's cousin leaned in towards me, holding a very peculiar rhythm of triple beats and long pauses as she spoke, 'In France, we like to add an alternative beat to show our understanding of the music, of its speech.' She nodded encouragingly, as if I was, at any moment, about to join in. 'I know it can sound like a bit of a phenomena to an English person, but it's very ordinary. Try it.' She beamed at me.

I eyed her suspiciously, gently putting my palms together and trying very hard not to make a noise.

'That's it,' she was delighted. 'Now establish the off-beat, it's harder than you think.' I looked over at Con, she was clapping away like a native.

I did try. I did my best to make my hands speak in little dancing formations, I tried my hardest to stay away from the obvious and compulsive rhythm I recognised. Something in me just could not leave the uniformity I'd learnt from years of music lessons at school. I couldn't help but giggle at the earnest, music-loving, faces of the pattern-deaf French.

Al and I lay by the river, helpless with laughter, every time we calmed down, one or other of us would start the time-challenged applause again.

'It was a beautiful day though, despite the clapping,' I leaned against him, the dry autumn grass tickling my neck.

Al reached his hand over, covering my fingers in his. We listened to the peace of the countryside, still warm as the night began to colour in the corners of the sky.

'My dad called you "son", did you notice?'

'Funny how I'm son just before I save his talentless bacon.'

'I'm tempted to argue that his jokes were very funny and far from talentless.' I grinned at Al.

'But you know that's ridiculous and that even the French didn't find them funny.' He kissed my shoulders, one hand already on the zip at the back of my dress.

I didn't want to spoil the moment by checking if we were hidden from sight beneath the tree. I chose instead to trust Al's judgement and unbuttoned his expensive linen shirt. If anyone had seen us, and we were a fair walk from the village, they would have understood how easily we were enchanted by the circumstance, by the soft warm air, the draped willow leaves, curved and gentle, brushing through each other without twisting. They would have been beguiled by the heron in his blue-grey bib standing sentinel by the water's edge. They would have heard the evening birdsong, the river – laconic with the lack of summer rain. An on-looker would not have heard me lift my lips from his open mouth and whisper, 'I will marry you.'

That night I dreamed of warm futures, children and cousins for the children, the safety of Al.

ALI

When I think back to Connie's wedding all I can recall is a red angry mist. It started with anger at my father, his stubborn rhetoric about marrying me to a religious woman. He seemed to miss the fact that I was already living with her, that it was a futile ultimatum. I then transferred my anger to Farzana. How dare she get married, really rub it in, bring home to my parents and me what I would never have.

I could feel storms gathering from the moment we got there. I had nowhere to direct my unhappiness, so I targeted Honour's family when she wasn't around, as though I had a nail stuck in my hoof. Honour was losing half of her, I should have been there to comfort her, assure her that I was there to fill the gap Connie might leave.

Instead I was annoyed and, in the pit of my stomach, I felt homesick.

Honour's dad kept putting his arms around my shoulders and patting me on the back, calling me 'son' and constantly asking for my opinion. It soon dawned on me that it was because my French was better than his and he was trying to communicate with Laurent's grandparents.

I had to keep telling myself that this was the happiest week of their lives, tried to transfer the excitement that my parents felt for Farzana's wedding onto them. It didn't work.

Things were going well during the civil ceremony, it was all very polite, and then we were herded off to the castle where Laurent's family had put on a feast.

I felt envious that maybe Honour and I wouldn't even get this far if she didn't budge on marriage and I started to feel insecure again. That fear that her feelings weren't as strong as mine. Even then, after so many years of her being with me.

So why couldn't she commit? Let me get the piece of paper that said it?

I sat through course after course of meat, the fat dripping, the steam wafting, the stupid waiters offering me everything. My mouth slavered at the beef, chicken and lamb dishes, I just wanted to tear the flesh from bone with my teeth. All of it was haram though.

I felt a bit put out that no one had bothered to make up a special plate of halal food for me. And what about Laurent's family? Half of his side were Moroccan Muslims? Were none of them here?

The pressure, the constant conversation and the heat were making me ill, and I wished for Jamal and weed and a car parked up by Plattfields Park. My head went light and I started to feel dizzy, my throat closing up needing something. I thought I would vomit or pass out.

Then they made me play guitar.

As usual it was Honour's father who opened his big mouth and called me son and told me to play. I would represent the family.

Sod off, I have a father, I have someone to call me 'son' and I will call my own children 'son' not Laurent's or anyone else's. I felt so angrily sick at that point. It was like he knew that my father had rejected me and that I was in a void.

Then there was peace.

There was an ideal.

There was just me and Honour and the world.

190

We lay by the river, on the grass, and we were in France. Beautiful, magnificent France. This was the France of fantasy, and it was serene.

Then she made it perfect.

She said she'd marry me.

Hooked up on the romance of her sister's day, she thought about it and she really would marry me.

But then spoilt it all.

'A small family wedding, but your family have to be there,' she said. 'I'll do this for them, for you.'

All the arguments, discussions, me pretending that my family loved her and wanted her to marry me, well, I had done it now. Honour wanted to marry me.

But a family wedding? That wasn't going to happen.

I was in tears before we walked back to the restaurant, she thought from happiness, but for me it was a vent for the exact opposite.

I had wanted nothing more than for Honour to marry me, to give me that certificate, make that commitment to me. I had it now, but how would she react when I said it would just be the two of us?

Chapter Fifteen

HONOUR

It shocked me, when I woke up, to think of Connie as married. It hit me harder when my second thought arrived; fuelled by champagne, high on emotion and carried away by sex on a riverbank, I had agreed to marry Al.

He'd been strange, almost distant. I supposed my turnaround had come as a major shock to him. There was nothing I could put my finger on; when I'd said it he'd kissed me long and hard, and when he'd pulled his face away there were tears in his eyes. He'd traced his fingers along the line of every muscle in my back as he zipped my dress up, ready to walk back into the restaurant as if nothing had happened. But there was hollowness to his smile, something in his eyes that didn't meet the rest of his face. He almost looked worried.

We'd decided, on our giggling walk back, that making an announcement would be inappropriate on Connie's big day and that it would just make it completely obvious how we'd occupied our time on our evening stroll. Until we got back to England it would be our secret and ours alone. I amazed myself at how thrilled I was. I knew that, over time, the debates and negotiations, the arguments and compromises over civil services and religious observance would take the shine off the idea but, for now, it was our news, our joint decision.

The morning sun flowed gently into the low-ceilinged bedroom when Al pulled the curtains back. I watched him from the bed, hoping it was my imagination that saw a tension, a tiredness in his shoulders.

'You okay?' I asked as he got back into bed.

'I'm exhausted. That was a very long day and now we've got to do it all over again.'

'Only it's going to be longer still. You might have to start drinking to get through it.'

'I might, in all seriousness, have to come back here for a kip.'

'I've seen the menu, it actually has breakfast on it for tomorrow morning. And the pudding from the meal gets served after the first lot of dancing. At eleven o'clock tonight.'

Al groaned and hid beneath the covers, the white linen pillow over his face. 'And then I fly to Manchester and have a week of my mother. Kill me now.'

The celebrations for Farzana's wedding were due to begin, seven days of ritual and tradition leading up to her marriage, a week after Con's. I still felt awkward, unhappy, discussing it with Al. The closer her wedding got, the more matriarchal Farzana became. I was comforted by her conviction that, one day far in the future, it would be important to the whole family that I had been at her wedding, snuck into a corner of a photograph, even though I wouldn't be able to speak to Al while I was there.

Al was quiet on the subject, taciturn and difficult if forced to talk about it; not the bold knight-in-shining-armour he'd been yesterday, entertaining the French people, holding the whole wedding party enraptured as he sang and leaving all the old ladies a little in love with him. When he dealt with his family, he seemed to me to become a boy; a silly snotty child, whiney on his high horse and unable to have a rational conversation.

We stayed in bed for a few hours after the flat-toned town hall bell had chimed us awake, determined to stretch out our seclusion to the last minute before we were due at the church. We didn't need the fresh croissants of breakfast, not hungry after yesterday's day-long dinner and still grinning with delight at our decision. We slept, on and off, cat-napping in the pool of sunlight that crept over the bed as the day lengthened.

'Tell me a secret,' I said, my back to Al, wrapped in his arms.

'I love you more than anyone else in the world?'

'That's not a secret, even your mum knows that.'

He moved in closer, blew on my ear, 'How about, when we're married you can leave your fancy pants West End job and stay at home churning out hundreds of babies?'

'And you'll pay all the bills? Deal.' I smiled at how different my reaction was now to what it would have been a few years ago, although I wasn't sure whether it was loving Al or finding out what the grind of working every day is really like that shifted my opinion. 'Do you realise that our kids will have one set of cousins who speak French and one who speak Punjabi? As a first language? That's amazing. Our kids will speak Punjabi, won't they?'

'They'll have to if they ever want to have a conversation with their grandmother. That's one mountain that you know who really won't go to, you know.'

'Mohammed,' I said in a joking voice, a Gothic inflection intended to mock his superstition. 'You should never say "Mohammed" when you're in bed in a love nest with your white heathen girlfriend, you know, terrible things could happen.'

He flinched at my blasphemy and I felt instantly sorry. He got out of bed and I knew I'd gone too far.

I watched him dress on the other side of the room. He always removed himself from a situation where I invoked his god or poked fun at his religion but still I didn't learn. I was like a child with a caged animal and a stick to push through the bars.

'I have to learn Punjabi before our children are born,' it was irresistible, 'otherwise how do I wring my dupatta and grind out the word beta through my gnashed teeth to make them feel properly guilty?'

'Drop it, will you?' He walked into the bathroom and slammed the door.

When we got to the church, there was already an invisible wedge of ice nestled between us. I'd gone too far in goading Al when he was already worried about spending a week at his parents' house. He was taking a taxi from the village to the airport and flying to Manchester, I would spend one more night with my parents before catching a plane to London and finishing up a few bits of work then joining him in a hotel.

I ignored the irritation that was prickling like static between us, concentrating on the spectacle unfolding before me. Yesterday's twelve-course dinner for fifty had been just the starter. Today was the proper wedding, a religious ceremony for Laurent's grandparents and a party for the whole town.

I let Al be dragged off by some of the old ladies who had fallen for him yesterday and walked over to Claire.

'You look exhausted,' she said, kissing my cheeks French-style.

'Thanks. What about "You look glamorous"? Or "That dress looks like it cost a fortune"?'

Claire laughed.

'It was a bloody long day though, wasn't it? And now look,' I gestured at the streams of people going into the church. 'This bit is huge. She told us it would be massive but this is crazy. There must be at least three hundred people.'

'Closer to four,' Claire said. 'And they're all having dinner. Right, I have to be waiting for the bride when she appears.'

I found Al and we made our way to the front of the church. It smelt glorious, scents rising from the posies tied artfully at the end of each pew and flooding into the Chancel from the enormous fountains of flowers at each corner of the blocks of seats and framing the altar. I could see my mother up ahead, marked out by her enormous fuchsia hat. Con had warned her that the French women would be unlikely to wear hats but she'd flustered and flapped and gone on about her 'only daughter likely to get married'. It was probably a fair decision; I was not keen on choosing a wedding venue that would warrant a hat and definitely not one that size or, for that matter, colour.

The church service that added the bells and whistles to Connie and Laurent's civil wedding was deeply moving. The solemnity of the cool church and the history of the words and incantations gave the day a humanist value as well as a religious one. They stood, stock still, at the front of the church for at least half an hour before the endless business of genuflecting and climbing back up. I loved looking at Con's face during that time, her radiance and the physical manifestation of how much she loved Laurent. I moved a little closer to Al, fracturing the ice between us, diffusing the static. I felt for his hand and twined his fingers into mine.

The Vin d'honneur was served by waiters, penguin-stiff, outside the church. While we'd been inside humming the tunes to hymns with words we couldn't understand, trestle tables had been laid with white napery and hundreds of bottles of champagne left to sweat in buckets of ice beside them. The canapés, regimented in their thousands and served by smiling professionals gliding through the crowds, were works of art. Piped mousses, creams of vegetables, cubes of foie gras chilled against the sun, nestled on flakes of pastry and troughs of thin biscuits fragile as sand.

The photographer had dispensed with formal pictures and was milling through the people snapping reportage shots. I saw her follow my mother's hat for a while before concentrating on the food and the glint of the tall glasses raised. She posed her lens on one man for a particularly long time, I looked beyond her to the subject.

The last time I'd seen Roman he'd been a student, back from Paris and his study of poetry to work on his uncle's farm for June and July. I had no idea that he and Connie had kept in touch, or even that they'd ever been particularly close.

Roman and I had been close. For a few weeks that summer we'd been very close indeed, mainly dictated by his rugged and inventive attitude to the whys and wherefores of sex, and shortly before I had discovered that he was only studying poetry to get closer to his favourite subject; Roman. Physically, he went beyond handsome and touched on beautiful, even more so six years later, but an inability to understand each other's language had been what kept us seeing each other. Once I'd worked out enough French to understand him, and he enough English to drone on for hours, I'd backed off and moved on.

I really didn't need to see him today.

I put off the inevitable through the long dinner, stayed tucked behind Al as much as I could or hid in the shadow of my mother's hat. By the time the dancing had begun and people had started to mingle I was fairly certain that Roman hadn't noticed me. When you have lived with it all your life, it is easy to forget things like being the identical twin sister of the bride.

'Ah, I have been looking for you all day. And now I find you, beautiful sister of the bride.' He kissed me, three times, and added to the intimacy by cupping my face in his hand, his thumb resting on my lips.

I jerked away. Two spots of red lit up my cheeks in an instant.

'Al, this is Roman, an old friend.'

Al's face was thunderous. Five years of imagined jealousy, of fantasy cuckolds, crystalised in the flash of his black pupils. 'Ali Hussain.' He put out his hand to shake Roman's, not dropping eye contact for a second.

'Al is my partner.'

'Ton copin? Ou ami?' Roman pulled at the French distinction between a platonic friend and a lover.

'Fiancé.' Al was almost trembling with tension.

'Ah, mais oui, congratulations. I knew it is too much to hope that my old love is here and she is alone.' Roman raised his champagne glass. 'To, with sadness, our past and,' he nodded towards Al, 'with happiness, your future.'

Al didn't join the toast.

A few more pleasantries, a nod to the beauty of the bride, a promise to seek me out to dance later and then Roman left us alone.

'What a wanker,' I said, smiling over my champagne glass.

'And one of your lovers.' Al pulled the word long with spite.

'Not a *lover*, you're making yourself sound ridiculous. A shag, a fuck. I don't know. It was before I knew you.'

'No it wasn't.'

We were walking away from the main group of people, trying to stay out of earshot from the small clusters of guests admiring the garden, gazing up at the windows of the vast house.

'You know what I mean. Before we slept together.' I had known this row would come. I had only slept with a handful of men, Al was the sixth, but it was inevitable that he would bump into one of them, one day. Why it had to be Roman – six inches taller even than Al, broad-shouldered and magnificent, with the slate-grey eyes of a wolf and the personality of a piranha – was known only to the Fates.

'I wasn't with you then. If you recall, I was fucking desperate for you and you were too good for me. I even asked you to come to France with me, remember? But you were too busy being matched up in Manchester.'

'Don't give me that. It's not my fault you fucked him.'

I had never heard Al swear in all the time I'd known him, in five years of being in love with him. I felt sick. It was as if one encounter with one bragging and ridiculous man, a man who had been at great pains to make it clear to Al that he'd slept with his soon-to-be wife, had wiped out all the love, smashed our future into vicious shards of something I could only be afraid of.

Al slumped onto a bench in the garden, the opulent surroundings at odds with his fighter's face, his tight and choking voice.

'He said he loved you. It wasn't a passing fling with the farm boy, was it?'

'He's French, he doesn't mean it like you think. Of course he didn't love me. He's just being a wanker. He's always been like that. He studied poetry, for fuck's sake.'

'So, you didn't even like him, you certainly weren't in love with him. But you had sex with him anyway. Where? Where did you do it? Go on, where?'

'What? Don't you dare ask me that? What the fuck has that got to do with you?' My memory flashed to the vineyard, to the barn, to the hay bales in the farmyard, to mine and Connie's tiny tent that smelt of nylon and wet socks. I wanted to say 'I fucked him everywhere'. But I held my tongue.

'In a field? In a French field? By a babbling brook?' I could feel the passion pouring off him as his anger turned to tears. 'Why did you have to do that? Look me in the eyes and tell me that you didn't. That I'm the first, the only one.'

I felt like I'd been slapped. 'You want me, at my sister's wedding, to stand hand-on-heart and swear that I've never had sex in a field with anyone but you?'

Al nodded weakly then put his head in his hands, hiding his eyes from me.

'You're being ridiculous. Fucking ridiculous.'

'You did, didn't you?'

I tried to grasp his wrists but he shook me off.

'You did.'

'Stop playing the fucking martyr. You knew. You knew I'd slept with other people. It was no different to sleeping with you. You could have been a one night stand; I didn't know then. You might have walked off in the morning but I took the risk. Just the same.'

'Just the same?'

'You're twisting my words. On purpose.' My throat was on fire, my skin taut and pricking. 'This is the twenty-first century, it doesn't even fucking matter. You were right all along with your pre-conceptions of all the gori slags.'

He stood up.

'I have an early plane to catch. I'm going back to the room.'

I didn't trust my voice to shout out after him. At the bottom of the garden, my mother looked up and caught my eye. She gestured for me to join her, my father and Connie and I wandered down, steadying my breathing as I went. I didn't see Roman again until three or four o'clock in the morning. A band had been playing and I'd been dancing with Claire and Connie and a surprising number of elderly French people, still up and still partying as the stars began to pale and the dawn threatened a fine pink line across the horizon. I was walking towards a cluster of tables to rest while the music changed over.

'Where's your man?' he asked. 'You look tired to be here alone.'

I swayed slightly; we had been drinking since the early afternoon and I had sunk my anger in a few more glasses of champagne than I should have. I reached out to grasp one of the chairs and steady myself but Roman grabbed my hand instead.

'If you were my beautiful lady, I would not leave you here *au seule.*'

'Al had an early plane to catch. That's all.' I looked down at his hand, swamping mine. His fingers were clean and neatly manicured, the muscles on the back of his hand stood out. I thought about moving my hand but didn't do it.

'You need coffee?'

I nodded and followed without comment as he led me, still holding my hand in his, to the bar and asked for two long black coffees.

We sat down at one of the linen-draped tables. The tablecloths were magically replaced with every sitting, every ring of red wine or over-flowing ashtray removed. The tidiness gave the garden a bewitched feel, the sheer opulence of it all made me slightly disjointed, undone.

'Pauvre petite Honour.' The way he stretched the last vowels of my name was annoying, oily. 'You are tired, yes?'

Roman moved his chair slightly and put his arm round my shoulders.

I was tired, but more than that, I was drunk and maudlin. I sighed and a tiny tear escaped down my cheek.

'I think you are fighting with the fiancé. Poor girl, and now you are sad.'

I leaned in to him, more than aware of his intent, perceptive to his seduction.

'We should walk, you are cold?'

There was nothing chill about the night but I allowed Roman to drape his jacket round my shoulders as much for the romance of the gesture as anything else. To spite Al I fitted myself into the curve of Roman's arm, moved closer to him, so close I could smell the soap on his skin and the washing powder in his clothes.

He slipped his hand down to my waist, curved his fingers round me. It transported me back to my younger self, to the first time I'd slept with him, to his showing me how inexpert the fumblings of the British boys before him had been.

'You are shaking.' He turned me to face him, his hands on my shoulders. 'Like me, you are thinking of us together, no? When we made love?'

I nodded, half in anger at Al, half forced by the alcohol.

And then we kissed. I tipped my face up towards his, pressing myself against him. I held the back of his head with one hand, my fingers gripping his hair, my other hand felt its way into his shirt, lay flat against the hard muscles of his chest.

My breathing was shallow, my pulse racing, it would have taken no effort at all to give in to Roman, to just fuck him in the nearest quiet place. No one would know.

His hand slipped onto the back of my leg, tracing my contours down and then up again, under my dress. His fingers pulled at the top of my knickers and he slipped his palm, warm, against my naked backside.

The feeling of his skin on mine was wrong. The taste of his mouth, alcohol and toothpaste, a trace of cigarette smoke, woke me, brought me back down to earth. I didn't want Roman. I reached behind me and grasped his wrist.

'Roman.'

'I have a hotel room.'

'No, Roman. I can't. I don't want to.'

'Your fiancé?'

I nodded, pushing him away from me with both my hands flat on his chest, he didn't resist.

He grinned, it made him more handsome. 'He is a lucky man. And you, you are a beautiful passionate woman. Come, I walk you back.' He made a Gallic shrug, clearly harbouring no ill feelings that the better man had won, showing he was still the chancer I'd known him as.

He offered me his arm and, like a prim Victorian, I took it, walking calmly by his side and trying not to think about the way I had felt about him just seconds before.

We reached the gate of the garden, I could see my hotel just across the square.

'It was good to see you.' He leaned down and brushed my lips with his, exhaling faintly as his mouth passed mine so that I smelt him on the fresh morning air.

I tiptoed through the dark restaurant, the blinds still drawn against the day and at the top of the narrow staircase, opened our door with the quietest of clicks.

The white chenille bedspread was unruffled, the plump pillows soft and straight at the head of the bed. Al's case was missing from the nightstand and the bed had not been slept in. I flung myself on the bed, fully clothed, and cried myself to sleep.

The last day in France passed in a horror of hangover, I ducked every time the door opened in case Roman came in but I didn't see him again. Years later I would feel slightly sick every time Connie's wedding album came out and I knew I'd see the black and white photograph of his fantastically symmetrical jaw and his looping curls of jet black hair.

I spent the day in sunglasses, sniping at my poor mother every time she spoke. Claire had gone back and Connie and Laurent had left for their honeymoon, I was left at the mercy of my parents, mine to entertain for one last, very long, evening.

'It's been incredible,' my mother had tears in her eyes. 'It's made the last twenty-seven years worthwhile.'

'Thanks,' I raised my eyebrows at her. 'Your sentiment is much appreciated by the spinster twin.'

'Actually,' my dad had his pompous voice on, made worse by his drinking and my delicacy, 'we thought it might change your mind. Or Al's.'

I was irritated by how transparent I must be, how shallow.

'Well, I have his sister's to go to next weekend too, so we'll see how that goes. Would you like that Dad? A full-on Muslim wedding with no booze? We could even do it in Islamabad; his cousin did.' My voice was petulant, I even hated myself. I wondered where Al was.

'Instead, you chose to spend the whole bloody weekend squabbling. Don't know when you're well off, girl, that's your trouble.'

My mother nodded her agreement, they'd obviously discussed it.

'We didn't squabble as you so annoyingly put it. Al had an early flight and I don't need to be back until tomorrow. Want to see the tickets? Do I have to prove it?'

'Just saying, that's all. We're not bloody stupid.'

'I think Daddy means to say that we're here for you, darling. That you can always talk to us. Don't you, David?'

My father wrinkled one nostril in an ambivalent facial gesture. 'Perhaps you should give a chap the benefit of the doubt now and again? It can't have been easy for him; surrounded by your family and,' he lowered his voice to a whisper. 'All those ghastly French.'

I was close to tears for my whole flight, for the Tube ride home, for the last sullen moments of wheeling my suitcase to our street. I was desperate to get into the flat, to check the answer phone, to hear his voice, catch the apology in his tone, go to sleep dreaming of how good it would be to see him.

To my relief the red flash on the answer phone showed five messages. I smiled involuntarily, feeling my whole body unknot with relief. I flicked the thermostat to start the hum of the heating, the warmth of France already just a memory, and found a bottle of white wine in the fridge.

I stretched out on the sofa for a second, enjoying the peace and the distance from my family; the last twenty-four hours together had stretched my patience beyond polite. I took a sip of wine and pressed the play button. There were three invitations to dinner from friends, one reminder call from the optician and one, pointless, announcement from my mother to declare their safe return to Britain. Nothing from Al at all.

I ran into the bedroom and checked my mobile. The same assortment of work and play, nothing from him.

I dialled his mobile. It was off.

I thrashed through my options. I could ring his parents' house. I could email Farzana and hope she checked her mail tonight, she didn't have a mobile. Or I could wait the evening out. Perhaps he couldn't remember my flight details; maybe he didn't realise I was home yet.

My train ticket to Manchester was for three days' time. Today was Monday, the hotel wasn't booked until Thursday. Surely he wouldn't wait that long. Surely he couldn't.

A tiny voice inside called to me softly 'this is serious, this is a real break.'

ALI

The morning of Connie's Church wedding, Honour lay in bed saying all the things I wanted to hear. She would learn Punjabi, and we would have kids who would speak two languages, our dreams of the future intermingled.

She felt as though she had given me everything.

It was afterwards that I had broken it to her, had put myself in her hands.

'My family... they won't accept it. Not unless you convert... I mean a civil ceremony,' I said.

She was quiet, and I could feel her body tense.

'Is there any point then? I mean we're okay as we are, aren't we? Let's talk about it when we get back. After Farzana's wedding.'

I kissed the top of her head, held her close to me, to hide the jolt as my deepest fears became reality. She didn't want to marry me just for me. She didn't want to commit to me officially.

And then there was Roman...

His wolf grey eyes, his smooth French drawl, that easy languid confidence. I swear the prick had undressed Honour while we stood there, imagining what her body was like. Except he didn't have to imagine. He was recalling.

Smack. Pit of stomach anger, envy and loss of sanity.

Images flooded into my head: Honour and her past, Honour and her lovers, Honour and her experiences.

I thought I had gotten over this, my virginal jealousy, maddening and overpowering. We had been there and done that, I had mastered it.

No, I had just mastered the idea of it.

In Roman (what sort of fucked up, up your own backside sort of name was Roman anyway?) I had seen the idea become real.

I stood there and while he letched over Honour, I watched him. Irritated by the fact that I had to look up into his eyes.

And Honour? She was giving him signals. Her eyes dilated, I swear, and she was brushing her fingers in her hair, at one point she touched her stomach and showed off the flatness of it. Flat against the beautiful breasts that went with it.

If it was a Bollywood film I would slap her or sing a song on a piano about how she had betrayed me.

And then back to Roman, with his nose and mouth and fingers…

And all the time her words, 'Is there any point then?' cutting me like shards of glass.

Is this why? Was she waiting for someone else to turn up? Was she waiting for Roman to come back? Is that why she couldn't commit to me?

And now what? Had he come back? I didn't understand…

I felt like a fool on the plane home.

I felt alienated from both my own people and hers. I was alone and even the prayers I said to ask for a safe flight sounded hollow in my head.

Losing Honour was traumatic.

I was crushed, images of Roman in my head. The jealousy burning like I imagined birth pains, coming at whim, wrenching and unstoppable.

Don't think of him crawling all over Honour. Don't imagine that wink he did when he met you, that said I've fucked in your garden. Don't think… but that's all I could think of.

Thank God the flight wasn't very long. I needed to escape the confines of the metal and engines, and get some clarity and boundaries.

I had left my beloved in the arms of a lion who had tasted her blood already.

They would surely sleep together tonight? I had acted like a dick and had made out that we were over. It was too late, Honour was gone.

Could it be that easy? I mean, she had wanted to marry me for my family's sake? That was a big step for her, right? She had changed her rules for me? For them?

My head felt as though it would explode.

Had I just ended it because I had presumed to second guess her?

And then images of Roman and Honour again. How could we be together if she had done that?

An animal began lowing inside me.

I had thrown it all away and I needed to free myself, avenge myself, take out the pain and move on.

I let the red mist and the hurt and desperation take over.

I used my mobile when I landed in Manchester to check Mehreen's whereabouts.

She was home.

So was I.

If Honour could seal our end with sex, so could I.

Mum.

She spoke to me.

She took me into her arms, kissed my forehead, and wiped her hands over my head. She did surreptitiously look over my shoulder, just for a second. It seemed like it had been an age since she had brought me near to her heart like this.

I had come alone, I had done the right thing, I was the eldest son back to see his sister married off. In Hindu tradition it was the brother that did the kanyadaan, walking his sister to the bridal car and off to her in-laws. Even as Pakistani Muslims, our customs and folklore still owed a historic nod to Hindu cultural practice, from the days when Islam had come to India via Sufi holy men. The Rajputs, my 'people' had come to Islam even later, my family only a couple of generations before my great-grandfather, and while they believed in one God, they also believed in their old traditions, the same practices for Rajputs whether in India or Pakistan, Hindu or Muslim. My culture was nothing if not complicated. Where was the room left to adapt to British life?

Farzana was no demure Bollywood sister type though, and there would be no kanyadaan. In the Pakistani tradition it was a Qur'an held over the bride's head by the mother's brother.

The wedding house became rooted in centuries-old rituals, memories, and things that mattered. Like a peepal tree in a dusty courtyard, everything began to revolve around it.

'Are you hungry, beta?' My mother said.

She called me beta. I know it sounds pathetic but it felt like it had been so long since she had actually been my mother, since she had chosen not to have an eldest son with a heathen woman. It felt great.

In truth it had only been a month.

But it felt like home.

That empty feeling in France, that homesickness that had invaded every cell from the moment I landed. Home was filled with everything I craved, undid all that.

I even loved the smell of cooking wafting through the house, the different music sessions my younger siblings were engaged in.

When the azaan sounded on an Islam channel for afternoon prayer, my soul leapt.

But my heart... oh, my heart was still empty... cold...

Mehreen had texted to confirm where we would meet tonight.

Dad.

He wasn't as welcoming as mum. He prayed and then we sat in the lounge, with its pale colours and wide vista from the front drive to the back garden. I used to think it was massive after they had first moved, compared to the small terraced house we had come from.

Now in the face of Laurent and his family heritage it seemed small again.

But there was sukoon, peace.

Dad had that ability to avoid small talk which I had never managed. If you asked him a question he would consider all the options and then give you a reply that was just right. He didn't bother asking how I was, or how Honour was. That would be a waste of time and words.

Instead he went straight for what mattered.

'Has she found a God yet?'

'No,' I said.

Silence.

There's a man who calls me son, you know. A man who shows off in France at his daughter's wedding that I can play the guitar, that I can speak French fluently. Who has no qualms in displaying physical affection.

I didn't say it but I thought it.

There's a man out there who can take your place.

I knew that was crap. There was no way anyone else could be my father. Because he was, really where it mattered, like the raising and guiding and all that he was.

I just chose to do the exact opposite of what he told me to.

And that other man, David Edwards, aka The Baron, came only with his daughter. And his daughter was a no show at the moment.

'I think it may be over,' I said.

'Is that a definite or is it just a misunderstanding?'

'I think it's a definite. We had a row, I stormed off.'

'I think maybe you should be more sure, my son. Before you think it has ended.'

Did he know what my intentions were with Mehreen?

'She wants to marry me,' I said.

No, must be past tense.

'She wanted to marry me. She said that she wanted to learn Punjabi, teach it to our kids.'

On cue there was a Noorjehan song coming from the kitchen.

'It was a big thing for her. She didn't believe in marriage. I guess she saw her sister's wedding, saw how happy she was, how happy everyone was... they went to a church. They did a ceremony there. Neither bride nor groom believes. The groom is half-Moroccan. Half-Muslim? Although, yeah, I know you're only a Muslim by practising and it's not a race. He didn't have anything against it though. None of them did.'

The TV was playing a Lollywood video.

Upstairs there was the sound of running feet and the gentle hum of different cultures.

Bollywood vs R n B.

Neither belonged to Pakistan. Or Britain. Both felt comfortable here though.

'I could have done that... we could have done that. Your grandkids would have spoken Punjabi. She wanted to do it for you guys...'

'Sikhs speak Punjabi. That doesn't mean they are Muslim. Yet if you had brought home a Sikhni, I would have accepted her. What I cannot accept is a Godless woman.'

'You keep saying that, Dad. Like she's a Satanist or something abhorrent.'

'Ali, we've been here before. Marriage is sacred. I will not accept a mockery. I need a moral code for my grandchildren. A marriage needs God's blessings.'

'It doesn't matter now anyway,' I said.

I was late.

I had to shower and change.

I had to meet Mehreen.

Chapter Sixteen

HONOUR

He didn't leave it three days; I knew he wouldn't, that he was too polite and too orderly for such an unresolved situation.

'I'm in Manchester.' His voice was expressionless; he added no colour or explanation to his statement.

'I thought so. How's Farzana?'

'Yeah, alright, you know. Frazzled.'

'And your mum? She excited?'

'Mmmm. I suppose.'

'Look...'

He stopped me. 'It's okay. We'll talk about it when you get here. Can you get a taxi to the hotel from the station?'

'Yes.' I was surprised.

'Just in case I'm stuck at some family thing.'

'Okay.'

I put the phone down. Neither of us offered an 'I love you' at the end of the call but I didn't know if that was through anger or fear.

I would normally ring Connie as soon as I quarrelled with Al. She and I would go over his behaviour, laugh or grumble about it and then take off at tangents on happier topics of gossip or of finding a chance to meet up.

When I arrived in Manchester, the trademark rain didn't let me down. A fine drizzle blew into my face as soon as I stepped out of the station to the taxi rank. A pathetic fallacy of my own; not cold, just miserable.

'It only rains twice a week here, love,' the taxi driver said, 'once for three days and once for four days.' He chortled to himself in the rear view mirror.

The hotel was decorated in the bland chocolate with ubiquitous flashes of cherry that marked out a particular top-end slot for hotel chains just after the millennium. Tall panels of smoked glass and leather furnishings were as close as it got to the homely comfort I could have done with at that moment. My heart was drawn back to the restaurant rooms of Candée sur Beuvron, to the genuine individuality of its sloped ceilings and poky bathroom, to the warmth of the sun.

The door opened efficiently, quietly, when I put my card in, no welcome, just clean lines, floor-to-ceiling windows and a neatly-made bed.

Anything logical in me had known that Al would probably be busy at his parents', that it would be difficult to get here; everything romantic was tortured that he hadn't found a way.

I sat on the bed watching poor daytime television until he arrived, flustered and unravelled.

'I'm so sorry, I really meant to be here. Every time I walked towards the door, my mother thought of something else that was urgent. Faz threw me out in the end.'

A tiny surge of tears gathered, filmy, across my eyes. Although he was being honest, I hadn't wanted Farzana to take charge; I'd wanted him to step up, to claim me, to carry me away on his white charger in front of all the neighbours while his mother watched, open-mouthed in horror.

'It's okay,' I said.

'It isn't.' He sat down on the bed. 'I should have been here.'

'It's not your fault.' I meant it, even though I resented it at the same time.

There was a pause, ended when we both said 'I' at the same

time.

'Go on.' He nodded, encouragement at me.

'I don't know when I got so angry.' I couldn't look into his face. 'I don't know what changed. What made me so furious.'

'I did.' He put his arm round me, drew me towards him.

'I think I made me cry.' I pushed him away. 'I kissed Roman. I cried after that.'

I felt the tensing in his body, sensed the pain pulling his muscles taut.

He got up and walked to the window. Below, streaks of traffic almost stationary mapped out the roadways of the city, their beeps and shouts inaudible from up here in our ivory tower.

He kept his back to me. 'And?'

I didn't know what to say. 'And nothing.' I left it at that.

'You didn't..?' He couldn't bring himself to say the words. He raised his hand to his mouth as if holding the rest of the sentence in.

'I love you. I only kissed him because I was angry.'

'And hurt.'

I nodded. I didn't want him to shoulder the whole burden, not be responsible for the way I had let myself go in Roman's arms, for how much, however fleetingly, I had let myself enjoy it.

He stayed facing the window. 'I hadn't met anyone before who, you know, who you'd... I'm not man enough for it. That's what it comes down to. I'm not mature enough to handle it.' He gave an ironic laugh. 'And I can't talk to anyone about it. Not my father, not my boss, not my cousins, because they... None of their wives.' He shrugged and left the words hanging in the air.

I decided not to rescue him. I stayed silent.

'And so I went to see Mehreen. And I, I...'

I felt sick. A breath caught, strangled in my throat. I was too frightened to speak. This was my real truth; I was totally shaken with the realisation that I would rather not know, that I preferred not to hear. If Al had slept with someone else we would work through it. I would do anything not to lose him. It crystallised in my mind in that horrible, silent, moment; I would even be the second wife, the mistress. Anything.

Both his palms were on his face, rubbing up and down, his fingertips in his hair. I couldn't see if he was crying or not, his shoulders were still. I couldn't move, couldn't walk towards him and take his pain, couldn't reach out and earth his agony. I had to let him speak.

'The time for secrets is over.'

ALI

Just like that, I let Mehreen change things between me and Honour forever.

It seemed like a good idea, like, hey, this is so easy to do. Honour did it, shagging someone who you're not in love with. It was easy, right? Get naked, get your freak on? And Mehreen wasn't a random, she was a girl who, well, let's face it, if I had the balls back when I was a yoof may have been my first, my wife even?

Gorgeous Mehreen, with her brown hair and her bright hazel oval-shaped eyes, her prominent but just right nose, her full mouth, her dimpled cheeks and her clear skin. Mehreen of the screen, the clothes and the air of self-confidence.

I kept putting the pieces together, the bits of Mehreen that meant I should fancy her, be passionate about her. They just didn't come together right though, I had to force the thought through.

Mehreen Khan, stepping out of my fantasies, out of my TV screen, into my life.

And tonight I wanted her; I wanted her with a passion. It was about righting wrongs from the past, it was about settling scores, balancing the scales.

It was about being a man.

I got to the restaurant before her. Obviously.

I was dressed a bit older than I normally would. Smart black pants, my best shoes polished, a white shirt, stiff collars and cuffs with cuff links, and to top it off a muted jumper. I would have streaked grey through my hair and brought a pipe if I could. A bit too far, but hey, she liked older men.

The restaurant was her choice, off Deansgate again. Inside the darkened brown and chrome interior I was the only Asian.

I felt hot, that same claustrophobic panic that I had felt at Connie's wedding, surrounded by people and meat and alcohol and another world, stoking my insecurity

I needed something to steady the blood that was pumping southwards, give me that push to go beyond that chalk line, make a move on her. Alcohol always seemed to work in movies.

I looked at the menu, but it made no sense. Did wine from Argentina taste different to wine from New Zealand or France? Should I just have a spirit or something? Or maybe wait for Mehreen? Share whatever she had?

She didn't disappoint when she turned up. Every man and woman was eating her with their eyes. I looked at them all, unable to look at her directly, taking her in from their reactions. Like the moon, you stare at it to see the reflection of the sun.

She was wearing red. It was a kameez, cut low at the front, silver sequins at the plunging neckline.

'You look hot,' I said.

It was true. She had all the elements of what a woman who was 'hot' should look like.

'I prefer elegant, or sophisticated, or beautiful. And of course I do, yaar, I spend a lot of time every day to look like this. It never stops. I gym, watch what I eat, don't smoke, use every cream in the world. I am an actress, and I trade on my looks. But you are sweet.'

The waiter came over, his antipodean tongue practically down her dress. She ordered a glass of wine, and I ordered the same.

She didn't even flinch, or question it.

'So, *kaise yaad kiya?*'

'I always remember you,' I said, but the heat crept up my sober face.

'I thought you might be doing the honours, no pun intended. Letting me meet your partner.'

Partner. Honour wasn't my 'partner'. We didn't have a business deal. She was…

'We split up,' I said.

'What did you do?' she said.

The wine arrived, the waiter taking a long time to uncork the bottle, fill our glasses.

'To lovers absent,' Mehreen said and raised her glass to clink against mine.

I picked mine up, the wine trickling down the side of the glass onto my skin. I wanted to wash it away, but I chinked my glass and watched her sip.

I brought my own glass to my lips and, as I began to tip it back, her hand came out, and touched mine.

'*Peene ki aadat nahin to kiyon peete ho? Devdas banna chahte ho?*' she said.

Why do you drink if you're not used to it? Yep, this was my cue. My gauntlet had been acknowledged.

I held onto her hand and put the glass down, secretly relieved she had stopped me.

The waiter looked at me with new envy as he took our order.

Mehreen's hand felt different to Honour's. It was softer, probably smoothed with emollients, and her nails were painted, probably fake. There was no comfort or reality there. Not like… not like cold hands that held onto you so they could be warmed by your body.

I let go, and she didn't react.

'What did you do?' she said again.

'Nothing. I swear. We had a falling out, it just wasn't working.'

'What did you do?'

I explained. She sat, drank and listened.

'Grow up,' she said at the end of it.

'Mehreen…'

'Seriously. So then what? You thought *let me hook up with Mehreen*. Darling, I'm liberal, but not loose. I feel insulted. What made you think I would sleep with you?'

She smiled as she said it.

'You know, Ali, let me ask you, again, why are you with her?'

'I'm not. Not anymore…'

'Don't be absurd, you are being ridiculous. Tell me, if you can't bear to be near her, if her past is such an issue, if you can't marry her, if she doesn't believe in a God, if, if, if… I am so frustrated listening to you. Why were you with her if there is so much wrong?'

I didn't know what to say. I took a sip from one of the glasses of water the waiter had left on the table, crunching down on the ice as I did so. I looked into the candle. I burnt my fingers putting it out. I looked into Mehreen's liquid eyes. I bared my soul.

'Because without her… she makes me who I am. She makes me a… she makes me different. She invented the perfect me…'

I put my head in my hands.

'She was willing to marry you for your family because she loves you, don't you get that? And she trusts you enough, she trusts your love for her, she knows you won't go anywhere, even if she doesn't marry you. Doesn't that make sense to you? Arre, it makes sense to me.'

We were standing outside after dinner. She had wrapped a shawl around her shoulders and chest, looking remarkably traditional.

'So, yaar, is everything sorted now?'

'I don't know, I can't get over… what if she slept with him? Again?'

'Ali… you don't know, so don't imagine. The imagination is there to help us survive, and it does this by exaggerating reality. Why would she? If she loves you, why would she? If she does sleep with him, she doesn't love you. So move on.'

'Oh God, Mehreen. Before you said that I didn't believe it, not really. What if she has? And how can I get over her past? What if I meet another ex of hers? I can't cope with the jealousy.'

Mehreen leaned forward and kissed me then.

It was a few minutes before she pulled away, before she unclasped my hands from her back, my pelvis moving against hers. I was like a teenager. I was embarrassed. I remembered the past.

She looked down and laughed.

'Now tell me, you've kissed me, I'm your ex, sort of. Do you love Honour any less?'

'No,' I said.

'I could take you home, yaar, and we could sleep together. And you know what? You still won't love her any less. You would have just slept with another woman, that's all. Do you understand what I'm saying to you?'

'Sort of…'

'It doesn't matter how many men she has slept with, they are nothing to her. Women love, and you men just don't get it, you don't understand how we will love just one man for an eternity if we have to.'

'I used to think I could love you,' I said.

The words sounded hollow even to my own ears. I couldn't love anyone like I loved Honour.

'You could screw me. Men can screw anything. Love though? I don't know. Even men with multiple wives always have a favourite. It's the way it is. Noorjehan, Mumtaz Mahal. They were Queens in a harem but only Noorjehan ruled and only Mumtaz had the Taj Mahal built for her. That was love.'

'Mehreen, that's different…'

'Love and sex are universal and timeless, from Adam and Eve to you and Honour,' she said, one hand still on my face.

'Ali, I bet you her past is her past. She doesn't lie in bed and compare you to them, except to say, Ali is my favourite wine and the others are just what I had to taste to get to him. That's how women are.'

'Mehreen…'

So she kissed me again.

This time though it was just her soft lips against mine, and I tasted her wine and lipstick, the sequins on her dress rough against my touch. My brain twisted away, looking for Honour.

'Don't be a fool, go back to her. And please, yaar, for everything that's good in this universe, don't ask her if she slept with that bloke.'

'You're amazing, do you know that?'

She just laughed.

'But of course. Allah Haafiz, meri jaan,' she said.

God look after you, my life.

Meri jaan.

My life.

Honour.

Just like that, a woman called Mehreen came and ended it all.

All my insecurities and my jealousy and my ignorance of how relationships work.

Just like that, I let Mehreen change things between me and Honour forever.

Chapter Seventeen

HONOUR

The older I get, the less surprised I am by the circumstances that one doesn't see coming. Even more so by the ways in which I react to them. If one of my girlfriends had said to me, 'my boyfriend kissed another woman in revenge for my having had relationships before I met him: he would have slept with her too but she turned him down,' I would have raged with indignation. I would have ranted and pontificated and I would have defied her, as a self-respecting woman, to go back to him. I think anyone would.

But Al came and sat beside me, trembling. In a dead voice he explained what had happened. He was brutally honest about his intentions, he described with close-to-fatal detail how he had felt as he kissed her, his longings, his private thoughts. He told me of his worst realisation that, when he faced his God, he would have kissed two women in his life – the love of his life, and another; a woman he chose just for physical pleasure and for revenge, an act that compromised his very belief system.

My greatest fear, the one that knocked me sideways with surprise, was my desire to get down on my knees in front of him and shout 'I'll do anything. I'll convert. I'll wear a veil. You can hide me in a flat and marry Billo.'

I could not trust myself to speak.

It was my Damascene moment, the one that I'd been waiting for. It was the moment I found my God, if finding your God is discovering what matters most to you in the world.

Slowly I realised that he was saying the same things, his version of the future finally and finely dove-tailed to mine. We both walked away from the arrogance that had held our stubbornness higher than love.

When I thought about Farzana's mehndi I imagined myself a family member. The idea of attending something so exotic – so very foreign – by myself, finding my way there without my native northern guide, made me feel wordly and sophisticated. I let that thrill distract me from the fact that there would only be women present and that there would be no filter of Al between his mum and me.

I took a bus from the city centre on my own, wanting to leave the reconstructed modern Manchester and feel the place that Al and his family had known before the bomb and the influx of European money and southern business. I pressed my face to the windows, looking out for the stop, the streets outside looked slippery, faintly painted with a moss that grew, despite the hammering of feet, in response to the constant drizzle.

Along the bus route, magnificent red brick buildings, monument to the industrial revolution, rose out of the dark pavements and towered towards the heavy sky.

The Hussains, Al told me, had once lived close to the city centre, squashed into a terraced house, back-to-back with a similarly shoe-horned-in and similarly immigrant family. As life had improved for his parents, they had moved further out of town, still in an area dominated by Asian people, but away from the lack of privacy and the clutter of their first home.

I stepped off the bus into a gaggle of youngsters waiting to get on. I tried to imagine, as I listened to the northern children shouting at each other, what Al and Farzana must have been like as children. Was their skin a mask of goose bumps and a slick of rain like these young people, proving their boldness by coming out without coats?

I practised my Punjabi phrases like a mantra, my lips moving silently as I paced towards their house; a stranger in town, talking to herself in two languages.

I walked until I saw the turning that led to Al's parents' house. The small garden wall was a miniature fortification. 'Good afternoon, Mrs Hussain,' I said with my brightest and most carefree smile as Al's mother opened the door, the hallway packed with people – women – behind her.

She pointed, wordlessly, at my feet. I knew to take my shoes off and I followed her hunched form down the hall. I looked down at my vividly painted toes rather than concentrate on her hostile back.

I couldn't see the set of her mouth from behind the gold-trimmed fabric of her dupatta but I could imagine it so clearly, the thin grim line of distaste. She opened the door of the large sitting room, and spat words of Punjabi, like bullets, to the women who sat inside.

The only person I recognised in the room was Al's youngest sister, Aaliyah. We hadn't really spoken on my previous visit; she and Zain had mostly limited their communication to whispers and giggles, even at the dinner table. This time, as she saw me come through the door of the sitting room, she scooted up on the sofa and patted the now-empty space next to her.

'Thanks,' I said, trying to make eye contact with the other women and smiling round the room. 'I'm incredibly nervous.'

Aaliyah giggled. 'You should be,' she said, pulling her dupatta up to her face in a gesture so like her mother's. 'They've been whispering and gossiping about nothing else all morning.'

I blushed horribly, dropping my eyes to my lap. Next to me, Aaliyah looked smug, mission accomplished. She fiddled with the gold jewellery on her hands.

'Your jewellery's beautiful,' I said in an effort to engage the obnoxious teenager. 'Is it real gold?'

'Mostly.'

'Are there any other girls your age coming? Any of your school friends?' I hoped that reminding her how much older I was would embarrass her into an armistice. 'How old are you? 15?'

'I'm 14,' she cocked her head to one side in a gesture of irritation. 'And no, they're not. I've had to put up with my mother marding on all morning, all week actually, about you coming and I wouldn't want to subject my friends to it too.'

'To be fair, Aaliyah, I'm here because your sister asked me.'

'And my brother.'

'Of course and your brother. He's my... We live together.'

She looked away from me, checking the impact of my words on the room. Several of the women were peering at us, leaning forward on the low sofas and eavesdropping.

'In fact, you should really come down to London and stay. Bring a friend from school or something.'

'Really? Could we?'

She visibly brightened and I remembered how shallow teenagers are.

'Really. And we'll go to the Hard Rock Café, Madame Tussaud's, those sorts of things. Then we'll sit in Convent Garden and celeb-spot. How about that?'

My first ally of the day was onside.

There was a rush of excitement and chatter and everyone got to their feet. Someone flipped a CD on and Farzana was ushered in, four women holding a sparkling dupatta over her head and an older woman walking in front of her picking coloured sugar pieces from a tray of Indian sweets and putting them into Farzana's mouth.

Farzana, always elegant and so beautiful, looked amazing. History and culture and art all fused into her outfit, her movements, her facial expressions. It was a picture of heritage, a beautiful collection of all of the best of thousands of years of culture, adopted by Muslims, framed in the Pakistani background of the family and presented in this quiet bungalow in a timid street of Manchester.

In the chatter of excitement that accompanied Farzana's grand entrance, people seemed to forget the fragile politics of my being there. Like Connie's wedding, joy was the dominant emotion, the guests throwing aside their other issues in order to add to it.

So I stood up, and, throwing my few words of Punjabi out beside me like frail walking sticks, I joined in.

An older woman advanced on me with the tray of sweets. It was the same woman who had walked in, backwards, in front of Farzana. The woman scooped sweets from the tray, her dark fingers like a beak, and put the sugary cube in my mouth. It was such an alien gesture, so odd. It reminded me of being a child and popping a boiled sweet into my dad's mouth as he was driving. He would always try and catch the ends of my fingers with his lips and I would squeal with disgust. Who touches your mouth? The dentist, sometimes a makeup artist or a beautician, maybe a priest if that's your bag. And a lover. But here it was normal for a complete stranger, her kameez and dupatta gold and green, to push coconut, spices and sugars, foods of opulence, luck and health, into every open mouth.

'I'm guessing,' she began with a smile, the tray of sweets swinging dangerously over my head, 'That you're Honour.'

'I am, how do you do?' I stuck out my hand.

'Shabnam,' she said. She grasped my hand momentarily before grabbing the tray again before it fell.

'Do you want some help?'

'That would be lovely. Can you take one side and come and give out the sweets? It'll be a good way to meet everyone.'

I couldn't see how to refuse. There was no way to object, to squeal 'no, no, I'm not shoving my fingers into strangers' mouths. It'll make me feel sick'. I tried to remember how grownup Al and I had decided we were, only yesterday.

Shabnam's accent was strong, with a hint of American drawl.

'Are you just here for the wedding? Or do you live in Manchester?' I asked.

'I've flown in from New York, although I live in Pakistan.'

'New York? Wow, one of my favourite cities.'

She beamed at me, 'Mine too. Have you been to Hong Kong?'

'Only as a layover.'

She let go of her side of the tray to make an expansive gesture with her hands. 'My two favourite places in the world. Cities so distinct they are characters in their own right. Almost people.' She shook her head in a now-familiar-to-me Pakistani gesture. 'Such elegance. Such excitement.'

I'd got more used to pressing the sweets on people now and Shabnam was right, meeting people was working, most of them had even begun to smile at me.

'So, whose side are you from? Bride or groom?'

'Oh, darling,' she laughed and fluttered her hand in front of her face. 'That little madam Aaliyah didn't tell you?'

I shook my head.

'I'm Bilal's mother. And Billo's, obviously.'

'Oh, I... I'm... I don't know what to say.'

'What should you say, child? That you fell in love with a kind and wonderful man? That you found the happiness Allah had in mind for you? Your embarrassment belongs in the old world. And the old world was a sadder place.'

I blushed to the roots of my hair, partly for having stolen her future son-in-law, but mostly in response to my relentless and entirely valueless prejudices; I couldn't even begin to think about those of my future husband. Sometimes it felt like I had to lead him like a child to an understanding of his own culture; his own eyes and ears as blinkered to its progress as his mother's.

ALI

Bilal was a shock to my ingrown stereotypes. I had more in common with him than so many of my own community who had been raised here, behind neighbouring walls and on familiar grey roads, parked with Toyota Corollas and Nissan Sunnys.

In true lady's prerogative Farzana's mehendi happened first, so I took Bilal for a lad's night out. He made me his sarwallah, best man. It was usually the youngest brother or nephew who did that, but stuck in Manchester with no friends or family except his parents, he asked me to do the honours.

I had planned a curry down in Rusholme, hanging with my cousins watching DVDs and telling gandey Punjabi jokes all night. These were the things I'd enjoyed when I lived here, the things it would be good to show an immigrant, a freshie.

'I'm really sorry, dude, to mess up your arrangements but I've been invited to the University of Manchester for the evening. I wondered if you'd come? I have to do a reading, won't take long, and then sign some books. Is that okay, man? Then we can do whatever you want.'

Typical freshie, I thought, to take a traditional, and family occasion and turn it into an opportunity to promote your business.

'Sure, no worries,' I said. He was a guest after all, and my plans were pretty fluid.

We never did make it to the Curry Mile. Bilal was like the literary equivalent of a cricket hero the BritPak students had been pining for all their lives. I was like the spare part that trailed behind them all the way to the Pak Soc disco... At least, I would have been if Bilal hadn't been so cool. I had to grudgingly become another victim of his charm – you couldn't dislike the man if you tried. I had to forgive him his film star looks, his gym-physique and his endless library of wit in the face of just how all-round grounded he was. How completely nice. I finally understood Farzana's devotion to him and accepted my mum and dad had done well for her.

I felt old in the dark and grubby Students' Union. I thought I still looked twenty, hadn't really aged that much. Until I came face to face with all these real eighteen to twenty-one year olds, and thought they looked twelve. Being nearly twenty-seven in this room meant I was 'pushing thirty'. Ha, at least Bilal was older, innit.

The music was a mixture of Pakistani, Bollywood, Bhangra and R n B; standard for any Asian nightclub.

'Dude, this is my last night of letting my hair down. Of enjoying my youth,' Bilal said, nodding at my soft drink. 'You want something stronger?'

We were seated at a table while the young students danced in front of us, neither of us daring to show what we thought might be grandad moves. Some of the dancers had learned whole routines from Bollywood films to show off tonight.

This Pak Soc was just like the one at LSE. I knew these people, their younger incarnations had been at uni with me. There were the BBCD ones, like me, or BuBCuDs, British Born Confused Desis (that's what they called us). In the main though they were genuine Pakistanis. Sons and daughters of generals, politicians, businessmen, lawyers. The movers and shakers of Pakistani society sent their kids abroad to get educated. Before bringing them home to make political marriages and take up Pakistan's best jobs, to rule via a morally corrupt system.

I totally got why they spent their years abroad drinking, doing drugs and letting their hair down Western-style.

'I don't drink, man, it's really not my thing,' I said to Bilal.

Bilal had that sing-song American-twanged voice that all-well-to-do Indians and Pakistanis seem to adopt.

I didn't like the idea of my sister's future husband drinking. Since when did I become so protective of Farzana? Maybe I was paying her back for being good to my girlfriend.

'And what if you get a taste for it, then what?' I asked him, sounding like some pious Imam. I wished I hadn't said it as soon as the words were out of my mouth.

'This isn't my first night of drinking, dude, it's my last. I went to uni in the States, three years of frat house parties and road soda. Anyway, Muhammed Ali Jinnah drank, before he became the father of the nation. It's not so bad. I won't drink back home, just like Jinnah, not once I'm married.' He looked at me. 'You've never drunk then?'

'No. You carry on if you want, not me though,' I said. 'I don't even like the smell.'

'Yeah, dude, the smell can be a problem at first. Until you meet my friend, Jack Daniels...'

Chapter Eighteen

HONOUR

Al was finding it hard to believe that I had a second ally in Shabnam. But then, he seemed to think that his mother was being perfectly pleasant. I decided to leave him in the blissful ignorance of his imagination; it was easier for him that way.

'I think Bilal and Shabnam are probably a bit of a shock to my poor old mother. I'm not sure how she'll deal with it all. She's probably thanking God that I didn't marry Billo now.'

'And feeling differently about you marrying me?'

'That's, unfortunately, not quite the same thing. Hey, man,' Al said to a man near the door. He pulled him towards him in a hug.

'Feeling okay, man?' The other man stood back, holding Al's arms with both hands. 'You look like you had a late night, man.'

'And whose fault is that?' Al asked as they hugged again.

Al turned towards me. 'Babe, this is Bilal.'

I couldn't decide which I was more stunned by; the fact that Al had slipped into such a Mancunian-Punjabi role that he had called me 'babe' or by Bilal's hypnotically green eyes.

'You must be Honour. I've heard so much about you; from my bride-to-be and from my best man. And my mother hasn't stopped talking about you. I'm so pleased to meet you.'

'You too. And I've got the English translations of your first two books. Lovely, I love them.'

We were stopped mid-conversation by a stream of aunts and little cousins. Al's mum caught sight of an important job to do at the very second she should have made eye contact and, apologising to Al with a rapid fire of Punjabi, she scurried away.

Shabnam showered me with kisses and introduced me to people as if I were her own family.

'Your son is absolutely gorgeous. I've never met anyone Asian with green eyes.'

'Billo too, they both have them. In Pakistan, it's seen as a sign of great beauty. It's common in Pathans and Afghans but very rare in the Punjab. The children you and Ali have will have the same.'

I looked round at Al to see if he'd heard her but he was awash with relatives, excited women ushering him onto a low wide stool next to Bilal's.

Aaliyah found a space to sit down next to me. A dark-eyed little girl clutched the hem of her pyjamas.

'Hello there, who's this?' I asked looking at the girl.

'This is my cousin, Afreena. She's three, aren't you?'

The little girl nodded, staring at me with round black eyes. I thought about what Shabnam had said and transposed my green eyes into Afreena's beautiful face.

'You look so pretty, Afreena. Have you had your henna done?'

She answered me with a solemn nod, she curled into Aaliyah trying to avoid my gaze and hiding her painted hands.

'Afreena has something she wants to ask you,' said Aaliyah.

The little girl shook her head vigorously and whispered hurriedly to Aaliyah in Punjabi.

'Shall I ask her? She's very nice and she doesn't bite.' Aaliyah peeled the younger girl away from her.

Afreena nodded, her eyes down and looking at the floor.

'Honour.' As Aaliyah spoke Afreena looked up hopefully. 'Afreena wants to know if she can touch your hair.'

I laughed out loud and, once I'd given the okay, Afreena spent the rest of the afternoon sitting on the back of my chair pulling and twisting my auburn curls.

Shabnam started dancing round Al and Bilal whilst everyone chanted. Aaliyah translated the words of the songs. I couldn't believe they were real; they sounded more like extraordinary Italian opera lyrics than traditional Punjabi chants. There were threats of fat wives and ugly children, hare lips and poverty, the political correctness of twenty-first century Britain had not been invited to the party. Al's mother pulled all the attention towards herself, weeping quietly amongst the revellers. I did my best not to even look at her.

The weekend passed in a blur of sounds, sights and flavours. Most of Al's family made huge efforts to include me, speaking to him in English if I was nearby and explaining the meaning behind various customs and traditions. The wedding ceremony itself, and Farzana made me a central part of it, was exotic and moving. The food was everything I'd hoped for and the music, the scents, the slurred flowery sounds of the Punjabi language all around me, made me feel as if I'd been transported into some kind of dream.

The people, the vast numbers of family and friends, were so different to anyone I was used to. It was an odd experience to count the white faces in a room, to be suddenly aware of my ethnicity.

I always felt awkward when a stereotype manifested itself in front of me, almost apologetic. But it was a fact that, for as many of his relatives were lawyers and doctors, there were another tranche in shiny shalwah kameez made of tight manmade fabric, the trousers too short over their cheap shoes; the whole ensemble sweaty under their slicked-down hair. A wincing embarrassment wriggled its way from inside to burn crimson on my cheeks.

'Mixed bag, aren't they?' Al said.

My blush deepened, he must have picked up something from my body language that illustrated my secret but uncontrollable snobbishness.

'You've gone really red,' he added, helpfully.

'Thanks.'

'Come on, we'll push through the natives and find the ones in Paul Smith suits. The ones you're more comfy with.'

I lowered my voice to a hiss. 'You can be a rude fucker, you know.'

'Their class was set in Pakistan, way back when. So when they came to the UK it all got a bit fuzzy round the edges. There aren't really any in suits, by the way. I'm just trying to make you feel better.' His teasing tone of voice showed he most definitely wasn't.

Throughout all of it, the spectre of his mother loomed, always looking at me through narrowed eyes, wringing the edges of her clothes and shaking her head whenever I caught her eye, avoiding me like the white devil of the long distant past.

The train back to London felt like the gateway to heaven and I spent the rest of the trip gazing in the direction of Manchester Piccadilly station from the hotel window. The south pulled me magnetically back as much as Al's mother repelled me.

The other relatives had fallen like nine-pins at Farzana's word. She had declared me a guest and Punjabi hospitality dictated that I must be treated as such, but no amount of *entente cordiale* or enlightened changes blowing in from Pakistan could budge Mr and Mrs Hussain. My face ached from the broad smile I plastered on whenever I looked at Mr Hussain, his wife I just avoided. I couldn't blame Al, it was just as bad for him, but their coldness upset me more than I cared to admit. I couldn't wait to leave Manchester and go home and I sat in the hotel counting the hours.

Two days later terrorists flew two hijacked planes into the twin towers of New York's World Trade Centre.

ALI

'Are you nervous?' I said.

'No, I have waited a very long time for this day. I love your sister, dude.'

Bilal didn't even blush as he said it. He was straightening his gold and maroon sherwani in the mirror. He had opted not to wear a sehra on his head, instead his long floppy hair was left loose.

A cousin had given him a facial in the morning so he looked a funny colour, sort of touched by an air-brushing pen, an even more youthful and vigorous version of himself.

I wore a kurta shalwar in gold with a maroon men's dupatta round my neck. I patted Bilal on the back and we headed out to the rented limo, tinsel on the bonnet.

Bilal's mother, Shabnam, stood outside with family friends and cousins who were going to be 'on the boy's side' for the wedding to make up the numbers. They lined the bit of road to the car in their myriad colours, hairstyles galore and jewellery fake and real. It was a scene from Bollywood, or like a row of Christmas Trees as we all liked to say on Eid.

The women had handfuls of red petals, throwing them over me and Bilal. We crushed them under our kussey shoes as we walked and the men blinded us with every type of photographic equipment available.

'You sure you're okay with this?' I asked again when we were in the car.

'Dude, stop transferring your own pussiness onto me,' Bilal said.

Ouch. He never failed to surprise me.

'Just because you are too chicken-shit-scared to tie the knot. I, my brother, have been waiting for this day for many years. Farzana is my everything, she is my Laila, Heer, Sohni.'

'They all died tragic deaths, without getting married,' I pointed out.

'She is my Noorjehan, my Mumtaz Mahal, my Bilqis,' he added.

'Bilqis? The Queen of Sheba? Does that make you Soloman? Astagfirullah.'

'Bakwaas, nah dude. You know what I am getting at right? To you she's your annoying sister, your rival. To me... to me Farzana... well, she is proof that God exists...'

I had to look away.

Bilal had his driver pick Honour up from the hotel we had been staying at, and I made sure she was safely in through the doors of the hotel the wedding was happening in. It meant walking her past all my male cousins who were waiting outside for Bilal to turn up.

Once she was inside, I went back to the car and escorted Bilal in as his best man.

There had been much debate over segregation. Mum wanted it, Shabnam said it was so backward, Dad said a compromise and make it optional. In the end it was cheaper to hire one function room than two, so the guests would be seated in mixed surroundings, with a few tables at the back for women who were strict about pardah and didn't like sitting with men.

The hall had been decorated with maroon and gold tissue hanging in great swathes over the stage and across the ceiling. The tables were impossibly over-the-top, stacks of red and white roses arranged on each.

The main stage had two thrones on it, gold and maroon, some distance from tasteful.

Zain was standing by the stage looking very smart in a suit (when did he grow up?) and with a white carnation in his pocket (showing he was from the girl's side).

'You look great. Are you being a good boy and helping Dad out today?' I said.

'I'm not a baby, bhaiya,' he said. 'I could have been sarwalla.'

'Hey, it was Bilal bhai's choice, and you are so much more useful arranging everything. Where's Jamal?'

'In the kitchens.'

'Helping with the cooking?'

'No, flirting with the waitresses.'

Yep, Zain definitely had grown up.

'Farzana bajee wants you to be there when she does her nikah,' he said.

Farzana had booked a room in the hotel to get ready.

We didn't knock, just walked in.

Honour was there. She had changed into a shalwar kameez, a dupatta on her head.

I wanted to go and kiss her but there were too many familial eyes, and an Imam, to do anything of the sort.

Farzana was wearing maroon and gold in her lengha, but her face was covered. The dupatta had been pulled down low, so just her mouth was visible, including the precious stones and pearls of the nath nose ring.

The Imam was sitting to her right, my father to her left. Mum was standing with Aaliyah and some of my aunts, including Shabnam, her eyes watery.

The Imam began, reciting verses from the Qur'an and then he asked Farzana three times in Urdu, 'Do you Farzana Hussain, of your own free will, and taking into account the dowry that has been paid to you, accept Bilal Rana to be your husband?'

Each time Farzana nodded her head and said, 'Jee'.

The third time a tear slid down from under her veil onto her cheek, and then my father hugged her close to him, with tears in his eyes also.

The mubaraks were flying around the room. Shabnam looked ecstatic, handing out a tray of sweetmeats to everyone.

'You'll be next,' she said, stuffing my mouth with a piece of barfi and winking where Honour was standing.

I couldn't help it, before we left, buoyed by Shabnam's prompting, I went up to Honour and told her she looked great. My cousins started giggling, and I didn't dare to look at my mother as I followed the Imam out of the room back to the main hall.

There was silence in the hall as the Imam repeated his three times question and answer session with Bilal, and then someone let off party poppers and everyone cheered and embraced. Metal trays with chuwarey – dried dates, were sent through the hall, with sugar sweets, almonds and raisins. Everyone gave Bilal a congratulatory hug, and a platinum band was placed on his finger by my mother.

'Look after her, you dog, or you'll have me to deal with. No, worse; Jamal,' I said.

'Ha, dude, Farzana scares me more than you or Jamal do,' Bilal said.

The music started up and Bollywood songs piped through the hall.

Bilal and I returned to the stage, and then there was clapping across the hall as Farzana entered.

She had pulled her dupatta back now so that her face could be seen, gold on her forehead, in her ears, around her neck, on her arms. Her make up was thick for the video cameras and her hands and wrists were covered in henna patterns.

She looked like a movie star and Bilal wolf-whistled next to me.

'She looks like a houri from heaven,' he said. 'Dude, I can't tell you how happy I am right now.'

Farzana was brought onto the stage by her friends, including Honour, and sat in the throne next to Bilal's. I was moved out of the way as the friends gathered around the bride and groom for pictures.

The traditions began.

Aaliyah stole Bilal's shoe and demanded money for its return.

'I will not be called stingy today,' said Shabnam, and opened her purse to give literally hundreds of pounds to my mother in return for the shoe.

A glass of milk was brought over. Bilal drank half and Farzana had to drink the other half. It would ensure their family never went hungry.

Shabnam put gold bangles on Farzana's wrists and on my mother's. Finally, she put a diamond solitaire ring on Farzana's wedding finger, all the customs had been met and my sister had a moment's peace. After dinner, I sat on stage with Bilal and Farzana, both now firmly enthroned, and on display.

'So, how do you feel?' I asked Farzana.

'Strange,' she said. 'I'm a bit scared about leaving behind everything I know. On a day-to-day level, Mum, Dad, you guys. I will be waking up in a house that isn't my father's, and eating breakfast that my mother won't have cooked.

'I just realised I won't be there for Aaliyah, you know when she's becoming a woman, all those thoughts and feelings. It's so confusing, and you can't talk to your parents. Or I won't be around to tame Zain, stop him turning into a MCP like most men. I hope Honour can be there for Aaliyah.'

She looked down at her hennaed hands. 'Isn't it funny how it was Honour that made us close?'

'I don't see Mum laughing. Or Dad,' I said.

'They'll come round,' she said.

I wish I could be as certain.

'Thank you, by the way,' I said.

'For what?'

'For including her. For supporting me. You gave her the rights she would have had if she was my wife. I'll never be able to repay you for that.'

'Oh, get over yourself, Al. I genuinely love her. Quite frankly, she'll be my friend no matter what happens between you two. She is the only thing that makes you bearable...'

'Thanks Faz,' I said, but we were both laughing. 'Right, you're supposed to look sad to be leaving your family, better get on with it.'

'I am a bit though, sad that is, all these people; our community. I'm giving all this up. I wonder how many marriages, births and deaths I'm going to miss. How many of the girls who did my mehendi and were there for my nikah... will I be able to return the favour?'

'You can fly back,' I said.

'It won't be the same,' she said.

'Okay, now you do look sad. Come on, Faz, it's a new start.'

'Don't worry, I have no regrets in that direction. I can't wait to start that part of my life. It's just, well I'm giving up so much. I think today, just for today, I need to mourn who I was. Otherwise I will linger and haunt my new self.'

Bilal put his hand over hers and squeezed it.

'You've made me the happiest dude in the universe, Mrs Rana,' he said, loud enough for just her and me to hear.

I nudged Farzana from where I was sitting.

'He's crazy about you, I hope you know that.'

'I always had a goal in life: marry someone who loves you more than you love them,' she said.

Bilal didn't even object.

'Do you think Honour loves me like that?' I said.

'No… but I know you love her like that…'

I tried to find Honour in the crowds who were now starting to come up and give money to Farzana, but I couldn't see her.

'And now ladies and gentlemen,' said someone into a microphone. 'It is time for the bride and groom's first dance.'

A space had been cleared near the stage, and there were a myriad of shocked faces everywhere. First dance? FIRST DANCE? My dad looked livid and my mother bunched her dupatta into her mouth in her trademark not-coping stance.

Only Shabnam was happy, even us youngsters didn't know what to make of it. It seemed so Western to have a first dance.

But with her head held high, Farzana was led to the cleared space by Bilal, and he held her close as the music began.

They had chosen *Kabhi kabhi mere dil mein*, the ultimate wedding number, although a bit clichéd. *Sometimes my heart thinks that you were made in heaven and sent to Earth just for me.*

There was nothing clichéd about the bride and groom dancing that day though.

I held the Qur'an over Farzana's bowed head for the rukhsati, it was a sign to everyone; we are handing her over under the protection of the Qur'an and God to her new life. It was also a warning. The Qur'an had stipulated rights for women in terms of marriage, property, inheritance, wealth, their day-to-day existence. It was a threat to her in-laws: don't stray from the rights she has been given by God.

My mother and Aaliyah held Farzana, all three of them weeping openly with my father's arms comforting them.

Farzana was put in Bilal's car, and I went and hugged my mum. She sagged against me, and the car drove off.

It was only going to drive around Manchester for an hour and then drop the bride and groom off back at the hotel for their honeymoon. The car leaving was just a token, a symbol to represent the old ways. The rules that had to be followed but that could be adapted for any situation.

My own included. The world was big enough for me and Honour to exist in it, for our rules to count and be real.

At that moment I thought that Honour and I would be fine.

Until the twin towers fell. Then I knew nothing would ever be the same for any of us.

Chapter Nineteen

HONOUR

My nephews were born within three weeks of each other, Jean-Paul in France and Zak in Pakistan. It had been almost eighteen months since the phrase 'War on Terror' had been released on a frightened world, since the crackling undercurrent of anger seeped through continents both just and unjust. We needed these births – these mixed-heritage boys of a peaceful future – and the joy on their mothers' faces, and the pride on their fathers', moving towards healing some of the cracks in our fractured world.

Being able to make a video call from home, however patchy and grainy the picture, felt like the stuff of childhood fantasies. I was able to talk to Farzana and watch her holding Zakariyya, or feeding him, and see him move around, gurgle and wave his little arms at the screen. I spent hours, one night when Al was out at a benefit, poring over the atlas, working out exactly how far away from me Farzana and baby Zak were. Six thousand miles, but six thousand miles covered by the instant miracle of the World Wide Web. The connection was unreliable, the sound would fade in and out before going off completely. But it was contact. It was a heartening reassurance that they were well and, most importantly, that at least for now they were safe.

We thought about going to Pakistan to see them, but travel over the last eighteen months had been more trouble than it was worth. Even catching the Tube with Al meant that people looked twice at him. We'd taken our last few trips as country cottage weekends up and down England and Scotland, preferring our clipped wings to the stories Al's friends told of being searched and detained at airports all over the world.

Al travelled with me to France to see Connie, so content, so illuminated, nursing my nephew amongst the wintered skeletons of sunflowers in her idyllic village.

'Jean-Paul's amazing, Faz. Just beautiful. I held him in my arms and just cried and cried.' I was talking to Farzana's two-dimensional image, my own reflection over-laid on her face in the screen.

There was a slight delay when she spoke, her lips fractionally out of sync with the sounds.

'I wish I could see him. I've sent her a card all the way from Pakistan. These babies are almost cousins; they should meet.'

'I wish they could too. And that you could bring Zak here to me. What a sad old auntie, nephews everywhere but not one nearby to cuddle.'

'I swear you sound more Pakistani every day.' Farzana laughed, her face looming in and out of the camera's focus.

'I think I feel it as well. I can't remember the last time I had a bacon sandwich. Living with the zealot isn't the easiest at the moment. No missing prayers, the whole of Thursday evening getting ready for Friday, prayer-wise.' I moved my finger up to wipe away the condensation my sigh had left on the screen. 'I understand it, I honestly do. Sometimes it's enough to make me put a veil on. Just to leer in people's faces and ask them what their problem is.'

'Is it really that bad? I don't want to move home and be a pariah. It doesn't sound like my England.'

'It isn't, it's different. On all sides – no one's particularly to blame. It just escalates all the time. How the *boys* were when it happened – I thought that would be the end of it but it was only the beginning. I thought only a few diehard zealots would continue it and the rest of the world would shout them down. And I didn't realise that we, the Brits, would be so involved. I still can't really believe it.'

Farzana nodded. In the background a tiny gurgle travelled across the miles. 'Hang on, let me get Zak.'

I watched Farzana as she walked away from the computer and bent over the basket on the sofa. She could have been in Manchester, I wished she was. She looked just as she had in England, her slick hair loose and tucked behind her ears, her waist enviably slim in jeans and a t-shirt, for inside the house, even though Zak was only six weeks old. It was hard to remember that outside her doors and windows lay the mild spring and modest dress code of Islamabad whilst outside mine a bitter February battered London's residents, their clothing chosen by the wind.

'Hey, hey, little boy,' she sang as she waved his tiny arm at the screen. 'Can you see your Auntie Honour?'

Tears pricked my eyes. 'Oh, Faz, he's even more beautiful than before.'

Zak stretched his wrinkled neck and arched his back. Farzana bent her head down to kiss his tiny face.

'Look at his hair, I can't believe how much it's grown. I'm scared he's going to turn into a boy while you're still over there and I'll miss the whole thing. I can't smell his baby smell through the computer.'

'Trust me,' Farzana laughed. 'Sometimes that's a good thing. We will come back, we really will, but it doesn't sound like we want to come back any time soon. You don't get stared at in the street for being a Muslim here.'

'And that's worth a lot at the moment.'

'What were you saying?'

'Oh, ignore me. I'm on about 9/11 still. We were at your parents' when we saw it, on TV. So it couldn't have been worse, you know?'

'The machismo?'

I nodded at the screen, forgetting the delay. 'Not your Dad, or any of the older people, but you can imagine what Jamal was like and even Al was weird about it for ages. It made me feel really scared; like they were religious loonies or something. I felt horrible being the non-Asian. They've got over it now, I think, but some of them were like ghouls. It's left a mark–across the whole country though, not just Al and me.' I leaned closer to the screen, screwing up my eyes to try and wish myself through the ether so that little Zak was in my arms.

'It's marked the whole world, Hon, not just the country. Are you still going on the Stop the War march?'

'God, I have to. I'm not going with Al though; he's going with a bunch of people from work. They're really nice people and I'd go with them normally but they've all kind of, well, taken control of their religious belief, reclaimed it if you like.' I made little apostrophes of my fingers to show her that I wasn't convinced by it all. 'Did you ever meet Ruby? She's an account manager. She's really nice.'

On the screen, Farzana shook her head. Zak nestled into her, his little fingers scrunching the material of her t-shirt.

'Anyway, she's really cool. Drinks, smokes, probably wouldn't even turn down a bacon sandwich. Yacein, Al's boss, turns a blind eye to it all and I'm sure she doesn't do it at work.'

We both laughed.

'Suddenly, she's devout. She wears her hijab dead tight round her head, no more business suits. I swear she spends days off in a bhurka.'

'It's the same here,' Farzana said. 'And I talked to my mum about it. She said everyone feels that their religion is under attack. And so they're going to defend it; step up and be counted in the name of Allah.'

'I feel for everyone. I really do. I just want it to stop before it gets any worse. Hence the march.'

It wasn't the whole world that was turning to war. My sister's adopted homeland had taken a firm stance of refusal. And yet, despite how much the war frightened me, how deeply opposed I was to its immorality, it wasn't the subject that dominated mine and Connie's conversation.

'Anything?' she asked, her voice passive even though I knew her as well as I knew myself and could imagine her pained face on the other end of the phone line.

I shook my head before I spoke, even though Connie couldn't see me. My 'Nothing' came accompanied by a sigh.

'Don't worry, it'll be all right. It's early days.' I had these same platitudes from my GP, from Al. I struggled to believe them. I'd felt the first yearnings for a child as soon as Connie had got pregnant. Maybe it was a twin thing, maybe it was simply nature. Hearing that Farzana and Bilal had joined the elite club compounded my need.

It wasn't a conversation Al and I had easily, it simply went round in circles of duty and need and world crisis. We reached an agreement of inaction; me being certain that not using contraception would mean I'd get pregnant as quickly as my genetically identical sister. Al convincing himself that not using contraception left the ball in Allah's hands; that His will would prevail.

Across the Atlantic, Billo and her Californian plastic surgeon had produced their first child and were onto the second. Farzana assured me that Billo bragged about it from her trout-pout pumped-up lips whenever she got the chance.

Al and I were no further on than we had been a year ago.

The Stop the War march was on a freezing cold February day. Even the proximity of millions of people surging and moving didn't add any warmth. Al had gone with people from work. My colleagues and I wanted to add more fun to the day, if fun can be the right word. We carried the kind of banners you would expect a graphic design agency to come up with, we were young and hip and shared a bottle of wine out between us into plastic cups when we stopped. It didn't mean we cared any less about the destruction, the iniquity and the terror of war.

The wind, as we waited to move off, chattered through our bones.

We fell in step with a Samba band and danced with them, hoping to slightly lift the chill. Neil and I took turns to sashay along hand-in-hand with the rest of our staff and the two interns who'd come with us.

'I was rather looking forward to seeing Al,' Neil said, a salacious rise in his eyebrows, his hips snaking to the drums. 'There's not so much eye-candy around as I hoped there'd be.' He leaned in conspiratorially. 'Khaki fatigues just do not do it for me, why aren't people turned out nicely like me? So thoughtless.'

'That's because it's a demo, darling.' I swirled under his raised arms, my fingers pivoting in his. 'We're thinking about world peace as opposed to your trousers. Or what's in them.'

'You might be.' Neil grinned and grabbed one of the interns. As he span him round to the Samba beat, the student's eyes looked panicked.

'And leave the office juniors alone,' I said, pulling him towards me instead. 'You scare them. It's a shame Al isn't here to distract you from your constant Attention-Seeking Behaviour.'

'I am surprised he isn't here.' Neil slowed down, walking forwards alongside the rest of us. The band's rhythm seemed to quieten once we were walking rather than dancing. 'It's the Islamic world we're defending, after all.'

'Amongst other things – alongside our rights and those of everyone in our country,' I reminded him, a slight 'tut' coming from behind my teeth. 'And Al is here. He's just with the serious people, not the ones who are using it as yet another excuse for cruising. I just wish I was too.' I stuck my tongue out at him.

Neil linked his arm through mine. We held each other close against the February wind. There were protestors on every side of us, a crush of cold breath, songs and grey pavements but still the icy gusts whistled through our bones.

The cold stuttered into my belly. I looked around for a cafe or a pub where I might find a loo. Most places had barred their doors, locked everything up against the tide of people. I found a seedy fried-chicken place. They were charging a pound for people to make their way through the back of the shop to the filthy staff toilet. Knowing that beggars can never be choosers, I went into the grubby stall.

When I had finished I wiped myself and saw, with another month's grief, the crimson flower of my body's betrayal on the white paper.

ALI

Manchester was the wrong place to be when 9/11 happened. Surrounded by my angry cousins, our 'community' under threat. We were scared.

It was also the right place to be. Feeling a part of this consciousness, this identity; an identity I hadn't been a part of since I was a teenager myself. Suddenly I felt I belonged, that it would be 'with my family' that I would survive the threat. Farzana's wedding music still playing in our ears.

Honour and I had been getting ready to return to London the next day when we saw the events unfold on the TV screen in our hotel.

She was in tears, horror struck, unbelieving. I grabbed her hand, headed like a magnet for my family.

We watched the people fall from the tower, we watched the planes crash into it, we watched the onlookers covered in ash.

Slowly it dawned on me that actually it was not America that had been hit. It was all of us.

At my uncle's it was a different atmosphere.

'It's not right for me to be here, Al,' Honour tugged at my shirt.

'It's okay, they don't mind.'

'I mind.'

'Because?' I couldn't understand what she was getting at, this was her time to side with Us. Us or Them.

'Because this is all men sitting around. Angry men. It just feels weird and I'm not going into the kitchen to help your mum and your auntie. I'm just not.'

'I don't know what to do.' I meant it. To go back to the hotel with Honour or to stay, talking politics with these frightened men, trying to make some sense of the new developments in an already tortured world.

'Stay. Seriously,' she squeezed my hand subtly. It hurt that she couldn't kiss me. 'I'll go back, ring my family. Call my mobile if you need me.' She looked straight into my face. 'I love you,' she whispered.

As we watched the world unravel on my uncle's television, we all got angry because they said it was Muslims, they started to bandy about terms like Al-Qaeda on the news.

None of us knew who Al-Qaeda were. We had grown up with Hezbollah hijacking airplanes and kidnapping people. They were always seen as bungling though, never very effective, and only good at creating lurid headlines.

Terry Waite, for God's sake, why would anyone kidnap him? It was madness.

Drip, drip, drip. That was what it was. I had never known a time when Muslims weren't thought of as *the other*, as evil, as terrorists.

These were our truths, the truths we grew up with.

Watching Muslims die in Iraq and Iran with rumours running rife that America supported both sides and armed both sides to keep them at loggerheads.

The Indian army committing atrocities on Kashmiri civilians.

Palestinians seemingly denied their human rights and freedom, forced to live under oppression.

The Arab world carved up by the British and then ruled by kings and despots from Morocco to Egypt to Saudi Arabia, all oppressive, all supported by the Americans.

Afghans used as chess pieces by the Americans, armed and supported as they fought the Russians, then left with a decimated population of mainly widows, unable to cope as a nation and turning to misogyny in the name of religion.

We had watched as the Serbians rained down terror, watched as the International Community refused to arm the Bosnian Muslims. Abdul and my other older cousins had all wanted to volunteer, and we knew so many friends of the family who actually went to fight on the side of the Bosnians at that time. We saw them as Orwellian optimists, fighting fascism in Europe.

The moral of the tale though was that even if your skin is white, your eyes are blue, your hair is blonde and there is nothing Muslim about you except your name, you will still be treated worse than a dog.

These were our lenses on the world, these were the injustices we had felt. Never corroborated, never backed up with fact, just the fiery rhetoric of an Imam doing his Friday khutbah. Cheap leaflets printed and distributed by unknown radicals outside mosques. Most ended up as litter, but some hit home.

Those who suffered from anger, revenge, needed an identity, something to believe and fight for, rebel against their community, or were just bored and needed some drama to feed their egos. Charismatic young men picked off by international organisations, as their pockets were filled with petro-dollars and their self-worth inflated. We all want to be special when we are young. They took the leaflets home and devoured them.

9/11 forced us to build another identity, to look deep and say *who are we* and *what do we believe* and *is killing in the name of Islam a part of that religion?*

No. No. No.

We had to stop our own killing. Killing Israeli civilians, killing Indian civilians, killing our own civilians. Without that we couldn't surely take the moral high ground?

'Can we look in your bag please?'

The cinema attendant looked about twelve. What the hell did he think he would find in there?

After coming to this cinema for years, just a few Tube stops from our home, the attendant did that. And everyone was watching.

I was bright red. I was angry but also embarrassed.

I wanted to make a scene, instead I just froze.

'Sir, can I please look in your bag?'

'No,' I said. 'This is ridiculous.'

'Please sir, it's cinema policy…'

'What? Since when? I was here two weeks ago. You didn't check my bag then, so what's changed?'

He didn't answer.

'Is it just brown people's bags you're checking? Or anyone who looks like a Muslim?'

Again no answer.

'You're not checking my bag,' I said again.

'I'm sorry sir, it's just company policy. All bags have to be checked. I can't let you in otherwise.'

I could feel every eye in that foyer looking at me in the dead silence.

It felt like a stand-off, who would budge first? I think people were scared of me, they probably thought I was a loose cannon, hey, maybe he has got something to hide.

There were stories filtering in on the Internet of women having their hijabs ripped off by skinheads, men with beards getting attacked, mosques being daubed with graffiti. Even Sikhs had been attacked in the USA with people thinking their turbans were Muslim.

This was Leicester Square though. This was my world. How the fuck had this happened?

Honour stepped forward. She lightly touched my arm, and then proceeded to open her bag and let the attendant shine his torch into it.

'Thank you, Madam,' he said.

I saw that he was as embarrassed as I was, he was as uncomfortable as I was. It was his job, it was just policy, and it was heightened security. He worked in a cinema for fuck's sake, he wasn't the Prime Minister.

I followed suit, and let him shine his torch into my bag.

'Thank you, Sir, enjoy your movie,' he said.

I can't even remember what we watched that night, because in my head I realised things were going to get worse before they got better.

It felt like going into battle.

The organisers said two million people would march, even though the government's ass-licking media said it was only ten thousand.

We were in Hyde Park, and we were telling Tony Blair that he was not going to war in our name.

I hoped Honour didn't know my father had come to London in a coach, used the Central Mosque facilities instead of our house, and was going to get back onto that coach and go straight home after the march.

Honour thought attending Farzana's wedding had mended some bridges, changed equations. I didn't want her to see that it was all a show.

What were the chances of them bumping into each other with two million people around anyway? She may be living with me but I swear if she saw Dad in a crowd of other bearded older Asian men she wouldn't pick him out.

I wished I could wander through London's streets hand-in-hand with Honour though. Instead she was off having fun somewhere no doubt, while me and Yacein were left with an ever-radicalised Ruby.

Ruby was re-interpreting Islam, reading crazy scholars like Asma Wadud from America, turning into a Muslim feminist.

From Party Girl to Funda Girl, Ruby was a drain.

Once she used to email us lewd jokes, now she sent us lectures on how to pray, how long your beard should be and how to give alms to the poor.

'Where's your wife?' said Ruby.

I assumed she was talking to Yacein, so did he.

'Hadiqa? She wasn't feeling too good, the kids are a little ill,' he said.

'I was speaking to Ali, I already texted Hadiqa to ask her where she is,' said Ruby.

She had a hijab on but was wearing combats with it. I had to hide a snigger when I first saw her.

'George Bush terrorist! Tony Blair terrorist!'

'Do you have to shout so loudly?' I moaned.

She just looked at me.

'Look up there, they have police photographers,' said Yacein.

I saw them lying flat with their police caps, aiming lenses at us.

'Click this, fuckheads!' said Ruby giving them the finger.

Some young guys walking near us started wolf-whistling and shouting encouragement to her. That's all we needed; fans.

Jamal called my mobile.

'Where you at, bro? Signal is wack. You seen Dad? I lost him.'

'I can barely hear you, and no, I haven't. Are you going to hook up with me afterwards or are you going straight back?'

'Nah, headin' to Edgware Rd for some shawarmas and sheeshas n then headin back,' he said.

'No worries,' I said lightly, my voice full of disappointment.

'This is crazy tho, bro, I can't believe it, how many people are here. I thought it would be some coaches from paki areas and that's it, but man this is everyone. It really...'

But the phone cut out.

I know what he wanted to say I think. It had brought home to him that he was British Muslim, and the British was important, and here he was in a crowd of a million, white, black, yellow, Hindu, Jew, Buddhist, and they all had one voice.

And it was a British voice.

'Oi, you,' Ruby said to a group of young Asian guys. 'Any of you got a lighter?'

They produced one, fumbling for the strange woman in hijab and combats.

'Cheers,' she said, and proceeded to take a firework out of her pocket.

'No, you aren't,' I said.

'Oh no, she di'ant,' Ruby mocked, as she lit the rocket and watched it explode over us.

She was cheered again.

'Imagine, in Baghdad, children will have to hear something like that for hours, as their city is destroyed,' she said. 'They will watch as their parents die and as their own limbs blow up, all because we want Saddam's oil.'

'Come on, sister Ruby, we must pray, the anger can't win,' said Yacein.

'I know but I can't help it. I'm fed up of men killing people for their own needs. And yeah, I said men, because it's always men. At the top in charge, it always is.'

I didn't argue.

'Man, I'm hungry, you guys okay if we stop at McDonald's?' she said.

'They won't let us in,' I said.

'You know what, Ali, sometimes you're a wimp,' Ruby said. 'And you'll be the first one stuffing fries into your face when I talk us in,' she added.

'True, I have to say,' said Yacein.

'Don't you turn on me too, bro,' I said.

It was things like that I remembered about Ruby, the incongruity, the struggle to find herself.

No matter what she wore though she was always Ruby, always herself.

Almost four years after that march Ruby would be in the carriage one of the 7/7 bombers blew up.

'He saw me, he made eye contact with me. He even nodded his head, as if saying salaam to me,' she would say when Yacein and I visited her in hospital. 'He was not a Muslim,' added with a determined voice.

She would die of her wounds two days later.

Chapter Twenty

HONOUR

Where other people might remember raw months of damning British history; invasions, bombings and slaughter that we were helpless to avoid as the theme of the millennium's early years, I just endured the waiting; relentless let downs over what seemed like a lifetime.

As the empty months drew on across another summer, we let more people into the secret of our hoping, my mother reassuring us that *it's not as easy as it seems*, Farzana telling me that *you never know how long other people have been trying for a baby*. Where we had put off marriage in answer to the instability of politics, now it seemed that a wedding would confirm my body's defeat, cement the stalemate of failure, and we stopped talking about it completely.

I threw myself into work. I persuaded Neil to take on a volunteer policy, American-style. The Tax man rewarded Neil for giving up his staff's time, a few hours a week, to a charity of their choice. I went to work for the Stop the War Coalition, hoping that my leaflets and mailshots might do more than Al's prayers and meetings. It kept me from staring silently at the calendar, wishing away each month, hoping it would end differently to the one before.

It did end, the waiting and wishing, just as my mother had assured me it would.

Doing the test on my own was not supposed to shut Al out, rather it was supposed to save him from the sadness, the wondering whether it was him or me, the sense of disappointment if my guess had been wrong. When he came home, he could see I'd been crying.

'What's happened? Are you okay?'

'I didn't want to get your hopes up.'

'Meaning?'

I nodded.

There was a shining in his eyes that reminded me of the first time I'd seen him, of his weak wink across the room. It was the glow of the future. We'd concerned ourselves with politics and protests, letting the weight of the world's problems remind us of the transient nature of ours.

'You and me?' He was too frightened to say it.

Tears rolled down my face and into my smile.

Al held me tightly and we sat, side-by-side on our bed, just dazed by fortune.

Al and I had travelled to France to see the tiny Jean-Paul unfurling like a bud into the world. I'd held the baby close to me, inhaling him, but mostly just looking in awe at the way mine and Connie's genes had replicated, the way that Connie's crazy red hair had morphed into the wavy soft black down on Jean-Paul's head. In the year and a half that followed, I occupied myself with his new tricks, his achievements and milestones, to try to forget the feeling of his first days when he looked so much like me. The drive from the ferry to Connie's house was only five hours, the flight even more convenient, we saw them often whether in England or in France. Jean-Paul's first words were French, his clothes and haircut so clearly European. He would be just two when Connie's second baby was born, two and a half when he met his cousin.

I was free now, to recall the power of seeing him for the first time, the landmark, the miracle.

'Should we open a bottle of champagne?' Al asked, still breathless with disbelief.

'But I could only have one glass.'

'With a side order of coal and pickled onions.' He put his hand on my flat stomach.

'I think that's all a myth, Con didn't have anything like that.' I lay back on the bed, my hands over his, wondering how I was ever going to fit a baby in before remembering that it was already there. There was already a baby growing under my skin. 'What if my craving's for bacon?'

'Oh, don't say that, that's horrible. What if it is?'

'I'm teasing you. I decided – a while back – during the long long planning that's gone into this... ' We both smiled. 'That I'm not going to eat pork while I'm pregnant.'

'You're kidding me.'

'Nope, I'm not.'

Al kissed me on the cheek. 'That's... it's, I don't know what to say. That's amazing.'

'It's half you, this baby. So it's only fair.'

'See? You're already the most perfect mummy in the world. And he or she isn't even born yet.'

'Besides,' I backed up my decision with logic, 'all these things, old wives' tales and stuff, have a basis in common sense.'

'Old wives' tales?'

'You know what I mean,' I said.

'Half the world, Jews, Muslims, Buddhists, Jains, Hindus, more than half the world I bet, don't eat pork. And now it's an old wives' tale. You're a nutter. But I'm glad your loony beliefs have led to this decision. So glad, I can't begin to tell you.'

I rolled towards him so that our faces were touching. 'So we only have one thing to worry about now.' But even the spectre of Al's mother sitting in judgement couldn't cloud this day.

'Have you told anyone else?'

'Of course not, silly. As if I would tell anyone before the daddy.' The word left us both silent, idiot grins in place of words and long pauses of imagination between each phrase where we saw ourselves as parents, pictured our child. 'I'll tell Con in the next few days but Farzana will be back at Christmas, I might wait and surprise her.'

'That's...' He counted on his fingers. 'Seven weeks away. You? Keep that kind of secret? I'll be able to hear her screaming from here.'

Suddenly, the baby seemed to touch everything we were. We pulled the contents of the fridge out onto the work surface; Brie, Chicken liver pate, a huge chunk of Stilton we'd bought down at my parents' from a deli, it all went in the compost bin. The photographs lined up on our shelves of our nephews at various stages of babyhood suddenly felt like a glimpse of our future, a clue as to whom this little person would become. Our whole flat felt different.

Later, I woke up in the dark, Al's side of the bed empty but still warm. The central heating clicked on with a buzz and, very quietly underneath the hum, I could hear the muffled notes of Al's guitar.

I clicked the spare room door open quietly. He was sitting with his back to the warm radiator, playing quietly and singing in a whisper over the melody he played.

He looked up at me, so much like when I'd first seen him, the dark fringe across his forehead, his eyes soulful and expressive. Dark deep eyes that my baby might have too.

'I'm sorry, babe. I didn't mean to wake you.'

'I don't think you did. It was the boiler clicking on. Have you been in here long?'

I sat down next to him, the radiator warm through the t-shirt I'd shrugged on to come and find him, the autumn making my toes cold. I planted my foot next to his, looking at the difference between them.

'I was looking at this room. Working out where to put everything.'

'Your guitars?'

'The cot, silly. And all the changing table stuff and drawers and things. I won't have the luxury of a music room anymore.'

I was silent for a second. I knew it doubled as his Prayer Room.

'And that led me to thinking about stuff, about us, the baby. About my incredible luck. And it made me snivel so I shut the door so you wouldn't catch me blubbing.'

He put the guitar down and put both arms round me. 'I'm trying to think of anything else in the world I might want. But I can't. I've got it all. How incredible is that? What a life.' He gave a little sniff as if his tears were on their way out once more. He coughed them away. 'It was like holding my breath underwater, waiting to get pregnant. Like my lungs were going to burst. I thought it might be my fault, or, well...' He looked down at his knees, his words evaporated.

'Well, what?' I curled into him, put my bare feet on top of his.

'This is going to sound so stupid.'

'I'm very used to that, darling.'

'I thought about all that superstitious stuff, the things my mum believes in, Evil Eyes and spells and all that. I started to worry there might be something in it and that I'd brought it into our home. Given it to you or something. I know I'm stupid.' A noise caught in his throat, a sob that he fought down. 'You can take the boy out of village but you can't take the village out of the boy, eh?'

'That's just what desperate people do. It's nothing to do with your background. I've been spitting at magpies, not walking under ladders. All that stuff. Looking out for black cats, picking up pennies from the street.'

'Really?' As he looked at me, a smile spread like life across his face. 'And I wasn't going mad or being weird?'

'I'm glad you thought those things. And glad you didn't tell me – they are a bit freaky.' I rubbed the tops of his feet with the bottoms of mine, our legs stretched out together. 'But it means you wanted this as much as I did.'

'I want this more than I've ever wanted anything in the world,' he said. 'Except for you.'

And we did cry then, but they were happy tears, they were the resolution of two years of wishing and hoping.

I couldn't wait seven weeks to tell Farzana, of course I couldn't. She and Bilal had decided to live in England for the next few years. Her decision, which had reduced me to tears on the day I heard it, was a combination of wanting Zak to have a good grounding in English and wanting her mother to help with her second son, Sam, who had arrived more quickly after Zak than planned. It was ironic really, while we had been having futile, answerless, tests for infertility all paid for by the NHS, Bilal and Farzana were spending thousands of dollars on ante-natal care they hadn't expected to need. But now we were all equal, all ready for the next stage of our lives. When we collected and opened the sea crates that contained all their family paraphernalia, there were bags and bags of baby shawls and outfits and amazing shalwar kameez for me, the golden threads of the fabric looped into beautiful patterns, the waists threaded through with generous elastic to accommodate my changing body.

Farzana being party to our guilty secret was a problem. We were in London, hidden away from pointing fingers and prying eyes, but Farzana was going back to Manchester to live near to her mother. We couldn't ask Faz to lie on our behalf, not even by omission.

'Are you scared of your mum finding out?' I asked Al. 'What do you think she'll say?'

'I cannot imagine. Or at least, I don't really want to, not while I can avoid it. It'll be my dad; all silent and disappointed. That'll be what gets me. My mum will flap and wail and be upfront about it. But, do you know what? It's nothing, not compared to this, to you. I'll sort it out. You just worry about growing my son. Or my daughter. I can't decide which one I want.'

'Or your mum might just say that babies bring their own love.' I knew I was being over-optimistic.

'She might,' he lied and squeezed my hand tightly.

We were walking through Greenwich Park. Squirrels darted along the top of green benches, the last of the leaves blown into heaps around the litter bins. I put my feet either side of the timeline and imagined being on both sides of the world.

'If we get the names sorted, it'll be more like thinking about an actual child; someone they know they'll love. Rather than just a lump. A lump being carried around by the nasty English heathen.'

'Don't be horrible. It's not like that.' He took my hand and we started down the hill towards the boating pond. We could see the swings in the distance, still, silent, as if waiting in the winter for our baby to appear and fill them with life. He sighed. 'It is like that, isn't it?'

I squeezed his hand tightly. 'For a boy, for a middle name, I want David, after my dad.'

Al didn't say anything.

'David? As in David, King of the Jews?' I was trying to get a reaction. 'Your dad will go nuts. He'll be down there,' I pointed at the swing sets, 'pushing his grandson on the swings with all the other grandads, watching the Mustafas and the Ayeshas and having to introduce his own little David.'

Al started laughing, his eyes disappearing in the crush of his smiles. 'You are so funny. I despair of you sometimes. David is an important prophet in my faith. Just like Jesus. My cousin Dawud? David. It's just about spelling.'

I shrugged. 'How disappointing. Oh well, we're not married, we're up the stick, we're going to have a baby out of wedlock. Maybe the name won't be the thing they mind most.' I snuggled under his arm, his coat keeping the wind from my cold ear.

'Kamila,' he said. 'Spelt with a K.'

'Millie? I like it. Is that for real? I've not met a Kamila.'

'I don't think I have either but it's a Pakistani name, definite.'

I pulled my scarf round my ears, the tree tops moved smoothly with a whisper of the sea. The sodden ends of fireworks from the huge Blackheath display were still stuck in the longer grass. The display had ended with a huge heart, tracked out in pink fireworks. 'How about Adam?' he said. 'The first man.'

'The whole world is engulfed in a hideous war on terror, America is hysterical and threatening to blow up everyone. And you want me to call my son Adam Hussain?'

ALI

In my mind my family had already expanded. I always had an image of the three of us in a bubble, our own little tribe staking our claim on the world. It was like Honour was carrying the baby on the inside, but it was my job to fend off the outside, to keep them both protected. The way we walked, the way I manoeuvred us, it was already three people. My mind went Honour, the baby and me.

Yet it seemed that the blind eyes that had been turned to our relationship status were now open and all seeing and more than that: JUDGEMENTAL.

Yacein I told first.

He was silent, typing away at his computer screen. About an hour later he took me for coffee and had a 'chat'.

'This changes things, my brother,' he said.

'Not really. It's great. We've been trying for so long,' I said.

I told Yacein I had been for tests myself. Just to make sure that I was in working order. It had been one of the most embarrassing and nerve-wracking moments of my life, but the tests had come back okay.

Then I didn't want to tell Honour that because I didn't want her to carry the burden of the failure, phantom blame on her shoulders. But, it transpired, it wasn't her either. It wasn't either of us.

I reassured her, repeated words our GP had said. It sometimes takes a while, two perfectly healthy people, doing everything right.

I hoped including Yacein in the darkness would make him appreciate the light.

'I see. And what name will you give this child?'

'We have a few on the list. You want to suggest some?' I said.

'People will ask, who is your father, who is your grandfather? It's the way it is.'

'My baby will have my name, obviously,' I said.

I was getting angry at Yacein's insinuations, more so because he was behaving in the way I expected my father to.

'But he belongs to his mother, it is her child. You are not her husband,' he said.

'You're speaking like some medieval sand bandit,' I said. 'This is 2005, my baby is mine, I'll give you a bloody DNA test if you really want.'

'And what if you break-up and get married to someone else? Have children with your wife? Islamically, your child with Honour will have no rights.'

'Honour is my wife as far as I'm concerned,' I said.

'Are you placing yourself higher than God now?'

'That's not what I meant. And maybe I don't believe in a God that will disinherit my child?'

'Astagfirullah, brother you are angry but do not commit shirk. It is the unforgivable sin.'

'I know that, I am a Muslim.'

'Are you? Islam is not about a birth right. You practice and you are a Muslim.'

'The five pillars don't talk about marriage,' I said.

'And what about at school? Or at the madrassa? Will you send your son or daughter to learn about their faith? And what about your parents? Will they accept a grandchild born like this? Think, Ali, this is no longer just about you and Honour. This is about a child. You need to give them the best start.'

'He or she will have two parents who want them and will love them, that *is* the best start.'

'And when they get married? What will be asked of them?'

'Do you really think we'll still be choosing spouses in twenty, thirty years' time?'

'Yes. We have been working this way for 1400 years. Some things will stay.'

I didn't want to follow his ways, these ways that were so harsh to my baby, to that spark of life inside the woman I loved.

God's miracle they called it, so the baby should be born with every right God gave to anyone.

'Okay, well I have done my best,' Yacein said. 'In that case, congratulations, brother, I am extremely happy for you both.'

He hugged me, and treated the office to cake and non-alcoholic sparkling grape juice later. In the toast, publicly, he called Honour my 'wife'. I felt slightly fraudulent when everyone patted my back, shook my hand.

Even Ruby was concerned.

'You know I'm down with you and Honour, it's your business right. But a baby, Ali, our people aren't ready for that yet. Seriously.'

'Honour told me,' Farzana said.

This was easier, it was over the phone.

I was on Kingsway, standing under the shelter of a closed bank's doorway, speaking into my mobile as the rain lashed the traffic and London.

'You're going to be a puppo. Aren't you happy?' I said.

'Of course. I even handed out mithai to my mother and toddler circle. I told them you're getting married?' she said.

'Come on, don't you start.'

271

RUTH AHMED

'I'm just saying. What other excuse do you both need? Have you told Mum and Dad yet?'

'I think you'd know about it if I had. They'll go ballistic.'

'Well, we have been preparing for that ever since you guys started trying to get pregnant,' she said. 'What are you going to say to them? Do you want me to tell them?'

'No,' I said. 'That much I do know. You don't think I'd get away with hiding a child do you? I mean I managed to hide a girlfriend for years…'

'Ali…'

'Jokes, sis,' I said. 'You didn't say all this to Honour did you?'

'Of course I didn't. It's not her parents who are going to be upset, it's yours. I bet her parents were chuffed?'

'You're so patronising, but yes, they were chuffed to bits.'

I watched as professionals in designer suits and heels jogged through the rain. There were so many people in the world, in this city alone.

How was it possible to latch onto someone, just one person, like I had with Honour? How did that work, that in billions of people there was only one who could mean so much to you?

'Look, Ali, even my mother-in-law said you should get married to avoid scandal. And you know how modern and liberal she is,' Farzana said.

'You told her? But she's bound to let it slip.'

'I trust her, she won't. She doesn't do idle gossip.'

'I don't care what she says anyway,' I said.

'What I'm saying to you is if she thinks like this, imagine what the cronies around Mum and Dad will say. Do you really want Zak and Sam going to weddings and the mosque and have people whisper about their cousin and their Uncle?'

'That's low, Faz, you can't use my nephews against me.'

272

'If it makes you realise what has to be done... please Ali... for their sake if no one else's. Don't make it so that they have to meet your children in secret, please. Every birthday, Eid, wedding, occasion... there will always be a fight – shall we invite Ali and his children or not?'

'I'm not bothered,' I said.

'I am. I want them here. But how many battles can I fight? For how long? I stood by you and Honour, I celebrated every victory with you both. I even prayed nafl that she would get pregnant, so you could both know the joy Bilal and I do. All I'm asking is that you think about what I said.'

'There's nothing I can do,' I said.

'Speak to Honour, tell her what this means to Mum and Dad. Please.' My sister was begging.

'Have you said this to her?'

'No, it's not my place. I look on her as my best friend, and if she was just my best friend I would behave the way I have done. I wouldn't be telling her to get married. But you are my brother, and so to you I *am saying* get married.'

'Your logic is as messed up as mine,' I said.

'Well, you know what's best. Sincerest mubarak though, I mean that. I can't wait for my niece or nephew to be born.'

I put the phone down, agitated after speaking to Farzana.

My child was mine, I claimed him or her and they had every legitimacy. My parents would die soon enough and if their aunts and uncles didn't want to know, well, sod it, we would create a new family.

Get friends who weren't like Yacein, friends who weren't even Muslim. Why not?

But I was adamant I would not pressure Honour to marry me. It had to come from her.

Chapter Twenty-One

HONOUR

We were cautious who we told, as most people are, until we had ticked past the twelve week mark and seen our baby in grey outline on a scan, its heart winking at us from another world. Farzana had known for almost as long as we had and I was conscious of the strain that winced across her face whenever we discussed 'family'. I was certain she was putting a quiet pressure on Al to tell his parents although he kept me protected from it.

Two days after the scan, buoyed by a great day at work and the grainy black and white printout of the baby propped up on the mantelpiece, Al decided to phone his parents.

'You want me to go in the kitchen or something?' I asked.

He was pacing the sitting room, the cordless phone like a weapon in his hand. I was sprawled inelegantly on the sofa, flicking peanuts into my mouth from a bowl that rested on my chest.

'No, don't be daft. It's not going to be that bad.'

I made a face at him, my eyes exaggeratedly wide, my smile goofy. 'Might be. Farzana seems pretty concerned about it.'

'She's just concerned about the effect on my parents, the gossips and stuff. Those communities don't change just because you move out of a village setting and into the affluent suburbs of another country. The women's attitudes stay just the same. Worse even. They've missed out on a big wedding, don't forget. Lost out on all the chance to dress up and whisper pointedly about the bride.'

'But they'll get used to the idea. Over time. And especially once they see the baby. Even the scan picture.' I beamed at the two-dimensional image over the fireplace, trying to communicate with it.

'You don't get it, you really don't. But I don't want it to be your problem. Don't let it worry you. They have their ways of dealing with things.' A shadow of words seemed to squash him, he slumped down next to me and sighed loudly.

'Will they cut you off?' It hadn't even occurred to me before that Al's parents could hold out after the baby was born.

He nodded, then tipped his head back, staring at the ceiling and breathing in and out through his mouth. He was trying not to cry.

'Disown you? And the baby?'

He nodded, slowly, silently. A sigh caught in his throat like a mute cough.

I reached out, covering his hand with mine. 'That's insane.'

'They have two other sons. Jamal will take my place, and the pressure will mount on Zain to hold up the family honour, get that Law degree, become a surgeon, whatever.' He shrugged and leaned forward, his head dropping into his hands, his fingers separating his black fringe.

'Our baby needs two sets of grandparents.'

I took his hand again and moved it, palm down, across my stomach.

'And God only knows what would happen to any family that had to rely on Jamal,' I said in an effort to lighten his mood. 'Listen, what would happen if we got married in the registry office? Just us. Would it count?'

'You said you didn't want to get married while you're pregnant.'

'I know, that was before I found out how damned hot I'd look once I'd stopped hanging over the loo and puking.' I smiled. 'And I do look hot, don't I?'

'You've never looked so beautiful.'

'And would a shotgun wedding in a grubby old municipal room be better than none at all? Soften the blow a little?'

'Fractionally less awful than the alternative. Maybe Faz could talk my mother down from the ceiling and get her to see that this kind of marriage will at least make the baby legitimate.'

I raised my eyebrows at his bald practicality.

'Sorry, you know what I mean. I was just thinking out loud. I'll stop.' He kissed me.

I hadn't wanted to get married after the shock of 9/11, it seemed better to mourn and wait, more appropriate. Once we'd embarked on our efforts to get pregnant, getting married seemed like a jinx, as though, if we accepted that happiness, we couldn't have any other. We were ready to do it now and we needed to do it now.

'Ring them then, quick. Before I change my mind.'

He sat bolt upright. 'You're kidding me?'

I shook my head.

He ran his hands through his beautiful hair. 'Thank you, darling. Right, I'll ring them. I have an awful feeling there's a double-edged sword hanging right over my head.'

I tried not to listen to the phone call and not to notice that Al's news was in the order his parents wanted to hear it not the way I would have imagined it in his heart.

Firstly, Yacein was promoting him, his salary would be ludicrous.

The second piece of reporting, we were getting married, just a small affair but legal and real.

Lastly, we were having a baby, not far along, quite a surprise.

ALI

'Dad?'

'Nah, man, it's me, Jamal. What's up, bro?'

'Get Dad.'

'Why wassup, you alrite? How's da missus?'

'Fine, everything's fine. Get Dad.'

'Sounds serious, k.'

Jamal shouting in the background for my father, Zain asking who's on the phone, my mother asking who's on the phone. I could picture it, people popping on and off stage, how the voices would travel up the stairs.

Where was my dad?

These weren't just any people though, these were my people, my blood.

Honour was in the sitting room trying not to listen in. I wished she was with me, holding onto some part of me just so I wouldn't be such a wuss.

Distance made it easy, using the flippin' phone made it *really* easy.

'Ali, *tu teekh ah?*'

It was my mother. That I didn't need.

'Yes, Ammi, is Dad there? I just need to speak to him.'

'*Kiyon? Kee hoya? Tu teekh ah?*'

'Yes, Mum, nothing like that. Just something important I need to say to him.'

'*Usski tabeeyat karaab ah, sir dukhriya. Kuch airi gairu gal na kareen,*' she warned.

'Trust me, Mum, his headache will disappear. It's just about work, I got a promotion.'

'*Acha, Mubarak huwey.*'

Mum didn't really understand what I did, and probably thought I wore a suit and acted as a bank manager or something.

'Ali,' said my father.

I could sense the entire family was in the room. I heard Zain and Aaliyah bickering, sniping at each other the way me and Farzana used to.

'Be quiet, I am on the phone,' my father said.

They were silent, he had that gravitas. Would I when it came to my turn to tell my child to be quiet?

'Dad, I got a promotion at work,' I said.

'Acha? Mubarak. Very good. How are you?'

'Happy,' I said.

The truth felt so easy.

'So, are you sending us some mithai? Why don't you come and visit, we will have a family get together.'

'Okay. There's something else too.'

'Yes? Is she okay?'

She? Well it was something. Okay, deep breaths.

'Dad… I'm… we're… we've decided to get married.'

Silence.

'Married?' he said.

'You go, bro!' I heard Jamal shout.

'I'm wearing a lengha!' Aaliyah said.

'I'm being best man!' Zain added.

Silence from my father.

'We've been through this before Ali. Or has she found a God?'

'No, Dad, it's going to be in a registry office,' I said. 'Just close family. Dad… she's pregnant.'

Silence… a long pause of my father weighing up his philosophies, balancing things with his God… and then…

'Mubarak to you both! That is excellent news, yes, yes, wedding is a must. Registry is fine, don't worry, we will get my brother to say a duaa, and I'll give her a cheque for your haque mehr and you will both have witnesses and say yes. Okay, this will be fine, I accept.'

'Dad... erm... thanks...'

'Is Honour there? Let me speak to her.'

'She's in the bathroom... you know pregnancy...'

'Yes, yes, of course. I have five children I know what happens. Well done, my boy, finally you are a man. And... I am glad you are doing this... thinking about somebody else for once.'

'Let me tell Mum.'

'No, no... you don't bother with all of that. I will sort it. Have you got a date?'

'No, we literally just decided.'

'Okay, well, do it in Manchester and do it as quickly as possible. Small registry and then dinner in a restaurant. No, actually, do it in London. Less tamasha, and nobody needs to know exact baby dates.'

We ended on salaams, and there felt, for the first time in so long, peace between us.

Chapter Twenty-Two

HONOUR

As with so many of life's nice quiet plans, events snowballed. The call-the-cleaners-in-as-witnesses day that I'd imagined in a haze of hormonal sympathy for Al took on a life of its own. Connie's second pregnancy was so far advanced that she couldn't possibly make it from France although dealing with her sheer grief at missing my marriage vows and her pleas for the date to be changed was terrible.

Farzana pointed out that it was the day that my mother was going to meet hers and that a skilled negotiator-cum-translator was essential to the smooth running of the day. I had to give her that one and add her to the guest list.

The obligatory Uncle, who graced every family moment and whose house I'd been to for Bilal's mehendi, was also non-negotiable despite the fact that I'd only met him twice in my life.

I woke early on the day of the wedding, savouring the quiet, appreciating the calm of our ordered flat. Al slept on beside me, his hair sticking to the white pillow, one arm stretched towards me. I practised my Yoga breathing, staring into space, holding the peace. I felt the strangest sensation, like a tiny electric butterfly caught inside me, struggling. A second time, no mistake.

'Al, Al,' I whispered, although I don't know why, 'it just kicked. The baby kicked me.'

The wedding vows passed without a problem. It was Al's parents' wedding not mine, although to say so would have been churlish. The least I could do was to cooperate with his mother's wishes in the few small spaces where compromise could be made without sacrifice.

I didn't catch her eye during the short ceremony. They had arrived late, straight from Manchester and there had been no time for chit-chat outside. Farzana stood as my witness and Bilal as Al's.

Zak toddled backwards and forwards throughout the service throwing himself first at Al's mum's legs and then at my mum's as they sat in a stilted and silent row. My parents knew how I felt about the whole thing and even my dad didn't tease me.

'Congratulations, Mrs Hussain,' said Al as the perfunctory service finished, 'I have everything I've ever wanted.'

'Are you Mrs Hussain?' Farzana asked. 'I didn't even question it, I just assumed you'd stay Edwards.'

'Professionally I will, but I want to have the same surname as the baby for home, you know, and its school and stuff.'

We moved towards the door of the registry office, blinking onto the street in the January sunlight. We'd booked a table at an Italian restaurant nearby that we knew well. It had halal food for Al's parents and Chianti for mine. I managed not to bump into Al's mum as we got out of the registry office door and was able to set off down the street without a forced, one-way, pretend conversation.

When we got into the restaurant, they offered us champagne and orange juice from a tray. I couldn't face the showdown and took an orange juice although every fibre of me cried out for alcohol to take the terrifying edge off the company.

'Farzana,' my mother said, 'would you come and translate so that I can have a chat with your mother?'

'My wife understands English perfectly, Mrs Edwards.' Al's dad said. 'She just does not speak it.'

'Sounds bloody perfect company for you, darling,' said my dad. 'You can go on for hours without interruption or protest from your victim.'

Both men laughed and I wondered which culture held the most archaic disrespect for women. From this angle, it was hard to tell.

I excused myself and took five minutes to go the loo. I said I needed to do my makeup but, really, it was just a chance to be away from them all for a few seconds. I stood staring into the mirror, my fingertips splayed out on the edge of the sink, my shoes kicked off.

The stress I was feeling didn't show. I looked radiant, even if I said so myself. My hair was piled in rambling curls onto the top of my head, a few tendrils whispering round my face. My make up was plain and English rose, my cheeks blushed faintly and my lips red. My skin was glowing and the tiniest amount of weight I'd put on around my face suited me. In the week before the wedding, a client had been chatting to me over my desk. Just before I stood up to shake his hand on a done deal and say goodbye, he asked me if I'd like to go for a drink. I'd grinned, stood straight and pointed to the small and beautiful bump curving with promise through my shirt. Now I could point to my wedding ring too. The thought made me smile.

I wondered what my mother and Mrs Hussain would be talking about and shuddered.

I stood behind my mother, she didn't see me as I heard her say conspiratorially to Mrs Hussain, 'You must be terribly excited about the baby. I worried so much; you do, don't you, as a mother? Two years is such a long time to try.'

My mother knew as soon as she said it. The silence was like a slow motion picture of someone trying to catch an object about to shatter into thousands of pieces. Mentally, she and I dived for the floor to scoop the words up before the impact; physically, we just stood, eyes and mouths wide open.

Mrs Hussain span round to face Al. She hurled words at him, '*Acha, phir neeyat de naal bacha plan kitta?*'

I caught the words 'bacha' – child – and 'plan'. I didn't get any more. I didn't need to.

'*Galti nayee hoyee?*' It wasn't a mistake? I got that one.

'No, it wasn't a mistake,' I said, anger blazing in my eyes. I wanted to shout at her that this wasn't her day, it was mine and that she should shut up. But it was her day. It was her day through and through. I dug my nails tight into my palms, imagining myself shouting at her, picturing Al's tortured face if I did. I took deep breaths and ignored her bad behaviour.

'Begum.' Al's dad stepped in. 'It is not of any consequence now. Our son, Ali, is married to this beautiful girl. She is now our daughter.'

Al's father's words were the oil needed to calm the waters. Everyone made a dedicated effort to talk loudly, even little Zak picked up the need to entertain and ran around, singing and smiling for all he was worth.

I sat down and took a huge gulp of my mother's Champagne. Zak slid onto my lap holding a breadstick for a sword.

'Swords, Auntie, fight me?' He parried the breadstick.

Why not, I thought, I've already gone two rounds with your grandmother.

I looked around the crumbs on the floor, the result of our duel. 'See,' I said to no one in particular, 'this is why you need a dog with children. No hoovering, no mess.'

'Do you like doggies, Zak?'

'Zak loves dogs, don't you?' Farzana said. 'Our next door neighbours have one and he adores it.'

'I thought all Pakistani people were terrified of dogs.'

'Just your husband,' Farzana said. 'I wouldn't have one in the house, well, not one of my own. I'd probably put up with a friend's for a few hours though.'

'How interesting.' I grabbed Al's hand as he walked past me, 'The things you find out after you marry someone.'

'Yes, but,' Al said, 'you can't have one in the house. It's written in the hadith literature.'

'Shouldn't have dogs in the house anyway.' My father chipped in. 'Stinking things, much happier sleeping in a kennel. They were always in kennels when I was a boy, the lucky ones anyway. The others were just outside.'

Al's father raised his orange juice. 'I think this dog issue, like so many things that keep us apart in this life, can be solved through love and compromise.'

'To love and compromise, as the wise man said!' shouted my father, standing and holding his glass out for a toast.

'Love and compromise!' we echoed. A tear wandered its way onto my cheek.

Al's mum sat in silence, her lips motionless.

ALI

I knew it wouldn't be so simple.

'I know you both have done the registry, but we need a nikah. So, this is how it is going to work,' my father said.

It was like a comedy sketch, with my mum giving Honour daggers, but kissing me on the face and genuinely happy about the baby. To me, she was the groom's mum and, hey, she would have been the evil mother-in-law no matter who I married.

'*Dil noon aj sakoon aa gaya*,' she kept saying.

My heart is at peace now.

Honour was giving my mother dirty looks.

And in my head I kept saying, *she is my wife, she really is my wife*. Throughout the whole day I felt another level of joy, the knowledge that my child was also here, watching his or her parents marry. My life felt complete.

I was in heaven, and as my family plotted around me I didn't care.

Farzana asked Honour three times if she was sure she wanted to marry her dunce of a brother, sort of just dropped it into conversation, and then came and told my dad it was done.

My father asked me, three times, did I want to marry Honour. This was more formal, out of Honour's hearing, but again done.

'Now, I know we don't stand on ceremony or tradition, but my brother would like to bless the couple if that is okay?' Dad announced.

'I think that's a fantastic idea,' said The Baron.

My Taiaji, his wife, and my oldest cousin Abdul with his wife Fouzia were the only extended family there.

Taiaji asked for silence and recited some verses from the Qur'an.

My father then presented Honour with a cheque.

'This is from our family for you, only you. Put it in a bank and if my son ever treats you badly, use this to leave the idiot,' he said.

I was laughing so hard I had tears in my eyes.

The haque mehr. was traditionally given to the bride on the wedding day by the groom, it was an amount that would be hers for her lifetime to keep in case things went wrong and she needed to stand on her own two feet.

Dad had done his little trickery, and in his head and everyone else's, we had done all that was required from a nikah.

He kissed Honour on the forehead, and joined my hand with hers.

'Welcome to my family,' he said.

Taiaji went next and said the same.

'I can see why Al fell so hard,' said Abdul. 'Welcome to the family, bhabhi.'

'Barbie?'

'Bhabhi means sister-in-law,' Abdul said.

After that there was laughter and conversation and food.

I booked myself and Honour into the Dorchester for the night.

'So how does it feel to be Mrs Hussain?' I said.

'Maybe you should be Mr Edwards, after all?' she said.

'I'll decide. I own you now remember. You are a Pakistani wife,' I said, jokingly.

'Then how come you're going to do what I say for the rest of your life?'

'Interesting,' I said.

We were lying on the rose petals Farzana and Aaliyah had sprinkled over our bed, staring at the ceiling, painting our dreams on it.

I stroked her stomach, hoping my child could feel my happiness, our happiness. Know that it was safe now to come into the world.

'Are you happy?' she asked.

'Honour... I've been happy since the moment I met you.'

Chapter Twenty-Three

HONOUR

I'd been awake most of the night but with excitement rather than discomfort. We had waited five days past the due date for this baby to come. Five days filled with phone calls from friends and family wondering if he, or she, had put in a secret appearance. Five days of re-folding tiny clothes and feeling a thrill every time I straightened the unruffled cot sheets or laid out the huge selection of talc and toiletries for the twentieth time. The tightenings across my stomach and into my groin were thrilling and I pottered, doing the things I was delighted I would no longer have time for.

At about half past four, as fronds of dawn began to whisper across London, I began my clear-out of the fridge. The yellow artificial light emphasised the freckled skin on my hands as I reached into its deepest corners. I savoured the smell of the cleaning fluid and its lime sharpness. After that, my nails looked tired and dull so I sat on the sofa and gave myself an early morning manicure. I lay on my side, my fingers splayed out to dry the polish and watched the graceful movements of the baby under my skin. The rhythmic contractions were the sweetest, lightest, pain and with one hand resting across the baby, smug in my ability to cope with labour, I dozed off on the sofa while the dawn broke properly into a cloudless sky.

I woke to a very different world. I curled, cursing, as a contraction hit me, beating through my muscles as if they would tear. After it passed I sat up on the sofa stunned, laughing quietly at my smugness and remembering, with a shudder, the labour videos we'd seen at the ante-natal class. At least I'd seen them, Al had concentrated his gaze onto the wall at the side of the screen. No one else had noticed, but I had and I teased him about it all the way home. I went to stand up and, as I pushed myself upright using the arm of the sofa as support, water gushed down my legs.

'Al! Al!'

He didn't come. Maybe time was slipping in length with the pain. I didn't know what Al was doing or where he was. I panicked and shouted again.

'Are you okay? Oh, darling.'

I pointed, tearfully, at the mess on the floor. 'I think my waters went.'

'I think they did, babe. Where do you want to be? You want to sit down here or..?'

As he spoke another wave of pain overtook me, my legs shuddered underneath it and I threw my arms around his neck so I could stay on my feet.

'We need a midwife. Or to go to the hospital.' I said, as soon as I could speak again.

'Do we need to time them? The contractions?' Al had picked up the phone.

I nodded.

The numbers for the Royal Free and our midwife team were written in an orderly list by the phone. My bag was packed with care, clothes collected, cosmetics and water sprays neatly stored, a book, headphones and music. That was the tasteful labour I'd worked towards not this hostile takeover by Mother Nature.

I was trying to find a comfortable position, the labour focussing my attentions solely on my body and its earnest task. I stood at the front window, my hands flat on the windowsill, my nails a traitorous red from the time when I thought I could do this, that it was going to be a walk in the park.

'How long do you think?' Al said into the phone. He paused to take the answer. 'Okay, and if anything changes we ring back?'

I looked at him, terrified that for some reason I was going to have to stay here, away from the pain relief I'd previously spurned, out of the care of the nurses.

Al came over to me. He let out a long sigh, trying to catch a calmness with his breath.

'Okay, sweetheart, it's complicated. First off, you've got to sit down, or lie down, if you can because your waters have broken. Just until the midwife can examine you.'

I nodded and took his hand, hoping to cover the six feet to the sofa before the next contraction hit. He looked worried, there was more to this; I could tell from his face.

'And?' I asked.

'Okay, the midwife has to come to us first. They're sending someone from nearby.'

The contraction I was scared of didn't come and I moved onto the sofa. I lay on my side, my knees up and my feet firmly planted under the soft cushions. I let Al finish speaking.

'I need you to listen, sweetie, and keep calm. There's been an incident. Several.' He moved forward and switched on the television. 'And the hospital is overloaded. The midwife will come here and assess you then we'll go by ambulance when it's time. Okay?'

I wanted to nod at him but I was transfixed by the images on the screen. As my next contraction flew through me, I struggled to focus on the war zone in front of me.

The television showed billowing black smoke, walking wounded and rescuers, stretchers with red blankets up high covering the whole incumbent. There were tunnels and broken bricks, bridges and buses, ripped metal, torn shirts, faint lights from dark haze.

The contraction faded. The images on the television maintained their description of hell. According to the lines of text rolling across below the pictures this carnage was London, my London, my home. I tried to hold the thread of my horror but the relentless contractions knocked it from me every time I tried to ask Al what was going on. His answers were washed away by the waves of pain.

Al held me, murmuring into my ears as each contraction grew then, as it subsided and I took a few seconds' rest, dashed to the window to look for the midwife. In those brief moments of rational thought, I wished we were at the hospital, along with our careful plans and meticulous packing, that the streets didn't hold the horror we had woken up to.

The midwife had a treacly Caribbean accent and a reassuring bossiness that spoke of order and common sense. She sent Al to make coffee while she examined me. The contractions were sending me into a dream state when they came, almost as if they were issuing me instructions, talking to me in the language of my body, a primeval awakening that shook me away from everything I knew and understood.

'You've done amazingly well. Five centimetres dilated, halfway there. Baby's well on its way. Do you know what it is?'

I shook my head.

'Names?' she asked.

I shook my head again. I couldn't trust myself to speak, the pain was climbing inside me. The poor baby had ceased wriggling, jammed against my ever-tightening sides.

The midwife unwound the wires of her monitor and began to rub the steel ball of the handset across my belly like a computer mouse. She took out a set of earphones and put them in to her ears, the other end clipped into the portable machine. After thirty seconds or so, she wound the instrument back up.

'Someone's not playing ball,' she said, taking her mobile phone from her bag. 'These portable devices aren't all that, if baby scrunches up in the wrong place you can't hear anything. We need to get you onto a proper monitor with a clip on baby's head.'

She called an ambulance, the same strong voice that she had taken care of me with commanding the medical team's attention.

The contractions continued like the tide. The midwife offered me a canister of gas and air but I was lost in my half-world, the world where there was only my baby, my body and the relentless rhythm.

I let myself relax in the ambulance, so grateful to be in the hands of the midwife and on the way to the hospital. The siren blocked out any intrusion from outside, the contractions wiped away my concern for London, for anyone. I could see Al trying to look out every now and again, peering through the darkened windows as the siren guided us through traffic gridlock and the fractured city. I tried the gas and air, sucking it deep and rising above the pain and confusion.

The ambulance crew ran through the interminable hospital corridors. I concentrated on staying hunched in the wheelchair, the strip lights and grey walls blending in with my waves of pain, the noise of the gas and air canister illustrating my desperate sucks.

I had expected to be in hospital for my whole labour but things were clearly well under way. Teams of people jostled around me, taking my blood pressure, asking me questions, monitoring the baby. It wasn't the calm I'd pictured, but then, the contractions weren't the delicate sweeps of forward movement I'd convinced myself they would be.

The bespectacled doctor stood in the double-width doorway of the room, he held one of the doors open. 'Mr Hussain?'

He wanted Al to leave with him. I nodded agreement and lay back, glad of the peace. Suddenly aware of the silence.

When Al came back in, I thought he was going to faint. He looked as if he would vomit if he opened his mouth, as if it was full of bile he was barely holding in.

He leaned over me, clutching my arm with one hand, the other cupping my face. His breath ratcheted out of his lungs.

'They can't find a heartbeat.'

Five words.

Five words.

They came at the start of a contraction and meant less and less as I sailed into the face of the pain again.

Then the quiet of the aftermath. The contraction gone. The five words still in the air. Tangible. The rising panic of their meaning. The terror of loss. The midwives began to slip back into the room. Grave faces, suggestions, solutions, platitudes well-meant, questions, contractions. No answers.

The Caribbean midwife we'd seen first spoke gently. I argued. I wanted a Caesarean. I wanted the baby. I wanted a second opinion.

Al stood strong as a rock, holding me, consoling, comforting, suffering silently and reminding me that there was still a real world somewhere.

She was called Margaret, the first midwife, the owner of the strong voice. She talked me down from the ceiling between contractions. She spoke in tiny phrases, short words I could still understand.

'Better for your mind and body to have a vaginal delivery.'

'Shortened recovery time.'

'We can give you drugs now, drugs you couldn't have had before.'

'It will all be over soon, you will have your baby in your arms.'

'No more pain.'

Al held my hand as Margaret released an arsenal of drugs, drugs that crossed the placenta, drugs that I couldn't have had if my poor baby were still alive.

I left the ethereal borders of 2005, of July the 7th, from The Royal Free, away from the hollow cheated experience, from the pain. Al had nothing. He stood beside me, his head high, his chin bold and strong, covering up the demolition in his soul.

It is snowing. Connie and I are squealing with delight, giggling and animated. We look through the condensation trickling down the kitchen window and watch the world turn soft outside. We run upstairs and find our summer clothes. Barefoot, in shorts and t-shirts, our red hair snaking out wet behind us, we run through the snow. Our mother is not a mother who believes in cold causing colds, our mother is a woman who lets us run free until our ringlets are black and flat with melted snow and our bare feet are red and swollen. We cuddle each other, Con and I, sitting inside the inglenook, our feet burning by the open fire, the pain shooting through our ankles as our nerves defrost. Still we laugh.

I'm nine, I'm brazen enough to take out the Connemara at our stables. I'm not big enough for her but I'm strong and I'm fierce. I grasp the bristled hair of her dark mane, I pull myself into the saddle, so far from the ground. I laugh. I'm high on the fear, I'm high on the chance to conquer this big angry horse. Sometimes she kicks if you're on the ground. Up here she can't hurt me. I start forward, pressing my heels into her flanks, moving her on, taking in the stale bread smell of her skin. She dumps me hard on the wood pile. There is an audible 'crack' and a chicken flies up from the logs, squawking and flapping its orange wings furiously. It barely leaves the ground. My wrist is bent, awkward.

I pull the belligerent horse by her reins back to the yard with one hand.

I'm tiny. Five? I am swimming in Lake Windermere. I can feel the sun tightening the skin on my back. My swimming costume is precious and new. It has blue and white stripes and a fairy skirt of red frills. I can't find the ground. The bottom has shelved away below, it has let me down. My feet bicycle beneath me, they cannot bring the lake bed any closer. My mouth and nose fill with water. The water is green, muddy; I do not want it in my mouth. Above me, my hair spreads out on the surface like drowned Ophelia. My father's strong hands scoop me up. They bang me hard on my back, swing me upside down until I cough, painfully and the last of the brackish water drips out of my mouth. It's still hard to breathe.

It's dark, I'm drunk. I'm at university. I thought I was big enough to walk across the park on the way home. I'm frightened and I try to run but I keep falling down, my balance is back in the pub with my friends. I hear noises in the rain, I see a group of men walking towards me on the muddy grass. I run. I manage to gain enough ground to get onto the lamplit street before them but not before I fall, taking the skin off my knee, dashing the cut with pebbles and gravel. Blood oozes out. Where the blood blooms, the stinging is fierce. I limp back to my student house, dragging my dead leg with the same gait as Frankenstein's Monster had.

I'm on the beach. Al is next to me. The pebbles are caving away from our feet, we are being sucked into the sea. We run to the pier to try and save ourselves. We stand on the lower deck, the furious sea below us, cheated of its victims. 'There's this girl in Pakistan,' Al says to me and he trips. The crazy shoes he wore for Farzana's wedding, the curled-up ends like Ali Baba's slippers, have caught in the slats of the pier's floor. The gold beads and cheap plastic diamonds are popping off the khussa shoes as Al wrestles them from between the planks. The sea is lapping at the curled leather ends of his shoes. Al has a magic carpet. 'Come with me,' he shouts. 'Come on my magic carpet ride. I can save us.' I climb, damp and cold, onto Al's magic carpet. I sit back on my haunches, my fingers digging into the swirling patterns of its weave. The carpet slides from the pier. It does not clear the rise of the waves. Its front touches the cold sea. It sinks, sinks, sinks, underwater. We fall and fall, the crashing waves close loudly over us.

Five words.

They can't find a heartbeat.

ALI

I woke up cold. The blankets had fallen off me and were in a heap on the floor. I put a hand out to touch Honour, but the bed was empty, the depression in the mattress still warm. She was having trouble sleeping; anxiety and excitement over the baby.

Usually I woke when she did, some primordial instinct kicking in to make me be there. I was worried for a second, wondering if something was really wrong. I used to worry I would be so fast asleep I wouldn't hear her screaming or needing me. She was pottering around, moving from the kitchen to the lounge. I could hear her. She liked to play classical music, didn't like watching TV. I knew what sort of baby she was trying to mould in her womb.

Reassured at her humming to the music I fell asleep again.

I'd be there when she wanted me, when it mattered. For now I enjoyed the double bed to myself. I had been working from home since the due date, not having to deal with the Tube and the rush hour still a luxury. So I took advantage of a lie in.

'AL! AL!'

I jumped out of bed, and rushed to be near her. I stood in the middle of our bedroom, sleep clouding my brain.

My phone was vibrating on the bedside table.

Maybe Honour hadn't called me?

I checked and saw I had missed calls from my parents, Farzana, Jamal, Yacein.

I checked my text messages.

'Are you okay? Have you seen what's happened? Call us.'

I didn't understand.

Honour called out again.

I switched on the TV in the bedroom, and froze.

Around me my world seemed to go in slow motion.

I read one of Yacein's texts. There'd been explosions on the Tube.

They were saying gas explosions of some sort.

Some said this isn't a gas explosion, this could be a terrorist bomb.

I watched as the smoke and debris mixed with the Emergency Services, journalists and ordinary people standing by.

People like us.

Everyone had a look in their eyes; panic mixed with practicality. You expected it in a war zone maybe.

But in London? Our home?

I switched the TV off. Honour couldn't know.

I padded into the room and saw her like one of those Bambi deers, all big-eyed and caught by a hunter's gun.

Her waters had broken.

My heart started hammering.

Stay calm, stay calm.

I pretended I had just woken up, made sure the TV was off, looked to see where her phone was. Our answer machine was blinking, five new messages.

The world was fucked up out there, something was happening. Explosions here, in London. I knew it wouldn't be the IRA this time.

I couldn't let Honour know.

I should have woken up properly when I found the bed empty.

The world seemed dull inside our flat, it was horrible to imagine what was happening outside.

I remembered the bomb in Manchester, getting caught up in it, how I had felt then.

I couldn't slip into that, Honour needed me.

I was getting more texts.

They said it could be an Al-Qaeda attack.

The bastards had come here? They had hit my home?

I read the texts as I cradled Honour, checking she was okay.

The mobile signal was intermittent.

This wasn't the best time to be giving birth.

I felt the panic like pins and needles in my veins.

How do I deal with this?

'Sir, there's been an incident, an explosion... We're overloaded, the traffic's at a standstill. Is your wife in any pain... I mean pain that isn't normal?'

'I don't know what is normal anymore,' I said.

'Okay, sir, we need to be sure she's in labour. Keep her calm, keep her breathing deeply and evenly. We'll get a midwife over to you first...'

'What about an ambulance?'

'Sir, some Muslims have blown up the Tube networks... Oh my God... Oh my God...'

'Muslims? You know that do you? What's wrong?'

'Another bomb just went off on a bus... in Russell Square they're saying... '

'Oh God...'

There was a commotion at the other end of the line, Honour was screaming as her contractions continued at this end and somewhere in between the two I was trying not to crumble.

'Can you... what do I do?' I said.

'Sir, I'll get a midwife to you... if needed we'll get an ambulance...'

'Okay, please be quick.'

'Your name, sir?'

'Al… Al…'

'What's your wife's name?'

'Honour. Honour Edwards.'

I didn't say Hussain. I denied myself, I denied my family. I was scared they might not come if they knew I was Muslim.

'How long will it be? And if something happens…'

'Call back, Mr Edwards.'

How to handle Honour?

I didn't want to stress her out, distract her, but I had to let her know there would be a delay.

I couldn't tell her about the explosions.

'There's been an incident. That's what the operator said when I dialled 999. I knew I should have called the Royal Free, but today… well, I didn't want to take chances.'

She didn't comprehend.

I risked switching on the TV.

There were random scenes of carnage, she must have thought it was an accident. That was enough, I switched it off.

'Yes, an accident, there will be a delay getting to us, they're sending a midwife,' I explained. Then seeing the concern on her face. 'Don't worry, I'm here, sweetheart, I'm here. I won't let anything happen to either of you, don't worry it's all okay. We're going to do this, we're going to bring life into the world.'

It seemed so hollow a statement when God knew how many lives had just been taken from the same world.

I should have hoped for a safe birth, instead I hoped the explosions weren't the work of Muslims.

I didn't respond to anybody, no texts, no calls. I couldn't face the scrutiny, I didn't want anyone to ask if I was okay, if things were going to be all right.

I wanted to be in a little bubble, just me and Honour and our baby. The midwife wasn't happy, she demanded an ambulance. She plastered a smile on her face, projecting calm, didn't explain why she had been sharp on the phone. She gave whoever she spoke to the address and she told them who I was.

Did they delay coming? Do we need another paki in the world? Another Muslim?

Fuck.

In the ambulance I carried on getting texts and calls, so I switched my phone off.

We heard sirens all around us, I tried to see if I could spot fire engines or police cars, but the ambulance windows were blacked out.

I held her hand and smiled at her: everything is okay, don't worry.

At the hospital they were very worried.

'It's crazy out there, a lot of our staff haven't made it in. Stuck on tubes and buses. But better stuck on one than blown up, hey, Mr Hussain?' said the doctor.

I just nodded.

'Sorry, doctor, I just had to call my daughter,' said the midwife coming back in.

'It's okay, half the staff are out on the scene,' Dr Patel said.

I just held Honour and stroked her moist forehead, letting her crush my hand bones as the pain wracked her body.

The moment I won't forget. Dr Patel locked his black eyes onto mine, and I saw in them a flicker of pity.

He called the midwife and nurses, and they ran tests and exchanged looks.

He called me out of the room.

He was very matter of fact.

'What can you do? Will you operate?'

'Mr Hussain, I don't think you understand…'

'Drugs? Can you not send electric shocks through the stomach? This is 2005, babies don't… Do something, man…'

I was shaking now, cold fear running through my body.

No. No, not today, this wasn't going to happen.

But it already had.

'I'm sorry, Mr Hussain. We have to think about your wife now,' said Dr Patel. 'I'll break this to her, gently, she has to give birth still…'

'Is there nothing you can do?'

'We can help your wife as much as possible,' he said.

I nodded, and wiped my face with my scarf. It wasn't enough, I gulped back sobs, but they came out as I leaned against the hospital corridor wall, my head against my arms.

Two minutes I let myself grieve.

Then went back in to save my wife.

I touched Dr Patel on the shoulder before I did.

'Let me tell her,' I said.

He opened his mouth, ready to spout something about procedure no doubt, but I must have shown my determination.

This was my family that was breaking, my child, my wife. I would break the news and then hold it together.

Hold Honour together.

Five words.

Five pillars.

Five rivers.

Five minutes.

'They can't find a heartbeat.'

Five words that were the hardest words I would ever have to say.

Five pillars of my faith that couldn't save him that day.

Five rivers, the Panj Aab, that didn't flow through his veins.

Five minutes that changed our world forever.

'Ali? *Shukur Alhamduliallh!* Where have you been? All day we have been calling you. We were so worried... so worried...'

'Dad...'

My voice broke.

'Ali? What's wrong? Is Honour okay? Her parents have called here, her dad's driving to London right now. We were so worried.'

'Dad...'

But I couldn't say it, I just started crying.

'Ali? Are you okay?'

'No,' I managed. 'I'm not okay, Abbu... and I don't think I ever will be...'

The world around us had crashed and the world between us had died too.

But who were we except just one more set of parents mourning for their child on this, the darkest day.

In words full-stopped by sobs like some emotional telegram of old I told my father.

'Sabar, beta,' he said, but I heard his voice full of grief at the other end. 'Allah's Will... I am coming...'

'No, Dad, it's not safe yet, I don't know... Allah's Will?'

'We never question it,' he said.

I realised the entire day not once, not even in my own head, not during the labour or in the ambulance or in the hospital...

not once had I turned to God... not once had I asked Him to save my baby...

My son...

Now it was too late.

Chapter Twenty-Four

HONOUR

The sadness began later, in waves as crushing as the contractions had been.

Al's face was the first thing I saw when I opened my eyes. Painted with grief, he was almost unrecognisable. I could have walked past him in a corridor. He was wearing the same clothes as yesterday. The smell of his black and white scarf, earthy and plant-like, brought back the labour. I had buried my face in that scarf as I clung round his neck.

Recollections popped into my mind like clouds, a puff of scent, a fuzzy shape, the floating cotton wool sounds I'd heard from within the drugs. The moment our boy had been born. The pride, the joy, the excitement on finding out he was a boy. For a frozen piece of time the room forgot. Congratulations from frail voices, admiration for his looks, his hair, his perfect fingers, his healthy birth weight. And afterwards we had to remember, the whole room, that he was dead.

He was born onto me, in the most natural of circumstance, his bare skin on mine. He was warm from being inside me. He cooled as I held him, as he met the world. And Al, he took care of us, whispered prayers through wordless lips over the boy's head, dropped silent tears onto his hair still slicked with the evidence of birth. The midwives and doctors slipped away. Al climbed onto the bed next to me, holding me and holding the boy. We slept, the three of us, together.

When I woke up, Al was sitting in the chair beside my bed. It was the early hours of morning. The baby lay in the plastic cot that had been prepared for him, whatever his outcome might have been. He was swaddled tight in white baby blankets, his cow-lick of black hair poking out over his face.

As the memories dropped in – one by one – of the day before, so the hope ebbed, piece by piece. Our plans, our ideas, my maternity leave, the nursery, everything needed to be rethought. Fitting the re-thinking into the interminable space of time available seemed so hard. There was no rush now. No race to get home, no despair that he wouldn't sleep through the night, no crying, no panic, no nappy rash.

'Have you told everyone?'

Al reached his hand out to cover mine and nodded.

'What did you say?'

He took his phone out of his pocket.

'I called your parents and mine. And Connie and Faz. The rest I sent a text.' He scrolled through the phone's messages looking for the sent box and passed it to me to read.

'*The worst possible news. Our beautiful son, Haroon (Harry) David Manzoor Hussain, was stillborn today at 4.18pm. He weighed 10lb 3oz.*'

My turn to nod.

'He's beautiful, isn't he?' I looked at Harry, at his tiny nose, his perfect eyelashes.

'He looks like you.'

'A bit. He has your nose. You look exhausted. Have you slept?'

'I'm fine,' Al said, although he clearly wasn't. 'I'll just stay here for a bit. I went home last night for a couple of hours. Do you remember? I've been dozing. And I slept while you were in labour. While you did it all on your own in the sitting room.'

'It was lovely then. Even the way it hurt, it was lovely.'

We held each other tightly until eventually drugs and tears over-whelmed me and I slept.

First thing in the proper morning, Margaret came back; just as caring and capable as the day before.

'He's beautiful.' She smiled into Harry's cot. 'You must be very proud.'

I stammered a little. 'We are but, well, I didn't think that was the right thing to be, you know, given that he's, well...' There was no need to say the word. It didn't even fit in the room, even with Harry's face, a still grey, as evidence.

'He's glorious. And he's yours.' Margaret had obviously dealt with this situation before. 'We're fairly certain about what happened, what went wrong with Harry's birth. The way your labour went, the way it changed? It all fits with a placental abruption, with the placenta just gently detaching too soon.' She touched my arm, her skin was warm. 'The doctors would like to have a look at him to help make up their minds. Could I take him away for a bit?'

'Will we have answers afterwards?' Al asked.

'You can choose to have an autopsy performed if you want to. It may tell you more, it may not. But sometimes there are no definite answers.' Margaret wheeled Harry's cot out of the room, looking just like a midwife, with a baby just like all the other babies.

'I don't want an autopsy.' I was adamant. 'I don't want anyone to harm him.'

Al nodded agreement. The light had gone from his eyes, his shoulders were rounded and his face drawn, his eyes swollen from crying. We were the picture of mourning.

'I need to call the Imam,' Al said, his voice hoarse. 'Can he... can he come and see Harry?'

'Oh, God, you don't need to ask me that. Of course he can.' My hand flew to my mouth. We had discussed how we would raise our son, we had decided we would be open and honest about our religious beliefs and that he would go to the mosque with his daddy and to madrassa, the Muslim Sunday School, and that, as a family, we would celebrate Eid and Christmas with equal verve. We had not discussed how we would bury him.

'Your parents are coming this morning. Do you want to have a shower or anything?'

'And Connie? Is she coming?'

'They all are. Farzana, my parents, yours and Connie. Everyone's coming.'

Al's mother's leather-lined face and vicious looks loomed into my mind. 'Okay, I'd best get washed.'

I unpacked the wash bag that held all my toiletries, the things I hadn't used, the tools of an elegant and fruitful labour. A natural sponge to suck water from, an Evian face spray, my headphones. None of it had mattered in the end. None of it had been important.

When I came out of the shower and walked into the corridor, I saw Connie pushing Harry back to my room in his cot. For a moment, in another world, I thought it was me, that Harry was healthy and awake in his swaddling clothes, that I was carefree and walking tall. Con and I fell into each other's arms.

We sat side-by-side on the bed.

'Have you seen Al?'

'He was in here when I got here. He's gone to see someone, a friend I think.'

'The Imam probably.'

Connie was evasive.

'I don't know what to say, Hon.' She kissed her finger and touched it to his cheek. 'He's so perfect. I'm so sorry.'

I shrugged, biting my lip. There was nothing *to* say. No plans, no comments, no marvelling at him arching his little back or nuzzling for food.

Margaret, with her kind efficiency had gently explained the drugs I would need to take to make the milk die down in my tingling breasts. The leaflets she had given me were spread across the bed. Con picked one up.

'Have they taken his photo for you?'

I nodded. 'And done his tiny footprints and handprints, but... Con?'

She looked at me, beyond worried, distraught on my behalf.

'He doesn't look like other babies, does he?'

She shook her head but didn't speak.

'He doesn't look, well, he doesn't look alive. I can't say it to Al, I don't want to hurt him anymore. But Harry's the wrong colour, the wrong... the wrong texture. In his photo he won't look like an alive baby. He isn't an alive baby.'

I burst into fresh tears, Connie rocked me to and fro like a baby of her own.

It was Farzana who would come to the rescue. Quietly and without fanfare, she would bring her inks and pencils with her from Manchester and sit peacefully in the Chapel of Rest drawing her nephew. Her picture of Harry is beautiful, it captures him and sums him up, it honours and keeps him. We treasure it.

To this day, when I see a winter cloud, heavy and sulphurous with snow, I look at its softly curved edge, tinged purple, and I think of his perfect cheeks.

ALI

My son was gone.

My baby boy, my inheritor, my legacy.

My tomorrow, my today.

My reason for living.

I was suffocating, as though the breaths he should have taken were now inside me, overwhelming me. But my son, my Haroon, I would have breathed for you, I would have bled for you, I would have died for you.

You never gave me the chance though, my son.

You never let me protect you, be there for you, hold your small hand and tell you it was all right because even in a dark sky you can find a moon and in the daylight you can find hope.

Didn't you trust me?

What did you hear in your mother's womb that made you so afraid, so determined not to come into my life?

If I had got out of bed and held your mother, would you have been more confident of me?

I never got the chance to call you beta.

I never got to hear you call me Abbu.

Haroon… you were my every second breath.

They said you left us as soon as you started to be born. Did you hear something on that spiritual plain, did you know how many souls were leaving around you? Did you choose to follow them because men like me had wreaked havoc on your world?

I would have kept you safe, my son, I wouldn't have let them harm you.

Or did you let go in protest, to say to this world enough? Enough death in my God's name? Enough anger and hatred?

No one can hear you now. Only me. Only your mother. Like our hearts beating, we can hear you.

I imagine a voice for you. I imagine how you would grow, from baby to child to infant to teenager to adult. There with you for your triumphs and disasters, your father, to be for you what my father was for me, what his father was for him.

To know it was okay, that you, my son, would bury me when the time came.

So why did you think it was okay to make me bury you?

With what hands can I wash your body, wrap you in a shroud and let the earth fall over you? With what heart can I walk away knowing you are all alone there? With what tears can I wash away the memories that never were?

Haroon… who can I call to look after me in life the way I must look after you in death?

If only I had seen you open your eyes, breath, cry…

You denied me a single breath, my son…

I am sorry… I am sorry for whatever I did that made you think you had to do that.

My heart, my soul, my life… how can I face tomorrow without you?

I watch you lying in your crib, your perfect fingers and toes, your perfect features. You are like a marzipan baby, so lifelike I could mistake you as being real.

But you aren't real.

You denied me that.

And I am sorry.

May my God protect you, and may He allow us to meet again.

I promise I will be as good a Muslim as I can, do my utmost to make sure that I am worthy enough to cross that wire-thin bridge, to see you again. To see you in heaven become the man you refused to be here.

Haroon... my every second breath... how can I live without you?

I ran into Yacein as I was about to leave the hospital.

He put his arms around me and I cried against his shoulder.

'It's okay, Ali, she will be okay,' he said.

'But will I? It's dreadful,' I said.

'Sure you will, you should be glad it wasn't you, you are unharmed,' he said.

I turned on him, pushed him away.

'Unharmed? I may not have bled and given birth, but I am not unharmed!'

'Birth? What do you mean?'

'Honour?'

'I was speaking about Ruby,' he said.

The darkness of my night intensified, like a grip round my chest, squeezing tighter.

'Ruby? What happened?'

'She was in the carriage... the one that blew up in Aldgate... she's here, in the hospital. I came to pray for her. Her parents are on their way; they called me, asked me to come... Why are you so sad if you didn't know?'

'Ruby? Allah...'

'Ali? What happened? Is the baby alright?'

'Yes, Yacein... the baby is perfect...'

'Mabrook, Alhamdulillah, that's good. Then Honour? Is she in a bad way?'

'Yes... so am I... but Haroon... my son... he's okay... but he's in heaven...'

Yacein's eyes filled and he allowed me to grieve again.

'I need to see Ruby,' I said.

We prayed together first and then went to find her room.

Ruby looked like she had been born tonight. There was so much blood, so many bandages, so many machines around her.

I jolted when she spoke, I thought she'd be too ill to move in any way.

'Ali...' she said.

'Hey, Ruby, look at you... what a mess, eh?'

Tears slid down my cheeks.

'I know... I can't remember much... did they say who did it?'

'There's rumours, nothing concrete...'

'Lies, accusations, not rumours,' Yacein said.

'When I got on the carriage... there was a man... he looked at me and smiled, even nodded his head... like he was doing salaam to me... is he okay? He was quite young...'

'We don't know, Ruby, no one knows for sure what happened. They thought it might be a power surge,' said Yacein.

'No, Yacein... I don't think it was...' Ruby said.

'No point worrying, you just get better, okay?' I said.

'Whoever did this... they are not Muslims... remember that...' she said.

The drugs took over and she fell asleep then.

Only her face was visible, the medical equipment acting as some hideous hijab for her.

'I'll stay with Ruby until her parents get here,' Yacein said outside. 'They're on their way from Derby. Go back to your family... I'll find you if anything happens here.'

'Make duaa for my son,' I said.

'Your son is in heaven, Inshallah... we should ask him to make duaa for us,' Yacein said.

How odd that Ruby was still alive, but my unharmed physically perfect son was not.

The new day brought my family, so I left Honour in the care of her sister as I went to meet my own.

'Al, she may be my sister, but I'm here for both of you,' Connie said.

I looked into Connie's face, to catch a reflection of Honour.

As usual there was none, the identical twins as different to me as any two women.

I couldn't reply, just nodded and walked away.

'Sons bury their fathers. This is not how it should be.'

Dad's words cut right through me, reminded me of so much. My grandfather's death, his own fears about me fulfilling my duty.

He held me tightly and let his sorrow show openly.

I had insisted they don't rush down when they heard, I didn't want them to worry. Dad had understood, despite my mother's determination, and they had left after the dawn prayers. Bilal was looking after my younger siblings and his own kids.

I didn't want him here. I didn't want him to feel the irrational jealousy I had of him. Father to two healthy children.

Jamal was red-eyed too. He had stepped up, driven the family from Manchester.

'I'm so sorry, bro,' he said. 'It's fucked up… I'm so so sorry.'

'It's okay, I'm glad you're here.'

'No way I wasn't going to be… the world is fucked up, Ali… have you been outside? They searched our car, when we got close to London. I kicked off, and they made me get out and searched me.'

'Everyone's scared, Jamal, it's not personal.'

'It's just messed up how they assume, you know? How do they fucking know it was Muslims?'

I didn't reply. Half of me agreed, half of me knew it would be. Ruby's words came to me then.

'The people who did this... they weren't Muslims... no matter what they claimed...'

Jamal didn't look convinced.

My mother was bawling, her voice loud and echoing and sad.

I didn't feel as despondent when she held me, just comfort, glad she was here, and glad she was sorry, upset. Her walls of stiff 'properness' had fallen for once, and the real woman was in mourning for her lost grandchild.

I could hear my mother's heart trembling as she kissed my face.

It wasn't just a lost grandchild. It was her first-born son's first-born son.

There was magic in that, something held dear by her and my father.

Farzana didn't wail, but she cried as she held me.

There were no words. There really weren't. For any of us.

I slept for a bit then, lying on the plastic seats in the waiting area, my head in my mother's lap.

I had to be an adult, be a father without a son, so for one last moment I needed to be a son who needed his mother.

Chapter Twenty-Five

HONOUR

It was Margaret who brought the news of the confirmed diagnosis, just as my parents arrived. Exactly as the midwives had suspected, the cause of Harry's death was a one-off. No one used the phrase 'one of those things' but we all knew it was there, lurking sadly round a corner.

As my labour had got underway, Harry's placenta had begun to detach and ceased to bring him the nutrients and the oxygen he needed. His death would have been peaceful, that was the most important thing for Al and me. The medical team had no reason whatsoever to suspect it would happen in a subsequent pregnancy.

Once the diagnosis had been given, the reasons found, we ceased to be patients. We just became some people, waiting in a hospital. My mother, suddenly older, her short auburn hair mottled with a sad grey I hadn't noticed before, sat by my bed with Harry in her arms; she cooed to him just as if he were listening and said her goodbyes alongside her hello.

My father looked so tall in the tiny room, his arms and legs angular with the stress, his face sombre. My dad suggested, when Al came back from wherever he'd been, that he, my mum and Connie, go and catch up in the canteen, leaving Al and me in peace for a while. We didn't resist; we were still in a state of shock, still trying to come to grips with the abrupt changes in our lives.

I realised that we hadn't picked Harry up since finding him swaddled and washed in his cot. We shut the door of our room and got into our little family group on the bed. Softly, we began to remove Harry's blankets, marvelling at his perfect arms, his sweet tummy, his wrinkled legs.

'I don't want to go home and leave him here.'

'It's okay, sweetheart, there's no question of having to go home. We can take as much time as we need, but...'

I knew something painful was coming.

'A Muslim funeral should take place as soon as possible. Sheikh Yasser's going to come by later and talk to you, to us. Okay?'

I was so far beyond arguing, I just squeezed Al's hand as a response. The last twenty-four hours were teaching me more about God than the last ten years had. The people who had God, they had reasons. They had someone to blame, something to rail against and someone to take responsibility for their anguish. The people like me, like my parents, we had science; we understood and we had to accept. Plain and simple.

I burned with one jealousy; Al believed fervently that he would see Harry again, alive and in the bosom of God. I would have loved to be able to take that simple comfort, given anything for it, but I couldn't just invent it, conjure it from a book of spells. I couldn't think about the difference between us. I had to let it go.

The Imam was a kind man and a wise one. He brought a rational response to a situation that I thought would be all the more emotional for his appearance. He was young and British, both of which, given that he was a Sheikh – a man of 'great learning' – and not just an Imam, surprised me.

'Asalama alaikum,' said the young man at the door. Connie had shown him the way in so he must have introduced himself to her. 'My name is Sheikh Yasser, I am the Imam of your husband's mosque.'

'May I?' he asked, indicating that he wanted to pick Harry out of my arms. I looked at Al before nodding to Sheikh Yasser. He lifted Harry to him. 'What a beautiful boy, who has clearly made his parents so proud. A first-born son who has made a family out of two people who were once just a couple,' he whispered to Harry's deaf ears.

Yasser turned to me, his beard incongruous on such an ordinary-looking young man, 'In our religion, it is important to say good things about the dead in order that the angels will listen and say "Aameen".' He said an Arabic prayer quietly over Harry and handed him back to me.

'Within our faith, we believe that everything belongs to Allah and that the life that you and I know, and treasure, is trivial in comparison to the wonders that await us after death. In a mixed marriage, I think this is harder than anything else to understand and to come to terms with.'

I almost gasped out loud. I wanted to scream at Yasser, to shout that, 'Exactly, that's my problem, that's what makes me feel isolated.'

'May we speak alone?' Sheikh Yasser asked me.

Al was up and out of the door in an instant; being years older than Yasser obviously meant nothing in the hierarchy. Connie went to follow him but Al quickly explained she'd have to stay as chaperone.

'Ali is a religious man and a cherished member of our community, something he will find a great comfort now,' Sheikh Yasser began as he sat down in the visitor chair, crossing his long legs.

I gave a hiccoughing sob, my throat smarted.

Yasser continued, 'It is hard not to resent someone with that level of protection, with that surety, when you don't have it, isn't it?

'I want you to know that it's okay to feel like that, that it's normal. Us, the Muslims, we have the Will of Allah, we have answers to all our questions. Time will bring you a similar peace, a philosophy if not a theology.'

His voice was kind, slow.

'Ritual helps with the grieving process; it's why it's there. Of course it honours God and protects the dead but, more so, it comforts the living. You need a marker, a ceremony, to help you move on from this, to begin to heal. The Salat-ul-Janazah, the funeral prayers, are a collective responsibility in our religion; it makes sure the whole community is involved. We'll say a different kind of prayer for Harry because of the circumstances of his birth. It would be nice if you could think of some words about him, you and Ali and your family, that you would like the angels to Aameen. Having a ceremony helps you celebrate Harry and it lets the community start to comfort you and Ali. It works. Have a think about it. And call me if you need someone to talk to.'

I nodded silently.

'You know we could have got to the hospital earlier? If it weren't for the bombers.' I surprised myself, almost as if these weren't my words. They were though, they were words that had struggled up from where they were buried, below my heart, fought their way to the surface and out of my mouth.

'Ali told me.'

'The Muslim bombers.'

'They didn't do what they did in the name of Islam. They did it through free will and specifically against the teachings of the Qur'an.' He smoothed down the front of his linen pyjama suit as if shaking off the blemish of the terrorists.

'I know that, I mean, I understand that they were representing something else, but... doesn't that still make it the Will of Allah? Isn't everything the Will of Allah? Isn't that your answer?'

'The Will of God, and the Peace of God, passes all understanding. That phrase echoes through all the religions, whatever they call their God. Think of it as an allegory, a sophisticated metaphor that means there is a comfort. There is someone with a plan who is taking care of you; whether you want to see that as Mother Nature, the Universe, any of the world's gods. A strong belief helps you to understand that this is not all down to mankind, that there is an order, even to the bad things that happen. And that, one day, He will reveal it to you without you having to take the responsibility or the blame.'

I had no answer to that. It felt almost like one of Al's cop-out answers, it didn't give me what I wanted.

Sheikh Yasser stood up. 'Do you ever look up at the stars and try to contemplate the ends of the universe?'

I nodded. Connie smiled.

'It's not possible. The ordinary mind, even a mind of science like your own, cannot process the scale and the space needed to understand infinity. Yes?'

Connie and I nodded our agreement.

'And yet, you still sleep at night. You can leave the thought behind and move on. But just because you're not thinking about it, that doesn't make the universe any smaller or any easier to grasp. We still have to believe what astrophysicists tell us; we still have to have faith.'

He shook my hand again and left, leaving words of Arabic hanging in the air behind him like a spell.

'He's a nice man,' said Connie. 'At least you can feel you can trust him.'

'They want to bury him tomorrow, Con.'

'I know.'

'He was only born yesterday. I've only had him for a day.'

'It's the same in France, sweetie. In fact, I think it's the same across most of the world. When Laurent's boss died – so suddenly – she was at work on Friday and buried on Monday. It's just the way they do it – in lots of different cultures.'

I put Harry back in the cot, conscious that he'd need to go back to the Chapel of Rest. Connie sat on the bed next to me.

'Bookends,' she said and laid her head against mine.

We were always called 'bookends' when we were children. Now we were less equal, no longer identical. On a see-saw now, I would be outweighed by Connie, Jean-Paul and baby Florence. I would be left dangling, childless, in the air.

'I didn't go straight to the hospital. When I was in labour, I mean.'

Connie snuggled into my shoulder, 'No one does, darling. In France they won't even bloody let you in unless you threaten to give birth in the doorway.'

'I painted my nails.' I spread my fingers out. The tip of my left index finger had a half-moon of white chipped from the red polish. 'And I cleaned out the fridge.'

'To be fair, it probably was time you cleaned out the fridge. You have lived in that flat for three years.' Her smile was weak but I appreciated it. It lit a part of me, breathed a soft life into a muscle of my cheek that had been dormant, too tired to move.

'Margaret, the nice midwife? She said, didn't she, it could have happened at any time but, whenever it did happen, it would have been too quick to do anything about.'

'Remember when I broke my arm?' I stared at the ceiling. 'When I got bucked off that pig of a horse? And I didn't cry.'

'When you fell off, you mean. I didn't see any buck.'

'I thought about it when I was in labour. I thought loads about being a kid.'

'Do you remember how annoyed you were? You stomped back to the yard, leading the poor horse in your good hand and then, when you'd got her in the loose box, you slammed the door with the broken one. Then you howled. I just stood on the muck heap laughing fit to burst.'

It was almost normal, that tiny exchange with my sister. I didn't see her anywhere near as much as I wanted to, needed to, and for the shortest fragment of time we forgot, or at least passed over, the circumstance of our conversation. Seconds later it was over, reality emerged and the guilt that had begun to eat away at me returned.

'I've got to go, Honour.' She hugged me tight. 'Laurent will be at Mum and Dad's with the kids any minute and Florence is going to be going crazy for a breastfeed.'

'Oh my God, you've done that? You've left a breastfed baby to come here, to be with me? Oh, Connie.' Fresh tears where I thought there were none left.

'Don't be daft, it won't ki... she'll be fine. She's six months old, she'll just pick up where she left off – don't you worry.'

'Of course, of course. Go on, get off.' We held each other tightly, then she was gone.

It was the first silence. The first moments of being alone. The devastating space in which to notice that the child I had carried, my constant companion for months, was physically gone. I curled onto my side and went to sleep.

I heard my father's voice in the corridor, booming, out-of-place, almost off-key. As Al's mother slipped, dupatta modest, through the door into my room I caught sight of Al's dad and mine outside the door. Manzoor and David – the two middle parts to Haroon's name, his identity. The two men were embracing each other, sobbing quietly into each other's shoulders, almost strangers, almost family.

'Beti?'

Al's mum was calling me 'daughter'. After her hostility, after everything, she dared to call me daughter. I didn't want to hear about her God, about his punishments and vengeance. I didn't want her to accept me because I had learnt my lesson, because I wouldn't dare to move outside of her precious Qur'an again. I couldn't scream at her to go away, my voice was broken, my fight sunk.

'My poor girl, I'm very sorry for you, Honour.'

It took me a few seconds to notice what was odd. Al's mum was talking in English, accented and fractured, but English. I stayed silent, pressing my tongue hard against the roof of my mouth to keep from crying.

'I have been a stupid old woman. And now I am receiving punishment.' The dupatta across the mouth, the familiar gesture that reminded me it was, really, her.

'May I come in? And sit? May I tell you of my times?'

Her English was sweet, an effort for her, anachronistic and unpractised. She took my lack of movement as permission.

'I came to Britain when I was fourteen. I married Manzoor in Pakistan, he was seventeen and brave for the future.'

I didn't care, I didn't want to listen to her but I didn't know what else to do. The details were hard to pull out of the peculiar English and her habit of moving her fingers in front of her face. I lay back on my pillows, closing my eyes to concentrate and picking the meaning from the sticky words.

She weaved the picture as best she could in her stumbling language; I was quiet and concentrated on her. There was no fight left in me to do anything else. I imagined the fourteen-year-old Noor, how pretty she must have been, how incredibly young and vulnerable. I think back to what mattered to me at fourteen; what luxury I had, what safety.

Noor was deeply in love with her new husband, Manzoor. She'd been afraid to meet him but, when she did, had fallen head over heels for his film star looks and his enthusiasm.

'My husband read paper after paper. Life is richer, safer, better for our children, in England.' She made a quiet clicking sound with her teeth. 'I was afraid and so sad. I had left my family, I was now wife, begum, and I no longer belonged to my Abbu, my beautiful Ammi. I cried for months in secret.'

She looked away from me, a sigh of the past, illustration of her loneliness, escaping her lips. She used her hands to help her fractured English, making the shape of a round dome to show me that she was pregnant when she came to this country.

'I am crying with joy to have a baby, a Punjabi friend to be my company. This baby is part of my family, I can take my family to Britain.'

Her voice dipped and flattened as she described her first sight of Britain; ugly cranes and grey buildings, rain in dank sheets that stuck her hair to her face. She showed me how she ran her hands along hedgerows in the town to try and send the smell of jasmine into the air; she told me how she went to the park day after day in the hope that the little red-legged partridges from her parents' home might appear. There was nothing that she recognised, nothing that she knew.

'I am hating the noises, the smells of Britain. I hold Manzoor tightly and I cry and he says that this is better for us, for the baby.'

I saw what the dupatta is for. She held it below her nose, allowing her to cry elegantly, delicately, and yet continue to speak.

Noor's voice was hypnotic. I could see the small dirty house she and Manzoor moved into, I could feel her longing for her parents' house in Pakistan with its servants and wide halls. She made little shapes with her fingers to show me the spiders that lurked in every grey corner of her house in England and the flat barren bricks that lined the yard. All she had was the baby; she sang to him in Punjabi, songs of flowers and hills and tall trees. I wondered for a moment if that was where Al's love of music came from.

She struggled to describe the seeds she managed to harvest from the fruit and veg she bought at the corner shop. Between my fledgling Punjabi and her rusty English we made a picture of metthi – fenugreek – withering on the kitchen windowsill, the roots rotten in water and aubergines, shaking and shuddering against the cold before collapsing. Noor told me that her own skin was the same, it paled and faded with the winter.

While Manzoor was at work she would sit at home with her loneliness. 'The only thing that grows is my baby, he kicks and rolls, he is Britain and the future inside me,' she said to me, her hand on my arm. 'When the time comes for him to be born, he is everything to me. He is my language, my links to the future and my past, my family. I am fifteen-years-old. I have two words of English; "Cocacola" and "thankyou"'.

She sobbed, her first loud one. I jumped a little. My fingers were screwed tight into the bed sheets. I was afraid for her, for her memory, for the girl she had been before Al was born.

And then I realised; this baby wasn't Al. It can't have been; she was too young.

'It is 1968, men do not watch the babies born. I speak no English, the doctor, the angry nurses, they speak no Punjabi.'

The fifteen-year-old Noor watched her baby born into silence. The nurse rushed him away from her, the doctor spoke relentless English at her that she couldn't understand. Eventually, she told me, someone fetched the eighteen-year-old Manzoor from the corridor and he had to explain to his child-wife that their son was dead.

My hand reached out involuntarily. I squeezed her fingers. She let my hand interlock with hers and gripped it tight.

'We do not talk of Muhammed, the first baby. It was not the way of our culture in those days. I mourned him, Manzoor mourned him, but we were alone in a foreign country. Manzoor washed and buried him, I did not say goodbye to my baby.'

I picked up Harry from his cot, laid him in her arms. She put her face on his and cried.

'When he is buried, this precious baby, will you come to my house, beti, to mourn with us as my daughter? I was too angry and stubborn to meet my grandson before his birth, too much I blame England for everything. I did not put my hand on you and feel him kick. Now to mourn together is all I can do for you, for our family.'

'Yes, Ammi,' I whispered.

ALI

Honour looked so much like a child herself, confined to bed, a white nightgown, like one of those maudlin Victorian dolls. Her cheeks were red, like someone had painted them, but I knew it was from rubbing, wiping away her melancholy.

I thought I would have a new sense of responsibility, someone to watch over and look after. I didn't realise it would be my wife.

I had done my despairing and despondent routine, cried more than enough tears, said enough words that showed weakness. That was over now, I had to step up, be the man, be the husband, be the father.

I couldn't change what had happened. I had to concentrate on the living.

I would give Harry his last rites, but his Heaven was assured. Now it was about my Heaven, my Earth, the lives of those around me.

No one seemed to have the strength to move forward.

My parents had aged overnight. I was looking at them fresh in the glare of the hospital lights. I was ashamed that I had put them through so much, forced my own selfishness on them. They who had given me everything, and what had I done to them?

Crushed their dreams of marriage and children. I couldn't do either properly.

Jamal, with his sad eyes and ghetto clothes, his addiction to his mobile phone. His head was somewhere else, fighting a war and maintaining a reputation. He wouldn't be able to do the duty that was mine by birth.

Honour's parents would give it a try I was sure, but they wouldn't know where to start even.

Faz sat in murmured solicitude, whispering and crying in turns with the rest of my family. She was so fragile, vulnerable, her heart torn between my son and her own children.

And Honour…

She had played her hand, I couldn't ask anything of her. My sole purpose was to make this as easy for her and get away from this hell.

'I don't know what happens, Yasser. Do we do a full janazah?'

Yasser was in his early twenties, with a beard and turban and long white flowing robes, a man who had studied with the best scholars in Damascus, Cairo and Mecca. He was born in London and was what the future of my religion looked like.

'No, when a child doesn't take a breath in this world, we consider him gone to heaven. There are no sins for Haroon to atone for, there is nothing to do a janazah for.'

'So what then? I can't just let him go, I need to do something. My wife… she needs something more too… the family do…'

'I will wash him and wrap him in a shroud.'

'My father… he went to Hajj, years ago. He said he wants part of his Ihram to be used, to wrap the body…'

Is that what it was? A body? It seemed such a grown up word for my marzipan baby, so small and new and unformed.

'Your father should keep the Ihram for himself, Haroon doesn't need the purity of the Hajj garments to wrap him.'

'My father wants to do this. He brought it with him. Can you imagine? The world is literally exploding around him and he remembers to do that?'

'Humanity is capable of bearing so much suffering, brother Ali,' he said.

'I know Yasser... but... right now I feel as though all the people in this hospital, my family, my wife's family, that they won't be able to deal with this.'

'They have the same faith in their God that you do,' he said.

'What about those that don't believe in God?'

'Allah created everyone, and He is responsible for all His creation. Whether His creation believes in Him or not.'

We were seated on the carpet of the prayer room, having just done Zuhr jamaat. I was surprised by the strong turnout for the congregation.

Inshallah.

God Willing.

God's Will.

I harked back to those times when I had abused the free will that I was given.

And the pain I had caused my parents. How many tears did my mother weep at my insistence that I would marry a Godless woman? My father, how many sleepless nights did he have? Was this my payback?

'Yasser, you never, out of everyone, not once... you didn't say anything to me when I was with Honour. Not once did you judge or tell me what I was doing was wrong, would land me in hell.'

'Allah is Judge enough,' Yasser said.

'Isn't it your job to guide us mere mortals when we go wrong though?'

'I am mortal too. I can give you my opinion. But you never asked for it.'

'You know we weren't married when we planned to have a child? Isn't that bad? Do you think that's why this happened? What do you think of me being with her?'

I didn't mean to challenge him, this man who had done so much good and who I was asking to liberate us all from our grief.

'Isn't it better she is with you, in the shadow of Islam, than not? Her children with you will be Muslims. Is that such a bad thing? What's the alternative? Ali, you know all this, why are you turning your mind to all this? I didn't come to lecture you, brother.'

'But it's forbidden. We marry Jews and Christians only. It's in the Qur'an.'

'And is that who you worship? An Allah who punishes his creation in such a way? We have Hell for a reason, the promise is that Muhammad's – *Sallilahu alayhi wasalam* – people will not be made to face their wrong doings except in the grave and on the Day of Judgement. Haroon did not die for your sins.'

'Then why did he die, Yasser?'

'Maybe he will be the one to intercede for you, ask God that his mother and father are granted Jannah on the Day?'

'I'd rather have him with me now,' I said.

'You will have him for eternity, Ali.'

Yes. That was what I believed, wasn't it? Yes, I would have Haroon again. Not the poor lifeless baby, but the son. It was a promise, a hope, a future. I could live out my days on that, that there would be a reunion.

'Pray, Ali, for yourself, your family and your wife. Haroon is safe where he is.'

I hoped so.

Yasser's words sounded so clinical, so by rote, rehearsed. He had probably said them to so many others, men like me who were left empty-handed, desperate for solace.

But there would be no words that could heal the rip in my soul.

So I took what words there were and repeated them to myself, like a mantra.

Haroon is in heaven, Haroon died for a reason, Haroon the intercessor.

But my heart beat to the rhythm of *Haroon, my son, where are you?* Your father is like a king with no kingdom, a night with no stars, a day with no sun.

Existing. Just existing. Empty. Completely empty.

Ruby was deteriorating. She didn't open her eyes when I went to see her, her breathing so shallow she couldn't speak anymore.

I told her I was there, and she nodded her head very slightly.

I leant close to her.

'Forgive me, my sister, for any wrong doings I may have done you intentionally and unintentionally. And in turn I forgive you the same, for any wrong doings I know of and those I don't. I will remember you in my prayers every day. I will be there for your parents, we all will. You have achieved martyrdom, Ruby, Inshallah you are guaranteed heaven. Just like my son. When you see him, tell him that I would have loved him and so would his mother. That either of us would have exchanged our lives for him, that he will remain in my life for as long as I breathe.'

Ruby moaned, as if she was trying to speak, but it sounded like an animal lowing.

'It's okay, I know, it's okay. I understand, and, Ruby, look after him for me… salaam, my sister, until we meet again…'

I felt the urge to kiss her forehead, but in reality I was not her brother so it would not happen.

Ruby moaned again as I was leaving the room.

They said she opened her eyes just once, seconds before she passed away. The angels had come to take her soul, so she opened her eyes to greet them.

Maybe Haroon had come with them, to welcome his aunt into the paradise that awaited them.

The gnostics' hearts with eyes are blest that see what other see-ers see not…

I couldn't protect Honour in London. I didn't have a network, not really. My family, my cousins, the people who had always been there, they were in Manchester. I wanted to take her there, keep her ensconced like women from the olden days kept in the Zananah quarter, behind purdah.

The men out front willing to die before anything was allowed to happen to them. It was the Rajput way.

'After the funeral, is it okay if we go to Manchester? They want three days of mourning...' I said.

Honour surprised me by putting her fingers to my mouth. It seemed odd, we had held each other and held our baby, but her fingers on my mouth... it felt intimate, private. It was the first time we had been like this since...

'Your mother already invited me,' she said.

A fresh pain. 'Maybe that was Haroon's master plan all along?' I said.

Chapter Twenty-Six

HONOUR

Neither of us had gone home to our flat in London. We were afraid of the world outside the hospital, a new world away from anything I thought I knew. I felt like I was crawling through life by holding on to someone each side, a parent, a sibling, an in-law or Al. I couldn't trust myself to stand up alone.

The kindness of people was something else that made me stagger. The gestures that I knew people felt were futile but, for Al and me, they were Harry's life. The gestures were the power he had given our families, their strength, his love.

Yacein came to the hospital and spoke earnestly, privately, to Al. Their department at the Islamic bank had opened a Trust in Harry's name; it would sponsor a cot in the Neonatal Intensive Care Unit, stretching into the future, the bank topping-up the fund on Harry's birthday each year. It gave us a direction in which to steer all the well-wishers, all the grief.

As we'd left the hospital, Margaret, our wonderful nurse, had come to see us. 'I'm so sorry things worked out this way,' she said, taking both my hands in hers. 'What a lovely family you have, and how lucky that they were all close by enough to come and meet Harry. Keep in touch with us so that we know when you have happier news.'

I thought of our families, of their personal and physical journeys to get to us in time, to be there when we needed them.

The Muslim women didn't come to the graveside; it was not their way. It was my mum, Connie and me who walked, in an auburn-haired row, through the wrought-iron gates of the cemetery and along the shingle path to the grave.

We had wondered whether we should bury Harry in London. Al's mother would have loved to have him near her in Manchester and the magic of London had gone for Al and me. London now was somewhere you looked over your shoulder, London was suspicious, London was somewhere where Al would sit alone on the seat of a bus, however crowded it might be, for the foreseeable future. But we trusted Sheikh Yasser and wanted him to officiate as well as being somehow afraid to move Harry too far from the hospital. Al's mum had explained to me how 'proper' mourning took place and with Sheikh Yasser's advice about ritual ringing in my ears, we wanted his words to be the signal for our mourning to begin.

I don't want to think about the bundle of white cloth that Al carried from the car. I don't want to remember how hard it was to stay upright as it went into the ground, how close I felt to being an animal, how near I was to losing the flimsy veneer of humanity.

Al and I kissed my parents and sister goodbye, promising to see them in a few days, trying to pretend they weren't as worn and broken as us.

Jamal drove us to Manchester in silence, even his driving out of character, sedate, respectful. Noor and Manzoor travelled back with Farzana.

I had completely forgotten about Aaliyah and Zain; they were frozen, terrified to speak to me or to their brother, so worried in case they upset us or put a foot wrong. The delicacy of the teenagers made the world seem even more fragile, the brittle ice of coping even more likely to crack.

For three days, I talked of nothing but Harry, pregnancy, birth, labour. I ordered my feelings, laid out in lists my needs and achievements, noted my losses and the gaps left to fill. I listened to other women, especially to Noor. I heard their explanations of things medical, theological, even just superstitious. They prayed, chanted and – most importantly of all – used Harry's name, spoke of him aloud and like a person.

'*Subhaan Allah*' Praise be to God.

'*Alhamdulillah*' Thanks be to God.

'*Allah u Akbar*' God is the greatest.

The chants and murmured offerings were noted with hard dry chick peas. At first it made no sense to me until Farzana explained.

'He doesn't need these prayers, because all babies are born without sin, guaranteed a place in heaven, but it's a ritual. For every prayer that goes out in Harry's name, a chick pea goes in this bowl. We count them afterwards so we can be proud of the achievement in prayer.' She moved closer to me and whispered, 'Actually, Aaliyah's going to count them, every night for three nights. Then she'll feel she has a role. That's what it's all for. So we feel useful, positive.'

My mother-in-law's take on the prayers was different. 'For every chick pea in the bowl, a pearl or a ruby is created in heaven for Harry. And for my Muhammed.'

Farzana had been nervous about my reaction to her boys. She thought they might upset me even more but she was so wrong. Zak was bright and entertaining, his every moment a handful, too naughty to be left alone for a second. Sam was still soft and round, young enough to smell like a baby. I held them both close as often as I could.

Al's parents' house was full of people. Neighbours came to and fro with food – a house in mourning cannot be used for cooking.

Mourners I had never even met before dropped in to tell me how sorry they were, how sad life can be. In the hospital, I had thought that I would never eat again, but the competitive chapattis of Noor's neighbours, the sharp lime smell of seared paneer cheese and the air thick with massala spices reminded me of the simple pleasure of food.

The women were in one room, wailing when the grief made them want to, the men in the other room, silent but for their prayer; the whole house was a vigil to our loss.

At night, Al and I would meet back up and hold each other, discussing the events of the day, wondering how to move forward. The nurses had talked incessantly of 'the next time'; in one breath they would say how beautiful Harry was and then talk about the next pregnancy. We'd found it odd, frightening even, but Noor told me of the seven years that passed before she had been brave enough to have another baby. Seven years that just centred on her grief for Muhammed, a pain that didn't abate until she held her Ali in her arms.

It was in the dark, in bed on the third night after we'd buried Harry, that Al told me about Ruby.

'I thought Ruby would ring. Or send a card. Maybe she has, maybe it's at our flat.' I said.

Al breathed out into the dark, pulled me closer.

'Ruby died.'

'What?'

'She was on the Tube. The one near the bank, Aldgate.'

I started to shake. He tightened his grip on my shoulders, closed his elbows together to hold my arms between our two bodies.

'She died just before the funeral. I couldn't tell you. I'm sorry.'

I was beyond tears.

'Was she? Did you see her?'

'Yes, a few times. She was in the Royal Free. I went with Yacein.'

'I liked Ruby.'

'I liked her too.'

'She was funny.' I thought for a second. 'You've missed her funeral, haven't you?'

'It's okay, this is more important. You're more important.'

'Al?'

'Yes?'

'Do you think this is the Will of Allah? Do you think Ruby is supposed to take care of Harry?'

Just a punching sob in reply.

ALI

I didn't trust anyone else to wash Haroon, to wrap him in a torn piece of my father's Ihram, to dab him with ittar, to bring him to me that day, except for Yasser.

Mum and Farzana stayed at a relative's house. We hadn't been back to the flat, couldn't imagine having lived anywhere but the hospital. Jamal and The Baron had taken the women to collect what we would need from home. Funeral clothes instead of cameras and celebration food.

Honour, Connie and their mother accompanied us to the graveyard. The Gardens of Peace in Ilford.

Salam, Peace, a word from your Lord... my favourite line from Surah Ya'Sin, the section of the Qur'an I would read every Thursday night for my son... the very heart of the book... for the very heart of me...

It didn't rain. I felt it should have, that the universe should have shown how much it empathised with me, displayed its own wretchedness. But it didn't.

Just another father burying his son.

Life and the world moved on.

I had carried Haroon's shrouded body all the way to the cemetery, and now we were here I didn't know if I could let him go. It was the closest he and I had been, the only real role I felt I had in his little life.

7/7 had meant it was difficult to get news around to all our friends, but Yasser had a regular congregation he brought along with him.

When it came to putting Haroon in the ground my hands started shaking. I froze, alone, lost. My father put an arm around me, and The Baron put his hand on my back.

I kneeled on the side of the small grave, and put my son into it, felt his form through the kaffan shroud, as though I was putting him into his cot, wrapped in blankets, ready for sleep.

I stayed like that while Yasser read verses from the Qur'an, some of them chosen by Honour from the translations she had read.

There was silence then, it was time to let my boy go.

But I would not disappoint my son at the one opportunity he gave me to be his father. I dug my fingers into the dry soil saying *Innalillahi wa innalillahilrajiun*. I let the earth fall from my fingers, listened to it make a soft whisper of contact against the cloth around my baby.

I stayed and watched until he was completely covered.

I wanted to run away, hide, not see it happen.

But I couldn't fail Haroon, I had to stay.

Then it was over.

Haroon was a mound of earth.

Haroon was not going to be held anymore.

Haroon was not going to be looked at anymore.

I walked away with a straight back and didn't cry.

That's my father, that's Ali Hussain, and I am proud to call him Dad. He held it together for me today.

That's what I wanted to leave Haroon with.

The drive to Manchester after the funeral was conducted in silence. I sat in the back with Honour, our hands linked, letting her rest her head on my shoulder, stroking her hair as she slept. Jamal didn't say anything, except to ask if we wanted to stop off at a service station at regular intervals.

I had to bite back the urge to make him turn the car around, to go back to the graveyeard, to unbury my son, to hold him just one more time…

After we got to the house in Manchester, Dad asked Jamal to get back in the car and drive us to Southern Cemetery. I didn't question it, I was just too tired. I handed my defeated Honour over to my mother and Farzana.

'Ali, I need you to come with me. I want to show you something.' My father was solemn.

I was in no mood to argue, and followed him, as we walked through graves that started to look more ancient and less well-tended as we progressed.

'There wasn't a Muslim cemetery back then, we just found a grave and buried him,' he said.

My mother had opened up to Honour, sharing a grief so deep even her own daughters didn't know. And now my father was about to do the same with me. I had suffered, I was marked by the same tragedy.

The graves around us had crosses, angels, green statues and markers. Everything looked so unkempt, old, decrepit.

Unloved.

Dad stopped before a tiny grave. There were fresh flowers on it, and incense sticks that had burned out days before.

I read the tombstone.

Muhammed Manzoor Hussain.

There was no date.

'He didn't breathe,' my father said.

Dad coughed, trying to stop himself from breaking down. I put my arms around him, the way he had done to me as I buried my son.

'Promise me… that you'll tend the grave… after… I didn't want any of you children to know. It was not the way, our way. I didn't think any of you could cope, were mature enough. But now…'

'I promise, Abbu,' I said.

We prayed at the grave of a brother I never had, and my father said we should be grateful, that Allah had blessed us thrice in this way.

'Thrice?' I said.

'My father, your grandfather… he lost his wife and first son in the Partition remember?'

'Three generations of Hussain men forced to bury their sons,' I said.

'Dadaji never got to bury his son. He was lost in the turmoil,' Dad said.

I couldn't buy into the blessing then, but later, much later it helped with the healing.

By the time we got back from Southern Cemetery, my parents' neighbours, friends, and all of our relatives – it felt like half of Manchester – had arrived to mourn.

As we got out of the car I was passed from one aunt to the other, from one cousin to the other, all wailing while clinging to me, their sorrow overpowering but touching in a way.

These people who had never seen my son, who had never seen my wedding even, they were so big-hearted they had come to cry for my baby and pray for him.

The three days passed like a dream. We were awake for practically twenty hours a day, praying, greeting, eating.

I had to miss Ruby's funeral so many of my prayers were also for her. By the end of the three days I had passed some invisible line, I had given my son my prayers despite being unable to help him in this life.

Aaliyah counted up how many times we had praised Allah, how many Qur'ans had been read, how many Surah Yaseens. Cousins in Pakistan who I had never met, Bilal's family too, they had all called up and told her how much they had read. It was like Eurovision, the votes being counted across the globe, and then Aaliyah presented the tally to my father.

On the fourth day the local Imam came to the house and said prayers for Haroon, gave out the figures for how much the community had contributed in prayers and then we fed the guests. My eldest cousin Abdul and his wife Fouzia had insisted that they buy and cook everything.

I saw Abdul differently now. I realised he would have been the same age as my brother, they were born at the same time. I wondered what shapes my brother's life would have taken, tried to map them to the cousin who would have been closest to him.

'Why don't you stay some more days?' my mother asked.

'I can't Mum. I need to get away, we need to be alone.'

'I understand. But afterwards, come back. Come back to Manchester, Ali,' she said.

I just kissed her on the cheek and held her to me.

It was tempting, I felt so much a part of these people again. And now Honour was part of them too, my mum making sure she was the first to eat and even making Zain go to the shop and buy quilted toilet roll for her.

But what I was too frightened to feel was any closeness to my wife, and I needed to repair something there. I thought Honour and me were bonded like rock. The last few days made me fear that we were held together by nothing more than whispers of silk.

My mind was reeling with one horrible realisation: she had only married me because of Haroon.

I had no idea where we were headed.

It was like we needed a rest home, or rehab centre. In a way we were in rehab.

And as the days dwindled towards the end of the week I knew only one thing: I couldn't return to our old life.

Haroon had taken Honour and Al with him.

I needed a fresh start, away from the memories that we had made for him, away from the home that didn't feel like my own anymore.

Away from the people that had been ready to welcome him.

Away from Honour and Ali.

Chapter Twenty-Seven

HONOUR

We took a plane straight from Manchester airport down to Kent. Neither of us wanted to see our flat or spend hours on the train. Neither of us thought we remembered enough of the old world to be able to drive. As the plane flew over London, we looked away as if the city wasn't there.

At my parents' house we walked a lot, lay on the beach talking, and sat at the end of the pier wishing for dolphins to swim past. We began to repair. We pretended to be different people as we strolled through the lanes together, the grass head high on the banks. We responded politely to strangers who asked, 'How do you do?' We didn't say, 'We are breaking in half, we are tortured, our world has been destroyed.' We just smiled and kept walking.

Over the course of the warm week, my mother bustling like a hen, my father in turns rude or pointed – back to normal – we started to defrost. For the first time in days there seemed to be a silence in my head, the hammering pain subsiding.

We spent as much time as we could in my old room, the room in which we'd first made love. It seemed the best place, in the summer heat with the curtain billowing gently like a floral sail, to start again.

'It's fucked time up, hasn't it?' I said to Al as we lay under the open window one morning.

'How so?'

'I was pregnant only ten days ago. My stomach was rock hard.'

Instinctively, protectively, Al moved his hand across the soft wastes of my skin, the empty slack that had grown our son.

'And now I don't feel like I know where I am. It's summer, but it's not my summer. Not the one I saw.' I felt better for having put my finger on the moment, identifying my stupor.

We drove back to the beach where we'd sat on the night we first kissed. We sat, staring at the sea, not speaking. Al threw angry stones into the shallow foam at the water's edge.

The cliffs of Cap Gris Nez climbed out of the sea in a grey haze just over twenty miles away at the tip of France. It was a horizon I knew well, one that had watched over me every clear blue day of my childhood.

'Shall we go to France?' I asked Al.

'For the day?'

'To live.'

'No.' He shook his head.

'For a holiday? See Connie and Laurent, the kids?'

'Maybe.' He kissed my ear, blowing gently onto my neck. 'Can I tell you something?'

'Yes.'

'I don't like France.'

I turned to look at him, disbelieving and almost shouting. 'Yes, you do.'

He put his finger on my lips and shook his head. 'No, I don't. You like France. You went there when you were a kid, your sister lives there, your nephew and niece are French. But I don't like France. In fact, I actually hate it. I hate the food, I hate the language and the stupid motorway signs. And, like a massive ignorant racist, I actually hate most of the people.'

I didn't know what to say. His finger was still on my lips, begging my silence.

'And most of all,' he said, 'Do you know what I hate most of all?'

I screwed up my eyes, laughing now.

'I effing hate the way they clap.'

I'd noticed, as I'd started to laugh again over the last week, that the emotions of pain and happiness were very similar. Like when you put your finger under a tap so cold you can't tell if it's burning or freezing for the first few seconds. People are right when they say that the opposite of hate is indifference, not love. And I knew now that the opposite of sorrow is not happiness, but peace.

This was the first laugh where I'd felt that it was definitely funny; that he, Al, was still funny. No tears gathered in the outer corners of my eyes above my smile.

'You want to hear a good story?' I asked him.

'Not about France?'

I shook my head. 'Germany.'

The sea twinkled at us, flashes of reflected sun changing the colour of the dank grey water, lighting it with a Mediterranean masquerade. The seagulls hawked their grating cries above us.

'Down there, round the corner at St Margaret's Bay, the beach I first took you to,' I gestured to my right where the cliff disappeared into the headland. 'There was a wooden tank there in the Second World War. There weren't enough armaments left, or enough metal or something, so the Home Guard built a perfect replica of a tank out of wood and covered it in camouflage and netting just like a real one would be.

'One day, a German plane flew over and dropped a wooden bomb on it.'

He roared with laughter. 'That is so not true. That story has all the hallmarks of The Bar... Your dad made that up.'

'I do know, you know,' I looked at him with hooded eyes, 'That you call my father "The Baron".'

I slipped out of his arms and lay back on the pebbles. 'What's more, so does he.'

We ate a late lunch on the beach. Fish and chips in sodden greasy paper, the batter soft and muted orange, the chips barely evolved from raw potato, warm and wet. The food was disgusting, our fingers pallid with grease. The pebbles dug into our backs as we stared at the sky, each of us imagining shapes from the clouds in silence, privately. We were still and, at last, as calm as the summer sea.

In the warm nights we dozed rather than slept, so that our conversations began to carry through dreams and our whispered words would wake each other up halfway through a sentence. The birds were fighting a war through trills and whoops, battling to be heard and to defend their territory of ripening fruits.

'Do you miss your guitar?'

'I'm not in the mood.'

'I miss your guitar. I miss you singing.'

He rolled over, opening his eyes. We'd got into the habit of talking with our eyes shut, fending out the day. 'I'll sing to you again, I promise. But I don't want to go back and get it, the guitar. I'm not sure I ever want to go back.'

'I'm not due back at work for...' I snorted, a little sadly, 'a year. We don't have to go back.'

He propped himself up on one elbow, his hand lightly on my breastbone, palm flat. 'I'm not talking about a year. I mean forever. I can't go back. I don't want my old life anymore.'

I traced the edge of his chin with my finger. Outside the sun was struggling up through the dewy haze of the morning.

'Like I said, we don't have to do anything.'

'I have to do some things, Honour. I have to move out of the flat, I have to get a proper garden. In fact, I have to leave my job completely and start again.'

I nodded my agreement, curling in beside him, closing my eyes.

'Honour?'

'Uh?'

'Would you have married me if it weren't for Harry?'

ALI

'David and I are going out for the day. Give you both space, hang around the house, use it as your own.'

'You don't have to, it's big enough for us not to see each other for a week,' I said.

'It's not that big really, but it will be good. You won't feel the pressure of being outside.'

'I guess. You don't have to, but thank you.'

She smiled, but not with her eyes. It looked wrong on her, this woman who had not once made me feel uncomfortable in her home or anything but a member of her clan.

'It'll get better, Al, it really will.'

'Very deep,' I said.

'It wasn't meant to be. The future is always difficult to picture, especially now. Just be careful you don't do anything in the darkness that you'll regret in the rays of the rising sun.'

She kissed me on my cheek, and then started to round up The Baron.

We sat watching DVDs for a lot of the day, wrapped in a wool blanket Honour's mother had knitted. It smelt funky, I wondered if the dog had used it, but it was cosy and it was just big enough for me and Honour to snuggle into.

I wondered at the pale yellow colour. The colour a grandmother might use to make a quilt for her yet unborn and unknown-gender grandchild?

We didn't speak much, Honour and I, just two cold hearts warming each other. I felt no desire for her, and that was a shock. There had never been a day, even in our worst fights, when I would have refused to make love to her, or confess how much she spoke to my carnal side.

But since…

There was nothing, just a vacuum of two bodies, two souls. No life. As if Haroon had taken that with him.

I wondered if that was why we had been left alone, a whole day of intimacy in this house might reawaken something.

Did Honour tell her mother about it? Was she afraid too?

I massaged her neck and shoulders, but she seemed to push me away, like it was painful, as if my fingertips stung her skin.

We cooked in silence a little while later, making scrambled eggs and ate them with salmon and tea. Sugary, milky tea. Asian style.

We had a nap, again holding onto each other. I took my shirt off because the room was close, and the sheets were making me sweat. She moved her hands away, unable to touch my bare flesh.

I couldn't sleep, listened to her breathing instead.

The Baron and his wife had been shopping, had driven the 70 miles to London to get a halal lamb leg and other bits of meat. They were going to do a Sunday dinner for us, the whole family, they said.

During dinner The Baron made some revelations of his own.

'Paula and I, well, we've decided we've had enough of this rambling old place,' The Baron said. 'It's a beautiful home and we have been so happy here. But there is a time for everything and now seems to be just perfect. We are downsizing, selling this place.'

Honour sucked in air, and dropped her fork.

'We've been planning it for some time. Moving on for some other young couple, someone who needs it more maybe?' he said.

'You can't, it's my home!' Honour shouted.

Her home? So that was that then. She had given credence to my paranoia, my irrational fears. This was her home, not the flat in London. Here in Kent, where her mother and father were. Where her sea and castle were. Where her memories of Connie were.

No memories of Haroon.

No memories of Ali?

'Honour,' The Baron warned. 'You haven't lived here for a decade at least. It's too much for your mother to look after.'

'And I told you, David, that this was not the time to make these kind of announcements.' Her mother was furious.

'All best out in the open, Paula.' The Baron made it clear this was not an argument.

'I know it will be difficult, darling, and it's such a hard time to hear it but really you'll see it's for the best,' her mother said.

'And then what? What will you do?' Honour said.

'We were thinking of a small cottage around here and then one in France, to be near Connie and our lot over there,' The Baron said.

'It would be lovely to split our time between the two,' said her mother.

'Connie? Oh of course, because Connie needs you, doesn't she? Because Connie has needs... needs like – I don't know – two children?'

'Honour,' I said.

It was the same warning tone her father had used.

'That's fine go ahead, sell my childhood, sell up my life. Abandon me. I'm useless anyway, aren't I? Because I couldn't even give you a baby?'

'You're being ridiculous, darling,' her mother said. 'That is not what it's about, and you know it.'

'All I know is that the one place in this fucking world where I feel something normal, something alive... you two are taking that away from me,' she said. Honour left the table, banging doors until she was back in her bedroom.

'Well, that went well,' said The Baron.

That night Honour lay with her back to me.

'I want this house,' she said.

'We can't afford it,' I said.

'If we sell up... you said you wanted to leave the flat, leave your old life. We could then. I'm sure my parents would be kind to us, give me my share of the inheritance or something.'

'Why would they? You have a husband now.'

'It doesn't matter, we'll do it somehow. I can't lose this house as well. I will go mad, Al.'

We lay with our backs connected at only one point of our spines. I wondered if that was the bone that if lost would mean we couldn't walk ever again.

'I think I just need to leave the flat. We can't afford for me not to work. And the charity jobs I was thinking of... well, they would be in London too. There's no way we can do this.'

'I'm not going to let anyone else live in this house,' she said.

'We can't, Hon, I would love to but it's not practical,' I said.

'I didn't say you have to live here with me,' she said.

I didn't reply, just eased myself away from her, the jointed spines uncoiled.

Would I fall over?

We lay in silence, our breathing that of people who were awake. Hers became heavier, the familiar sign that she was dozing, then it was back to awake.

'There's nothing you could have done,' she said. 'I was fine. I wasn't in pain.'

'I can't help it. I'm obsessing over everything. The trips around the country? The stress of the wedding? Any of it?'

'No, Al, we didn't do this,' she said.

'How do we get past it? I'm scared for us, Hon.'

She didn't move closer though and eventually sleep took hold of me.

I left Honour in Kent.

There was no other way.

Trying to open the door to the flat in London was another frozen moment. I stood there for ages, thinking what would happen, how I would react. The last time we had been here there was Honour in labour and 7/7 on the TV.

Ruby and Haroon had been alive.

I eventually turned the key and walked in, switching on the lights as I did so.

There was an odd smell in the rooms, musty and cold.

I put-down my suitcases then crawled into the bed that I had once shared with my wife and son.

Now it was just me, alone. I would deal with the practicalities in the morning, but tonight I wanted to pretend that things were as they had always been.

The office was muted when I went in, everyone busy suddenly, the usual banter dead.

Yacein hugged me the Islamic way, three times, twice to the right shoulder and once to the left. It reminded me of the men who had hugged me like that in Manchester, during the days of Harry's funeral. Yacein led me into one of the meeting rooms and ordered drinks.

'It's no use, brother Yacein,' I said. 'This world… just walking in through those doors, the metal detectors, the interrogation by security. It brought it all home to me… and the whole set up…'

'I understand, and if I'm honest I have felt the same many times. Maybe you need some more time? It's only been, well, barely a month. There's no rush.'

'No, Yacein, there's no point, man. I've done nothing these past few weeks except think. Think and pray.'

He sighed.

'I do understand, Ali,' he said.

Drinks came and we indulged in black coffee and Turkish delight. It reminded us of a boys' weekend we had had in Istanbul a few years back. Nothing dodgy just architecture, food and laughs, an Islamic version of a lads' holiday. Before all this.

Ruby had made a big fuss about none of the office women being asked to go, so they had gone off to Sharm El Sheikh for a girly weekend and sent us pictures of themselves in burkhinis in their hotel swimming pool.

'How is Honour?'

'In Kent,' I said.

Nothing else was needed to be said. She was my wife but she wasn't with me, she was somewhere else. Yacein didn't pry because he wasn't built to.

'So what will you do? Why don't you take a sabbatical? Six months, a year even? I will fill your job and you can come back when you are ready.'

'Shukran, my brother, but seriously I will never be ready. Not after this. What we do, deal with money, make money, lose money. It's so… please don't be offended, but it's so empty and pointless.'

'You used to pride yourself on developing those sort of products,' Yacein said.

'I know. But I've lost the spirit, the desire. I don't give a, well, you know what I mean.'

He nodded, drank and then looked at me intensely.

'I am going to make a suggestion... wait, let me finish... you don't speak till I stop speaking?'

'You sound like a dictator, typical North African,' I said, but gave him my full attention.

'For a while now our backers, the board, they have wanted us to give something back. They have set up a fund, where the zakat percentage of our bank's profits go. They want it spent on inter-faith projects, helping the poor. They also have a sadqah fund that people give to.'

'Brother Yacein... Me?'

'Why do you think I'm telling you, I don't waste my time. They need someone they trust... no, someone I trust, to run it.'

'And I get to choose the projects?'

'Yes,' he said.

'So if I want to give money to One Voice I could?'

'One Voice?'

'They are a group in Tel Aviv, bringing Palestinians and Israelis together, dialogue and two states.'

He shrugged his hands, as you wish.

'And if I want to give to Christian Aid, help them with their projects?'

'As long as it doesn't break bank policy, then everything is okay. I trust you, Ali.'

The alternatives in my life went through my mind. Unemployed, alone, despairing, watching daytime TV. That couldn't end well.

Or helping people, like genuinely making a difference. Imagine waking up and doing that every day?

'Okay, I'll do it.'

He nodded his head; there was no other outcome, he knew.

'You also can do this from home if you wish… You don't have to be in London,' he said.

His words were careful, loaded.

'Thanks. But for now, I think I want to be here. Just for a while.'

'Keeping Haroon close?'

'Yes,' I said.

'You know he receives your prayers and blessing no matter where you are?' Yacein said.

I coughed, embarrassed, not wanting to pursue this.

'So what odd acronym have they given this fund then?' I said.

Yacein smiled, but there was some wistfulness in his eyes.

'They let me choose the name. It is the Ruby Fund,' he said.

There was never any question after that whether or not I would take the job. I knew I could never recover if I stayed in the flat in Pimlico, suffused with memories of a life with Honour, a life that for the last three years had been about starting a family. Remembered moments floored me at the oddest times like concealed assassins. I stayed there for just that one night, and found myself somewhere else to live the very next day.

In the early evening, after praying Asr in the East London Mosque, I would go to see Haroon. Sometimes at the grave I would find flowers left by someone else, and I would know Honour had been to London. I only felt a bit sad she hadn't let me know and met up with me.

She didn't mention anything when I went to Kent at the weekends either.

It was what it was.

I sat and stared at the boxes, the plastic bin liners, stocked up neatly in the Pimlico flat. I couldn't let them go, but I had to.

Honour sounded tired when I called her, as though she had just woken up.

'Sorry, I didn't mean to disturb you,' I said.

Since when did that become necessary? Apologies for interrupting her life?

'It's fine, I was just with my mother. Are you not coming home?'

Home. She had made her choice then. That's where she was settling, where she felt safe. I felt sick, my throat drying as I spoke, as every part of me ached for her. Just hearing her voice, imagining where she was standing, what she was wearing, inhabiting a space I wanted to be part of.

'No,' I said. 'I'm going to sort out some stuff. I was thinking of… Harry's things. The baby things.'

I heard her intake of breath, sharp, short.

'They're just lying here, I think we need to decide what to do with them.'

'No, you're right, I've been wondering what happened to everything. And I think I'd like them to go to a children's charity. I hope you're okay with that?'

'Of course, whatever you want.'

'Thank you. Why don't you come home afterwards? We can still spend some of the weekend together?'

It would take me an hour to make the drop at a charity shop, driving to Honour afterwards would be natural. This was another goodbye. We should be together.

'I think it might take a while to sort everything. I have some work to do too.'

Once she would have convinced me that no it wouldn't take long, that they had the internet in Kent, I could work there. Instead she accepted my decision. We both knew there was no excuse to be apart, yet both stayed silent.

'Okay, well I'll see you next week then?'

'It's a fundraiser dinner next week,' I said. 'You could come down if you wanted?'

'Maybe. I'll think about it, let you know later in the week?'

'Yes, sure.'

There was static and silence, Honour's breathing in my ear. It felt intimate.

'Do you want to keep anything?' I said.

'No. He didn't use any of it, did he?'

'I suppose. Okay, I'll get it sorted. I love you.'

'Yes,' she said, and then ended the call.

It was weeks before I saw her again.

'Ali, where is my daughter?'

'Dad, she's – erm – in her house, I suppose? Has Faz not been around for a while then? Or has Aaliyah runaway?'

We were on the phone. I stayed in London as much as I could, hadn't even visited Honour for two weekends now.

It was significant, the first time we had been apart for longer than a week since…

She didn't ask me why I wouldn't be with her, and I gave her a flimsy excuse, said I had too much work on.

'Not Farzana... not Aaliyah… my other daughter,' he said.

'Dad…'

'You brought her into my life, Ali. You know all that time you fought for her, when you stood by her, when you married her… you made me so proud, beta,' he said.

'Dad, please… look, I'm tired,' I said.

'You made her our daughter, and now what? When did you last see her?'

'I don't know. Not that long ago… a week… maybe two… I can't be near her without thinking of Haroon… I wonder if that's

358

why it happened, because of how we lived our lives. How can I go on with her, Dad?'

'How can you go on without her, Ali? This is wrong. Do you hear me? She is your wife, she is the mother of your child. I did not raise you to run away from your responsibilities.'

I sighed into the phone.

'*Main tak gaya, Abbu,*' I said.

'We all get tired, but we get up and carry on. When my father came to Pakistan he had lost everything. Imagine if he had behaved like you, just given up. But he didn't. He remarried, he had other children. You don't stop living because people you love have,' he said.

Now I felt small, useless, yep, selfish again. I had been through something, yes, but it wasn't the end.

'Our family, we are very resilient,' Dad said. 'You, my son, are strong, I know because you are just like me, just like your grandfather. We have hearts of steel now. When I came to England, I insisted your mother come with me. I didn't want to let her be alone. You do the same. Bring my daughter home, Ali.'

'Dad…'

'Bas… I've said it. You are not welcome in this house until you bring my daughter with you,' he said and disconnected the line.

The Pimlico flat would never feel like home again, no matter how much time I spent away from it. There was no point keeping it, so I put it on the market, pricing it just right, and in those heady times it had sold within hours.

My final visit was to make sure there were no traces left of 'Us'. I had given Haroon's baby things away like Honour had asked me to.

With Honour's things packed off to Kent it seemed even more barren. The closets that she rammed with her junk, bits of clothes in every corner, shoes that tripped you up at night, all of it was gone and the rooms looked huge, cavernous. I missed her then, like an ache inside me.

Only a few last bits of my stuff remained, and I packed those away to take with me.

I did a last tour, walked through every room, fingering the baby-proofing, the furniture that would stay here. I hoped it would bring the couple moving in as much happiness as Honour and myself had experienced here.

And prayed they would never feel the sorrow.

I closed the door behind me, dropped the keys through the solicitor's letterbox.

I sat in my car for a while, and I felt the loss acutely again. I caught sight of the rose bush on my backseat.

I had one last stop to make.

There were flowers on the grave that weren't from me again. Honour, another trip she hadn't told me about. I shook my head.

'Your mother, hey, Harry?'

I planted the rose bush, packed the earth tightly around it.

'They say the flowers will pray for you as they grow, Harry, not that you need it, hey? You're probably lapping it up in heaven right now. Maybe you can toss your old man some of the prayers, innit?'

I patted the ground and made it as flat as possible.

'Daddy is going away now, Haroon. I probably won't be able to visit you all the time, so I'm hoping the roses keep you company. If you have time, you know to get away from the houris in heaven.

But you'll always be my every second breath, Haroon. I take you with me, so don't worry, Daddy is always there for you.'

I kissed the marble tombstone, the one that had his name in gold, just like my brother's.

No dates. Just like my brother's.

I looked back once, just hoping.

But there was no little boy ghost waving at me.

I texted Jamal to say I had left London, was on my way now, to let my parents know.

The motorway wasn't too full when I eventually saw the signs. I looked at the ones telling me about the M1 and the M25, the roads that led me to a father and mother who had changed the measure of their relationship with me. We were equals now, almost. They still got final say, but it was habit for them to follow my lead, get behind my opinions. Their prodigal eldest son had come home in more ways than one.

I peeled off into the left hand lane, 'Dartford Crossing and The South East', and let the M1 go to the north without me.

I put my foot down on the accelerator as I thought of my family, and I headed back home.

Chapter Twenty-Eight

HONOUR

Two months or so after Harry's birth, I was desperate to go back to work. The hours just rolled by around me, clicking through the days of summer relentlessly. When I counted in my diary how many lifetimes had gone by in this new collapsed timeframe that I lived in, I found that only 67 days had passed. I needed some recognisable structure to the pattern of my day but London was a problem.

The public transport system of Kent, although geographically close to the capital city, ratchets through an archaic route of country towns and seaside villages, leafy and lovely but time-consuming, as it collects commuters who may as well have walked to work.

I braved it one day and walked through the last of summer in Soho to my old office. Bright young things with wasp waists and white teeth, designers and runners and shop assistants and waiters, everyone groomed, neat, presenting the best of themselves to the world. It wasn't me anymore. At my desk, I met the lovely girl who'd got my job to cover my maternity leave, her face a giveaway pink that told me she knew where my baby was. The job was hers until I was due to come back after my maternity leave.

Neil called out to me from the back of the office. 'Look who it is! Wait there, gorgeous, while I get my coat.'

He grabbed his chi-chi jacket and, kissing me hard on each cheek, hustled me back through the door.

'Pub, sweetheart. You look like you need a drink. Six drinks.'

We tumbled into Ronnie Scott's. Neil threw me onto the nearest chair and gestured wildly at the barman, blowing him a kiss when he nodded that he'd understood Neil's frantic waving, translated it into 'a bottle of Frascati and two, goldfish-bowl, glasses.'

'Where, my living angel, have you been? You look like you've been having your hair cut by Edward Scissorhands.'

I laughed and it made the skin of my face feel papery tight. 'I've been having my hair cut in Kent.'

'Kent?' Neil made a face, 'I don't know it. Is it south of The River?'

Neil and the others in my office had been wonderful after Harry's death. They had raised funds for the NICU cot and sent beautiful, Soho-sophisticated, flowers to my parents' house. The flowers sat, incongruous, on my parents' kitchen windowsill, the vase slightly off-centre where it was resting on a broken tile. I hadn't felt ignored or abandoned by the office for one second, their emails with newsy banter still arrived and Neil's obscene texts about his love life still chirruped into my inbox, sometimes making me laugh – and sometimes making me shudder – but never letting me feel alone.

'Are you still at your parents?' Neil asked. 'Where's the glorious Ali Baba? How can he tolerate your father?'

Neil had only met my father once, after a work do. On the way back to the hotel, but still mercilessly close to our office where the staff were outside smoking and worse, my gin-sodden father asked me loudly if 'that short fellow is a ruddy shirt lifter?' I never found out from Neil whether it was 'short' that offended him or my father's ingrained homophobia – Army issue circa 1965.

'Al's moving away from me, Neil. I can feel it. He says he isn't but he is. And I don't help.'

'Well, don't fucking let him, sweetheart. Go and get your man back, whatever it takes. Where is he? Is he in Manchester, lost on Canal Street? Does he need a guide?'

'He's in East London.'

'Jesus Christ, as if the man hasn't suffered enough.'

'Fuck off, Neil,' I smiled. I felt like Honour Edwards, Senior Creative Designer, again. We'd finished the bottle, Neil signalled for another.

'Are you going to drink until you pass out on the floor of my sitting room?' Neil asked me.

'Yes, I promise.' I tied my hair back with a scrunchie as if it would help me drink more earnestly to be properly prepared.

'Good girl. And while you're unconscious, I'm going to have telephone sex with the divine Ali Baba when he rings your mobile.'

'Deal,' I said and clinked glasses with him, actually, really, truly laughing.

I was as good as my word. Whether Neil kept his or not, I didn't like to ask.

When I woke up, my face was stuck to the leather cushion of Neil's sofa, my hair matted at the ends with a horrible suspicion of vomit.

'Rough as a badger's arse?' He put a cup of tea down beside me. I nodded.

'I'm proud, sweetie, I must say I'm proud. I haven't seen you do that for years. Drinking, check. Turned down the Columbian Marching Powder, check. Out-danced anyone in the club who didn't, check. Wailed, check. Wept, check. Gnashed teeth, check. Sick on my bathroom floor, check. You're a lady.'

'What am I going to do, Neil?' My eyes hurt, my throat was sore and I could feel the blisters on my heels where the blanket

Neil had thrown over me was touching them. 'I just don't know what to do.'

'First you can apologise to the nice lady on the reception desk at the Groucho. Phone and tell her that you've finally remembered you didn't bring a coat after all.'

'Oh, God.'

'And then you can wash your hair, fuck off back home, and get started on some freelance work for me.'

'What?'

'You heard. Then I can keep the new girl, she's a thousand times better than you ever were, and so much prettier, and you can tick over until the gorgeous adorable Ali Baba gets you up the stick again. And while you're at it, Honour...'

'Yes?' I said through my state of awed shock.

'Give him one from me.'

The kitchen was full of the smells of baking when I got back. My mother was carefully pasting a sheet of greaseproof paper with smears of choux pastry that would puff up into buns shaped like teardrops.

'Good time?' she asked.

I smiled, it was the same tone she had used when Connie and I were teenagers, when we crawled in dishevelled or a day late.

'Is Al coming home tonight?' she asked.

'No, Mum.' There was a petulant prickle to my voice. 'Al doesn't live here remember? He lives in a hovel in Mile End where he beats himself with hessian sacking and eats frogs.'

It was as if I hadn't spoken at all.

'I expect he'll come on Friday. I'll do something nice for tea.'

'Marriage guidance buns? Anti-divorce cake? That's about all that's going to save us. Anyway, on a lighter note...' I poked her in the side with my finger, her apron string giving me a sudden vision of 'home'. 'Neil's given me some freelance work. A lot of freelance work, actually. I'm a human again. I have a purpose.'

My mother slid the kettle across the Aga top onto the hot plate, almost immediately, it began to steam.

'Come and sit down with me, I made biscuits.'

'Chocolate?'

'Are there any other sort?'

We took our tea and sat down at the long kitchen table. Close up, its grain was stippled with marks, gouges and pinpricks from mine and Connie's cutlery, and from countless children before us.

'Going back to work will do you the world of good,' my mum said. 'Give you an identity again.'

I sighed hard. 'As ever, Mum, that is – exactly – what's missing. When I see women in the street, or start talking to friends with babies, they don't want me to say, "Oh, yes, my little boy was born. But then he died." It's like it's catching, the gloom, like you'll infect their baby, their life.'

It hadn't taken long to realise that the childless mother is like the single magpie that people spit at or salute; antipathy or deference but no social embrace. The people Al and I had met at the ante-natal classes had been kind; they had all responded to our loss with cards or donations, but after that they had melted off, embarrassed at their own good fortune.

My mum let me speak. A torrent began, a flow I couldn't stop.

'And Al, he doesn't understand. We've come out of this as different people. Having Harry has added to my life. I wouldn't not have had him. He was mine and I grew him and I am more of a person for what I had of him.

'I think all Al feels is loss; that Harry has taken everything, not added to him in any way.' My fingers were scalding round my teacup, I pressed them harder against the china. 'And he just keeps saying to trust him. "Trust me, trust me, I have to do this", well, I don't want to trust him. I don't care what he's doing. Last night I went out and I wasn't someone's wife and I wasn't half a bloody Muslim and I drank and I swore and, and, I was sick on Neil's floor.' My mum and I both laughed.

'Oh, my beautiful girl.' My mum put her hand on mine. 'I know you're fed up with hearing it but it really is all about time. I'm sure you had a lovely evening with Neil and back in London and all of that, but at night? In the dark or when the chips are down? Neil won't be there then.'

'No, he'll be out on the pull, or snorting coke in a bog somewhere. He'll be having a good time though.' I smiled weakly.

'Exactly, but Al? Al will be there. Just give him time. He'll come good. I remember when you first brought him here; he was like a little foreigner. I couldn't understand it at the time, how he could be British and be that, well, that different. And he was so frightened of everything, like a little lamb ready for slaughter. And do you know, now, what's the only thing that hasn't changed? The expression on his face when he looks at you.' She pushed my hands back across the table and looked me square in the eyes. 'I think you forget, darling, that once upon a time he decided to give up a place in heaven to be with you. He chose a few fleeting years on this Earth with you over an eternity without. That hasn't changed. Just give him time to settle his demons.'

We both became aware of the acrid smoke from the Aga at the same time. If my parents had had anything as new-fangled as a smoke alarm it would have been screaming at us.

'Bugger!' My mother pulled the blackened choux pastries from the oven.

'That's the marriage guidance buns fucked then, Mum.'

367

I went to my room. I thought about lying on the bed and crying, more out of habit than anything else. Instead I pulled the sheets of paper from the file I'd brought home and started to dissect the brief. I started jotting notes onto post-its, thoughts of typesets, fonts, a reminder to ask my dad to get my old drawing board out of the barn and, while I thought of it, to give me his accountant's number so I could register myself as a business. I was lost in a reverie of shining office block dreams, fantasies of a huge staff, all working together to eradicate the Comic Sans font and make the world a fantastically graphically designed place, every restaurant menu a triumph, every greengrocer's apostrophe at home.

Downstairs my mother squealed like something from an Agatha Christie murder, the noise vibrating up through the gaps in the floorboards. I could hear my father shouting but couldn't discern his mood or catch any words.

I threw the papers down on the bed and ran down the stairs in case I missed some form of event.

Al stood by the kitchen door. His face was white, his chest heaving. He looked like a madman.

Both of my parents were focussed on him, my mother flapping and my father booming instructions and advice. As they peeled away, leaving my view of him clear, I saw his face. The fierce eyebrows, the wide forehead, the symmetrical features that made him so beautiful were still there but his mouth was twisted in an effort not to faint, his skin pallid. He was trying not to look directly ahead or at his own body, doing anything to avoid the bundle squashed against his jumper, his gaze fixed in panic a few inches left of centre. I looked down and realised what all the fuss was about.

In his arms, pressed nuzzling against his chest, Al held a puppy, its tiny black nose poking out between his wide strong fingers, its eyes like beads, its fur velvet.

'He's all I can give you. For now.'

ALI

Kent was the safest place for Honour and I knew, from the moment she said it, that we would end up buying her parent's house.

I couldn't refuse her anything. Even a dog.

There was a time when we seemed to be living two separate lives. I was working and living in London all week, then driving to Kent at the weekends, trying to reconnect with my wife, trying to fan the embers of what lay between us. In odd moments on the Tube, or walking through London's parks, or tending my son's grave, words like separation and divorce started to emerge like spectres. I put them away from my mind as quickly as they had come, giving them a conscious form would mean they became a possibility.

I had spent years claiming Honour from the world, the outside world, to make her mine because she pulsed through me like life. Then what was I doing now? Pushing my life over a precipice, watching as she fell and shattered?

The first weekend I didn't go to her was the worst. I got my keys, got ready to go. Then stopped. I went to my front door so many times; all the while I sat on my sofa, watching mindless TV or reading, I could hear the hours passing around me.

Just go and see her.

All weekend I was waiting for something – which was stupid, because I was waiting for myself to go and be with Honour.

Or maybe I was waiting for her? I texted her, called her. Told her there was too much on at work, we chatted for hours. Desperate to keep that connection? Maybe she knew this was wrong too? But she didn't say.

The second weekend was easier. It became ten days of being apart. It sounds such a small number when it's said, just ten days. Until you break it down. How many heartbeats did that entail, how many times did I breathe petrified that I was breathing without her? It was too long.

It was after my father made me wake up to myself that I realised she didn't have the strength to heal us by herself, that if we were going to make it I would have to be the one to make things work.

Honour had done her bit, she had wrenched a part of us from her body and let it go. I couldn't ask her for anything else. It was my turn now, and it was time for grand gestures. I had to give her something that would go some way to plugging that void in her. In us.

The dog was in a basket downstairs, and I was wrapped around Honour.

'I've given notice on my flat in Mile End,' I said. 'My lease ends next month.'

'Is the Pimlico one…?'

'Yep, all done.'

'What about Yacein and the bank?'

'I can work from home four days a week, only have to be in the office one day,' I said.

'Will you be able to cope? Stuck with me four days a week? My father? My dog?'

I kissed the back of her neck, and pulled her closer to me.

'I will have an office in one part of the house, and so will you. The dog will have a kennel. And in the opposite side of the house I am going to have a prayer room. The rest we can fill with your junk and our kids.'

'Kids?'

She turned around to face me. We hadn't lain like this in a long time, our noses touching, our mouths breathing onto each other as we spoke. My hands found her body, and I started to touch her like I used to.

She put her lips to mine, and I responded.

It all pales before her who succours my soul.

Chapter Twenty-Nine

HONOUR

It was around the six month mark that I started to fill the Harry-shaped holes that I found in every single day. Perhaps it was passing the milestone of Christmas, or maybe just the tumult of running a business and making plans for our new home. Neil had passed over one huge client account to me; having worked for him for so long, I knew this was the result of him sleeping with the client and things not running smoothly, towards true love. His habit of seeking pastures new before he'd fully seen out the possibilities of the old was working in my favour and I was struggling to keep up with the work.

I'd persuaded my parents to turn the old music room into a makeshift studio. It had had nothing in it but a dusty piano, haunted by the fleeting attention of two little red-headed girls, bookends on the red leather piano stool, never moving on from 'Chopsticks'. A few stacks of sheet music, brittle with the dust of jumble sales completed the faux-Dickensian picture of home-spun entertainment and civilised pastimes. It made an ideal studio, the mullioned window panes, cracked in parts, some with fragments of the Victorian glass missing, faced directly south, the sun streaming to each spidery parquet corner.

My dad's study was at the other end of the house, beyond a series of doors that led from room to room without corridors. I walked through the lounge, ducking my head in the doorway, looking down at my dad's tea so as not to spill it. My own tea cup was in my other hand.

The beamed ceiling of the sitting room was the focal point of the house. The cracks and fissures of the wood, the smoke damage from centuries of fires in the inglenook, the clefts and splits, all intricate parts of the house's history. Here and there were the copper edges of pennies or the tarnished silver sides of five pence pieces. Every year, my father would pick Connie and me up, resting us, one at a time, against his shoulder so that we could press a coin into a crack in the wood. We thought this was a magical ritual, invented to bring us luck, until years later when he explained that it was a builders' trick as old as time. If the house's ancient frame moved more than a fraction of a millimetre, the coins would drop out.

Al and I had looked at other places in the area once we'd decided we really would stay. Some were as big as my parents' house, a few with more land, one even had a swimming pool. But they had all been finished, a palour of hotel-beige carried through into every room, a homogeny of leather furnishings and chrome radiators all but eclipsing their oak beams and sloping floors. My parents' house was the only one we found that ticked every box, in need of renovation and with a future not yet prescribed but rooted in a past that gave it gravitas, a house we could make into our very own home.

I knocked on the door of the study with the back of my hand and the tea splashed slightly onto the tiled floor; I pushed the door open.

My father was supposed to be packing away his stack of papers, books and newspapers, trying to cram four decades of detritus into cardboard boxes, leaving behind for the skip what my mother called 'the Rammel'.

'Bloody hell, darling,' he said. 'If I'd known your bloody mother was going to make me do this myself, I'd have chosen to die in the house.' He took the tea from me and peered at it, trying to find fault with its colour.

'You haven't made much of a start, have you?' I said. I picked up a yellowed fragment of newspaper from his desk, two girls had been highlighted in the black and white photograph, their faces ringed round with felt-tipped pen. 'Our one-mile swimming badge. What were we, eight? Maybe nine?'

My dad shrugged, detail being something his wife had remembered for him for the last forty years.

'The kid you've ringed, there.' I pointed at the row of children, proud gapped-tooth-smiles, holding their swimming badges against their costumes. 'That isn't even me. It's not that hard, Dad, we are identical twins. It's like one of those intelligence tests where you have to find the shape that matches the first one. You only had to find the second kid that looks exactly like Connie, not some vaguely ginger one in the corner.'

My dad peered at the cutting then shook his head. 'Bugger this tea, I've had enough. Let's see what there is in the drawer.' He reached into the bottom of his desk and pulled out a half-empty bottle of whiskey. 'Join me?' He gestured at my mug.

I took our cups and poured them into the already-dead pot plant in the corner. I gave them a little shake before holding them out for the whiskey.

He slid down against one of the bookcases, sitting on the floor with his legs out in front of him. He patted the carpet beside him. 'This is a rum old turnout, isn't it?' He clinked his tea mug against mine and I drank, feeling the whiskey burn the back of my throat.

'Drinking whiskey on the study floor with your daughter?'

'Selling my house to a rather charming young couple who I am incredibly proud to call my own.' More toasting, the chime of the china a cue to drink again.

'But who you wish had bought it with contents.'

'Jesus Christ, yes. Then you could have just torched the lot, I'd be none the wiser. Look at all this stuff.' His hand landed on a pile of ochred papers, corners tired and curled. 'These are my parents' death certificates, and birth ones. It's all here, all the family history. Very strange stuff, things I haven't looked at for forty years. Since we moved in.'

I browsed through some of the papers, blowing dust from the worst ones.

'We didn't know we were having two of you, you know.' My dad held a little stack of pink-edged cards, gawdy with the 1970's, glittered and musty.

I opened the first one. 'To David and Paula, congratulations on the birth of your twin girls, with love, Mummy and Daddy.'

'Can I keep these?' I asked.

'Of course, they're yours really I suppose. And Con's. We only found out there were two of you just an hour or two before you were born. Some sharp-eyed midwife poked around and found an extra elbow or some such; no one had scans then, or not anyone we knew. Bit of a shocker, all in all. You have to get on with it, don't you? We none of us get what we expect in this life.' He pursed his lips, giving me a thoughtful look. 'Took us a long old while to find each other again, your mum and me, after something that big.'

He poured another whiskey in each of our cups.

'What's with the concerned father routine? It's making me feel weird and that's Mum's job,' I said, smiling to let him off the hook. 'You don't have to worry about us, Al and me. It's a long haul, but we'll get there. Many rivers to cross and all that.' The whiskey was tightening a band across my forehead. 'We've got something else to think about now. Moving on and everything, it makes it feel like we can think about us again and not just not having Harry.' I looked around me. 'This place is going to take some renovating. I'm sure once we start cleaning it, it'll just fall apart. It's going to cost a fortune but it'll be worth it.'

My dad gargled for a second with his drink. 'Interesting, the money thing. I mean your move; Al becoming the country squire. Where would you have gone without the money? You can't glide from class to class, culture to culture, without money. Whoever or wherever you are. A universal truth.'

I looked across the rows of leather-bound books on the shelves in front of me. There was a tiny plaster bust of Beethoven on the floor, I remembered it from when Connie and I had run into this room once, slamming the door. The bust fell from its shelf, its nose and ear forever chipped. After that we'd been banned from the study, at least twenty years ago. It felt strange to be sitting in here now, with permission and my father's single malt.

'There are no other Asians in this village,' my dad continued. 'Come to that, there's no one from Manchester, not that I can think of. It's going to be odd for him. He's made a lot of sacrifices on your behalf. Done a lot of growing up.'

'Both sides, Dad. Not just him.'

'Not just him at all, but when he first came here...' He topped our mugs up. The whiskey was definitely taking hold. 'He was like your little pet.'

'Dad!'

'It's true, Mum and I were stunned. All those big oafy public school types; and then the little northern boy, scared of his own shadow. He held his own though, more to him than I ever thought. Just as well, really, considering.'

'God, I'm actually a bit pissed.' I tried looking through one eye with the other closed. The room straightened slightly.

'Good show.' Another clunk of cups.

'This is going to be a prayer room, Dad. The study. I'm going to sand the floor and make it a place of contemplation for Al. I'm going to decorate it as a surprise.'

'That's what it's been for me, a prayer room. *Please God, don't send the phone bill. Please God, don't let me have to pay for my daughters' weddings.* All manner of prayers have gone up in here. *Please God don't let my teenaged daughters find my single malt.*'

My dad reached over towards a carrier bag propped up against the bookcase.

'I wanted to give you this, darling. I bought it on Charing Cross Road in an antique book shop, just after you'd decided on names for the baby. It seemed the wrong time, well, you know, after he'd been born. Now's a good time.' He passed me the bag.

Inside was a beautiful book, large and filled with coloured plates depicting the scenes from its pages. The curled inscription on the front read 'One Thousand and One Nights.'

'Dad, it's beautiful. How old is it?'

'I think it was printed in the twenties. It's the same one, the same edition, that I had as a boy. It was my favourite. You know the stories?'

I moved my hands to show that I knew something of them, but for him to tell me more. I leant my head against his shoulder, a child again, and listened to him tell the story, the big book open across our laps.

'The Sultan took himself a new wife every night. In the morning he'd have her beheaded.' He laughed to himself, a little wistfully. 'Scheherazade put herself forward one day to be the new Sultana. That's what they're called, Sultan's wives.'

I imagined Al's voice saying, 'He so made that up. That is so your father.' It made me smile.

'On the first night, she called for her sister to bid her farewell but, instead, Scheherazade began to tell her sister a story. The

Sultan listened to the story, mesmerised. By dawn, he was transfixed and begged Scheherazade to tell him the end. She said that she would have loved to but, unfortunately, it was dawn so she must die. The Sultan let her live for one more night. This time, she finished the first story and started a second. And so on. For one thousand and one nights. By the time she'd finished, the Sultan was hopelessly in love with her and everyone lived happily ever after.'

I turned the shiny pages, the smell of antiques and old houses wafting up from the crease, gold-brocade and jewelled furs in every illustration. I thought of how much Farzana would love this book.

'Do you know who her hero was? The swash-buckling adventurer of Scheherazade's tales?'

I shook my head.

'Haroon. That's why I bought it. I want you to have it now, now you're so focussed, so much happier. Now I'm slowing up on the worry. I'm not frightened for you anymore. Nor for Al.'

'It's beautiful, I'll treasure it.' I leaned against him, sipping at the whiskey. 'Am I odd, Dad, wanting to live in my childhood home?'

'I think it's thoroughly understandable. And it's not as if you're keeping it as a museum. Or like you never left, you hadn't lived here for over ten years. You've got Manzoor's money to leave with if Al grows up like me.'

'Do you know what? He could do worse.'

ALI

It was supposed to be my glory moment when I got to Manchester to tell my parents about us buying the big house, moving out of the city. To see in my dad's eyes the pride that I had come good, saved my marriage. I wanted to be the centre of attention but I was far from it.

'You know, beta, I think really you and Honour are a modern day Elizabeth Bennett and Mr Darcy.'

I nearly dropped my china cup.

Did my mother just speak to me in English? What the hell was happening?

Farzana was rolling her eyes, and giggling into Sam's head. But he was getting annoyed, a sign that he was growing up, didn't want his mother to be so touchy-feely. He was watching Zak and me build up my old Scalextric set.

They reminded me of myself and Jamal.

'You should read what I wrote about the way British Pakistanis live today, you will love it.'

'Okay, Mum,' I said.

'Don't encourage her,' my dad said, but he couldn't hide the affection in his eyes.

'You be quiet, Ali's dad. You have had me since I was fourteen, made me bear you children and clean your house.'

'Ah, but, Begum, who will love you for forty years like I have?'

My mother blushed, it was freaky.

What had happened to this family? I blamed Honour and Farzana. They had said to my mother that the reasons she didn't get an education no longer existed, that she was a woman of means and had the world available to her.

Mum had caught a re-run of *Pride and Prejudice* and said she wanted to read the book. So off she went to college, adult education, English for non-native speakers. She found it too basic, as I knew she would. I mean you don't live in a country for forty-odd years without knowing the language, not really.

Dad pretended he hated it all, and pretended to be fed up with the constant demands to practice words and read bits she'd written and cook his own dinner. But every time he whinged his eyes did just the opposite.

'That's my wife, my begum, look at her, she's a genius.'

That's what came across.

Dad, in turn, became domestic house-husband extraordinaire. He started attending curry cooking class (run by a white English woman) and was soon the master chef in the house. Everyone was banned from his kitchen.

I hated it, this paradigm shift. Your parents were meant to stay the same.

Farzana thought it was hilarious. Our parents had become English eccentrics. Finally.

I guessed it would be good for Zain and Aaliyah though. Both myself and Farzana had struggled with identity so much. I had gone in search of what it means to be British, what my country of birth had to offer. Farzana decided to explore her roots and tried to love living in Pakistan, but in the end she too realised she was too British to live there. Jamal had been in the middle, and had turned to African-American ghetto culture. He had done a volte face of late though, and grown a beard.

As part of the complete turnaround, Jamal had fallen for one of Bilal's third cousins, from a village in Pakistan. Her family were delighted to receive an offer from a man with his own small chain of butcher's shops and four takeaway chicken restaurants.

'Allah's will,' he said, stroking his beard.

'And if you think I will make my bahu cook and clean after you, well you have another thing coming,' Mum said. 'I have already enrolled her in English classes at the college, and I will make her do IT or something.'

'Begum, don't interfere in their relationship,' my dad warned.

'Manzoor…'

We gasped.

Not once since she had married my father at fourteen had she used his name. Farzana nearly dropped Sam, and Jamal choked on his biscuit.

'Well, how long can I keep calling you Ali's dad or jee or miah? Anyway, you are now in charge of cooking and use your own children to do the chores. My bahu will be going out to work.'

'Mum, you've lost it,' I said. 'Totally bonkers.'

'Yes, but you are not so old that I can't give you two thapars,' she said.

'Dad, I need some cash, I'm going out, innit,' said Aaliyah.

'Where are you going?'

'Honestly, you're like that Taliban sometimes. I'm going to Doyin's. Look, her mother is outside waiting to take me there, okay? I've got my mobile, and you can check my Facebook status if you really want to know what's up. Honestly, you so – like – oppress me,' she said.

My father just gave her some cash and she stomped out.

'If I had spoken to you like that you would have beaten me,' Farzana said.

'What to do? This is how teenagers are now,' my dad said.

'Who is Doyin?' I asked.

'Aaliyah's best friend, a Nigerian girl at her grammar school,' said Faz.

'Where's Zain?' I needed to know where everyone was in this crazy family.

'He's off to football practice, or is it karate?'

'I never got karate lessons. You said it was too dangerous and when I said I wanted to play football you said it wasn't for Asians and made me play cricket,' I said.

'Well, you and Farzana have shifted the goal posts,' said my dad.

I looked at Faz who gave me an equally hard-done-by look in exchange.

It was true, we had carved our place in the world, forged a new species, the British Pakistani, which meant the ones that followed had so many more options. But it was clear that this was just us, just our family. You couldn't do it for society. Every family would need the first girl to go to university, the first boy to marry and not live at home. Everything that we had done would have to happen on a micro level.

Not in the same way though; there would be people who looked so different to us on the outside, but were still Britpaks.

And the Jamals, the generation in the middle, the most confused of all, would eventually get their role models that didn't involve gangsters or terrorists and they could wind their necks in.

I had seen it happen here in the Hussian household, and it would happen like dominoes in other families too.

And none of it, no matter what we did, meant that we weren't Muslims. I had turned to my faith with a vengeance after events, and I found solace knowing that this wasn't 'it', that there was more to existence, a real purpose to life.

It was about balance and I reckon I had achieved it and my family had reached their own conclusion in their own way.

As for Zak and Sam? Well, who knows where they would end up, with their French and Moroccan extended family, one grandmother in New York or Hong Kong depending on her mood, the other at university. I looked into their future and it was such a blur, so exciting and vibrant and unknown, I prayed that they too would find God to cling to. It kept you sane when you had so much identity conflict going on.

'So are the flights to Pakistan all booked then?' I said.

'Yep, Dad did it all online. He got us the cheapest deals and then spent two weeks telling us how much he had saved,' Jamal said.

'If you do get cold feet, just say so, yeah? Me and Faz will smuggle you out,' I said.

'Speak for yourself, they are my in-laws. I'm going to shop him if he messes up,' Farzana said.

Zak started zooming his cars over the tracks, but they kept bumping against a piece that wasn't laid down properly and he sat down with an Einstein look on his face, trying to work out how to fix it.

'Mashallah, he looks well cute,' I said.

Zak gave me a dirty look.

'He's gone beyond that age now, so has Sam. I'm not having any more, so it's up to you now to produce cute babies,' said Farzana.

I sipped my tea and didn't meet anyone's eyes.

'All in time, beta?' Dad said.

I stretched out on the new sofas, and enjoyed the sun pouring in through the bay window. There was ease and comfort in the room, this was home, this was a family.

But I had my own home and my own family to go to.

I was holding Honour, the day her parents left and the deeds were signed and we became official owners of Baron House (yep, we renamed it for him). We stared in silence at the space that was now ours, and I put my hands on her stomach, and stroked the future. I became the first Asian in that part of Kent, and that opened the doors for others.

An Indian family moved into a house not far away soon afterwards and people stopped staring at me or asking me where I came from.

They knew I was Ali Hussain, married to Honour Hussain, and living in the house that had belonged to the Edwards.

That we were their heirs.

'Why do you love me?' she said.

'Because you complete me,' I said.

'Snap,' she said.

I didn't say anything.

I always like her to have the last word.

HONOUR

I walk the dog here every morning. It helps me think, to plan my day, to order the past and the present when I am still sometimes daunted by the future. This secret place is an old chalk pit; Kent is full of them, the scars of an industrial past swallowed up by redundancy. Some of the larger ones have been developed into estates of ticky tacky houses, their identikit gardens petering out into the cliff of the old excavations. Others, like this one, are privately owned and forgotten, grown into a wilderness of memories, brambles and rusty iron. It is the kind of place where Connie and I searched for Stig of the Dump when we were children and that maybe, one day, my children and their cousins will tear across with sticks for swords and imaginations for enemies.

When I was small, these chalk pits had pools of muddy water in the bottoms, hollow reeds of giant hogweed reaching out of them like the mountains of the moon. Decades of hot summers have long since dried up the stagnant ponds and marooned their skating insects but the memory is still strong of my sister and I finding a rotted steel bathtub and trying to float it, holes and all, across the pond, propelled and punted by hazel sticks we'd pulled from the innocent trees. When I catch my arms or legs on brambles, I still feel the same way as my childhood self did, a thrill, a moment's furrowed concentration as I remove the tiny thorn. I feel alive.

The dog loves it here too. His tail beats furiously, a tattoo of warning; look out rabbits, look out birds, fly in fear from me. When he turns to check that I'm still behind him, his face is that of a black bear and his tongue lolls sideways in the dog version of a laugh. He is only ten months old but, despite being a puppy, he is biddable and steadfast. A solid and typical Labrador.

I am climbing back up the sloped side of the crater now, my breathing more rapid than it was, my calf muscles tightening with the effort of traversing the more rugged parts, now and then I have to drop a hand down to the chalky soil as it rises up to meet me to keep my balance. My whole childhood was like this; outdoors, tactile, as full of adventure and risk as I wanted, free to make my own mistakes. The peace of the chalk pit helps me think back across the process that made me as bold as that child again.

The letters, phone calls, emails, started a month or so ago. Everyone being, oh so casual, wondering what we're doing in a few weeks, where we might be. They are funny, Farzana and Connie, if a little patronising. When they get together they are like two textbook old women, one French, one Pakistani, each typical of their race; cooking, gossiping or ladling out advice from behind a garden wall.

I think we're not supposed to notice, Al and I, that it will be Harry's birthday. For me, the choices are simple; I don't want to spend the day clock-watching, ticking off minutes in a real-time reconstruction and reliving those terrible hours. I want a house full of laughter and light, I want to feel sunshine and prospects. Al struggles with a pointless guilt even now; I don't want him to remember the vivid piercing sorrow of the hours he passed, with no one to help him, watching Harry be born. The journey to this time in our lives has been a difficult one and today I want to celebrate its joys and triumphs, not its despairs.

Connie and Laurent arrived last night, Connie a little green from the effects of the car ferry on her third pregnancy. And now we're standing on the drive, watching the children dig through the flowerbeds with our Liberty cutlery canteen, bought in another lifetime. We are all waiting for Farzana and Bilal to arrive. The sun has done us proud today, the ground is baked and cracked and we have to lather the children with sun cream before they can even step outside the door.

I've spent a long time on these flower beds, as has Al; although his real dedication shows when he heaps his garden produce onto the kitchen table. He brings in perfectly white new potatoes, dusted with cool earth and drops them next to violently red tomatoes that split open where the July sun has over-ripened them. Every day there are curled salad leaves, vivid green and still damp from watering; each leaf, each muddy clod, a million miles away from who we used to be.

A car crunches down the drive, the noise the epitome of middle England. We didn't change the drive when we renovated the house, preferring to see the weeds poking through the gaps and the bare ruts carved by time, just where they have always been. Inside, the house is almost unrecognisable, clean and ordered. We didn't strip out its soul, just fixed and mended, healed and helped; installed glass shower cubicles instead of the perished rubber hoses pinched with Jubilee clips onto oblong Victorian taps; light sockets that never crack and fizzle, doors that close neatly against the draughts of winter. We managed to make it ours.

The car door opens and Farzana steps out, elegant and poised, her gold-strapped sandal reaching out from the bottom of her summer-patterned harem trousers.

'Nice job,' she smiles looking around her, 'Lady of the manor.'

I rush forward and kiss her, almost tripping over Jean-Paul who is running to the car, fighting his way through Bilal's legs to get into the backseat where Zak and Sam are still in their car seats. Jean-Paul tries French first, then remembers. Zak, who has talked – no doubt relentlessly – in Punjabi all the way from Manchester makes the transition flawlessly to answer.

The adults hug and chatter while the two little boys slide away, walking hand-in-hand on to the grass by the dog's kennel, to where Jean-Paul has left his digging tools. They look at the hole together, discussing which Liberty's knife, fork or spoon would be most effective to carve through the dirt.

Zak and Jean-Paul are so alike, their eyes are an identical shade; Connie and Bilal's green mingled and misted with the profound brown colouring of Farzana and Laurent. Their tough little bodies are matched exactly for height and a newcomer would be hard pressed to tell them apart at a glance. A second set of twins, separated by nationality, language and culture, united by being Harry's cousins.

We are planting a tree today to mark Harry's birthday. My parents claim to be signing vital papers for their French house but I think, really, they are simply leaving the young ones to it because Al's parents can't be here. Noor and Manzoor are leaving for Jamal's wedding in Lahore in a week and there seems to have been a calm conspiracy of convenience between the older generation, marked by their absence. Poor Habiba, Jamal's bride, has all of our sympathies and the idea of Jamal as someone's husband is the butt of all of our jokes. We will join the rest of the family in Pakistan to celebrate before Habiba comes back to Britain with us, another Mrs Hussain, another sister-in-law.

Al goes into the barn to collect the sapling. He has researched his choice of tree long and hard and has chosen a Kent Cobnut, grafted onto a Twisted Willow stem. The technicalities of his preferred option mean nothing to me, but the nuts are my favourites.

'Ali looks amazing. So healthy,' Farzana whispers to me, watching her brother's broad-shouldered and assertive stride.

'Everything's different for him. He buries all his work stress in the garden at the end of the day.' I laugh. 'Con, what's that thing Dad always says about the frog in the boiling water?'

'Charles Handy,' she says. 'If you drop a frog into a pan of boiling water, it'll jump straight out. But if you heat the water slowly with the frog already in the pan, it'll stay there till it dies.'

'I think that's how his old job was. Neither of us noticed. Now he's just fulfilled on every level, he has everything he wants.' I can't keep eye contact with them and turn away. They know I'm hiding something but they won't ask. They want to tease a revelation from us, slowly, savouring every second.

'He's started to sing again too.' I smile.

Laurent brings the champagne. He carries the glasses splayed out upside down from his fingers with a Gallic style. He holds his hand out to his wife, my sister, to fill the glasses and pass them round.

I put my glass to my lips but do not drink.

'Not thirsty?' Con asks, winking at Farzana.

I mouth 'fuck off' at both of them.

Florence sits underneath the newly planted tree, putting stones in her mouth. Sam fusses round her in Punjabi, his baby words meaning nothing to either of them, his chubby fingers hooking saliva out of her mouth in an effort to get the pebbles.

Al and I stand, entwined, and watch them. We imagine the trunk of the tree thickening, its branches reaching out towards the warm sky and the nuts, green-wrapped and bitter, raining onto the grass each season.

I leave Al to look after our family just as I know he can. I excuse myself and take the dog for a walk in the chalk pit. Everyone lets me go, they know I am all right, that I will be where I need to in my head, and then come back to the party. It is a strange day; it has a nomenclature of its own. To the rest of the country, it is 7/7. To us, it is the seventh of July, Harry's birthday.

This walk is my prayer.

I call the dog back and hush him. A heron stands, ecclesiastical in his grey robes, his sombre pointy face watching the last of the tadpoles-turned-frogs limp to the surface of the pond. I barely breathe as I look down the bank to where he stands, fishing, hardly more than ten feet away from me. I fumble for my phone to take the bird's picture but, as I click to the right screen, the bird takes flight, ancient, smooth and noble, leaving no trace but for my memory.

Yesterday we drove to London, to see Harry's grave and check the rose bush, to share our secret with him. We're not ready to tell anyone else, to dilute the thrill by sharing, although I have the distinct feeling that most people have guessed, certainly all the women in the family. For now, although not for long, it's our secret.

Al, of course, would say that his God already knows.

About the Authors

When Ali Met Honour is the first novel by Ruth Ahmed; the pseudonym for the writing team of Anstey Spraggan and Dimmi Khan. Anstey and Dimmi met whilst on the Creative Writing Masters programme at Manchester Metropolitan University.

Anstey Spraggan teaches creative writing in the community and for Canterbury Christ Church University. She lives near the seaside in Kent with her husband and a huge sigh of relief that their five children have left home.

Dimmi Khan is a published short story writer. He has studied at the Manchester Grammar School (after receiving a full bursary), is a graduate of the London School of Economics, and has Master's degrees in Islamic Studies (Birkbeck College, University of London), Information Systems (University of Westminster) and Creative Writing (Manchester Met University). He is currently studying for an MLitt Terrorism Studies at the University of St Andrew's by distance learning. He also has a lifelong passion for Archaeology, Human Evolution, Ancient History and Bollywood.

Acknowledgements

Dimmi would like to thank:

God, for everything.

Mum and my family for letting me pursue my writing: you are the best people I know. Tony Etchells: the English teacher that started it all. Anstey Spraggan for obvious reasons.

Special thanks for their encouragement and reading: Shaheeda Sabir, Amit Shah, Anita Majumdar, Doyin Max Lino, Sonya Brown, Dawn Varley, Graeme Shimmin, Andy Dickinson, Ronita Dutta, Ruth Smith, Calum McDonald, Najma Khanzada, Naz Ogazi- Khan, Sophia Khan, Mohammed Vic Khan, the Whole Kahaani, Colin Cross, Sally O'Kane and Ifrah Mukri.

Anstey would like to thank:

Ella and Ruby for reading it (and Joe, Lucy, and Charlie even though they haven't). Also, all the Mhor Maniacs, Amanda 'Lade' Atherton, Annie Barber, Annie Townend, Bex Rechter, Carl Ashmore, Catherine Rose, Chris Wallis, Clodagh Murphy, Colm Redmond, Emma Fairbrother, Fionnuala Kearney, Hattie Douch, Helen 'Maggot' Mosley, Jacqui Christodoulou, Jane Morris, Jane Reeves, Kate Lord Brown, Kathy O'Donnell, Keris Stainton, Louise Swingler, Nick Royle, The Ning Girls, Steph Ebdon, Sue Hawkins, Yvonne Light, and especially Janet Lewis.

Thanks to Nadeem Khan, without whom this story would never have been.

Most of all and always, I'd like to thank Colin Cross - for everything.

We'd both like to thank:

The Arts Council of Great Britain, Jane Gregory and Stephanie Glencross, Kate and Mous Elouaaer, and – hugely – Farhana Shaikh.